Beyond the Horizon

Beyond the Horizon

Riders of the Mauvaises Terres:
A Barton Family Saga

BILL BISHOP

RESOURCE *Publications* · Eugene, Oregon

BEYOND THE HORIZON
Riders of the Mauvaises Terres: A Barton Family Saga

Resource Publications
An Imprint of Wipf and Stock Publishers
199 W. 8th Ave., Suite 3
Eugene, OR 97401

www.wipfandstock.com

PAPERBACK ISBN: 978-1-7252-6325-3
HARDCOVER ISBN: 978-1-7252-6326-0
EBOOK ISBN: 978-1-7252-6327-7

Manufactured in the U.S.A.   10/07/20

This book is dedicated to
my daughters
Sophianna and Monicamay.
Never give up on your dreams
and always strive to reach
beyond the horizon.

Contents

Preface

THE PROTAGONIST OF *BEYOND the Horizon* is my great grandfather, John Barton, who was born in Fort Dodge, Iowa in 1868, and died in Rapid City, South Dakota in 1956. John married in Iowa and had seven children—three sons and four daughters. He homesteaded at Three Tree Creek in Rainy Creek Township, Pennington County, north of the town of Wall in western South Dakota from 1907. He proved up his claim in 1912 and continued to work the land until 1932.

I have spun both fact and fiction into this epic old west tale, drawing from historical facts about the Barton family as well as facts surrounding Jesse James; Cole Younger; Bloody-Bill Anderson; General George Armstrong Custer; Lieutenant Gouverneur Warren; Dr. Ferdinand Vandeveer Hayden; Colonel Ranald S. Mackenzie; Joseph Smith; Mr. Lyne T. Barret; Captain Leader McNelly; Don Juan Flores Salinas; J. R. Hebbron; Samuel A. Maverick; Owen G. Chase; Seth Bullock; Little Wolf; Dull Knife; Sitting Bull; Crazy Horse; Wovoca; Big Foot; Henry Ford; Theodore Roosevelt, 26th President of the United States; and many more.

The tale spans the period from 1884 to 1912, covering the twilight of the Old West and the dawn of the Modern Age. The completion of the Northern Pacific Transcontinental Railroad; the explosion of railroad networks west of the Mississippi; the great blizzard of 1887, resulting in the end of the age of Great Plains cattle barons; the 1890 Wounded Knee Massacre, marking the end of Indian armed resistance; the 1891 ratification of the 1889 treaty which opened up new lands for homesteading west of the Missouri River in South Dakota; and the long-awaited building of railroads across the Badlands of western South Dakota in 1907, all played a role in shaping the western United States and especially the state of South Dakota as we know it today. Little-known to most Americans, let alone most Dakotans, is the critical role Theodore Roosevelt played in the settlement of the western territories. His own life experiences on his Elkhorn Ranch on the Little Missouri River in Dakota Territory informed many of his policies as president from 1901 to 1909, including his immigration policies that brought millions of immigrants, many seeking free agricultural land, into the United States. Immigration peaked at an annual record of over 1.3 million in 1907 (a record not exceeded until 1991 and not exceeded again since). Changes to the Homestead Act to make the settlement of the nation's new lands west of the Mississippi productive, especially the arid lands west of the 100th Meridian, helped to drive immigrants into lands formerly thought to be wastelands, unsuitable for productive development.

In writing this fictional account, I found it necessary to include a few historical facts, believing we are all products of the times in which we live. John Barton was no exception. This is a work of fiction, none of the characters or events depicted in this story are intended to represent any true persons either living or deceased or their true actions or intentions or any actual historical events. This novel is at best a flight of fancy based on historical facts surrounding John Barton's life and times.

The author's intent is to entertain, not to inform readers of the accurate recounting of historical persons, facts, or events. The author reserves the right to leave the writing of history to historians. As to those things that may be plausible, the author believes the realm of the possible is limited only by an understanding of the facts and your own imagination.

BILL BISHOP
Rapid City, South Dakota
July 22, 2019

October 1, 1879

Lizard Creek, Webster County, Iowa

A Father's Dream

It had been a long, unseasonably hot and humid day. With scattered clouds in the west lit up burnt orange as the sun slipped beyond the distant horizon, Bill and Johnny called it a day, loaded up their tools, and headed back to the house. As they drove the buckboard wagon into the yard, Pappy, with little Benjamin holding onto the hammer loop on his coveralls, came from the back of the house, where they had been working on mending a fence. They both waved as the buckboard pulled up in front of the barn.

Alda was just finishing up sweeping the front porch, when they pulled into the yard. Catching Johnny's eye, she pointed at the broom she was holding and then back at him with a smirk on her face. He reluctantly nodded his acceptance. Porch sweeping was a chore Alda and Johnny shared; trading the never-ending duty had become an unwelcome ritual between them. Johnny knew it was his turn; he also knew that sweeping was one chore he couldn't wait to escape forever. He could give a hoot if dirt piled up a foot deep on the porch; his ma, however, saw it differently: A clean porch signaled a tidy home and he had long ago accepted there was no changing her mind on that point.

It wasn't long before everyone had entered the house, washed up, and got ready for supper. After settling into their customary places round the dining table, all eyes soon turned toward Pappy. Everyone knew that, given half a chance, Pappy wouldn't be able to stop himself from sharing a wild and wooly tale or two with his grandchildren. Bill also enjoyed Pappy's stories and liked telling his own whoppers whenever he could. The kids loved to listen to the many wild adventures and especially about Pappy's memories of the old days and the old ways before settlers began filling up the land.

"Grandpa, last time you finished tellin' stories, you promised to tell us more about the lands of the Lakota Indians," Johnny said, looking expectantly at Pappy.

Johnny couldn't wait to ride west all the way to the booming goldfields in the Black Hills. He wanted to learn more about what Pappy knew of the little-known land west of the Missouri in the Dakota Territory and the Indians that lived there.

"I've told you a hundred times about my travels with Lieutenant Gouverneur Warren during our expedition into the Black Hills region in 1856 and 1857," Pappy chuckled as he recalled telling his grandchildren more than once all about the expedition and even about the endless arguments between Lt. Warren and Dr. Hayden.

Lt. Warren was a soldier and civil engineer who had been charged with making an accurate survey of the topography around the Black Hills and with gaining insights into the makeup of the rock and mineral formations in the region. Dr. Hayden, by contrast, was a scholar who had joined the expedition wanting only to add to his list of fossil discoveries.

In previous years, Hayden had joined several fossil-hunting expeditions in the Mauvaises Terres, the Badlands of the Dakota Territory. Like other early explorers, he sought the fame and notoriety he would gain back east for discoveries of the remains of creatures that had lived in the far-distant past; creatures that had over eons fossilized and been turned to stone.

"I love the strange fish imprints you discovered by splitting rocks in half and all the other strange imprints of shells, plants, and sea creatures," Alda said. "We have some of those, and shark's teeth too, and even some seashells you collected in the desert with Dr. Hayden."

"Yes, as I told you, the Black Hills was an island long before the continent of North American rose out of the sea," Pappy said, pleased that he had piqued Alda's imagination and curiosity.

"It's hard to believe the Black Hills had been a tropical island surrounded by a sea rich in life," Alda said with a wistful look in her eyes that told everyone she was awed by the wonder of such an ancient, alien world.

It was times like these that Pappy loved the most: times when he could encourage his grandchildren to stretch their imaginations and curiosity about the wonderous world in which they lived. He believed this was the most important and valuable gift he could ever give them.

"The giant tortoise shell fossils Dr. Hayden discovered and insisted on bringing back even though they filled up a whole wagon bed is one of my favorite stories," Johnny piped up. "Especially when Hayden refused to give up the fossils even when the Lakota threatened to burn down Fort Pierre."

"Yes, that was a tense time," Pappy agreed.

"Warren's knockdown, drag-out fistfight with Hayden over the whole affair was really something," Johnny added.

Johnny had recently learned the reason the Indians had threatened to overrun and burn down Fort Pierre, where Hayden had insisted on having the tortoise shell fossils taken, before having them moved east. As it turns out, the turtle is a particularly potent and important symbol to the Lakota people.

Pappy had explained that the Lakota divided the year into thirteen months or thirteen new moons, with twenty-eight days from one new moon to the next. Like all native peoples, the Lakota found meaning and a unity in natural things; the turtle, called *keya* in the Lakota language, with its thirteen large scales on its back and twenty-eight small scales around the edge of its shell, symbolized perfectly the Lakota people's understanding of the cycles of the moon and hence the universe in which they lived.

Because of this and other beliefs about the natural world, including the Lakota belief in Turtle Island—a belief shared by many native peoples in North America that the Earth itself rode on the back of a giant turtle—the turtle had come to represent a guardian of life, longevity, and fortitude. The Lakota often wore amulets in the shape of a turtle for protection, much in the same way a Saint Christopher medallion was worn by many Christians.

Johnny hungered to learn these deeper insights about the Lakota people and their beliefs in the land to the west; the land, he hoped he would someday call home.

"Don't forget about the dragon bones," Benjamin chirped, almost jumping out of his seat, not wanting anyone to forget Pappy's stories about such wonderous beasts.

"That's right, Benny, we wouldn't want to forget how your grandpa helped dig out dragon bones in the Mauvaises Terres belonging to reptile-like creatures as big as a house," Bill said acting like a huge beast with his fingers curled like claws as he scanned the children, one by one, as if ready to pounce.

Benjamin giggled at his pa's goofy antics while Johnny and Alda looked on, enjoying the innocent fun.

"Don't forget kids, Pappy even told us about how the Lakota refused to let the Warren Expedition fully enter their scared Black Hills," Bill continued, hoping to prod Pappy into telling the kids something about the religious beliefs of the Lakota people.

"That's right," Pappy said. "They blocked our advance on every attempt to trek deeper into their sacred hills. Even though we outgunned the Indians, Warren knew we were outnumbered, isolated, and had limited ammunition. We simply had no way to escape. If hostilities broke out, regardless of the body count, we would've had no chance of surviving. Warren did his best to pass through Lakota lands with as little trouble as possible and made every attempt not to unsettle the Indians, who kept an eye on our every move. This is the reason he was so upset by Dr. Hayden's antics. I'm here today because Warren knew when to keep his power dry," Pappy finished with a dead serious look on his grizzled face.

"Why would the Lakota risk so much, the deaths so many warriors, just to keep Warren from entering the Black Hills?" Johnny asked, knowing this detail was important.

"Well now, that is the question, isn't it?" Pappy said slowly, feeling the tension rise around the table as everyone grew increasingly eager to know the answer.

"It's the question that calls for an answer that runs deep, an answer that simmers at the center of a people's beliefs, an answer the white man may never fully understand," Pappy added.

After slowly looking from each eager face to the next, Pappy became silent and then in a low voice began to weave his story about the mysterious Lakota people and the lands of the Dakota Territory west of the Missouri River.

"The Lakota call the Black Hills the *Paha Sapa*, a sacred place which hides a deep, dark cave from which their people emerged into the world," he said as he once again held his grandchildren under his spell and filled their young, eager minds with stories and myths from distant lands.

"Grandpa, how'd the Indians find their way out of that deep dark cave?" Benjamin asked, his little face etched with concern.

"The Spider Trickster, Inktomi, changed himself into a wolf and descended deep into the earth to where humans were living and tried to convince them to follow him to the surface where they would discover the wonders of the world," Bill replied matter-of-factly, having heard the story before.

He was pleased Pappy had decided to share it with the children. Benjamin, having heard his pa's answer, turned to Pappy for confirmation.

"That's right. The Lakota believe in Inktomi, a shapeshifting spider, that can change himself into anything," Pappy said, his eyes large and round. Benjamin mirrored the look in Pappy's eyes. "Tokahe was the first man to follow Inktomi to the surface," Pappy continued. "He later returned to his home deep underground and brought six more men to the surface. They became the people of the Seven Council Fires, known as the *Oceti Sakowin*, the tribes of the Great Sioux Nation as we know it today."

Pappy had learned the origin myth of the Great Sioux Nation from an old French fur trapper during the Warren Expedition who had lived among the Lakota people long before any other white man dared to venture uninvited into their lands. He knew the Sioux Nation was made up of several tribes with three distinct dialects: the Lakota, Dakota, and Nakota. The name *"Nadowessioux"*, meaning "Snake" or "Enemy", was used by Ojibwe tribes, including the Chippiwa and others, that inhabited the lands from the mouth of the St. Lawrence River on the Atlantic coast across the northern Great Lakes region, to refer to all the peoples that made up the Lakota, Dakota, and Nakota tribes west of the Great Lakes. This Ojibwe word was later shortened by early French explorers to Sioux and came to be used to refer to all the tribes west of the Great Lakes.

Though the origin of the name Sioux for the Lakota people was based on a derogatory name, the moniker continued to be used when referring to the Lakota, Dakota, and Nakota peoples, even though it was not the name they used to refer to themselves. The largest group, the Lakota, or Teton Sioux, made up of seven tribal bands, lived in the Dakota Territory. The Dakota, or Santee Sioux, the second largest group, lived in Minnesota and Nebraska. The Nakota, the smallest band, lived spread out across the Dakota and Montana Territories.

Though he wasn't sure he had the Lakota origin story exactly right, he figured it was fairly close to what the old frontiersman had told him. Accurate or not, it made a good yarn that would captivate his grandchildren's young imaginations and hopefully inspire them to be more open to new ways of thinking and to always be eager to look beyond the horizon.

"Are all spiders tricky like that pa?" little Benjamin asked with a worried look on his little face.

"No, son. Only Inktomi, and he lives with the Lakota so we don't need to worry about him playing tricks on any of us," Bill said to his youngest son.

Benjamin was three going on four and full of curiosity. Bill could see that he was exceptionally bright for his age and growing smarter by the day. Bill knew Benjamin had been born with a veil, something very rare. Babies born en caul, with amniotic membrane still covering the head or even the whole child at birth, have been believed to be auspicious in many cultures around the world down through the ages. Bill had high hopes for the boy.

"Like the Lakota, the Otoe tribe have seven clans with each clan represented by its own spirit animal: The Bear, Beaver, Elk, Eagle, Buffalo, Pigeon, and Owl," Pappy said with a huge grin. "Your grandma, being part Otoe, was a member of the Eagle clan. That means you kids are all members of the Otoe Eagle clan—something you should never forget."

"It seems the number seven is important to the Indians," Alda said.

"Yes, for many Indian tribes the number seven has meaning. The fact is, it's an important number to many peoples around the world, including Christians. Everything comes in sevens in the Bible: seven plagues, seven brides, seven angels, seven trumpets," Bill said.

Pappy listened rubbing his chin. "Yes, seven comes up in many stories and for many peoples. Interestingly, the Otoe once had an eighth clan, the clan of the Snake, which no longer exists. Why the Snake clan disappeared is a dark tale. It's a tale full of mystery," he teased as he readied himself to spin a new yarn.

"You two stop filling the kids' heads up with all these wild stories," Lucy yelled from the kitchen where she had spent most of the day canning vegetables for the coming winter.

"The kids just want to learn more about the Dakota Territory," Bill yelled back.

"Bill Barton, you know the Lakota people have been as mad as hell since the Custer Expedition discovered gold in their sacred *Paha Sapa*," Lucy shot back.

"Yes, well—" Bill started to reply.

"Yes, well, my foot," Lucy interrupted. "Since the news of gold in the Black Hills spread far and wide, miners, outlaws, charlatans, and rogues of every sort and stripe have rushed into those sacred hills and started tearing the hell out of things.

"Yes, well—" Bill tried again.

"Yes, well, for the past five years, the only news we've heard coming out of the Black Hills is that the unwelcome invaders have been fightin' and killin' one another for every gold nugget they can lay their greedy hands on," she concluded with emotion.

"Now, now, calm down, Lucy. There's no arguing the Dakota Territory is a lawless land and that gold fever has a way of driving men crazy. There's no denying the frontier is still wild and lawless. It's been that way down through history whenever new lands and riches become free for the takin'," Bill said, agreeing with Lucy in his own way and knowing his remarks would do little to calm her down.

"You'd have thought that Custer getting' himself and two hundred sixty-eight of his men kilt would've slowed down the rush of fortune hunters into the region," Lucy said from the kitchen doorway as she stood with her hands on her hips.

Bill could see clearly that Lucy's belly had grown to the size of a small watermelon as the twins she was carrying made ready their entry into the world. When she leaned with her back against the doorframe, he admired her profile. A day never passed that he didn't count himself as being one of the luckiest men alive for having Lucy Breeden in his life. She meant the world to him and he knew she always would. He also knew he needed to tread carefully if he wanted to stay on the right side of her hair-trigger temper.

"Fact is, the victory over Custer by Crazy Horse and Sitting Bull only made the settlement of the Black Hills and all the lands in the Dakota Territory even more urgent for the government," Bill said. "With railroads laying track on all sides of the Black Hills region, the government's been forced to step up its military campaign against the Northern Cheyenne and the Lakota Sioux. The government's mandate is to bring order to the untamed lands by whatever means necessary."

He knew very well, as did Lucy, that the settlement of the lands to the west would be a long, bloody affair, as it had been since the first white man set foot in the new world.

"They may bring order after a spell, but the killin' isn't over by a long shot," Lucy quipped as she returned the kitchen.

Lucy felt the twins move inside her and feared for their future and that of all of her children. Life had always been hard on frontier families. Her life had been tough at times. She knew taming the lawless lands to the west would be an even tougher challenge for her children.

"I still think the youngsters need to be ready to stake their claim in those lands. New lands in the Dakota Territory will open up for settlement one day, sooner than anyone thinks," Bill said wanting his children to be as excited as he was about the prospect of settling the untamed lands to the west.

"Well, we'll see," Lucy said, wanting to drop the topic, knowing the children were hanging on their every word.

She worried that Johnny, who had already voiced his desire to fulfill his father's dream, would be heading west sooner than she hoped.

"Believe me, it'll go quickly when it happens. Hell, after Colonel Mackenzie and his Fourth Calvary defeated the Northern Cheyenne on the Power River in Wyoming Territory, it didn't take the government long to send 'em packing to join their Southern Cheyenne bothers in Indian Territory," Bill reminded everyone with a sense of confidence.

"All well and good, but you know damn well many of those same Northern Cheyenne have already come back north and after one hell of an upset led by Little Wolf and Dull Knife ended up being settled in Montana Territory," Lucy reminded Bill as she returned to the doorway.

"Well . . ." Bill said, knowing Lucy was right.

"Well . . . is right. You know the Lakota aren't going to give up as easily as the Cheyenne. Custer wasn't the first one to find out the Lakota know how to fight; and he won't be the last," Lucy said.

"But Crazy Horse . . . " Bill said, feeling the sting of Lucy's accurate recounting of recent events.

"Yes, Crazy Horse. Now there's a subject. He might be dead, and the Great Sioux War ended two years ago with the Lakota forced to cede the Black Hills and their lands outside the Dakota Territory. Don't forget, they didn't do it willingly. The government annexed their lands and established fixed Indian reservations just the same," Lucy said, conceding recent setbacks.

"Yeah, well . . . " Bill started.

"Yeah, well, you can be sure Sitting Bull and the Lakota haven't given up their resistance to the military occupation of their land west of the Missouri," she added still wanting things to be different.

"That may be, but the numbers say it's just a matter of time. The northern and eastern regions of the Dakota Territory are already filling up as new immigrant homesteaders continue to pour in from the east. The land to the west of the Missouri River will also open up for settlement one day, of that

I have no doubt," Bill said, still confident he was right and that his children would be among the first settlers of that new land.

"Lucy, you know Bill has a point, the final settlement of northwestern Missouri happened quickly and in much the same way," Pappy said wistfully.

"The Otoe tribe fought hard for the land they had been promised along the Missouri River, but in the end, they were forced to move to Indian Territory, much in the same way the government tried to treat the Northern Cheyenne," Pappy continued, his voice growing more agitated with every word. "Once the government strips a tribe of its ability to fight, destroys its food supplies, and takes its horses, shippin' em to Indian Territory is easy."

Though he was an old man now, he remembered as if it was yesterday how the five counties that made up northwestern Missouri had been purchase from local Indian tribes, mainly the Otoe, in 1836.

The Platte Purchase, as it came to be called, added over three thousand square miles of new land to the state of Missouri, an area nearly equal to Delaware and Rhode Island combined. Among the many irregularities involving the purchase and annexation of Indian lands by the slave-state of Missouri was the expansion of slavery into the former Louisiana Territory north of the 36th-and-a-half parallel in violation of the Missouri Compromise of 1820.

The Missouri Compromise was worked out by Congress to maintain a senatorial balance of power between slave and free states at the time. Statehood was granted to one free-state, Maine, and one slave-state, Missouri, with the proviso that the 36th-and-a-half parallel would act as the dividing line for the future creation of slave and free states west of the Mississippi River. The slave-state of Missouri, being mostly north of this parallel, breached the agreement when it incorporated former Indian lands located in the Louisiana Territory north of the 36th-and-a-half parallel.

"Pappy, you're right. The Otoe Indians got a raw deal when they were forced to move down to Indian Territory," Bill said. "There's no doubt the Otoe were cheated out of their land, with alcohol playing a big part in the tribe's demise."

Bill knew how deeply Pappy felt about the loss of early frontier life and the many wrongs suffered by Indian tribes as their lands were taken and their traditional ways and spiritual beliefs were swept aside by an unyielding tide of European settlers.

"You're damn right, they were cheated. It still gets me riled up every time I think about it," Pappy said.

"I know Lucy's ma was part Otoe and that you lived and traded with 'em in the old days. My kids, and hell, in many ways all of us, are part Otoe. We may have been invaders, but we're part of the land now. We have to accept others will come and they too will fill the land," Bill said.

"Will there be no end to it? There's still plenty of land east of the Mississippi to settle. Why continue to push into the wild lands to the west?" Lucy asked, frustrated and afraid for the future of her children.

"Since the end of the war, come hell or high water, the whole nation seems to be following the sun west. Otoe or no Otoe. Cheyenne or no Cheyenne. Lakota or no Lakota. The old native ways will give way to a new modern age, it's just a matter of time. The nation is moving west, there is no stopping it," Bill said flatly.

"I know you're right, Bill. They just keep coming. Their numbers have grown beyond counting. I just refuse to understand how in tarnation it's happening so fast," Pappy said shaking his head.

"Mostly it's new immigrants by the tens of thousands arriving on ships from Europe every day, many of 'em are farmers. They'll have to move west to find new land," Bill said, knowing new waves of settlement were coming and that there was no stopping them.

"I guess, every rail spike that's been driven to pin down the steel ribbons of the white man's iron horse has been a nail pounded in the coffin lid on a past few'll ever know and fewer'll ever remember," Pappy lamented.

"You're right, Pappy. The railroads, more than anything else, have been responsible for bringing civilization to the untamed lands," Bill agreed.

"Civilization, you say. Yes, the white man's civilization," Pappy said shaking his head, unhappy with taste of the words in his mouth.

"The Union Pacific's Transcontinental Railroad changed things forever. The building of the Northern Pacific's Transcontinental Railroad has also opened up the Dakota Territory to the north. Earlier this year they crossed the Missouri River at Edwinton and are well on their way to joining up with track being laid from the coast in Washington Territory," Bill added.

"So, what you're sayin' is that the lands of the Lakota have already been hemmed in across both the north and the south," Pappy said flatly.

"That's right, steel rails surround the Black Hills and western Dakota Territory on three sides and have permanently sliced through the migration routes of the great buffalo herds, causing their numbers to decline by the year," Bill said.

"Then, there's little doubt settlers in large numbers will soon pour into the lands of the Lakota from the east, the north, and the south," Pappy concluded, his voice fading to a whisper, as he looked out the window at nothing in particular.

"The next ten years will reshape the map of the Dakota Territory as we know it," Bill said matter-of-factly.

Bill was confident homesteads would soon be sprouting up out of the prairie all the way to the horizon and beyond. The direction of their conversation and Pappy's remarks reminded Bill that time was growing short. He hoped his children would still have a chance to stake their claims in the new lands. Considering the speed things where moving, he worried they may not grow up fast enough to do so.

Just as Bill was having these thoughts, Johnny reminded everyone that the next generation also sensed the urgency and had its own ideas about the future.

"Pa, I can't wait to ride into the Dakota Territory to stake my claim. Do you think there'll be any land left when I'm finally able to strike out on my own?" Johnny asked.

The question hung unanswered for a long beat as Bill looked into Johnny's eager eyes and at his smooth, whisker-free face that belied his grown-up manner and his desire to appear older than his years.

"No need to worry son, it'll be some time before they homestead west of the Missouri River in the Dakota Territory," Bill replied.

Knowing the settlement of the eastern and northern regions of the Dakota Territory was already well underway, Bill wasn't entirely certain when settlement of the lands west of the Missouri would happen.

The fact his eldest son couldn't wait to head west filled Bill with pride. He had every confidence Johnny would one day build his future out west. Johnny had always been a boy in a hurry to grow up. He had a lust for life and an overpowering desire to ride beyond the horizon to make his own mark in the world.

Day by day, Bill saw more and more of himself in the boy. His eagerness for adventure, his curious and inquisitive mind, and his stubbornness were all traits Bill saw in himself. Though there was plenty of good in the boy, he also knew, like himself, the boy had an outlaw streak in him; a wild streak he would need to learn to tame as he grew into a man.

"Well, that may be, but as soon as I can strike out, I plan to do so. There's no time to waste and I got a hankerin' to make my mark in this world. No one's going to stop me when it's time to go," Johnny said looking straight into his pa's eyes with determination.

Bill knew what the boy meant and knew that he meant it. There would be no way to hold him on the farm after his sixteenth birthday. From that date on, they would have to let Johnny cast his destiny to the wind, as was the right of all free men, Bill thought.

What Bill dreaded most was that Lucy wouldn't be thrilled having her baby boy leave home so young. He figured he still had four years to get Lucy used to the idea that striking out to make your mark in the world was a man's God-given right. Johnny would have to grow up and learn to stand on his own two feet in the world. Bill and Lucy would need to let him go when the time came. As with all things, they would all have to cross that bridge when they came to it.

March 7, 1884

Lizard Creek, Webster County, Iowa

A Son's Dream

JOHN BARTON HAD ALWAYS been a boy in a hurry to grow up. He had made up his mind on what he wanted to do with the rest of his life on the day his father first told him of the new lands out west that would one day be open for settlement. He swore to himself that on that day he would ride into the Black Hills and the lands of the Mauvaises Terres in the far western regions of the Dakota Territory the first chance he got.

That chance came when Tom Burton, an old friend of his father from his time in the Union Army, agreed to take on John and his cousin Jasper Waite as cowpunchers if they could get to his Rocking T Ranch south of San Antonio by mid-March. Burton had plans to drive a herd of over five thousand head of longhorn cattle up the western Chisholm Trail all the way to the southwestern corner of the Dakota Territory just south of the Black Hills.

Though John was only sixteen and Jasper only a few months older, they were big for their ages and could put in a day's labor equal to any full-grown man. Burton's offer was that if the boys did a man's work, they would be paid a man's wages. With their fathers' blessings, the boys signed on to the drive, despite still being more than a little wet behind their ears.

John was determined to never give up on his boyhood dream of one day staking his claim in the Dakota Territory. The Dakota gold rush had been a lively topic over the dinner table during his childhood, with his father often claiming that, had he been a younger man, he would have joined the miners and fortune hunters who flooded into the Black Hills with dreams of striking it rich. Though John had been only eight years old when the discovery of gold in the Black Hills first filled the newspapers, he was old enough to feel the excitement in his father's voice every time he talked about the Black Hills and Mauvaises Terres, the French name for the lands west of the Missouri River and east of the mysterious Black Hills; lands that had come to be known as the Dakota Badlands.

Throughout his boyhood, his grandfather, who everyone called Pappy, had filled John's young mind with his stories of the Black Hills and the lands of the Mauvaises Terres, lands he had experienced firsthand as a U.S. Calvary trooper, during Lt. Gouverneur Warren's early expedition into the unknown region in the 1850s. The picture Pappy painted in John's mind was one of a wonderland of lush, green, rolling plains, teeming with buffalo, pronghorn antelope, mule deer, and countless varieties of wild fowl, all awaiting the first homesteaders to stake their claims to the virgin soil of this prairie paradise.

John knew of the stiff resistance from the native tribes in the region and of the many claims and counterclaims and territorial disputes. He was convinced, like his father, that as railroads extended their reach into these untamed regions, homesteaders would follow to fill up the land, as they had done since the first arrival of Europeans in the New World. He refused to believe that the Badlands had nothing to offer. He was confident once they were settled, they would yield their bounty as had other untamed lands as each new wave of settlers move ever westward.

"Jasper, you ready to ride?" John hollered as his reined up in front of the Waite place.

The Barton and Waite kids had grown up together. Being blood-kin, they had formed a tight-knit clan in southwestern Webster County, Iowa and were known far and wide as a tough bunch to handle should you ever get on their wrong side.

Wilber and Nancy Waite had twelve children, all born roughly a year apart. Bill and Lucy Barton had only half as many with six children, having gotten a later start. Lucy said she had no intention of catching up with Nancy, but did hope for one more child to make it a lucky seven, the number of children she and Bill had planned to have soon after they first met and fell in love.

As it turned out, Jasper, the Waite's fourth child and the nearest boy to John's age, was only a few months older than John. The two boys had grown up together like brothers, spending nearly all their time together when freed from their many daily chores.

"Yea, yea, I've been waitin' on ya for over an hour," Jasper hollered back as he rounded the barn door, leading his fully outfitted grey and white Appaloosa into the main yard.

"Well then, mount up partner, it's time to ride," John said as he nodded at the growing crowd of Waites that had assembled on the front porch of the Waite house.

Jasper's mother ran to her son and gave him a final hug. John could see the love between them and knew his own mother felt the same way about him.

"You boys take care of one another. You'll be on your own out there. You'll need to count on one another," Wilbur said, unable to help himself from reminding the boys one last time to watch each other's back.

He knew neither of the young men had been away from home, but like Bill, he had agreed his son had the right to make his own mark in the world. Wilbur walked over and reached up to shake hands with John and then turned to shake his son's hand, gripping his shoulder firmly. He knew the next time he saw the boy he would be a man.

"We'll be alright, pa. We've been watching each other's back since we were kids," Jasper said as he swung up on his horse.

"Well, partner, are you ready to ride?" John said, eager to get started.

"You bet, partner. Giddyap!" Jasper hollered, as he spurred his horse, wishing to get on the move before tears started flowing, especially his own.

"Yee Haw! Texas here we come!" John yelled, as he waved his hat high and spurred his horse, following Jasper out of the gate at a gallop.

The Waites waved and watched the two young men grow smaller as they rode toward the Barton place. Wilbur and Nancy knew they would face this same day many times in coming years as their children, one by one, set out to make their way in the world.

John and Jasper would stop by the Barton place and then ride southwest across Lizard Creek on their way to Kansas City where they planned to take the train to San Antonio. From San Antonio, they would ride their horses south to Tom Burton's Rocking T Ranch. Though neither of them had ever wrangled a Texas longhorn steer, the boys couldn't wait to join the trail drive to Dakota Territory.

Riding into the yard in front of the Barton house, John and Jasper were met by the Barton clan all gathered in front of the house. John's mother had a small bundle in her arms and motioned for John to get down from his horse. As John stepped down, Lucy hugged him tight one last time. Bill and Pappy came over and shook hands with both John and Jasper. Lucy insisted the boys take the bundle of food she had packed for their ride.

"Thanks for fixin' up some food and such, Ma. Jasper seems to never get enough to eat," John said with a chuckle as he took the bundle from his mother.

"I try to grab whatever vittles I can whenever John's around. Heck, talk about appetites, he'd eat my hat if I didn't keep it on," Jasper quipped.

Everyone got a kick out of the friendly banter between the two young men and could see that they would make good companions on the trail.

John stepped back up on his big black Morgan and promised to write once they got to San Antonio.

"Well, I guess since we're headed down yonder, we should say, *adios,*" John said as he turned his horse and trotted out of the gate with Jasper not far behind.

"Good-bye!" everyone boomed in reply.

"Take care of yourselves!" Lucy yelled, holding back her tears.

"Good luck, boys. Keep your heads and you will do well!" Bill yelled, unable to resist giving out a final bit of advice.

"*Vaya con Dios,*" Pappy yelled with the wave of his hat, remembering another time and another place long ago.

Pappy watched with the others as the two young men rode out and headed southwest. He imagined being young again. He could feel the wind in his face, the horse flesh under his command, and his heart beating strong and steady. He knew these two boys would come back as men; men hardened from the trail; men wise to the ways of the world; men ready to take on any challenge. He only hoped he would be there when they returned so he could shake their hands and listen to their tales of the Mauvaises Terres.

John and Jasper, following Bill's suggestion, rode southwest across the north branch of the Raccoon River and down between the Tarkio and Nodaway Rivers, crossing the state line just north of the little town of Tarkio in Atchison County, Missouri. Following the Missouri River south, they rode into Saint Joseph to spend the night. Their plan for the next morning was to follow the Little Platte River that ran down through Buchanan and Platte countries to the crossing at the port town of Independence on the Missouri River. From there, it would be a relatively short ride on into Kansas City, where they planned to catch the train all the way south to San Antonio.

As John and Jasper rode into Saint Joseph, they found the streets bustling with actively. Saint Joe, as the town was known, was at its zenith, with fortunes being made as merchants played middlemen for the growing trade flowing from both the east and the west. Huge mansions lined the high streets as ladies and gentlemen in fine attire ambled along gas-lit avenues. For John and Jasper, Saint Joe was a sight to behold.

"I ain't seen so many grand homes," John said in awe as he surveyed all the conspicuous wealth on display. "They're like castles."

"With so many folks headed to Oregon and all the cattle going east and the fur trade booming, folks around here can't help but make money," Jasper said.

Jasper had summed things up in a single sentence. Saint Joe had become a jump off port for the Oregon Trail and the cattle trade had grown rapidly with the growth of the railroads. The fur trade, though it had come to play a lesser role in the town's economy, was the foundation upon which Saint Joe had been built.

"Well, let's find a hotel. I'd like to see if we can get us a drink at one of Saint Joe's finest saloons," John said, hoping Jasper would like the idea.

"Sounds like a hell of a plan, pard," Jasper replied with a grin and nod.

Jasper had a hankering to wet his whistle for the first time in his life. He figured if he and John were playing the role of men it was time they started acting the part.

After settling into the Occidental Hotel, they decided to walk over to the house where Jesse James had been shot just two years earlier. The boys had heard many stories about the days of the James-Younger Gang and the many daring escapades of Jesse James. Like most folks, for John and Jasper, Jesse James was a legend.

John had learned his father had somehow known Jesse and Frank James after the Civil War. Pappy had also told him that Cole Younger had tried to track his father down after he ran off with his mother, as it seems she had caught the outlaw's eye, though he never had the chance to act on his desires. Considering his father had served in the Union Army during the Civil War, John often wondered how his father had become wrapped up with *desperadoes* the likes of Jesse James and Cole Younger, who had both been former Confederate guerrilla fighters.

These were things that had never been fully explained. John was certain his father was hiding more than a few dark secrets about what he did in the years right after the Civil War. He hoped his father would tell him one day. Either way, the death of Jesse James had brought an end to a legend and a post-war time of lawlessness by former Confederate guerilla fighters.

"It's a hell of a thing to be shot by one of your own men for reward money," Jasper said as the two men headed back to Main Street.

"Yeah and in the back no less," John said.

"No tellin' how many men Jesse gunned down in his lifetime," Jasper said, thinking out loud about how things had been more violent in the past. "They say he was one mean sonuvabitch."

"He hated blue-belly Yankees, that's for sure. They say he rode with Bloody Bill Anderson at the age of only fourteen," John said. "After the Union Army gunned down Bloody Bill in 1864, they found a rope on him with fifty-four bloody knots tied in it."

"Damn," Jasper retorted. "Think about it, pard: Jesse outlawed for nearly twenty more years after Bloody Bill was gunned down. If'n Jesse had a knotted rope, his rope must've had a damn sight more than fifty-four knots tied in it."

"You might be right. But, as Pappy always says, live by the gun, die by the gun," John said.

Thinking about Jesse, John wondered if he would ever be able to kill a man no matter the reason. He also wondered how Jesse had been able to live with himself after killing so many.

"How about the Bison Bull Saloon?" Jasper said gesturing at the batwing door of one of many fine drinking establishments lining Main Street.

Smoke and piano music rolled out of the door as the sounds of deep manly laughter and the high-pitched giggling of the finer sex mixed with the aromas of grilled steaks, stale cigars, sweet perfume, sour beer, and raw whiskey. John, trying to act nonchalant, followed Jasper through the batwing door and into the melee, a boy who would soon learn what it takes to be a man.

The saloon was packed. Barmaids in low cut blouses served a jumble of tables while a scrum of men crowded around the long bar as the bartender and his assistant pushed drinks out into the rowdy mob. Jasper and John worked their way to the bar and finally caught the eye of the wax-haired, barrel-chested bartender who they had heard called Ned by several of the customers.

"Ned, two cold beers," John called out, ordering the way he had seen other men do as they gathered around the bar.

"Comin' up," Ned barked without looking up. Soon two mugs of lukewarm beer slid down the counter. "Twenty-cents," Ned said as he looked John square in the face. "You sure you can hold that liquor, son?" he quipped with a grin.

"We'll give it a hell of a try," John said dryly, keeping his cool and holding eye contact as he tossed twenty cents on the counter.

"Best to drink those quick 'fore they go flat," Ned said before turning to tend to the urgent needs of the next thirsty patron.

"Heck, we should'a done this a long time ago, pard," Jasper said with a chuckle. "These places'll serve anyone with a little lose change in his pocket, even some young jake with a babyface like yours."

"Speaking of babyfaces, you looked in the mirror lately? Your face is as smooth as a baby's behind," John retorted, grinning.

"Not sure what kind of baby behinds you been lookin' at, pard, but they must've been some hairy little critters," Jasper quipped, mirroring John's look.

"I said smooth. I didn't say if'n that baby's behind had any fuss on it or not. Cheers, pard," John said with a huge smile as he raised his beer mug in a toast.

After they clinked mugs, they both took a long draw. The beer was bitter, but somehow rich with a zesty flavor, a flavor neither man had ever tasted before. They soon discovered it wouldn't be hard to follow the bartender's advice as their mugs quickly emptied.

"Damn, man, that's a mighty fine brew," John exclaimed, smacking his lips as he wiped foam off his upper lip with the back off his hand.

"A man could grow fond of a drink as fine as this one," Jasper said as he snickered at the wide-eyed expression on John's face.

After downing their first beer, they both soon ordered another and then another. Unaccustomed to the effects of alcohol, the two young men soon became tipsy and loud as they each laughed at nearly everything the other one said. Though they were obviously happy drunks, there are men in this world who get mean when they drink. The last thing a happy drunk wants to run into when he's three sheets to the wind is a mean drunk looking for a fight.

"Hey, watch where you're steppin'," a mangy-looking cowpuncher growled as he shoved Jasper in the back, causing him to spill his beer and stumble into another hard-looking character who soon took offense.

"Whoa, big guy, what the hell's going on?" the hard-looking *hombre* barked as he jumped up out of his chair.

John, struggling to fight off the effects of the alcohol, soon snapped out of his jovial mood and quickly assessed the swiftly escalating situation.

"Beggin' your pardons. We just be on our way," John slurred, hoping to find a way to maneuver Jasper and himself out of the crowded saloon without touching off an explosion of violence.

"Alright then, no harm done, goddamn it. Just be on your way," the hard-looking *hombre* growled, as he settled back down in his chair and took a generous gulp of whiskey.

"Not so fast, you two yahoos. That big sonuvabitch stepped on me," the cowpuncher bawled as he pointed at Jasper.

It was obvious to everyone in earshot the drunken cowpuncher was brewing for a fight.

"I apology for being so clumsy, sir. Let me buy ya drink," Jasper offered with a friendly smile as he held out his right hand to guide the offended cowpuncher to the bar.

Without warning, the cowpuncher hauled off and hit Jasper square in the mouth, throwing his head back and splitting his lower lip, causing blood to spray out. Surprised and rocked by the blow, Jasper staggered back a step and then came up swinging. His first punch landed square on the cowpuncher's nose, smashing it as flat as a pancake against the man's ugly face. His second blow caught the cowpuncher in the ribcage right at his solar plexus, busting ribs and doubling the cowpuncher over as he gasped for breath.

Jasper delivered his third blow with both of his balled-up fists crashing down on the cowpuncher's lower back. Like piledrivers, his fists sank deep into the man's kidneys, as the force of the blow pushed him headlong into the floor. Hitting the floor hard, face-first, the cowpuncher soon curled himself into a fetal position, twitching and groaning in agony like a wounded animal between ragged gasps as he struggled to catch his breath.

John had nearly been knocked over by a second cowpuncher who had come charging out of nowhere with pistol drawn to the rescue of his fallen comrade. Grabbing the handle of a mop leaning up against the bar next to him, John swung it down hard on the cowpuncher's extended forearm, sending his pistol flying. From the cracking sound that echoed off the walls of the saloon, and from the fact the oaked handle of the mop was still in one piece, there was little doubt the bones in the man's forearm had been broken. Clutching his forearm, the cowpuncher turned to meet John head on just as John swung the mop handle around like baseball bat, smacking him upside his head and dropping him where he stood.

With the would-be gunman lying at his feet, knocked out cold and bleeding from his right ear, John gripped the mop handle and surveyed the saloon, as he guarded against anyone else venturing to jump into the fray. The hard-looking *hombre* they had riled up earlier made no move to join the fight and with a crooked grin on his grizzly whiskered face he shook his head and nodded to both John and Jasper before taking another gulp of whiskey. The other customers also seemed content with their role as spectators. John breathed a sigh of relief when no one else made a move to lend the cowpunchers any aid.

John had known Jasper since childhood. Like his father, he was a big-boned man who could take a blow and dish one out just as well, and more often than not, better than most. He had never seen anyone who could take Jasper in a fair fight. Jasper was no idiot giant, however. He tended to surprise everyone with his sharp mind and his ability to pick up new things quickly. Though the saloon's clientele had grudgingly made room for the fighting men, in the main, business had continued unabated, with drinks flowing without missing a beat. When the dust finally settled, the burly bartender sprang into action.

"Alright, alright, the show's over," Ned barked as he came around from behind the bar. "Everyone, step aside now. Make a hole while I clean up this mess," he added, motioning for everyone to clear a path to the batwing door.

Without further fanfare, he grabbed the collars of both cowpunchers and quickly dragged them out into the street. After dumping them next to a nearby watering trough, he motioned for a Deputy Sheriff, sheepishly patrolling the other side of the street, to take the rowdy cowpunchers to the drunk tank. After getting a nod from the Deputy, he quickly returned to the saloon and his station behind the bar.

While the bartender was busy cleaning up the mess, John and Jasper slipped out of the saloon and hightailed it back to their hotel. They both knew it had been a close call. Had the cowpuncher's friend used his pistol or had any of the other customers joined in, there was no telling how things might have turned out. Jasper's lower lip was split and bleeding, but if that was the worst of it, they knew Lady Luck had shined on them this time around. They also knew she was a fickle maiden, who may not always be so kind.

After a restless night where neither man got much sleep, they got up at the crack of dawn and without a word quickly checked out of the hotel and hit the trail. As the sun lit up the eastern sky in streaks of crimson and gold, they rode south out of Saint Joe toward the Little Platte River, which they planned to follow to the crossing on the Missouri River at Independence.

Figuring the two cowpunchers wouldn't be released from jail until later in the day, they planned to put as much distance as possible between themselves and any potential acts of retaliation. They had no idea how big the cowpunchers' outfit was or if they had friends who might take offense at their shabby treatment. If they were Texans, the chances were high the two cowpunchers wouldn't let things drop easily. Texans were notorious for carrying a grudge. Getting even would be a high priority for such men. John and Jasper just hoped they would never run into the two mangy coyotes again. John worried, considering how quickly the one cowpuncher had pulled his pistol, that should he ever run into the man again, it might not end in a duel of simple fisticuffs.

John had planned to swing by Pappy's old cabin just to see where his mother had grown up. He had heard many stories about the area and was looking forward to finally being able to see things firsthand. Though he hadn't told Jasper, he also wanted to find the flat stone his mother had used for washing clothes along the Little Platte, the location where according to his father's many stories he had met Lucy for the first time. In his mind's eye, John thought he had a good idea where the stone might be located along the river in relation to Pappy's cabin.

"I think the cabin is just up yonder," John said as he motioned with his arm and pointed to a trail up through the trees branching off the main road.

"Let's take a look," Jasper replied.

It wasn't long before they rode into the yard of a cabin surrounded by several pole barns and outbuildings. A large black dog came around the cabin and started barking. The occupant of the cabin was soon out on the porch holding a shotgun in his right hand.

"You folks lost?" the man said in a stout voice.

"No, my grandpa is Joseph Breeden, he homesteaded this place. I've heard so much about it over the years, I just wanted to see it for myself. My name is John Barton," John said with a big smile on his face.

"So, you say you're one of Pappy's grandkids," the man said.

"That's right and this is my cousin, Jasper Waite," John replied.

"Well, step down and have a look around if ya like. Buck won't bite, his bark might sound tough, but he's as gentle as a kitten," the man said. "I'm Frank Clark, I bought this place from your grandpa about eight years ago."

As John and Jasper dismounted to have a look around, Frank added almost to himself, "My wife and kids are at a church social. I'm not partial to the new preacher, so I usually stay to home when they go."

John and Jasper walked around the place and could see the rich fields, that now lay fallow, stretching out across a rolling countryside. It was a well-maintained and beautiful piece of land and John could see the care his grandfather had taken in building a life for his family here. Buck, his tail ever wagging, followed them wherever they went and turned out to be a gentle as Frank claimed.

"This is a damn nice place," Jasper offered. "Too bad Pappy had to let it go when he moved."

"Seems a shame, but than none of us kids were old enough to work it and he couldn't do it alone. We have no other kin in these parts," John said.

"Tough to let a life's work go," Jasper said.

"No doubt, though I think Pappy is happy with his decision to come and live with my folks and us grandkids," John said. "He's a man of no regrets. He always says, 'What's done is done; what's next is the most important thing.'"

"I always enjoyed his stories about his adventures on the frontier," Jasper said.

"He has never stopped wanting to venture beyond the horizon; he truly loves the frontier. I guess I'm a lot like him," John said, thinking about Pappy and how his abiding influence had shaped how John had come to see the world.

After taking a grand tour of the place, they soon returned to the cabin, thanked Frank, mounted up, and headed back to the Little Platte. A row of low-lying brush separated the Little Platte and the main road. Cutting through the brush to look along the bank of river a number of times, John soon discovered the impossibility of finding the flat stone where his mother had done her laundry long ago. Jasper wondered what John was looking for and why it was so important, but said nothing, figuring it was something he needed to do. Giving up, John joined Jasper on the main road.

Worried about being followed, they took turns to check their backtrail after leaving Pappy's old place. Though he had wanted to find the flat stone where his parents first met, John accepted it was better that he hadn't. He had heard about their first meeting and what it had meant to them. He figured it was a memory and place better left for them, alone. He hoped that one day he and his future wife would share such a special memory.

As they rode south, John's mind drifted in and out of such thoughts until Jasper signaled they had reached the crossing to Independence. Wanting to stay ahead of any possible pursuers, they crossed the river by barge and rode straight through the port town of Independence and on to Kansas City without stopping.

"Independence was to be the new Zion for the Mormons until the Governor of the state of Missouri ran 'em out," John recalled as they passed quickly through the town.

"I heard that too. What happened?" Jasper asked wanting to learn why the Mormons had made a speedy exodus from Missouri and ended up settling way out in Utah Territory.

"Well, according to Pappy, back in 1831, about a year after Joseph Smith was visited by the Angel Moroni who instructed him to write the Book of Mormon, Smith proclaimed a 'New Jerusalem, a land of peace, a city of refuge, a place of safety for the saints' would be built in Independence, Missouri," John said as the two men rode on toward Kansas City.

"I take it folks around here didn't want so many Mormons comin' in and crowdin' them out," Jasper quipped. "It also seems the Eden they were building for themselves around here wasn't very acceptin' of the Mormon brand of Christianity."

"You're right on both counts. They sent the whole Mormon bunch packin', lock, stock, and barrel," John said without emotion. "I guess the Mormons will have to witness the Second Coming from their new Tabernacle in Salt Lake City."

"No doubt they'll try, but I'm not sure they can see Independence, Missouri from the other side of the continental divide," Jasper chuckled.

Jasper than suddenly got a serious look on his face and turned to meet John eye to eye. John had seen that look before and knew Jasper had something important to share.

"You know, pard, people'll believe in damn near anything. My pa believes in God and in God's will, everything follows from that. There's no accounting for his blind faith and no changing his mind. If something happens, and I mean to tell ya, if'n anything happens, God willed it. Once a man truly gives over his heart, truly gives it without reservation; his faith'll drive him beyond reason," Jasper said his expression still serious.

After riding in silence, he took a deep breath and concluded, "I can truly understand how strongly the Mormons must feel about their newfound faith. I can also understand how folks around here must've felt about believers in a faith so at odds with their own. Both sides have the right to believe in whatever God they choose. Fact is, faith has little to do with what's right or wrong."

Jasper's words hung in the air, expressing a truth that was understood without the need of deeper thought. John had himself witnessed how people had given their hearts to one another, or held a faith in something beyond their own understanding, and had, come what may, unwaveringly followed their beliefs to the bitter end.

The giving of one's heart was no simple matter. Finding a cause or person worth giving it to or believing in was no simple task. Indeed, it was the destiny of every man to search for that in which he might entrust his heart and himself fully. Though he wondered what his destiny held in store for him, he believed, like his father and his father before him, his destiny would be of his own making, somewhere beyond the horizon. As far as entrusting his heart, he knew that day would come when he found his other half.

March 8, 1884

St. Joseph, Buchanan County, Missouri

Axes to Grind

RUDY WOKE UP WITH a splitting headache and soon realized his nose was broken and probably more than one rib. His lower back throbbed with stabbing pain and he wasn't surprised when his piss was ruby red with blood. He was a man who had taken a hell of a beating and wanted nothing more than to even the score.

"Willie! Willie! You awake?" Rudy yelled at the inert form curled up in the far corner of the cell.

"Just let me sleep, Rudy. We ain't goin' nowhere," Willie whined.

"We got to get out of here. Them greenhorns that sucker punched us might still be in town," Rudy urged, noting that Willie's right forearm had been trussed up in a makeshift splint and the right side of his head had a huge egg-sized welt that had already turned several godawful shades of yellow, purple, and orange.

"Can't you see what that mop swinging bastard did to me?" Willie said between clinched teeth. "That bastard broke my arm and coldcocked me when I wasn't lookin."

"Like I said, we need to get out of here and track them bastards down and make 'em pay for what they've done," Rudy said, certain Willie would soon be onboard with his plan to get even.

Hours passed as the two men discussed possible ways to even the score. It wasn't until mid-afternoon that Sheriff Bates ambled in and unceremoniously unlocked their cell door.

"Good afternoon, gentlemen. The Bison Saloon isn't pressing charges and Judge Morton has no time to deal with your public intoxication charges today, so you're free to go," Sheriff Bates said with a smile. "Oh, and don't let the door hit you on the ass on your way out of town. I want you boys cleared out within the hour," he added, his face hard, his jovial smile nowhere to be found.

Once they hit the street, they went straight to the stockyards to pick up their pay vouchers from their last trail drive. They had helped herd over three thousand head of cattle out of eastern Colorado through the winter cold. The markets back east where demanding beef and though herds were generally not moved after the first snow flew, they had signed on for double wages for the late winter drive. With their pay vouchers in hand, the two men made a beeline to the First National Bank of Saint Joseph, where they soon drew their pay in cash.

"The next drives north out of Texas will be gathering their herds about now," Willie said.

"My thoughts exactly, I was thinkin' we might mosey on south to hire on to one of those drives," Rudy said. "Hell, we got a fist full of cash and time on our hands. We might just have a little fun on the way," he added with a chuckle.

Willie, nursing his broken forearm, wasn't in the partying mood. The doc who had patched him up had told him the bones in his forearm were badly fractured and might not heal right. He worried that he may end up with a bum right arm. He had seen plenty of men with crippled limbs; it wasn't the kind of future he had ever thought might be his own. As the men rode south, the pain in Willie's arm throbbed with every bounce in the saddle, despite liberal swigs of opium-laced laudanum every couple of hours.

Though he had little chance to ask around before their hurried departure from Saint Joe, Willie had learned that the two men they had fought with and who had gotten them both thrown in jail answered to the names of John and Jasper, and that they were headed to Texas to drive a herd of cattle north into the Dakota Territory. No one knew their last names, nor did they know the name of the outfit they were headed south to join. They only knew the men were headed for southern Texas by train from Kansas City. Willie felt they had enough information to track the bastards down. He felt the biggest clue they had was that there simply weren't many outfits pushing that many cattle that far north, especially into the untamed lands of the Lakota Sioux.

"Let's just get down to Texas as quickly as possible. I'd like to lay up in Mexico for a month or so to let my arm heal," Willie said, not wanting to upset Rudy who had a hair-trigger temper when he didn't get his way.

"I'd like to find out which drive our friends signed on with. The quicker we get down there the better chance we'll have in trackin' them down," Willie added, hoping to focus Rudy's mind on their plan to get even and off his clear desire to spend his hard-earned wages on booze and whores, which, if left to his own devices, he would do with abandon the first chance he got and would continue to do until he was dead broke.

"You're right Willie. Let's get you down to Mexico where a little senorita can doctor ya until you're all patched up again. While you're on the mend, I'll scout for outfits headed north until I sniff out those low-down varmints. Once we have 'em in our sights, they won't know what hit 'em," Rudy said enthusiastically, before laughing with abandon at the thought of getting even.

Willie joined in laughing as much about their dogged determination to even the score as their miserable physical condition. Rudy rode bent over nearly double in his saddle, his ribs heavily wrapped and his flattened nose pinched upright in a blood-soaked, splinted bandage. Willie, with his head wrapped in a turban-like bandage, rode while nursing the throbbing pain in his shattered right forearm that had been trussed up in a splint, its bandana sling tied around his neck. He couldn't deny, the two of them were a banged up, mangy lookin' pair of ragged cowpokes. Even so, all things considered, it felt good to have a plan and a clear goal in life, he thought. He then wondered, as he cradled his busted arm, if he really believed it.

With cash in their pockets and time on their hands, they rode toward the crossing at Independence with only one burning desire: revenge.

March 8, 1884

San Antonio, Bexar County, Texas

All Hat, No Cattle

TOM BURTON WAS A man used to being in charge. He had bucked and gouged his way to the top of the heap. At the age of fifty, he bestrode a cattle empire that controlled holdings that stretched from the Mexican border in Texas all the way to Colorado and Wyoming. His dream was to push his holdings into Dakota Territory and then on into Montana Territory and even beyond.

Being a short-statured, barrel-chested man, he never liked to deal with other men standing face to face. To gain the advantage, he always arranged for seated meetings where his chair was slightly elevated or gatherings on horseback where his horse was at least a hand or two taller than the others. His deep, commanding voice and confident manner, along with his handsome, stone-hard face, impeccable handlebar mustache, broad shoulders, and bulging fencepost forearms tended to intimidate lesser men. To maintain the illusion of his superiority and strength, he often held arm-wrestling contests among his cowpunching crews that he arranged to win on a regular basis.

His inferiority complex and vanity aside, he was a shewed business-man and a man true to his word with those who had earned his trust. He would do anything for his friends, if it also benefited himself, of course. His largesse didn't extend to those who hadn't won his trust or hadn't dealt with him honestly. For them he held no compassion and would seek to even the score the first chance he got.

Though he owned fifty thousand head of cattle and controlled over two hundred thousand acres of land, he hadn't been able to gather the ten thousand head of longhorn cattle he needed for his drive to the Dakota Territory. Gathering feral longhorns from southern Texas bush country had become next to impossible in recent years. The region had been picked over and worked by countless cowpunchers gathering feral longhorns for cattle drives headed north, leaving very few free-ranging longhorns to be found. The thick, thorny brush and endless draws and arroyo made the search all the more difficult. Despite having worked the region south and southeast of San Antonio for over a month, his men had gathered less than a thousand head. With the goal of gathering a herd of eight to ten thousand head, he worried that setting up his Dakota venture may cost him far more than he had planned. Though Burton owned land aplenty, and had cattle on his ranches in Wyoming and Colorado, he had very little working capital. Being strapped for cash made his situation dire. He knew he would need a large herd if he wanted to corner the market in the new High Plains region. Cattle were already flooding into ranches being set up north of the Black Hills. He needed to establish his cattle operations in the southern Black Hills as soon as possible.

The Trans-Nueces, the strip of land between the Rio Grande and the Nueces Rivers, had been a favorite hunting ground for feral Mexican long-horn cattle since the U.S. annexation of Texas and the establishment of the Texas border with Mexico at the Rio Grande River in 1845. The unilateral movement of the national border from the Nueces River to the Rio Grande River further to the south was the final spark that ignited the Mexican-American War that end with the Treaty of Guadalupe Hidalgo in 1848. As a result, Mexico was forced to cede not only the territory of Texas, but a whopping 55 percent of its claimed national lands in North America.

Burton found himself weighing the price of sending men in quick forays across the Rio Grande to drive as many feral cattle back into Texas as they could find. It would be a risky move that could touch off a major confrontation; however, if successful, it could quickly swell the number of cattle in his current gather, and as importantly, at a price that was hard to argue with. Feral cattle cost him nearly nothing beyond cowpuncher wages. The more he thought about his plan, the broader a wily grin spread across his cold hard features, remolding them into a jolly smiling face, something few people had ever witnessed.

He would send teams of three riders each south of the border to scout out feral cattle over the next several weeks, then at the first new moon, the teams of riders would move as one and push as many cattle as possible north across the Rio Grande and into Texas, where other riders would be waiting to quickly gather and move the herd further north into the Trans-Nueces and then on to San Antonio. Everything would need to move like clockwork with every team driving their gathered cattle out of Mexico on the same night.

The movement of the cattle across the border wasn't an operation that could be done over several days or weeks, it needed to be a lighting strike that would leave little for the Federales and Texas Rangers to discover. They would move like ghosts without a trace. Once they drove the animals into the Trans-Nueces, the vast stripe of land between the Rio Grande and the Nueces River, there would be no way for any authorities on either side of the border to determine where the feral longhorns had originated from.

The plan was just audacious enough that it might actually work. He figured, with the era of feral longhorns free for the picking coming to an end, the rewards of one last big gather south of the border were well worth the risks.

March 8, 1884

Kansas City, Johnson County, Missouri

At the River's Bend

KANSAS CITY WAS THE largest city John and Jasper had ever seen. The stockyards were sprawling and said to be second in size only to Chicago. The fine mansions that lined the main avenues told the two men that the city had grown rich as the county pushed ever westward.

Still concerned the two cowpunchers they had fought with in Saint Joe may be on their trail, they rode directly to the West Bottom, where the new Union Depot stood like an ornate castle out of a fairytale. Tall towers shot up on all sides of the building with a huge clock tower straddling the main entrance that soared nearly out of sight when looking up from directly below. In awe, they entered the huge central terminal, rubbernecking at the architectural splendor that met their gaze in every direction. Though it took them some time to find the right ticket window and to buy their tickets, it wasn't long before they found themselves back on the street.

With over four hours before their train departed, they decided they would take a quick tour of the downtown district. The closer they came to downtown Kansas City, the busier the shops and traffic on the streets. They had been told 12th Street had many diners, saloons, and taverns. With their minds focused on dining on thick beef steaks with a couple mugs of cold beer to wash it down, they soon settled into a table near the back of the main dining room of the Lady Luck Tavern.

Having escaped from Saint Joe without either the law or angry cowpunchers immediately on their trail, they figured it was only apropos to dine at the Lady Luck Tavern; she had definitely pulled their fat out of the fire at the Bison Bull Saloon. Both boys, being more than a little superstitious, believed that paying their respects to Lady Luck seemed the right thing to do.

"What ya havin'?" a busty waitress said as she leaned into their table.

Taking in her substantial cleavage, her ruby red lips, and powdered face, Jasper could only stare bug-eyed, unable to speak.

"We'll have a couple of medium-rare Kansas City strip steaks and two mugs of cold beer," John said, noticing Jasper's face growing redder by the second.

"I'll hotfoot that right to ya," she said smiling and giving Jasper a sideways look.

Jasper's face had grown crimson by the time she performed a little twirl in front of him and barked out their order to the cook in the back of the tavern.

"Damn, Jasper, what's got into ya?" John asked with a concerned look on his face.

"She's, she's, she's about the most beautiful woman I've ever seen," Jasper stuttered, his face slowly returning from crimson to a rosy pink.

"Yeah, she's pretty I'll grant ya that," John said, knowing there is no accounting for another man's tastes in women. *Beauty is indeed in the eye of the beholder*, John thought. Though he, too, found the waitress pretty, he was convinced right then and there that whoever had first spoken those words knew what he was talking about.

"Yeah," Jasper said dreamily. "She's perfect, absolutely perfect."

About halfway through their second mug of beer, Jasper's confidence found its voice. When the pretty little waitress made her way back to their table, he was ready.

"You boys finished," she said pointing at their empty plates.

"Yes ma'am, and those were mighty fine steaks, mighty fine," Jasper said beaming at the little waitress like a schoolboy hoping the teacher would give him a gold star.

"I'll let the cook know. He'll be happy to find out at least somebody likes his cookin'," she joked, smiling at Jasper, her eyes locking on his and his eyes locking on hers in what John would later describe as a kind of blissful fog of two lovebirds lost in their own world together.

"By the way, where you handsome boys from?" she said, leaning in so close to Jasper as she picked up his plate that several strains of her long blonde hair brushed his flushed cheek, causing the hue to darken as Jasper's heart raced.

Jasper, with his eyes glued on hers and intoxicated by the scent of her, would have at that moment followed her to the ends of the Earth if she would have only led the way.

"I—I—we're from up north," Jasper finally offered.

"Yep, we're riding through on our way south," John said, glad that Jasper had enough sense not to provide too many details about who they were or about what their future plans might be.

His father had warned him to be careful not to share too much with total strangers. His father never failed to add, "If you want to avoid trouble, it's always better to err on the side of caution."

"You boys staying in town for the big dance?" she said, looking straight at Jasper, her lips full and inviting, her eyes never leaving his.

"Dance? They havin' a dance tonight?" Jasper said a bit too loudly as he sat up straight in his chair.

"Yes, they have a big dance at the Meridian Saloon every Saturday night. I'd like to go, but I haven't got a partner," she said her eyes still locked on Jasper's.

"We have a train to catch tonight, but we have time for a few dances. I'll be your partner," Jasper stammered, his face still flush. "I apologize, but I haven't asked for your name,"

"I'm Maryanne and I'm pleased to meet ya," she said with a shaky voice. "What's your name?"

"My name's Jasper, Jasper Waite, and I'm indeed honored to make your acquaintance," Jasper said, trying to be as formal and proper as possible with the woman of his dreams.

"My name is John," John volunteered, though neither Maryanne nor Jasper seemed to notice.

Relegated to mere spectator, John watched as the budding lovebirds seemed to drift, suspended in their own world, utterly infatuated with one another.

"I get off soon. Meet me on the porch of the Great Western Hotel on the corner of 10th Street in thirty minutes. The dance has already started," she said as she swept up their plates and was gone before either man could answer.

Jasper seemingly unable to break her spell, followed her every move as she daftly bobbed and weaved through the tables and into the kitchen.

Once she was no longer in sight, he turned to John and he said, "Let's go."

After slapping two shinny Morgans on the table the two men headed for the door. Back on the street, Jasper was a man on a mission, as he marched directly to the porch of Great Western Hotel on the corner of 10th Street and Main. Grabbing three empty chairs which lined the outer wall of the hotel facing the street, the two men each took a seat while Jasper jealously guarded an empty chair he had pulled up next to his own. Jasper was more nervous than John had ever seen him before.

They hadn't been seated for more than a minute, when a young lady in thick makeup came sashaying out of the hotel flashing her long slender fishnet-covered legs through long slits that ran down the sides of her sequin-dress as she strode over to them. Held by two thin straps over her shoulders, she carried a tray on which was arranged a variety of tobacco products. Bending over in front of them she gestured to the many products on offer; her eyes and the way she shimmied her substantial and near naked breasts told them the items on offered included things far beyond the mere pleasures of tobacco.

Jasper seemed not to notice the tobacco lady's many and alluring wares, his mind filled only with the anticipation of meeting Maryanne again. Unable to completely steady his shaking hands, he bought a pouch of tobacco, rolling papers, and a small box of stick matches. After the cute little tobacco lady settled up with Jasper, she turned and winked at John and gave him her sweetest come-hither smile.

"Women around here sure are friendly," John said as he watched the little gal sashay down the porch and back into the hotel showing more than a little of what she had on offer.

With trembling hands, Jasper fought to roll himself a cigarette, something he had done only a few times in his life. Finally getting a botched-up smoke put together, he lit up and took a long-ragged drag which caused him to cough nearly uncontrollably. Steadying himself, he took a second drag that seem to agree with him better.

Blowing out a huge plume of smoke, he offered John the tobacco bag and papers. John took the tobacco and papers and quickly rolled himself a smoke. The tobacco was strong and tasty, and John enjoyed playing the role of a grown man.

He and Jasper had already come a long way, and having a smoke out in public seemed to confirm they were now men, grown up and out in the world. Unaccustomed to smoking, the two men became a little dizzy and soon focused on relaxing and enjoying the hubbub around them. Time seemed to slow as they let the tension of the past two days drain into the well-worn boards of the porch.

"Jasper, Jasper, I'm so glad you waited," Maryanne said as she bounded onto the porch.

Seeing her, Jasper sprang to his feet and took her hand ever so gently and guiding her into the chair next to him. He was mesmerized by her beauty and her irresistible feline-like allure.

"Let's go to the dance," she purred, her breath warm on his ear, and then stood squeezing his hand and pulling him up out of his chair. Holding hands, the couple stepped off the porch as though they had known each other all their lives. John, feeling like an unwelcome house guest, followed them to the Meridian Saloon, wondering where this chance meeting of lovebirds might lead.

Music and light spilled out into the street as they approached the Meridian. The high-pitched laughter of young ladies having a good time filled the air. The fiddler was calling the dance as couples dutifully followed his cadence.

allemande left, allemande right

Swing your partners to and fro

Meet 'em the middle and do-si-do

Promenade!

Maryanne pulled Jasper into the press of bodies and John watched as they were absorbed into the tangle. Jasper was easy to track since he stood a good head taller than average, which was a comfort to John, who reminded himself they would need to get back to Union Depot in less than two hours. They had already arranged for their horses and gear to be loaded once the train was ready to leave. As for John and Jasper, they only needed to board the train on time. John began to wonder if Jasper would be willing to leave with him, when the time came to board.

Jasper could feel Maryanne press her body hard against his every time they came together which excited him like nothing he had ever felt before. Looking into her eyes, he could see she, too, liked him, and he wished he only had more time to find out everything about her. She wasn't the first girl he had liked, but she was like no other girl he had ever known. She made him feel important and proud, proud that she had chosen him when so many other men had surely vied for her hand. He felt he had to be honest with her; he needed to tell her he was leaving town that night. He was afraid if he did he would lose her. He never wanted to let her go.

"Maryanne, I know we just met, but I feel like I've always known you. I like you a lot and want to get to know you better, but me and my pard have to board the train soon. I'll be away for many months," Jasper said struggling to be honest.

Maryanne stopped dancing in mid-swing and guided Jasper to the far edge of the dancefloor.

"Jasper. Kiss me now you fool," she said as the two of them fell into each other's arms. He kissed her like he had never kissed a woman before. His split lower lip was tender, but he couldn't help wanting her lips touching his. He knew he would never be able to forget her taste, her scent, her tenderness.

"I don't want to ever lose you," he said meaning every word, but knowing he must do what he had signed on to do. He had to go to Texas and complete the drive.

"My darling, I never want to lose you either. When's your train?" she said with urgency, tears running down her cheeks.

"In about an hour," he said looking into her big blue eyes and nearly losing himself in them.

"My room is near here. Come on," she said without a thought and pulled him out the back of the saloon and down the alley.

John suddenly became concerned when he lost sight of Jasper in the crowd of dancers. Frantic to find his partner, he wrestled his way through the crowded saloon circling the dance floor and coming up with neither Jasper nor Maryanne anywhere in sight. With their train ready to roll in less than an hour, he wasn't sure what to do. Stepping outside, he caught sight of Jasper and Maryanne headed up the street.

"Jasper! Jasper! Where you headed?" John shouted.

"I'll see you at the depot. Go ahead and I'll catch up," Jasper said and then turn and hurried up the boardwalk in the opposite direction.

Seeing there was little he could do, John started to head for the depot and then changed his mind midstride. Now more than ever, he was determined to watch his partner's back. He had no idea who Maryanne was or what she might have in store for Jasper. Turning back, he caught a glimpse of the couple as they ducked into an alley up the street. Running to catch up, John slowed his pace when he reached the corner of the alley. Peeking around the corner, he watched as Jasper swept Maryanne up into his arms and carried her up a stairway and into a side door on the second floor of what looked like a women's boarding house.

Looking up at the windows on the second floor, he soon saw the glow of a lantern being lit. John decided to wait in the alley to guard against any foul play. They had pledged to watch each other's back. He would keep his end of their bargain, even if it wasn't necessary. Their train would leave in a little more than forty-minutes. He figured they could make it to their track in ten minutes, if they ran like hell. He decided to give the star-crossed lovers a generous twenty-minutes before he got in the middle of things.

Time crawled. John, still in possession of Jasper's tobacco, rolled himself a smoke and tried to relax. Getting into fights, running from vengeful cowpunchers, chasing after women, drinking, and smoking, *What next?*, he thought.

All in all, their world had become a damn sight more complicated since they left Webster County. Thinking about everything that had happened over the past two days, his mind drifted from one thing to another. Looking at his watch, he was shocked to realize, he had waited for Jasper more than twenty minutes. They had to get on the move, and now!

Rushing up the back stairs, he ran smackdab into Jasper, who was making a mad dash out the side door. With no time to say all the things that might have been said or might have needed to be said, they both turned and bounded down the stairs and out into the street. Quickly getting their bearings, they ran toward Union Depot as fast as they could possibly run all the way to track number five, where the Missouri Pacific's train to Denison, Texas was already pulling out of the station.

In an act of desperation, the two men jumped headlong onto the narrow deck between the end rail and the back of the caboose just before the train cleared the end of the platform. Disheveled and laying prostrate, they looked up and met the conductor's stern glare as he stood over them, hands on his hips with a deep frown showing under is bushy-mustached face.

Frantically, they searched their pockets and, almost in unison, offered their wrinkled and bent up tickets to the conductor, who reluctantly punched them and without a word, turned, and entered the caboose to return to his duties. After regaining their feet, the men dusted themselves off.

John and Jasper remained silent for a long moment as they stood watching the train weave its way through a series of switching stations on its way south out of Kansas City. They stood at the back of the train and watched a thin sliver of a crescent moon slowly rise in the east, its delicate, tranquil, and silent beauty standing in stark contrast to the sharp clanging of crossing bells, screeching of steel, and chugging of the train's mighty steam engine as it gathered speed.

Unable to hold back any longer, John turned to Jasper and asked, "And so, what about this little heifer named Maryanne?"

With that, the two men burst into a belly laugh that doubled them over. Neither man could believe how close they had come to missing their train. It seemed Lady Luck still had their backs.

Still trying to catch his breath and wiping tears from his eyes, Jasper said, "She's the love of my life, pard. I'm coming back here as soon as we complete the drive and I'm going to marry the little heifer named Maryanne!"

John could see at once that Jasper was dead serious.

Before John could reply, Jasper declared in a loud shout as if to tell the whole world the wonderful news, "She is everything a man could ever want, and she loves me!"

"That's wonderful, but are you sure? You just met her, and we'll be gone a long time," John cautioned.

"That may be, but she'll wait and so'll I. We belong with one another. I knew she was the gal for me, the first time I laid eyes on her at the tavern," Jasper said matter-of-factly.

John knew better than to ask how things went at the boarding house. Considering a lot of lovin' and gettin' to know one another can happen in a long twenty minutes, he figured they had had plenty of time to consummate their new relationship. The way Jasper was acting and the fresh kiss mark on his neck confirmed that the couple had done just that, and much to Jasper's likin' if the sparkle in his eye was any indicator.

"I have her mailing address and plan to write every chance I get," Jasper offered. "She'll send letters to the towns we'll stop at along the way, once I know the route our trail drive will take. We'll keep in touch until we're together again. You'll see," he assured John, confident he had it all worked out.

The two men had to wait until the train stopped at Olathe, Kansas to quickly hop off the caboose and run up the platform past the livestock and luggage cars to the passenger coaches and their reserved compartment seats. The journey would be a long one, taking nearly three days with train changes at Denison and Galveston, Texas before arriving in San Antonio. The men were relieved to finally be able to settle in for the journey.

Seated opposite them in their compartment were a couple of business-men headed to Melrose in Nacogdoches County, Texas where they wanted to look into the operations of an active oil well. John and Jasper had heard about the growing use of oil and about the growing influence of the Standard Oil Company that seemed to be trying to corner the burgeoning new market. That Texas, like Pennsylvania, Ohio, and Indiana, had oil wells was not something they had ever heard about, however.

"Yes, we understand that a Mr. Barret has had a producing oil well in Nacogdoches County since 1866," Timothy Gillam said, emphasizing the discovery of oil in Texas was not a recent event.

Timothy Gillam was the smaller and older of the two men, and was clearly the man in charge. He wore a three-piece pinstriped suit which displayed his gentlemanly status. His hair and mustache were carefully groomed, even his skin seemed smooth and blemish-free. Though his overall appearance was impeccable, the thing that was the most noticeable to any working man was that his hands showed no signs of use and his fingernails were meticulously manicured and clean; something rarely seen west of the Mississippi.

"That's right, if Mr. Barret can find oil in Texas, we think we may have an opportunity to find more," Mr. Harvey Bliss offered. "If you boys would like to invest in our little venture called the Kendall Refinery located on Kendall Creek in Pennsylvania, we'd be please to sell you shares. It'd be a wise investment, that I can assure you. We set up our operations in 1881 and we have big plans—big, big plans—and Texas just might supply the oil we're lookin' for."

As it would turn out, Timothy Gillam and Harvey Bliss had a nose for crude; Texas would emerge as a major global producer in coming years. It wasn't until the January 10, 1901 Spindletop gusher however that the Texas oil boom finally got underway. In 1901, Texas production shot up more than four times to more than four million barrels, due almost entirely to the Spindletop strike. By 1902, Spindletop produced over seventeen million barrels, or 94 percent of all Texas production, pushing prices down to three cents a barrel, an all-time low. After the boon brought by the Spindletop strike, one major oil strike after another followed in coming years.

Harvey Bliss was also dressed in a business suit, though its fit was less than perfect. He had obviously put on weight and looked as though he had been poured into undersized britches. His hair was well-groomed and face clean-shaven, his pudgy cheeks even carried a rosy glow, one that matched his thick lips and dimpled chin, which he dabbed incessantly with a white handkerchief that never seemed to leave his right hand.

"Your kind offer sounds very promising, but we're fresh out of cash and lookin' to make our fortunes in the cattle business," John said with confidence.

"Cattle, you say," Bliss said. "They already have all the cattle they can handle down in Texas, don't they?"

"That's why we plan to gather as many of 'em up as we can and drive 'em further north," Jasper said.

"Yes, that sounds like a good plan. Beef prices are higher the further away you get from Texas," Gillam said wading into the conversation.

"That's the gamble we're makin', gentlemen. It's why we're headed south," John said trying to sound like the man he wished he was, and like a man who knew what he was talking about, which he wished he did.

"Well, it seems Texas might hold a cornucopia of opportunities, enough for all of us," Bliss chuckled.

"Indeed, there're opportunities to be had for those who can see 'em," Jasper added.

"Yes, as a good friend of mine used to say: In a country of the blind, the one-eyed are kings," Gillam shared, smiling.

Being a well-read and highly educated man, Timothy Gillam always liked to throw out a pearl or two whenever he got the chance. The old French proverb was one such pearl he had often shared.

"So they are," John said, liking the expression as it summed up well the value of being able to see when others could not.

Over the next two days, the men talked about many things, including the upcoming presidential election between Democratic candidate Grover Cleveland and Republican candidate James G. Blaine. As their conversation drifted across a wide array of topics, Gillam threw out his pearls of wisdom whenever he saw an opening.

Many of the topics discussed were beyond John and Jasper's experience or knowledge, but listening to the men debate one topic after another opened up whole new vistas of thought and knowledge to them. John and Jasper would later discover that more than a few of Gillam's pearls of wisdom would turn out to be more valuable than either man could have ever imagined at the time.

March 11, 1884

San Antonio, Bexar County, Texas

Cold Welcome

ARRIVING IN SAN ANTONIO mid-afternoon, they were met at the station by a rough-looking, scar-faced, one-eyed Mexican named José Rodriquez. Beyond helping them gather their gear and round up their horses, he had little to say. When asked, he informed them that Don Tomás Burton was away and would be back to welcome them the next day. After riding straight south from San Antonio for over an hour, they came to the main gate of the Rocking T Ranch, one of several ranches owned by south Texas cattle baron Thomas Burton. José showed them where to put up their horses and led them to an empty bunkhouse that had beds enough for at least twenty men. Picking a couple of bunks on the far end of the main room, they quickly settled in and stowed their gear.

Following the irresistible aroma of fresh-baked bread, the two men found themselves at the side door of the main house. An elderly white-haired butler named Jarvis appeared in a well-pressed waistcoat with tails and escorted them to a long table just off the kitchen where meals were served to ranch hands working on the place.

Once again, they found themselves alone. Just when they began to wonder what would happen next, a short, stout, middle-aged Mexican lady who introduced herself as Lucia soon appeared with large plates of fried chicken, biscuits and gravy, green beans, and a variety of other side dishes. After several attempts to speak with Lucia, they soon discovered she spoke no English, or at least pretended not to speak the lingo. She served them in silence and before long Jarvis returned to escort them out of the main house.

John and Jasper found themselves perplexed. They had been treated well enough by everyone they met, and yet it seemed they weren't exactly welcome. Weary from their long journey and with their stomachs stuffed to bursting, they fell into their bunks and were soon fast asleep.

Both men were up at the crack of dawn and excited to get started.

"Hey boys, you up?" a voice boomed from somewhere outside the bunkhouse.

"We're up and lookin' to get started," John yelled back.

"Good, good. See you at the main house for breakfast. We'll talk there," the voice replied, drifting off, as if the speaker had already turned to walk to the main house.

"Well, I'm not sure, but I think that was Tom Burton. We best get washed up and hustle on over to the main house," John said.

"We're doin' it, pard, we're really doin' it," Jasper said, clearly still in disbelief and excited about all that had happened to them in the past week.

In less than five minutes, the men washed up and hustled over to the main house, as giddy as two kids on the first day of school. As they entered the dining room, Tom Burton was already seated at the head of the table with José seated to his right. José's single ravine-sharp eye locked onto the two boys and tracked them to their seats. John couldn't help wondering if they would ever win him over.

"Welcome boys. I'm Tom Burton and I guess you already met José yesterday. I'm happy you made it down here without any trouble," Tom said extending his big meaty right-hand.

After handshakes all round, everyone settled into their seats. John and Jasper sat across from José with Burton at the head of the table. Burton wanted to hear all about their trip. John provided an outline of their journey, leaving out their barfight and hasty departure from Saint Joe and any details about Jasper's Kansas City love affair.

"Good to hear you were able to avoid trouble. Tough thing to do for any young man these days. Seems there's trouble everywhere," Tom said studying the two young men and leaving the impression he might have more to say.

"Yes, we saw plenty of trouble, but tried hard to sidestep it," Jasper said. His split lip was on the mend and he had covered up the kiss mark on his neck with his bandana. He worried Burton might notice and ask about one or the other, or both of these obvious features, but tried to act nonchalant and as innocent as a pious choirboy.

"Good, good," Tom said, nodding. Looking at John, he added, "Your pa sent me a telegram and wanted me to let you know all is well back home and that he wished both you boys good luck."

Their conversation continued through breakfast with Burton recounting how he knew Bill Barton during and after the war and how he owed Bill a favor. He was pleased he could repay an old debt to a friend. What he didn't tell them was that Bill Barton had saved his life and in many ways was the man who got him started in the cattle business nearly twenty years earlier. Tom Burton, like Bill Barton, had been a spy for the Union during the war and, like Barton, had also tried his hand at cattle rustling in the South after the war.

Barton had helped him move nearly a thousand head of rustled cattle into Indian Territory. It was during that foray into southern Missouri that they were ambushed and nearly killed. Barton had saved the day by charging the bushwhackers, guns blazing, killing several before the others broke and ran. Burton had been shot, but was able to escape with the herd. Barton ended up with a hundred head of cattle as payment, but Burton had never repaid Bill Barton for saving his life. He felt helping Bill's son fulfill his dream of staking a claim to land in the Dakota Territory was the least he could do. He also couldn't be happier that he now had a couple of Jokers up his sleeve; riders he could trust without question. In a game where Jokers were always wild, they could help a man turn a losing hand into a winner nearly every time.

Before excusing himself, Burton informed them that he had business in San Antonio and wouldn't be back for a couple of days. In the meantime, twelve to fifteen riders would be moving into the bunkhouse sometime tomorrow afternoon. He asked José to show the boys around the ranch and to make sure they were introduced to the riders coming in. José graciously accepted his duties for the day. It was clear, however, that José wasn't happy about having to play wet nurse to a couple of greenhorns. John and Jasper both knew proving they could do the work and winning José's favor wouldn't be easy. Come what may, they were both determined to do just that.

"When I get back, I'll fill you in our plans for the gather over the next month. We'll start moving our herd north by mid-April," Tom said with confidence.

With that, he headed for the carriage waiting for him at the front of the house. John, Jasper, and José followed.

Standing on the front porch, they watched Burton's carriage disappeared over the first rolling hill. John and Jasper felt as though they too were on their way. John dreamed of Dakota Territory and his plan to stake his claim. Jasper couldn't wait until he would be able return to Kansas City and hold Maryanne in his arms again. José, knowing he would have to follow the Don's orders, wondered why Don Burton, despite his debt to Bill Barton, would hire a couple of *niños* when he could easily hire skilled *vaqueros* that to a man could do twice the work in a day that either of the *gringo* greenhorns could.

Shaking his head in disgust, he motioned for John and Jasper to follow him to the barn. After saddling up their horses and filling their canteens, José pointed to a ridge on the horizon and nudged his horse into a fast trot. John and Jasper kept pace as the men rode in silence.

"José, you don't seem very happy about having us here," John ventured.

Though he worried about prodding José with pointed questions for fear of the answers he might get, he figured they needed to know what was troubling José and what he really thought.

After riding in silence for several minutes, José finally turned in his saddle and replied, "You're right. I don't think you know the first damn thing about cowpunching and you damn sure don't have the sand to make a drive all the way to the Dakota Territory."

His words cut deep and John and Jasper both wondered if he might not be right.

"Well, as they say, time'll tell," John said while trying to look straight at José in a show of bravado he really didn't feel.

Meeting José's single unblinking eye square on, John found it difficult to hold eye contact with the one-eyed *hombre*.

"*Sí, Sí, el tiempo dirá,*" José said, nodding as a grin spread from under his long mustache across his pock-ridden face. Without further comment, he turned forward in his saddle and spurred his horse.

"Things are goin' to be downright tough around here," Jasper said, coming up beside John.

"We'll just have to get a damn sight tougher," John growled, his face and the tone of his voice both cold and deadly serious.

Pulling down his hat, John spurred his horse in an effort to catch up with José.

"We'll kick the shit out of him, if we have to, pard," Jasper said more to himself than to John, who was already gone.

Determined not to let his partner down, Jasper pulled his hat down tight, and spurred his horse into a gallop.

When they finally arrived at the distant ridge, José was waiting for them. Holding out his right arm, he waved it in a broad arch and told them that Don Burton's Rocking T Ranch covered all the land they could see in every direction, sixteen thousand acres in all, a full twenty-five sections of land. The thought that one ranch could cover twenty-five square miles of land was beyond anything they could imagine.

In Iowa, an average farm was one hundred sixty acres and a large one was three hundred twenty acres, or half a square mile. Some large places had been able to gather six hundred forty acres, a full section or one square mile, through marriage and such, but they were few and far between. Nothing prepared them for land holdings beyond what a man could see in every direction from the top of a hill.

What also caught their eye was that there were very few cattle on the open rangelands. Given that the plan was to drive over four to five thousand head of longhorn cattle north out of the Rocking T Ranch in roughly a month, they wondered where all the cattle were. It was a question they would soon have an answer for, an answer neither man could have ever expected, and one that would require a choice neither would be prepared to make.

March 12, 1884

Primavera, Nuevo Laredo,
State of Tamaulipas, Mexico

Borderline

WHEN RUDY AND WILLIE finally arrived in Laredo, Texas, they wasted no time in buying fresh horses, crossing the border, and settling into the small pueblo of Primavera. Despite being only fifteen miles east the border crossing at Laredo, the locals spoke little English and lived in a world very different than their northern neighbors. Life was simple in Primavera. Willie needed simple. He needed time to heal his mangled arm. He needed a good woman to tend to him and to comfort him at night. Like any wounded animal, he needed time to lick his wounds.

With his hard-earned money burning a hole in his pocket since departing Saint Joe, Rudy couldn't wait to get Willie settled in, so he could return to the hurly-burly saloons of Laredo and to all the trouble he could find there. He also wanted to begin the search for John and Jasper, the two yahoos who had run off without paying a price for their cowardliness. He swore to the devil himself that if he ever tracked the two sucker-punching bastards down, he would make them pay for what they had done.

With Willie under the care and in the arms of a homely yet motherly senorita nearly twice his age, Rudy paid in advance to ensure his partner's needs would be tended to during his absence, both morning and night. Promising to return in two to three weeks, he rode out without looking back.

While changing the dressings on Willie's arm, the senorita discovered that his arm had become badly infected and had started to smell of rotting flesh. After the local doctor looked at the wound, he met Willie's worried eyes with a growing concern in his own.

"*Debemos amputar de inmediato,*" the doctor said with urgency.

Willie, running a high fever and nearly delirious, didn't speak Spanish; even so, he understood all too well what the man had said. *Amputar* could only mean one thing: the doctor would have to take his right arm, *immediato*—immediately.

"Is there nothing that can be done?" Willie begged, knowing it was far too late.

The rancid smell of rotting flesh filled the room and was overwhelming.

"*No, debemos amputar ahora,*" the doctor said, shaking his head.

"Amputate now," Willie lipped.

The doctor nodded his head in agreement, and said, "*Sí, amputar ahora.*"

Willie, fighting through a feverish haze, could only weakly reply, "*Sí, amputar ahora.*"

With that, the doctor quickly flew into action. After the senorita fed Willie several stiff gulps of his opium-laced laudanum mixed with the strongest tequila she could find, the doctor wasted no time in taking off Willie's arm at the elbow. Studying the amputated forearm, the doctor noted it was no more than a mush of rotting flesh, with its bones a shattered mishmash of shards; there had never been any hope of saving the arm. He cursed the so-called *medico* who had treated the man. Had the infection gone untreated for another couple of days, it would have been too late.

With his fever broken, Willie awoke two days later only to realize the horrible nightmare he had lived through in his restless sleep hadn't been a dream at all. Though he could still feel the fingers of his right hand, his right arm ended at the elbow. Search as he might, his right hand was no longer there. He had never seen a one-armed cowpuncher and wondered, now that he was a cripple, what life held for him.

There was only one thing he was certain about: he would find the bastards who ruined his life and see to it that their lives were also ruined before he would allow himself the joy of killing them both. He prayed Rudy would soon return with word that he had tracked the bastards down.

Now that he only had a cauterized stump to heal, he would be able to ride sooner than he expected. Rather than waste good time while he waited for Rudy's return, he would practice day and night, fast drawing and shooting with his left hand. He may not be a cowpuncher anymore, but he still had one good arm and he could damn well learn to draw and shoot faster than any two-armed varmint. Now that he was nothing but a one-armed cripple, the two cocksure, sucker-punching greenhorns who had caused him so much trouble would never see him coming.

March 12, 1884

Don Martín, State of Coahuila, Mexico

Mexican Hat Dance

LOOKING OUT OVER HIS vast holdings of rangeland in the State of Coahuila bordering on the Venustiano Carranza Dam near the little pueblo of Don Martín just south of Villa Juarez, Don Enrico Martín Lopez knew he would need to be patient, something he had never learned how to do very well. He had come from a rich, privileged family and had never lacked for anything, including men who would do exactly what he told them to do without question. The note he held in his hand had come at a price, but then the information it held was to him priceless. He had for years tried to outfox Don Tomás Burton, but had been vexed at every turn. They had both fought across the border in an endless tit-for-tat that all too often left Lopez the loser.

Burton had committed many sins and had stolen countless cattle from south of the border. He had even been one of the central Texas cattle barons who back in 1875 prodded Captain Leander McNelly to lead a force of renegade Texas Rangers across the Mexican border to drive more than two thousand head of so called stolen cattle back into Texas. As it turned out, many of those cattle bore Mexican brands and had never been north of the border; many of them had belonged to Don Lopez.

The armed conflict triggered by the illegal raid resulted in the death of Don Juan Flores Salinas, one of the most famous cattle barons in all of Mexico. In time, the battle came to be known as the Las Cuevas War. None of the cattle taken by the Rangers were ever returned and none of the nearly one hundred Mexican lives lost in the conflict ever avenged. What burned in Lopez's belly like a searing ember that couldn't be extinguished was the desire to make greedy *gringo* demons like Don Burton pay for their careless disregard for Mexican lives and Mexican sovereignty.

In recent years, the size of cattle herds on both sides of the border had grown beyond the carrying capacity of the land, resulting in overgrazing and overproduction, driving down prices and driving many smaller ranches out of business. With huge landholdings and enormous herds of cattle on both sides of the border, Lopez knew that Mexican and Texan cattle barons would continue to fight for dominance and survival. He could also clearly see the handwriting on the wall: the era of the longhorn was quickly coming to an end.

Texas ranchers were already building herds of Hereford Longhorn hybrids and other blooded stock. Fences were going up north and south of the border as ranchers sought to control scarce feed and water resources. Unlike the ranchers in Texas, Lopez and his Mexican compatriots no longer had untamed lands to conquer to the north—these had all been stollen by their northern *gringo* neighbors. The 1848 Treaty of Guadalupe Hidalgo between Mexico and the United States of America, which ended the Mexican-American War, forced Mexico to cede all its lands north of the Rio Grande all the way to the west coast; lands that now made up all or part of the states of Texas, California, and Colorado and the territories of Arizona, Nevada, New Mexico, Utah, and Wyoming. Having lost over half of Mexico's national territory, the Mexican government's central challenge had become holding onto and defending the sovereign territory it still held. In northern Mexico, the biggest challenge faced by Mexican ranchers was from Texas cattle barons like Don Burton, who believed they had a right to all the feral longhorns they could gather wherever they could find them, north or south of the border.

For many years, Lopez employed spies to work on several ranches controlled by the largest cattle barons north of the border. He had placed his biggest bet on a ranch hand who had been working on the Rocking T Ranch for many years and who had gained the trust of Don Burton. The note he held in his hand was worth every ounce of gold it had cost. The information it contained held the potential of ending Don Burton, once and for all. The note outlined a bold plan to gather feral longhorn cattle in Mexico over a number of days with the goal of driving over two to three thousand head of cattle north across the Rio Grande into Texas in a single night.

The audacity and brashness of the plan was genius in many ways. No one would expect such a move by any of the established cattle barons. Indeed, the price of failure would be utter ruin for anyone who dared to pull off such a foray in breach of the Treaty of Guadalupe Hidalgo. There would be no way the U.S. Government would allow anyone, even a well-known cattle baron with political connections, to stir up any further trouble on the border especially after the insubordination of Captain Leander McNelly and the debacle of the bloody Las Cuevas War.

Don Tomás Burton had kept his hands clean of the bloodstained Las Cuevas War, at least in the eyes of the public, despite having taken the lion's share of the stolen cattle. In Lopez's mind, there was no denying Don Tomás Burton had blood on his hands. Since the Las Cuevas War, it had become Lopez's single-minded obsession to catch Don Burton red-handed on the wrong side of the border. He wanted nothing more than to have Don Burton arrested, his reputation destroyed, and his cattle empire seized and sent into bankruptcy. Such wonderous thoughts brought a broad, toothy grin to Lopez's hairless, wrinkle-free, effeminate, smooth-featured face.

His informant had earned a bonus for such valuable information. He would need to pay him well to ensure the man continued to owe his loyalty to the highest bidder. Knowing that Don Burton was pondering such a wild scheme was interesting; however, without more details, there was little anyone could do to thwart his plans. The vast empty lands on both sides of the border made it nearly impossible for local ranchers and the Federales to guard against forays across the Rio Grande from Texas. This was also true for the Texas Rangers north of the border, who found guarding against bandits crossing the Rio Grande from Mexico just as impossible. He would need to know when and exactly where Don Burton planned to pull off his outrageous theft of Mexican cattle. He also needed to know why Don Burton needed to make such a risky move, considering cattle weren't exactly in short supply on either side of the border.

This latter thought caused Lopez to think more deeply about Don Burton's motivations. Could it be that the great cattle baron Don Tomás Burton was overstretched? Was he financially strapped? Why was he so desperate for cattle, when he controlled herds in the tens of thousands across several states and territories? Where was he driving the cattle he planned to steal? An endless string of questions filled Lopez's mind. He needed answers and he needed them fast. His biggest concern was that those answers may come too late.

The sooner he could arrange to send his usual payment with a sizable bonus to his informant the better. He was confident that in this battle with his *gringo* nemesis, the advantage was on his side for a change. He was confident that this time, Don Tomás Burton wouldn't see him coming.

March 12, 1884

San Antonio, Bexar County, Texas

Best Laid Plans

TRAIL-WEARY COWPUNCHERS, ONE AFTER another, rode into the Rocking T Ranch all morning. José greeted them, and as per Tom Burton's request, introduced each man to John and Jasper. Of all the riders, John hit it off best with Gus McKay, a man who had rode the Chisholm Trail to railheads in Kansas many times over the last ten years. Though he had never been in the Dakota Territory, he had been to Fort Laramie and west of the Black Hills in Wyoming Territory. He knew a great deal about trail drives and surviving on the open range.

Wanting to go into ranching himself someday, he had taken cattle as payment on his past five drives. He had over five hundred head of cattle and hoped to nearly double that number during the coming calving season. He planned to add even more cattle to his growing herd as payment for the drive to the Dakota Territory.

Once he had over a thousand head, he planned drive them into Thunder Basin in Wyoming Territory, north of Fort Laramie and west of the Black Hills, where he had scouted out good rangeland that had good graze and plenty of water—all for the taking, he told everyone who cared to ask. He wished for nothing more than to find a good woman and to hone a new life out of that wilderness. The twinkle in his eye when he talked about building his future ranch in Wyoming left listeners with no doubt that he would one day build his ranch just as he imagined.

Gus's stories convinced John that his own plans to stake his claim to land in the Dakota Territory were just as possible. Thoughts of such an adventure excited him and reminded him how far he and Jasper had come and just how far they still had to go.

All together fifteen riders had settled into the bunkhouse since early dawn. They all spoke of the coming gather and were all ready to get started. José knew many of the men well. As the day wore on, José tended to spend most of his time with Ben Thompson, who went by the handle Rowdy, and Bob Thompson, who went by Bo. Being identical twins, Rowdy and Bo were like two peas in a pod. They looked alike, sounded alike, acted alike, and tended to dress much the same as well. They were partners and the best horse wranglers in the outfit. They would manage the horse remuda and ensure every cowpuncher on the drive had at least three good horses to ride in rotation at all times.

Just as the men were ready to head to the main house for dinner, a chuckwagon rumbled into the yard.

"Howdy, boys. Sorry I'm a bit late to the party. I'm Sam Black. Just call me Cookie," the gruff-looking, grey-haired, heavily bearded driver said without missing a beat.

"Well, Cookie, you might have the wrong place," José said as he stepped forward.

"This is the Rocking T Ranch ain't it?" Cookie asked jerking his right thumb over his shoulder at the carved sign above the main gate.

"Yea, this is the Rocking T, but we haven't hired a cook, leastwise not one with a chuckwagon," José said with an edge in his voice.

Chuckwagons were nice to have on a long drive, but they tended to slow a drive down and were hell to deal with in wet, muddy weather. To top it off, mule teams didn't usually mix in well with a large horse remuda. They tended to be nothing but trouble.

"Well, there must've been a change in plans. Tom Burton hired me yesterday and told me to get out here to help with the gather and if things went right, he may hire me on to accompany the drive all the way to Dakota Territory," he said taking off his hat to wipe his brow.

It was tough not to notice that the skin on the top of his bald head appeared nearly snow white compared to his dark brown, leather-tough complexion.

"Well, pull up your wagon, we're on our way to supper," José said.

"Yea, Cookie, come on and join us. This might be the best meal you'll have for the next six months," Bo said, causing a ripple of laughter to run through the men.

"Just wait till you taste my flapjacks, sonny," Cookie said, shaking off the barb, as he hopped down to join the men.

Once again, the men had a good laugh as they made their way to the main house.

The next morning, Tom Burton joined the men for breakfast, having returned from his San Antonio business trip late the night before. Though a few men had questions about the coming gather, Burton let everyone know that he would outline his plan for the gather after supper that evening. In the meantime, he asked the men to check over their tack and clean up their gear, since things would be busy in the coming days.

Most of the men assumed Burton had several smaller herds he would need to have brought into the Racking T Ranch over the next several weeks. None of the men figured feral longhorns would make up a large percentage of the herd, since there were fewer and fewer feral longhorns to be gathered, and being wild, they tended to resist being bunched with other cattle and were difficult to herd.

That evening after supper, much to everyone's surprise, Burton informed them he had a bold plan that would result in more than half of the herd being made up of feral longhorns from south of the border. He would pay a hundred-dollar bonus, plus wages, for any man who would be willing to gather feral longhorns south of the border. For those who stayed on the north side of the border and helped drive the gathered herd further north once they crossed the Rio Grande, he would pay a twenty-five-dollar bonus, plus wages.

The men had the option of taking their pay in cattle or cash or a mix of both. Every man agreed these were generous terms, but then, Burton's bold plan could cost them their lives if things went sideways. To a man, they knew there was always the chance things could go wrong. Rustling cattle in Mexico was high-risk, but the money was tough to turn down for flat-broke cowpunchers.

With the men in agreement, Burton went on to outline the basic plan. Four teams of three riders each would be sent into the State of Nuevo Leon south of Laredo. Each team would work to gather feral longhorns and push them long arroyos to gathering points near a series of natural lakes. The gathered cattle would then be able to be driven north, hopping from one gathering point to the next until they came to the Arroyo El Lobo that flowed north into the Rio Grande about forty miles southeast of Laredo. At this point the number of longhorns in the herd would have swollen to two or three thousand head and possibly more.

Once the herd was driven across the Rio Grande, the plan was for riders waiting on the north side of the border to converge on the herd and drive it northwest to Lake Zachry as fast as the animals could be run. On the southside of Lake Zachry, the longhorns would be checked for brands. Those without brands would be considered feral and would be bobtailed. Marking cattle by trimming their tail hair by cutting straight across the end tassel of the hair was a common practice that ranchers used to show which unbranded cattle are meant to be kept. Burton's intention was to bobtail the feral longhorns to show they now belonged to him and would be branded the first chance he got.

Any Mexican-branded cattle would be rounded up and driven east as quickly and as far away from the main herd as possible. Branded cattle would then be left to wander the brushland of the Trans-Nueces for ranchers and Rangers to round up.

Burton anticipated that once Mexican ranchers discovered they had cattle missing, they would be up in arms. Federales would demand that officials on the U.S. side of the border return any missing Mexican cattle. With Rangers and Federales focused on getting the branded Mexican cattle back to their rightful owners south of the border, there might be little interest in chasing bandits who had vanished into a moonless night.

In the meantime, the herd of bobtailed feral longhorns would be driven northwest to the Rocking T Ranch. Should Rangers stop the herd at any point, they would find only bobtailed feral animals. There would be no way to prove where the cattle had come from since feral longhorns still roamed freely on both sides of the border. When Burton finished, he had to admit to himself, the plan was genius. He was certain it would work.

"What gathering points have you picked out?" Gus asked, having ridden the high plains desert of Nuevo Leon and knowing well the arroyos and lakes in the region and the overall lay of the land.

"The first team of riders will push all the feral longhorns they can scare up along the Arroyo El Recodo to Cuevas Lake, which will be the first gathering point and furthest south," Burton said. "The second team will follow the Arroyo El Huisache to Bordo La Caldera, which will be the second gathering point, and the third team will follow the Arroyo El Berrendo to

Biordo Presa Grande, which will be the third gathering point. The fourth set of riders will gather from south to north along the Arroyo El Lobo to the last fork before the river runs to the Rio Grande, it is at this final point that the full herd will be gathered and pushed up the Arroyo El Lobo and across the Rio Grande."

When he finished, Burton studied the men's reaction to his plan and waited for any further questions.

After a long pause as the magnitude and audacity of the plan sank in, José stepped forward and asked, "When do we get started?"

José's simple question broke the silence that had filled the room and released a cacophony of sound as the men all seemed to start talking at once.

"We start sending our teams into Mexico on March 19th during the half moon. They will work down each arroyo with the goal of herding their cattle to each gathering point by no later than the evening of March 27th. At midnight on March 27th, with the new moon, the teams will push their gathers to the Arroyo El Lobo final gathering point and then, as a single herd, across the Rio Grande," Burton said nodding at José in appreciation for the question. "Are there any further questions?" Burton yelled above the din, wanting to ensure everyone was comfortable with the plan and the timeline.

Burton knew he was asking these men to risk their lives. He needed to allow those men who were having second thoughts a chance to voice them and to bow out gracefully if they choose to do so.

"I have only one damn question and I need to have an answer to it, right now," Gus barked, standing up from his seat at the table and causing the room to once again fall silent.

"Well?" Burton asked, wondering where things were going.

Gus had been one of his best hands over many years—if he wouldn't go along with the plan, many of the other men would soon bow out.

"When in the hell are you going to break out the whiskey, so we can seal this deal?" Gus roared.

Gus's words hung in the air for a single beat until everyone in the room broke out into uproarious laughter.

"Lucia! *Whiskey para todos!*" Burton hollered with a huge smile on his face. "Whiskey all round!"

With his command still echoing off the walls, almost like magic, Lucia came bounding out of the kitchen, wheeling a chart with two full uncorked bottles of whiskey and a tray of shot glasses. The men cheered wildly and quickly grabbed and filled their glasses.

"To success!" Burton said holding up a full shot of whiskey.

"*Salud!*" the men said in unison.

With that they all emptied their glasses and quickly filled them again. The deal had been sealed and the party had begun. Lucia knew only one thing, as she headed back to the kitchen, two bottles of whiskey wouldn't be near enough.

A few days later, after the men had retired to the bunkhouse and everyone had settled in for the night after a long day's work, a lone rider slipped out into the night, mounted his saddled horse, and soon left the Rocking T Ranch behind him. Riding hard, he arrived in the booming town of Pleasanton, the county seat of Atascosa County, just thirty miles south of San Antonio and only three miles east of the Rocking T Ranch.

Entering the Longhorn Saloon, he took a stool at the far end of the bar. After ordering a rare special label whiskey, which sent the bartender searching for the bottle, he quickly exchanged a sealed envelope for a pouch full of gold coins with a scruffy-looking cowboy who had come up to the bar from one of the back tables to order another drink. With the hour being late and the saloon nearly empty, the exchange caught no one's attention. As far as anyone in the saloon knew, the two men at the bar were total strangers.

"Bartender, I'll have me another whiskey," the cowboy slurred, pretending to be drunker than he was.

"Hey, cowboy, I think you might've had enough for one night," the bartender offered, as he studied the man leaning on the bar on wobbly legs.

"Mind yer own damn business, bucko. Just pour the drinks," the man blubbered, sounding indignant at the suggestion he was a man unable to hold his liquor.

The bartender gave the cowboy a long look and then filled his glass without another word. Slapping two bits on the counter, the cowboy staggered back to his table, bumping into chairs and tables along the way.

The lone rider spoke to no one, stayed for another drink, and, as quickly as he had come, he left, the night swallowing him once again. As he rode back to the Rocking T Ranch, he could feel the weight of the gold coins wrapped in the money belt strapped around his waist. He knew he had received a sizable bonus and looked forward to an even bigger payday.

Mulling over the events to come, the rider couldn't help but chuckle at the thought of Burton being so confident his plan was foolproof, when in fact he had already been fooled. He had trusted too much. Such is the burden of the rich: in their endless desire to acquire more and to hold on to all they possess, they are doomed to never knowing whom they can really trust. He couldn't get over Burton's hubris—the man had never seen him coming.

March 19, 1884

Laredo, Webb County, Texas

Tex-Mex Tango

JUST NORTH OF LAREDO on a high plateau overlooking the Rio Grande and the endless Mexican brushland that stretched south from its southern bank, Burton sat astride his favorite appaloosa as he gave final instructions to each team of riders before they rode into Mexico. Bo and Rowdy had been teamed up with Tommy Water Horse, a Shoshone Mexican breed, known as Baagahni, who earned his living as a scout, horse wrangler, and all-around ranch hand. It would be their job to go furthest south and to gather as many feral longhorns as they could scare up.

Burton's choice of the trio for the first team seemed the best fit when he learned that several ranchers along the Arroyo El Recodo had recently rounded up a huge herd of wild horses. He figured since they were gathering all the cattle they could lay their hands on they might as well add as many horses as possible. They would need over sixty head for the drive. Bo, Rowdy, and Baagahni where the best horse wranglers in the outfit and the only ones who knew how to best run horses and longhorn cattle together.

The second set of riders were three skilled cowpunchers, led by Joe Bishop, who was one of the few men in the outfit who knew the State of Neuvo Leon like the back of his hand and spoke passable Spanish to boot. John had learned that Joe had already staked a claim in the southern Black Hills in the Dakota Territory, near where his brother Eugene ran a small hotel with a bar called the Standard Gauge Saloon. Joe's team was sent to work its way along the Arroyo El Huisache to the gathering point at Bordo La Caldera.

The third set of riders was led by Gus McKay. They would work the banks of the Arroyo El Berrendo to the gathering point at Biordo Presa Grande. Gus was also made responsible for ensuring the three gathers would move as one toward the final gathering point at the last fork on Arroyo El Lobo before it flowed into the Rio Grande.

Burton then turned to John and Jasper and told them they would be riding with his most experienced hand, Kit Larson, who knew everything there was to know about the cantankerous nature and habits of longhorn cattle and about gathering and herding the crafty and obstinate critters. They would gather cattle along the Arroyo El Lobo which ran southeast, parallel to the Rio Grande. Should anything go wrong they had the shortest distance to ride, and therefore best chance, to get back across the Rio Grande before being caught or killed. The other teams would be working deeper into Mexican territory, making their chances of escaping back across the Rio Grande slim at best should things go haywire.

Once Kit Larson and the boys rode out, Burton turned to José Rodriquez, who had sat astride his horse next to Burton, giving an encouraging word to each team of riders before they rode out. He had even wished John and Jasper good luck.

"Well, it's done. We'll need to get riders into position south of Lake Zachry in a few days. The night of the new moon is just eight days off," Burton said.

"Yes, the plan is good. All should go smoothly," José said.

"It seems sound enough, but then, every road has a curve," Burton said with a distant look in his eyes.

"Will you be riding into Mexico?" José asked.

It was a strange question, but not completely uncalled for. The operation had a lot of moving parts and it could be reasoned that Burton might want to take a more hands-on role.

"I thought I might cross over so I could be at the final gathering point on the Arroyo El Lobo. It'd be good to ride with the full herd across the Rio Grande and on up to Lake Zachry," Burton said giving José a sideways glance.

"Why don't you ride down to the Arroyo El Recodo and help Bo and Rowdy wrangle horses? Might be tough with only three riders to handle both longhorns and horses," he added, rubbing his chin and looking at José.

"*Sí, eso sería una buena idea,*" José said, his attitude clearly brightening.

"Yes, I agree, it's a good idea. Let's hit the trail in a couple of days. In the meantime, let's take in the sights of Laredo. The town has grown since I was last here," Burton said as he nudged his horse forward.

The two men worked their way down the slope and on into Laredo, each man believing he had the world by the tail, and only one of them certain that he did.

Unknown to anyone, including John and Jasper, the fourth team wouldn't be gathering longhorns along the Arroyo El Lobo, but would instead work the Arroyo Blanco further to the northwest. Both arroyos ran into the Rio Grande with the Arroyo Blanco north of Lake Zachry on the U.S. side of the border and the Arroyo El Lobo further south.

It was Burton's plan to have the full herd gather on the north side of the lake, not on the south side as he had told everyone. Only Kit Larson and Gus McKay, his most trusted men, knew about the last-minute change of plans. Gus would guide the combined gather of the first three teams to the southern branch of the Arroyo Blanco, rather than the southern branch of the Arroyo El Lobo. He knew this would throw off any possible double cross in the works. Having John and Jasper ride with Kit, Burton figured even if they discovered the change in plans, they would go along with the ruse without sharing this vital information with anyone.

If there was a snake in the mix, Burton figured that snake would wait to strike when he could catch all the men and stolen cattle together just before they crossed the Rio Grande. Burton thought he knew who the snake was, but would play out his hand and let the cards fall where they may.

After spending three days in Laredo, José headed across the border. Burton watched him go and wondered if his hunch was right. Returning to the Laredo Grand Hotel, Burton had no intention of riding into Mexico. Such a move would be suicide. He would ride to the north side of Lake Zachry in a few days with the riders who had opted to stay on the U.S. side of the border. From there, they would wait for Gus McKay and whatever herd the men were able to gather.

Baagahni had led Bo and Rowdy to the head waters of the Arroyo El Recodo. The men could see that the brush was teeming with longhorns. The ranchers in the area hadn't taken the time to brand the natural increase in their herds over the past several years since the market for prime beef had collapsed. Without brands, the longhorns could be passed off as feral and free for the taking. None of the local ranchers in Nuevo Leon ever expected a foray by marauding *gringos* from north of the border this far into Mexico.

Bo and Rowdy were sure the other teams would find the same rich pickings. None of the ranchers in the region were wasting their time branding cattle they already held on their land and that wouldn't be readied for market until prices came back. The men had to admit, though they had had their doubts, the simplicity of Burton's plan was genius.

Burton had counted on the custom of small ranchers not to immediately brand the natural increase in their herds. These unbranded longhorns were technically free for the taking. As they worked the banks of the arroyo, their herd of mostly unbranded cattle grew rapidly in number. On the fourth day, they came upon a loose herd of wild horses numbering in the hundreds. They cut out over two hundred head and continued to push their herd of longhorns and horses toward the gathering point at Cuevas Lake, picking up more and more loose longhorns along the way.

John, riding on his tall, jet-black Morgan, cut down a tight draw only to find five more longhorns hiding in the brush. Chasing them out from under their thorny cover, he drove them to where Jasper could snap their noses with his looped rope and push them into the growing gather. They had worked steady, day and night, for six days with little rest. During one of their short breaks, Kit had revealed to them that they weren't on the Arroyo El Lobo, but were gathering cattle on the Arroyo Blanco. He told them of Burton's suspicion that they had a traitor in their midst. He also shared that Gus would drive the combined gather of the three other teams to the southern fork of the Arroyo Blanco and that they would push the combined herd over the Rio Grande north of Lake Zachry and not south as Burton had shared with everyone.

John understood why Burton would want to be cautious. Too many men knew the full plan. The temptation for a double cross was high, considering the high stakes involved. The stealing of over four thousand head of cattle was more than a simple hanging offense. The tension along the U.S.-Mexico border was already at a boiling point. John wondered how he and Jasper had gotten themselves wrapped up in the whole mess, but then again, they had been given little choice in the matter.

"We're coming to the rendezvous point. We'll hold up when we reach there tomorrow noon. Gus should reach us by some time after midnight tomorrow. We'll have to be ready to push 'em hard, when Gus rolls in. There'll be no time for chit-chat. When they get here, we'll push our herd into the main herd and ride as one," Kit said.

Kit had been impressed at how the boys had worked nonstop and how they had been able to quickly pick up many of the tricks of the trade. So far, their little trio had had no trouble as they gathered cattle and moved south, though he worried that the growing size of their herd would attract attention sooner or later. They would have to work their cattle under the cover of trees and shrubs along the river's edge and try to lay low once they reached the rendezvous point in broad daylight. Knowing there was little he could do if things went sideways, he was left to pray to a God he didn't believe in that things would somehow work out.

"It'll be tough holding a herd this size in one place for half a day. It might be better to push them over the border now," Jasper said.

He could see the graze wasn't good and the animals would be getting restless if they had to stay out in the open all afternoon. The gather had been an overwhelming success. They figured they had well over a thousand, possibly as many as fifteen hundred head. If the other teams were as successful the full herd could number over six thousand. Jasper couldn't imagine how they would be able to hide such a huge herd for much longer.

"We'll need to push the cattle under the trees and brush along the river and hold tight. The herd must cross as one. You heard Tom. He knows what he's talking about. We can't take chances going across separately," Kit snapped.

Jasper felt the edge in Kit's voice and knew he was right. They had no choice but to wait and hope for the best.

At midnight on March 27th, Gus first felt a vibrating rumble under his feet and then heard the sounds of a massive herd of longhorns headed his way. His team had gathered over two thousand head of longhorns over the past week. They had readied their herd to join the one coming so they could push the merged herd forward without any undue delays. The first thing Gus could make out was Tommy Water Horse waving his hat high and riding hard at the head of a massive wall of longhorns. It was a dangerous move, but Gus was glad the man had the guts to pull it off. It had given his team the early signal they needed to get their cattle moving.

Pushing their relatively smaller herd into a full run, Gus's team merged their gather seamlessly into the body of the larger herd, swelling its ranks as it flowed by like a raging river of hooves, hides, and horns ready to burst out of its banks at any minute. Riding drag and following close behind, Bo and Rowdy snapped their ropes as they pushed a horse remuda of over two hundred head up tight on the heels of the longhorns running ahead of them. Gus was flabbergasted by the huge number of animals they had been able to gather.

After the herd passed, he rode up beside Bo and yelled, "My God, man, how many in the first two gathers?"

"We have no idea, but it's well over five thousand head, not counting over two hundred horses," Bo hollered back.

Gus just shook his head in disbelief and spurred his horse into a gallop as he raced to the head of the herd. Frantically waving his arms, he directed the riders to push the herd to the northwest. Though the men had thought they should be turning the herd further southeast, they followed Gus's orders without question. He had been put in charge and they knew this was no time to have any differences of opinion. They had avoided bloodshed and indeed trouble of any kind up to now and the riders just wanted to reach the final gathering point as quickly as possible so they could finally push the herd across the Rio Grande and into Texas without getting caught or killed. Their huge payday seemed close, and yet still too far away.

After waking up in the alley of a popular Laredo saloon, Rudy dusted himself off and spent the morning tracking down his horse. Once he was able to finally crawl up into his saddle, he rode south across the border. Arriving back in the pueblo of Primavera in the late evening of March 27th, he soon discovered that he now had a one-armed partner.

On first sight, Willie could hardly recognize his partner. Rudy's nose had healed badly. It now sat askew in the middle of his homely face; its bridge permanently dented, causing a high-pitched whistling sound to radiate out in every direction whenever Rudy breathed heavily through his nose. Neither man could believe the price they had paid for getting into a bar brawl with what they had considered to be a couple of northern green-horns still wet behind their ears.

"I musta asked a hundred outfits, but none of 'em had run across our friends, John and Jasper," Rudy said frustrated that he had come up with a big fat zero after beating the bushes for weeks..

His temper ran high at the thought of John and Jasper slipping through their grasp, sending his nose into a whistling bout.

"We'll track 'em down. And when we do, we'll kill 'em," Willie said.

He now wore his holster low and strapped to his left leg. He had prac-ticed pulling and firing his Colt .45 with his left hand until his fingers bled. His speed and aim had improved by the day. He was getting faster with ev-ery draw. His goal was to become deadly. Rudy took in the transformation. Willie wasn't the same ol' good-natured Willie anymore. He had become hard-edged. Even the creases in his face had deepened and seemed sharper and meaner. He was a man on a mission. Rudy knew Willie wouldn't rest until the greenhorns were dead.

"I heard they're hiring riders to herd cattle into their stockyards to be shipped north from the new railhead town of Hebbronville. Some bigwig named J. R. Hebbron claims cattle drives are a thing of the past. Everything will be shipped by rail straight out of Texas," Rudy ventured, wanting to show Willie times may be changing, though they still had cards to play.

"So, what are you sayin'?" Willie shot back, wanting to hear something that might point them in the right direction.

"I'm sayin', we ride over there and look around. Hebbronville is already one of the largest cattle-shipping centers in Texas. If it's the boomtown they say it is, we just might get a lead on the whereabouts of our long-lost friends," Rudy suggested.

Rudy still felt sick every time he looked at Willie's stubbed arm. The sight of it made him queasy somehow. Though he wanted to divert his eyes, he couldn't help staring at the mangled lump of flesh, where Willie's right arm now ended. He worried about how useful a cripple like Willie would be when the chips were down.

"Let's leave tonight," Willie said as he started gathering up his gear.

"Tonight! Hell, I just got here. Can't we wait for a few days? I'd like to get me some senorita lovin' 'fore I head out again," Rudy said, surprised Willie wanted to take off in the middle of the night.

"We've lost enough time. I'm goin' tonight. You can come or stay, that's up to you," Willie said, leaving no room for negotiation.

Time froze as the two men looked at one another for what seemed like an eternity. The only sound a pulsating, high-pitched whistle as Rudy struggled with his next decision.

"We can save time by riding south about fifteen miles to cross the border where the Arroyo Blanco flows into the Rio Grande. From there we can ride past the north end of Lake Zachry and then straight east to Hebbronville. It's rough country, but we should be able to make it in a couple of days," Rudy said, having made up his mind that he would stick with Willie at least until they killed the lowdown scum they were looking for.

Sporting a fresh shiner and two loose teeth from his last bar fight in Laredo the night before, Rudy was a man who simply lacked the ability for self-reflection. His troubles would forever be someone else's fault. He believed he was a man who made his own destiny. Reluctantly—for now, he thought—he would follow Willie's lead. The last thing he would tolerate for long however was to take orders from a cripple. Rudy couldn't wait until he was finally free of the need to kill the bastards who had caused them so much pain. He also wanted to be rid of his crippled partner as soon as possible. To Rudy, Willie, with only one good arm, was no more than half a man. He hated cripples; most of all, he hated the sight of them.

A little after midnight, the two men saddled up and rode south. The moonless night was pitch black and as silent as a dead man's tomb. Riding slowly at a steady gait, they took their time as they worked their way toward the crossing at Arroyo Blanco. Wishing only to get to Hebbronville as quickly as possible, they were oblivious to what Lady Luck, through her careful weaving of timing and circumstance, had in store for them on this fateful moonless night.

He had ridden hard, changing horses twice along the way, to get word to his paymaster, Don Enrico Martín Lopez, as fast as he possibly could. Upon learning the details of Don Burton's plans for his cattle-rustling foray into the State of Nuevo Leon, Don Lopez quickly shared the information with the Federales. He then assembled and outfitted over a hundred of his best vaqueros and set out for Arroyo El Lobo to join the coming battle.

After arriving at the Arroyo El Lobo, Don Lopez and his vaqueros quickly joined the ambush that had already been set up. Two Gatling guns had been brought in by the Federales, along with over two hundred heavily armed troops. General Luis Perez Figueroa had assumed command and made it clear this would be a glorious victory for Mexican sovereignty and the Mexican people. As a token of appreciation for doing his patriotic duty, it was agreed that Don Enrico Martín Lopez would be awarded the lion's share of the unbranded cattle they captured in the operation. Don Lopez couldn't have been happier at how things were working out.

The rider had assured Don Lopez that Don Burton himself would meet the bandits and their stolen herd of Mexican cattle at the southern fork of the Arroyo El Lobo on the Mexican side of the border. Don Lopez had hired sharpshooters who could hit a moving target at three hundred yards to take down Don Burton if they failed to capture him. Don Lopez was under no illusion that some of the *gringo* bandits would inevitably escape back over the border into Texas. Come what may, he wanted to make damn sure Don Burton wouldn't be one of them.

Willie's horse was the first one to hear a low rumble coming from the southwest. His ears rotated wildly before he let out a long whinny. Rudy's roan soon followed suit. Both men were immediately on the alert for a possible ambush.

"Hear anything?" Willie whispered as he brought his horse up beside Rudy.

"No, but the horses are acting like there's something coming from the southwest. Damn strange. It's not weather. The only thing I've seen is heat light along the western horizon," Rudy said.

Both men were feeling spooked by the darkness that enveloped them and by their unfamiliarity with the surrounding terrain. Suddenly, the low rumble grew into a bellowing stampede of long-horned muscle headed straight at them. With the deafening roar of charging animals surging at them, their horses twirled in circles, not knowing which way to run. Having a tough time controlling their mounts, they too had no idea which way to ride.

"Sounds like a stampede!" Rudy cried out just as the solid front of hundreds of long, sharp horns enveloped Rudy's horse as it reared up in a hapless attempt to repel the surging wall of death.

Willie looked on through the dim light as his partner's horse was gored and literally ripped apart, bringing it and its rider down. Rudy, thrown to the ground, never regained his feet, his body trampled by countless grinding hooves. Gone in a flash, he never had a chance.

Willie, having no idea what to do, had given his horse its head, hoping it would find a way to escape. Luckily it had. He found himself on a narrow ridge that had become an island in the middle of a raging river of beef. In the inky black of a moonless night, he could make out only the shadowy figures of riders driving the herd straight down the Arroyo Blanco for the Rio Grande. One ghostly rider after another pushed the herd faster and faster as the number of cattle seemed to have no end. Mesmerized by the never-ending flow of cattle and stunned by what had happened to Rudy, Willie had no idea what to do next. He worried about being discovered and what might happen if he was. Just when he thought he might be in the clear, one of the riders seemed to spot him and then turn his horse directly toward where Willie had found refuge.

Unable to see the rider's face until he was only a few yards in front of him, Willie found himself looking straight into John Barton's eyes. It took only a split second for the two men to recognize one another. Willie knew at once he had come face to face with the man who had taken his arm and ruined his life.

"So, we meet again," Willie barked as he let loose of his reins and in a flash drew his Colt. Surprised to run into a *gringo* rider this side of the border, John soon realized the man was the cowpuncher who had drawn a gun on Jasper back in Saint Joe and was now drawing on him.

Without further warning, Willie fired twice just as his horse reared up, nearly throwing him off, causing his shots to go wide. His stub arm, useless in grabbing the reins, left Willie nearly helpless and unable to gain control of his mount. John, seeing the other man had only one good arm, quickly drew his own pistol and fired. The shot missed its mark, but hit the back flank of the man's horse, sending both horse and rider galloping northwest as the horse cried out in pain. With only one good arm, Willie, in a failed attempt to get control of his horse, lost his Colt while struggling to grab ahold of the reins.

Having no weapon and a horse that was badly wounded, he had no way to pursue his nemesis. He had no choice but to wait out the stampeding cattle. He would need to check on Rudy's remains and collect Rudy's pistol and money belt and hopefully find his own Colt. He could then ride back to Primavera to get a fresh horse. Considering the massive size of the herd being pushed over the border, he was sure he would be able to follow their trail. Now that he finally had a bead on his target, he had no doubt whatsoever that ol' Lucky John would soon be meeting his Waterloo.

John wondered how in the world the cowpuncher from Saint Joe had suddenly turned up in Mexico. That he shot at him made it pretty clear the man held a grudge. The man's stubbed arm told John the grudge ran deep. The damage he had done with the oaken mop handle had been much more serious than he had imagined. John prayed he would never run into the one-armed outlaw again. If he did, considering everything that had happened between them, he knew he may have to kill the man in order to kill the hatred that now festered inside of him.

Burton waited at Lake Zachry with eight mounted riders ready to quickly sort and bobtail the unbranded cattle as they came in. Burton's intention was to bobtail the feral and unbranded longhorns to show they belonged to him and would be branded the first chance he got.

He had instructed half of the men to quickly sort and herd all the branded cattle to the south side of Lake Zachry to a point on the north bank of the Rio Grande, close to where the Arroyo El Lobo flowed into the Rio Grande on the Mexican side of the border. He figured the Federales who were probably assembled on the south fork of the Arroyo El Lobo would soon discover the animals and would demand their return. The diversion would tie up the authorities and the ranchers on both sides of the Rio Grande while things were sorted out and the rightful owners identified, giving Burton and his men more time to push their herd of unbranded bobtailed longhorns further north before being discovered.

General Luis Perez Figueroa, decked out in his finest military uniform, had been pacing back and forth in front of his jet-black stallion for over two hours. He had been too late to engage the Rangers who had marauded across the border and bloodied sovereign Mexican soil in 1875. Had he been able to engage Captain Leander McNelly and his ragtag troop of Texas Rangers, the Las Cuevas War would have been a real war and not an embarrassing bandit raid that resulted in the deaths of over a hundred Mexican civilians and the theft of over two thousand Mexican cattle. The U.S. Government had never fully acknowledged the illegality of the intrusion, nor provided adequate reparations. This time he would have the upper hand.

"Where are they?" Don Lopez said through tight lips as he gave a sideways look at his informant.

"It's going on three o'clock in the morning, they should be here any moment," the informant said, realizing he had been repeating this same reply for the last two hours.

There was no arguing that the herd should have arrived well over an hour ago, according to Burton's timetable.

"There must be something we can do," Don Lopez said in frustration.

"General, we need to send out scouts. Single riders to check further west, north, and points between," the informant said, hoping the General would agree.

"Yes, take three other riders to see what you can find. Have the riders go fifteen miles in every direction and report back," General Figueroa ordered, worried the *gringo* bandits may have already slipped through their fingers.

Within minutes the informant mounted his horse and followed by three other riders rode to the fork in the river the assembled troops had surrounded. After a short discussion between the riders, they split up, riding in four directions. Don Lopez's informant rode straight north.

The informant sensed Don Burton had changed his plan and that the herd had been turned further north to cross at the Arroyo Blanco which would still allow Burton to use Lake Zachry as his sorting station before pushing the herd north to San Antonio. The informant was angry with himself for underestimating Burton. He wondered how he could have convinced himself that Burton was such a fool that he would give out his final plans to everyone in advance. He had to admit, it was he who had been the fool. His problem now was in dealing with Don Lopez and General Figueroa after such a debacle.

Arriving at the southernmost fork of the Arroyo Blanco, the informant found only a deep gouge where thousands of longhorns had trampled everything in their path. The gouge ran straight toward the Rio Grande. The bloody carcass of what appeared to have once been a human being lay pounded into the dirt. The body, or at least what was left of it, was the only sign that riders had accompanied the massive herd of longhorns as it stampeded across the Rio Grande and on into Texas.

The informant wondered how he should play the new hand that had been dealt to him. There was no way he could return to General Figueroa and Don Lopez with the news Burton had slipped their trap; the chances of things turning out well for him after delivering such a message would be slim at best.

With the Don and the General both losing face, they would need someone to pay for the insult; he would be the obvious scapegoat. If he followed the tracks of the herd, he could catch up at some point. The odds that Don Burton was unaware of his betrayal were also slim at best, making the outcome just as fatal.

"Hold it right there, *amigo*," Willie said as he slowly stepped out of the shadows.

Willie couldn't believe his luck when a lone rider stopped right where he had just picked up Rudy's pistol. Though he still hadn't found his own Colt, Rudy's would do just fine.

Taken by complete surprise, the informant instinctively reached for his pistol. Willie fired three shots at point-blank range into the rider's chest, throwing him off his horse. The rider was dead before he hit the ground with his pistol never clearing leather. In a further stroke of luck, the rider's horse stayed put having been trained not to be skittish around gunfire.

Willie quickly checked the dead man's body and found a money belt bulging with gold coins. Liking the man's hat and leather vest, Willie stripped the body, taking everything of value. He even took the man's eyepatch as a good luck talisman. The one-eyed Mexican had been his first kill. Willie was determined the man wouldn't be his last.

Wrapped in gold coins, dressed in new duds, astride a fresh horse, and armed with plenty of hardware and ammunition, he decided he would stay out of sight and trail the herd to see where it was headed. There was no reason to return to Primavera. Cutting his own wounded horse loose, he crossed the Rio Grande and headed for Lake Zachry. The Mexicans would soon be on the warpath and looking for *gringos* to blame. He knew it wouldn't be long until Rangers would be sent to try to track down the stolen cattle. He wondered who had pulled off what might have been the largest cattle theft in history. He also wondered how they thought they would get away with it.

Wasting no time to put the Rio Grande behind him, he spurred his new horse into a fast trot and headed north. He reached up with the stub of his right arm to touch the eyepatch, his blood-stained lucky talisman, he now wore around his neck. Having notched his first kill, he was confident Lady Luck was now on his side.

As the golden glow of dawn grew in the east, the stars faded as they merged into the brightening sky. General Figueroa waited until the sun broke over the horizon in the east to give the order for his troops to stand down. There would be no victory this day. One rider had already come back empty handed. The rider who had checked along the Arroyo El Lobo from the north all the way down to the Rio Grande came charging back at a high gallop. Seeing the rider coming fast, the General ordered his men to make room for the rider as he raced toward the General's colors.

"*General, cuernos largos en el lado norte del Río Grande!*" the rider yelled.

Hearing the rider's yell and the direction he rode in from, it was clear the stolen cattle had already crossed the Rio Grande and were on the Texas side of the border. He knew it would be a long day, since any cattle left behind by the bandits would all bear Mexican brands. It would now be up to him to spend the day dealing with Mexican ranchers and Texas Rangers to identify the rightful owners.

Knowing the rider had found longhorns near the north side of the Rio Grande made Don Lopez's heart sink. Don Tomás Burton had won once again. Don Enrico Martín Lopez would now have to return home with another stain on his reputation and without a reward of what may have amounted to several thousand head of cattle. Despite the shame that he must now bear, he felt the most valuable thing he had lost was the fame that would have come with a long overdue victory over marauding *gringos* who had disrespected Mexican sovereignty.

What troubled him most was not knowing why José Rodriquez had double-crossed him. He had paid the man well. Just as he was mulling over how he would kill José the first chance he got, a third rider came in with a report no one wanted to hear. A huge herd of cattle had been driven across the Rio Grande at Arroyo Blanco, the river just north of where they stood. The rider estimated the herd must have been several thousand head. The rider also reported he had found the body of José Rodriquez with three gunshots in his chest. His body had been stripped of clothing and valuables. Someone had even taken his eyepatch. Another body had been found nearby, a *gringo* that had been trampled badly. The rider figured the man had probably been one of the bandits who had been killed in the stampede.

Both General Figueroa and Don Lopez knew that with José Rodriquez dead, there was little chance of ever finding out what had happened. The only clue Don Lopez held onto was the bizarre fact that someone had taken José's distinctive eyepatch for whatever macabre reason. He would need to find the man who now possessed that eyepatch. He was certain that if he did, he would find more than a few of the answers he sought.

After sorting the cattle at Lake Zachry and sending the branded cattle south back toward the Rio Grande, the unbranded herd had been pushed north as fast as the animals could be driven. For the next three days, unseasonable rain showers helped to erase the sizable trail left by over nine thousand head of tightly bunched longhorns. Burton, acting like a man possessed, drove his riders and the herd hard, wanting to get as deep as possible into Texas before running into any Texas Rangers.

Amazingly, they arrived at the Rocking T Ranch, a hundred and fifty miles north of Laredo, without incident in less than five days. Over the next week the men worked in shifts branding animals nonstop. Combining his earlier Texas gather with the Mexican haul, and after paying off several of the riders with cattle for their own operations, Burton ended up with over ten thousand head of cattle ready to move north into Dakota Territory.

For a man who had lacked a herd of cattle to drive north into Dakota Territory only a month ago, Burton had been able to conjure up over ten thousand head, virtually free of charge. He always loved it when a good plan came together, especially a plan pulled off on the other side of the law, and, even better, on the other side of the border. Having started out as an outlaw, it had always been tough for Burton to walk the straight and narrow.

Of course, if things went as planned over the next couple of years, he would have a fortune big enough to buy whatever law he desired, a thought that caused him to laugh out loud.

March 23, 1884

Laredo, Webb County, Texas

Mystery Mavericks

BERT BLACKWELL, TEXAS RANGER, wasn't the kind of man to go looking for trouble; being in the business of trouble, it always had a way of finding him. The ruckus on the border south of Laredo had riled things up like nothing had in recent years. Over eight hundred head of branded Mexican cattle had been found on the Texas side of the border. After considerable wrangling with the Mexican authorities, the cattle were rounded up and herded back across the Rio Grande into Mexico without further incident.

The problem was no bandits had been apprehended and no cattle, other than branded cattle, had been returned. General Luis Perez Figueroa and the Mexican Government were demanding a full accounting. They demanded to know why no missing mavericks had been returned. How anyone would be able to know one maverick from another was a problem no one had an answer for on either side of the border.

To mark their property, as a custom, ranchers on both sides of the boarder branded each calf crop, every year. The practice of not branding this natural increase started with a rancher named Samuel A. Maverick, who during the Civil War, let his calf crop go unbranded. Other ranchers followed suit due mainly to the fact that Texas, as a member of the Confederate states, found itself without markets for its cattle during the war. As a result, the value of longhorn cattle plummeted. Year after year, the natural increase filled the countryside with tens of thousands of unbranded cattle.

Mexican ranchers soon found their cattle as worthless as those on the Texas side of the border. They too left the natural increase in their herds unbranded. After the war, rounding up unbranded cattle became a bonanza for those who had the wherewithal to drive them to markets further north. The huge herds being driven to railhead towns in Kansas soon gave birth to the Chisholm Trail.

As a joke, all unclaimed, unbranded cattle came to be called mavericks. The moniker soon stuck and became the term used for all cattle that were without brands. Whether an unbranded animal was a feral longhorn or a maverick was impossible to tell. Unbranded cattle belonging to any rancher who had failed to brand his annual calf crop were, as far as the law was concerned, free for the taking.

Bert had two leads on the possible identity of the bandits. His first lead was the badly trampled body that had been found on the Mexican side of the border near the south fork of the Arroyo Blanco, the point where it was now believed the herd of stolen Mexican cattle had been driven across the Rio Grande. Though the body had been mangled nearly beyond recognition, the remains were taken to Laredo in hopes someone at one of the many saloons where cowpunchers gather might know the man. Surprisingly, the bartender and several patrons of the Double Eagle Saloon in Laredo were able to identify the body as belonging to one Rudy James, a cowpuncher who liked to start fights every time he got drunk. Rudy's distinctively dented and twisted nose had made his identification undeniable. According to the bartender, he had been thrown out of the saloon the night before for starting a fistfight, which, the bartender added, ended badly for ol' Rudy, as nearly every fistfight did.

Bert figured it was highly likely Rudy was in on the raid into Mexico. The facts surrounding his death made that pretty clear. Bert also figured Rudy's well-known partner, Willie Dunhill, wouldn't have been far behind. No one had seen Willie at the Double Eagle Saloon the night before, but had heard Rudy talk about him and how they were enjoying a little well-earned senorita time in Primavera south of the border. This placed Willie Dunhill in Mexico near Arroyo Blanco at the time of the raid. If he could track down Willie, he might track down the herd and the whole damn thieving bunch.

His second lead was the body of José Rodriquez. José had been shot three times in the chest at close range. The body lay face down in the mud near Rudy's mangled body. José's body had been stripped of nearly all its clothing. A wounded horse that had been shot in its right rear flank was also found when its cries led Rangers and Mexican authorities to where it lay dying in a nearby ravine. It was assumed the horse had belonged to José. What was left of Rudy's horse's carcass had been found near the Rio Grande where the stolen cattle had crossed into Texas.

According to Mexican authorities, José Rodriquez was one of Tom Burton's close lieutenants, which pointed to Burton as the culprit behind the foray into Mexico. Why José would have ended up dead after the cattle had already crossed the border, no one on the Mexican side could answer.

His problem now was what to do next. Several Rangers had followed the tracks of a herd of cattle and riders that had headed straight north from Lake Zachry until pouring rain washed out their tracks. The dark of the moon made pursuit over the next night impossible. By the time they had combed the countryside the next day, more than two days after the raid, there was nothing to be found.

Knowing Willie Dunhill may have taken part in the raid and Tom Burton may have been behind it was a good start. Proving it, without the cattle or witnesses, would be difficult. If they had taken only mavericks, and now that the animals were deep inside Texas, there would be no way to prove which side of the border the cattle came from. After discussing the facts of the case with several other Rangers who had been charged with getting to the bottom of the raid into Mexico, it was agreed that Bert Blackwell and Phil Roberts, an experienced Texas Ranger and a good gun hand, should try to track down Willie Dunhill. In the meantime, a two-hundred-dollar reward would be offered for information on Willie's whereabouts. Wanted posters would be sent to sheriffs' offices throughout Texas in the coming weeks.

Bert figured it was just a matter of time before they tracked down Willie Dunhill, who would likely be on a cattle drive or looking to join one headed north to railheads in Kansas. Tascosa in the Texas panhandle, the crossroads for cattle headed north, presented them with their best and last chance to track Willie down before he crossed over into Indian Territory and beyond their jurisdiction. The one advantage they had was that if Willie got that far north, he would think he had gotten off scot-free. He would never see them coming.

Bert was informed a group of Rangers would also be paying a visit to Tom Burton's Rocking T Ranch south of San Antonio to have a word with the man. Mexico was demanding answers. Bert had his doubts that they would ever corner Burton without a witness. That fact made tracking down and taking Willie Dunhill alive all the more important.

April 8, 1884

San Antonio, Bexar County, Texas

A Cowboy's Life

DURING THEIR FIRST MONTH at the Rocking T Ranch, John and Jasper received a crash course in longhorn cattle wrangling. They also learned that Tom Burton was a man who wasn't afraid to bend the rules and even break them, if it served his purposes. He always played to win, no matter what the potential cost. The Mexican foray had been a high-risk play that John and Jasper had often talked about when they were away from the other riders. They still couldn't believe they had agreed to become cattle rustlers and were now wanted *desperadoes* on both sides of the border. That they had gathered over nine thousand head of cattle and over two hundred horses on the wrong side of the border and somehow lived to tell the tale was beyond anything they had expected to find in Texas.

With cattle selling at over twenty dollars a head up north, the profits Burton would haul in from the foray could easily be calculated. Considering cattle in Texas were plentiful and selling for roughly two to three dollars a head, no one could understand why Burton had needed to take the risk of stealing Mexican cattle, especially at the risk of the lives of his men. The only answer anyone could come up with was that greed drove everything the man did. He was a man that never had enough, could never get enough, and would never be satisfied with what he had.

"We're moving out in the mornin," Jasper said as he stepped off his horse.

He had just ridden in from the ranch's southwest quarter where half of the herd was being grazed.

"Gus was just here. He said Cookie'll join the drive. They were in town all day stockin' up on supplies," John said, happy to share the good news.

Cookie had become indispensable for the riders who had been working day and night to get the cattle ready for the trail. The man always had a hot pot of coffee on and could rustle up something to eat at any hour of the day or night. Many of the riders had spread the rumor that Cookie never slept.

"Damn good to hear. I was afraid we might be eating hardtack all the way to the Black Hills," Jasper said with a chuckle. "If Cookie wasn't so damn homely, he might even make a good wife," he added.

"Speaking of wives. Have you heard from Maryanne?" John asked, knowing Jasper had been waiting for a reply to his letters since they arrived at the Rocking T.

With the drive pulling out the next day, John had learned that there wasn't a cowboy mail drop on the route they would be taking until they reached Tascosa in the panhandle of Texas, over five hundred miles north of San Antonio.

"No, nothing yet, but I'm sure she's been busy with work and such. I plan to send her a telegram from San Antonio tomorrow morning to let her know to send her letter to the cowboy mail drop at the sheriff's office in Tascosa," Jasper said, his voice full of good cheer and high hopes.

"Good idea," John said, wondering how long it would take before Jasper accepted Maryanne may not be the girl of his dreams.

The fact that Jasper had left Maryanne a ten-dollar gold piece to cover postage and such just before he ran to the train station in Kansas City made John think Maryanne may have been a different kind of girl, though he didn't want to believe it. That she hadn't written in a month, however, wasn't a promising sign.

The next morning the longhorns moved out. Cookie, driving the chuckwagon, was placed at the head of the column. He knew the trail and would help keep the drive headed in the right direction. With over ten thousand head in the drive, finding a route with plenty of water and graze would be a challenge. Baagahni and Joe Bishop had been sent to scout ahead of the herd, since they had the best knowledge of the lay of the land and knew where the best water and graze might be found.

It had taken over a week working with the cattle to find the drive's natural leaders. Kit Larson had been put in charge of this important duty. Once several natural leaders were identified, Burton declared the outfit's readiness to, "Head 'em up, and move 'em out."

As the leaders set out, it didn't take much to encourage the rest of the herd to follow. Kit Larson worked as the herd's pointer, directing the natural leaders to stay the course. Gus McKay and Lance Freeman, the outfit's most experienced hands, rode swing and worked to shape the herd in a steady flowing column behind the leaders. In the coming days, Kit knew a true lead steer would emerge from the natural leaders, making all their jobs easier.

Six flank riders, Charlie Wingate, Lester Beaman, Teddy Ingles, Frank Lee, Pete Russ, and Wayne Garcia worked further back along the column, three on each side, to keep the cattle bunched and moving forward by chasing down and encouraging cattle that tried to quit the herd to get back in line. With over ten thousand animals, more than double most cattle drives, the column soon stretched nearly two miles long.

John and Jasper, the youngest and greenest riders on the drive, were paired up with two other young riders, Clay Olsen and Junior McCain. As was customary in the code of cowpunchers, the youngsters had been relegated to riding drag, the dirtiest, toughest, and most undesirable job on the drive. The job of a drag rider was to push the cattle forward and to turn back any cattle trying to quit the herd. Within the first couple of hours on the trail, the young drag riders all learned that their days would be spent chasing an endless cycle of quitters while living in a cloud of dust that nearly blotted out the sun. Even with his bandana pulled up tight over his nose and mouth, John could taste every inch of the trail.

The horse remuda followed the drag riders at a distance, with the Thompson twins, Rowdy and Bo, riding on each side, circling the perimeter to keep the horses bunched and moving with the herd as close as was prudent. Cowboys had learned early on that horses and cattle, especially longhorn cattle, don't mix, leastwise not on friendly terms. Keeping the horses away from a swarming sea of deadly horns was a full-time job. Stampedes were never far from everyone's thoughts. If the herd suddenly bolted as one, no one wanted to be caught in its path. Over the years, having the horse remuda trail the main herd had become a simple precaution that had proven its worth.

At the end of the fourth full day on the trail, John and Jasper finally got their first break to catch some real shut-eye. The night was warm, as a rusty orange ball of a moon sprang fully formed from the eastern horizon. The restless sounds of milling and snorting longhorns filled the air.

As he had done every evening, Gus warned everyone to be on the lookout for cattle trying to quit the herd in the middle of the night; he reminded them it would take at least two to three weeks to break the ornery varmints into the daily rhythm of their new lives as members of a herd, especially since most of the animals were still on the wild side and used to their independence.

Using their saddles as pillows, John and Jasper lay stretched out on their bed rolls. The full moon grew brighter as it steadily rose higher in the sky, with its long shadows growing shorter by the minute.

"I've eaten more dirt in Texas than beef," Jasper said with a snicker.

"No one said it'd be easy," John said with a grin.

"That, pard, is an understatement," Jasper said matching John's grin.

"Is that right? Well, either way, I'm plum tuckered out from chasin' down an endless string of less-than-polite long-horned critters," John said, giving Jasper a sideways glance, his face serious.

"And that, pard, is a euphemism," Jasper said, matching the serious look on John's face, causing both men to break out into uncontrollable laughter.

Still trying to catch their breath, Gus came by and was glad to see the two young men could laugh at their miserable plight. He knew what it was to be one of the youngsters in the outfit and to ride drag for weeks on end. He could see these two had the sand to do the job and most importantly the right temperament and attitude.

"Good to see you boys enjoying yourselves on your Chisholm Trail Holiday," Gus chuckled. "I'm sure the scenery from the back of the herd has been darn right breathtaking," he added, pretending his remark was an innocent one.

John, Jasper, and several other riders within earshot all guffawed at Gus's clever remark.

"Yea, I've heard tell that the beauty of that lovely haze at the back of the herd can just take a fella's breath clean away," Kit offered as he walked by, carrying a fresh cup of coffee.

"It surely can," Gus agreed with a grin.

Once again, everyone had a good laugh. The laughter had helped to cheer John and Jasper up. Exhausted from four days of backbreaking labor without a chance to rest and with the tension in their bone-weary bodies now relaxed, they were soon dead to the world.

Maryanne had been swept off her feet the first time she laid eyes on Jasper Waite. She couldn't get his handsome, chiseled features and deep blue eyes out of her mind. Their time together had been brief, but she would never forget how he held her in his strong arms and how tenderly he had kissed her. She wanted more than anything for them to be together again. She hadn't written to Jasper for fear he held no real feelings for her. He had had his fling in Kansas City and like all the cowpunchers she had served at the tavern, he was just another tumbleweed blown in by the wind, and not the kind of man to put down roots. The telegram she held in her trembling hands told her she had been wrong about Jasper Waite. He wasn't just another tumbleweed. He loved her and couldn't wait to get back to Kansas City to hold her in his arms once again. With hope in her heart, she soon put pen to paper.

Following the broken and nearly washed-out tracks of the herd as it moved north, Willie arrived at the gates of the Rocking T Ranch. He now knew where he could find Lucky John and Jasper, his brawny idiot sidekick. It would be just a matter of time before he would have his opportunity to even the score. Ol' Lucky John got off a lucky shot that had for the moment postponed the inevitable. He wouldn't be so damn lucky next time, Willie promised himself.

To keep an eye on the movements of John and Jasper and to learn more about all the comings and goings at the Rocking T, Willie purchased a pair of field glasses in San Antonio. He lay on a high bluff with a view of the main house, bunkhouse, and surrounding corrals, barns, and sheds. The more he watched John and Jasper strut around the yard and joke with the other ranch hands, the more he missed his old cowpuncher life.

He had been a damn good cowpuncher and had always enjoyed the camaraderie of working with other men, working hard, and doing the job right. Rudy had been the irresponsible, wild one and had been a mean drunk. Rubbing his mangled stub, Willie knew he had paid a high price for putting up with Rudy's wild side. Knowing nothing would ever bring his arm back, killing the bastards who had made him a cripple would at least give him the satisfaction that he had leveled the score.

By the time the herd headed out, Willie had decided that making his play in the open might not be his best option. With fifteen other riders able to give chase, the odds of a one-armed man escaping would be slim to none. Having learned where the herd was headed from a loose-lipped bartender in the nearby town of Pleasanton, and figuring the herd's likely trail, Willie made up his mind to make his play in Tascosa. A public execution by a one-armed cripple would be his ultimate revenge. Gunning down John first would guarantee the big galoot Jasper would come running, which would make gunning him down all the easier.

Weeks flew by and the routine of daily life had beaten any thought that life could be any different completely out of the drag riders. They moved like zombies; their minds numb. John had never been so bone-weary. Having Jasper to talk to helped to relieve his loneliness and countless aches and pains, but did little to bring any joy to his miserable life. At times, he had his doubts about his Dakota dream.

"Word is Cookie's breaking out the dried apples tonight," Junior said as he swatted the nose of an unruly longhorn trying to quit the herd, turning the animal back in line.

"I can already taste hot apple pie; even through the noble and glorious scent of fresh cow dung," John said with a chuckle.

"Damned if'n I can as well," Junior yelled back as he rode off, chasing after another quitter that decided to make a run for it.

"What'd he say?" Jasper yelled from John's other side.

"Apples tonight!" John yelled back, extending his arm and holding up his right thumb.

"Apples! Alright!" Jasper yelped.

"Apples tonight?" Clay chimed in as he rode by chasing yet another quitter.

"That's right!" Jasper replied.

"Can't wait!" Clay hollered, as he drove the quitter back into the herd.

None of the men would have ever believed that thoughts of an apple pie at the end of the day would ever mean so much. At that moment, it meant everything. After learning what waited for them at the end of the day, all four men rode taller in their saddles and worked with renewed vigor. They had something to look forward to for a change.

Living in the moment was important, it focused a man's mind and opened him up to deeper understanding. When he thought about the impact the news of apple pies at the end of the day had had on himself and the other drag riders, John realized having something to look forward to was the spark that gave meaning to life.

As he pondered this thought, John recalled an expression Timothy Gillam had shared with them on the train to Texas. "Make your plan, work your plan," Gillam had said. A man with a plan always had something to work toward, something to look forward to.

John had believed a man should live his fullest every day and enjoy the now. Gillam's words had reminded him to never forget that living a life with a plan, no matter how loosely organized, gave life meaning and direction. His plan had always been to get to the Dakota Territory to stake his claim. He was now headed toward that destiny, a destiny of his own making.

He had to chuckle at his silly daydreams and the many meanderings of his weary mind. There was only one thing he was absolutely sure of, he looked forward to having apple pie at the end of the day.

With that, he pulled his bandana up tighter around his nose and mouth, snapped his looped rope, and yelled out, "Get along, little doggies!"

On the thirtieth day of the drive huge thunderheads rose up in the west and threatened bad weather ahead. They had made good time and were only fifty miles outside of Tascosa. As the wind and pelting rain came up, the longhorns turned their backs to the storm and began to drift with the wind. Kit Larson fought to keep the lead steer on course. Gus McKay and Lance Freeman riding swing worked to support Kit's efforts to keep the herd moving in the right direction. All of the riders were soon working overtime to keep the column from breaking up.

With the wind suddenly blowing at near gale force, the clouds opened up with rain, pouring down in buckets, hammering everything in its path. Just as Kit, working in tandem with Gus and Lance, attempted to get the lead steer turned to mill the herd, an effort that they had hoped would bunch the herd until the storm passed, a huge bolt of lighting struck a lone tree not fifty yards from the front of the herd. An intense flash of white light exploded into dozens of glowing blue balls of energy that rolled out across the ground in every direction. The ear-shattering clap sent a physical shockwave through the herd.

Instantly, the lead steer bolted followed by ten thousand nervous animals. A full-fledged stampede broke out, pushed by the wind as driving rain peppered the hides of the raging animals. Wayne Garcia, Frank Lee, and Teddy Ingles, the flank riders on the leeward side of the herd, were suddenly in the path of a mindless wall of horns. Spurring their mounts into a full gallop, the men sought to find openings in the ragging line of cattle to get clear of the stampede. Charlie Wingate, Lester Beaman, and Pete Russ, the flank riders on the windward side of the herd, could only watch the unfolding nightmare, helpless to lend their comrades a hand.

Wayne and Frank somehow dodged most of the charging horns that dug at the sides of their horses and their leather chaps until they were finally in the clear. With blood oozing from rips in their chaps, both men nursed their badly injured horses. How they had found the way out of the path of the stampede neither man could fully explain.

Teddy wasn't so lucky. With his horse badly gored and bleeding, Teddy attempted to sidestep further damage only to run into a huge steer that ducked its head and came up with Teddy's horse impaled on his left horn. Teddy, still in the saddle, attempted to ride his mount like a bucking bronco. With a sudden twist, the steer tossed the horse free, throwing Teddy high in the air. Landing sprawled out like a ragdoll in the path of the stampede, Teddy quickly sprang to his feet, pulled his pistol, and started firing into the raging animals headed straight at him. With no way to run clear of the swiftly moving stampede, his only hope was to down one or two of the animals causing the herd to split around their fallen carcasses and hopefully around him. Though it was a valiant attempt, the riders could only watch as Teddy's pistol barrel flared repeatedly until he was swallowed up by the mindless wave of frightened animals.

Teddy's death hit the outfit hard. They were so close to Tascosa after covering over five hundred miles from San Antonio without incident. Every man knew the work they did was dangerous, they only hoped they would be among those who beat the odds. Teddy had been a happy-go-lucky cowpuncher who dreamed of one day setting up a ranch in Montana Territory. He had joined the drive so he would be able to continue on to Montana to join his brother who worked as a foreman for the Northern Pacific Railroad. Teddy's dream had ended quickly and without warning. John and Jasper understood for the first time just how fragile life really was, and how it could be taken away in an instant. There were no guarantees in life, only choices—the outcomes known by no man.

The stampede had sent cattle in nearly every direction. A majority of the herd had run east with the wind. Since the herd was near Red River

Crossing, Tom Burton directed the riders to work the south bank of the Red River, where the cattle would naturally gather. Baagahni and Joe Bishop were sent to the north bank of the Brazos River, the river they had crossed the day before. The cattle were soon found in groups of varying sizes as far as ten miles from the main trail. Other animals were scattered between the two rivers over a wide area. Very few animals had run south back toward the Brazos River, saving the need to send more riders back the way the herd had come. The horse remuda had been gathered quickly due to the skill of the Thompson brothers in keeping the remuda bunched even when they bolted with the rest of the herd.

After three days of chasing down strays, Tom, Kit, and Gus all took counts of the gathered herd. Taking an average of the three totals, Tom was satisfied they had rounded up most of the animals. If their counts were right, they had lost only twenty-six animals, a miracle considering the herd numbered over ten thousand head.

"We move out to Tascosa tomorrow. We'll drive the herd north of the town and take turns going into town to get supplies," Tom said as he surveyed the men. "I don't need to tell ya, it's fine to have a few drinks and kick up your heels a bit, but if any of you yahoos end up in jail, we'll leave ya on your own to sort out your troubles with the law," he added, making sure every man understood the ground rules.

"We're a family, boys. Stick together, watch each other's backs, and never leave a man behind," Kit said as he stepped up in front of the men and took a seat at a small table that had been set up next to the chuckwagon.

"For those who need it, step up and I'll advance forty dollars per man, four ten-dollar gold pieces. More than enough money to get any man whatever he desires. Spend your money wisely, gentlemen," Kit continued as he laid down his pay ledger and a leather pouch full of gold coins.

After the men received their advances, the main topic on everyone's mind was what they would do as soon as they hit town. Having a beer or two was high on everyone's list. They had been on the trail thirty-five days and couldn't wait to escape the drudgery of their daily grind, even if it was only for a few hours of reprieve. They were a third of the way to their destination in the Dakota Territory; they wouldn't get another chance to visit a town until they hit Dodge City, Kansas, roughly two hundred fifty miles north of Tascosa.

Jasper couldn't wait to get to the cowpuncher's letter drop at the sheriff's office. John wanted to buy some rolling tobacco and drink a beer for the second time in his life. He also wanted to take a look around the boom town.

Jasper agreed to meet John at the Mustang Saloon, after he collected his letter from Maryanne. Both men had learned that the saloon had the coldest beer, best liquor, and most shapely women in town. None of these things interested Jasper, who only had thoughts of Maryanne and her letter, which he knew would be there. Gus had spread word among the riders that he would be collecting letters from everyone for the next couple of days and would see to it they were posted before the herd pulled out for Dodge City. Jasper planned on taking Gus up on his offer.

With dreams of a bright future ahead, both men slept soundly with no sense of the coming storm.

May 13, 1884

Tascosa, Oldham County, Texas

Appointment with Destiny

BERT BLACKWELL AND PHIL Roberts rode into Tascosa three weeks before Tom Burton's herd arrived. They had asked around and no one knew Willie Dunhill, nor had they seen anyone who fit his description. With no leads to follow, the plan was to lay in wait for Willie, whom they believed to be a member of the Tom Burton outfit and a witness to the raid into Mexico. Bert decided to stake out the Mustang Saloon, the main hub for cowpunchers drifting through town. Phil staked out the cowpuncher's mail drop at the sheriff's office. His plan was to question the riders coming in to check for mail. Willie's wanted poster had been nailed up prominently above the mail drop, making it impossible for anyone to miss it.

The word from San Antonio was that Tom Burton had gathered a herd of over ten thousand longhorns and planned to drive them through to the Dakota Territory south of the Black Hills, where Burton had set up a new cattle ranch. The collective thought was that Burton's cattle drive would come through Tascosa by mid-May. Burton would then follow the Canadian River north into Kansas. Both men knew Tascosa would be the last chance for the law to prove Burton was behind the Mexican raid and to catch Burton before he slipped across the state line and beyond their jurisdiction.

After consulting with Tom Burton, Kit Larson had the riders gather the herd along the Canadian River north of Tascosa. The graze was good and would last several days. Keeping the cattle gathered along the river's edge helped to keep the animals bunched and discouraged quitters. Once the riders' rotation schedules had been set, the first group of Burton's men where turned loose on the town. Kit, Gus, and Lance prayed the men had the God-given good sense to stay out of trouble, or at least stay out of serious trouble.

Tom Burton accompanied the first group of riders to town. Once the men arrived in town, the cowpunchers scattered faster than a mule deer being chased by a pack of wolves. Burton soon found himself riding alone.

After being established in 1876, Tascosa had grown rapidly to become a central commercial hub in the Texas panhandle. The natural Canadian River crossing aided the boom town as cattle drives drove an increasing number of longhorns through Tascosa to the railhead in Dodge City. Tom Burton had invested in several businesses in Tascosa and was proud to see a new stone courthouse under construction. He would work to bring rail connections to the town in coming years and looked forward to turning a handsome profit on his commercial investments.

Tying up his horse in front of the First National Bank of Tascosa, he planned to take care of banking business and then check in on the General Store and Mustang Saloon in which he was a silent partner. Just as Burton stepped down from his horse, he was dumbstruck by the vision of another man wearing José Rodriquez's distinctive hat and black leather vest. He also noticed José's silver inlaid eyepatch hanging around the man's neck, like a trophy. That the man had only one good arm couldn't be missed.

José would have never willingly given his treasured hat and vest to any man, let alone his eye patch, facts that confirmed for Burton that José was dead and this one-armed cowboy had somehow killed him. Burton was relieved to know his José Rodriquez loose end had been tied off, permanently. Finding out who exactly this mysterious one-armed cowboy was and what his connection might be intrigued Burton. With his curiosity piqued, Burton decided to follow the man to learn what he could.

John and Jasper had been among the riders who had accompanied Tom Burton to town. Arriving in town, Jasper rode straight to the sheriff's office and John straight to the General Store. John figured he would buy his tobacco and then amble over to the Mustang Saloon for a cold beer. He no longer felt like a boy acting the part of a man. He was a man who was out in the world, who aimed to make his mark. As he had these thoughts, he found himself straightening his posture and squaring his shoulders as his lean, six-foot-four frame strode down the boardwalk. He hadn't shaved for over a month and planned on getting a haircut and a shave before returning to camp. Though he wasn't yet seventeen, his beard was heavier than most.

Jasper was momentarily shocked when he stepped up to check whether there were any letters for him. The wanted poster hanging above the letter drop featured a strikingly familiar face. The name under the drawing was Willie Dunhill. The poster indicated authorities were interested in questioning Mr. Dunhill concerning a recent cattle rustling raid across the Mexican border. A two-hundred-dollar reward for his capture was offered. Jasper had no idea how Willie Dunhill, one of the cowpunchers who he and John had fought with back in Saint Joe, could be wanted for information about a Mexican cattle rustling foray, Willie had nothing to do with.

"May I help you?" asked a deputy who had been assigned mail drop duty for the day.

"Ah, yes, do you have a letter for Jasper Waite from a Maryanne Fairmont of Kansas City, Missouri?"

The deputy looked over his shoulder at Phil Roberts, who sat at the sheriff's desk reading the newspaper, and indicated with his eyebrows the cowpuncher might know something.

"Let's see what we have. Maryanne, pretty name. She your wife?" the deputy asked, trying to seem nonchalant as he dug through a box of letters.

"No, no, just a good friend . . . of the family," Jasper offered, wondering why the deputy would ask such personal questions.

"Young man, do you know the *hombre* on the wanted poster?" Phil asked, pointing at the Willie Dunhill poster as he stood up and walked over to the mail drop desk.

"No, can't say that I do," Jasper answered a bit too quickly.

"Take a closer look. You seemed to recognize the face when you first saw it," Phil pressed as he studied the reaction his words might have on Jasper's face.

"No, I thought he looked like someone I knew, but I never knew a Willie Dunhill," Jasper said, meeting the Ranger's eyes straight on in an attempt to convince the lawman he knew nothing about the outlaw.

After a long pause, Phil said, "Well, if you happen to recall anything, there's a two-hundred-dollar reward leading to the capture of Willie Dunhill. Well worth considering."

"By the way, what outfit you ridin' with?" Phil added, as if asking only in passing.

"Tom Burton's," Jasper replied.

"Burton, now there's a man who knows cattle. Where you headed?" Phil questioned.

"We're headed to the Dakota Territory somewhere south of the Black Hills," Jasper said, wondering why all the questions.

"That's a fair piece. You boys take care. We heard there's a band of Comanche renegades between here and Dodge City," Phil said.

"I'll let everyone know. Thanks for the heads up," Jasper said trying to maintain his composure.

Jasper didn't like the Texas Ranger or his suspicions one damn bit, but figured it was better to keep things friendly.

"Ah, here we go, a letter from Miss Maryanne Fairmont of Kansas City for a Mr. Jasper Waite," the deputy said as though he was proud to have finally found something.

"How much do I owe ya?" Jasper asked as he took the letter.

"Four bits," the deputy said as he pointed at the crudely handwritten sign next to the mail drop.

Fifty cents to retrieve a letter was more than a little expensive, but Jasper figured it was a bargain considering there was no other way to pass mail between cowpunchers, who were always on the move, and folks who were trying to stay in contact with them. After forking over fifty cents, Jasper left the sheriff's office clutching the letter he had awaited for so very long.

Taking a seat on a bench in front of the General Store along the boardwalk, Jasper carefully ripped open the envelope and pulled out a two-page handwritten letter. Reading slowly, he learned that Maryanne had been busy at the tavern and she missed him very much. She hadn't received any of his earlier letters. She admitted without receiving word from him, she had come to believe he held no real feelings for her until she received his wonderful telegram. The last paragraphs of the letter set Jasper reeling.

I love you, Jasper Waite, more than anything, more than life itself. I want us to be together always. You told me you come from a big family with eleven brothers and sisters. I hope you love children as much as your parents did, as much as I do. I want to have your child and to be your wife one day. If we had a child would it make any difference what it was, a boy or a girl? Would you still love me if we had a child together, even if it was before we were married?

Please reply to this letter soon after you receive it, so I can reply to your letter quickly. My hope is for you to receive my next letter when you arrive in Dodge City.

With all my love, Maryanne

Jasper reread the last paragraphs of Maryanne's letter over and over again and came to only one conclusion: Maryanne was with child, his child. He knew he had some hard thinking to do. Tucking the folded letter into his shirt pocket, he rose from the bench and came face to face with John, who was coming out of the General Store.

"Jasper," John said startled at nearly running his pard over.

"Oh, John. I wanted to read Maryanne's letter and thought I would use the benches here," Jasper said absentmindedly as he buttoned his shirt pocket. "You do some shoppin'?" he added quickly.

"Yea, picked up some tobacco and some throat lozenges the shop-keeper swore by. The trail dust is killin' my throat, pard," John said.

"Let me pick some up and a few other things and then let's go have that beer," Jasper said, hoping John wouldn't ask him anything about Mary-anne's letter just now.

"Sounds like a plan. I can taste that beer already. Go on in and do your shoppin'. I'll wait out here and have a smoke," John said, as he took up a seat on the bench and pulled out his tobacco and papers.

Sitting on the front porch of the General Store, John rolled himself a smoke and lit up. Just as he blew out a large plume of smoke, he caught sight of the one-armed cowpuncher who had tried to kill him in Mexico, heading up the boardwalk on the other side of the street. Not far behind him was Tom Burton keeping pace. Seeing the two men moving in tandem in the same direction at the same speed, John got the impression Burton was following the one-armed man.

Suddenly, a big man with a Texas Ranger badge pinned on his vest came bounding out of the sheriff's office and into the street.

"Texas Ranger! Willie Dunhill, hold it right there!" the big man yelled, his right hand on the butt of his revolver.

John watched as Willie took another couple of steps and then swirled around with pistol in hand. The Ranger was ready and lighting fast on his draw, firing twice, before Willie could get off a shot. The Ranger's hot lead hit Willie in his guts, knocking him back into a porch post. Just when John thought Willie was a goner, Willie quickly raised his pistol and fired twice, hitting the Ranger square in the chest. Dead before he hit the ground, the Ranger fell backward with the look of utter shock and surprise on his face.

Willie, like a wild animal, swiveled around with pistol in hand looking for his next target. In a chilling instant John would never forget, his and Willie's eyes locked.

"That you, Lucky John?" Willie hissed.

Stepping into the street, he motioned at the dead lawman and pointed his pistol at John and added, "You have something to do with all this?"

John, unarmed, stood on the boardwalk facing Willie, who motioned for him to join him in the street.

"I don't want any trouble Willie. It's Willie, right?" John said, having never known the name of the man who seemed to want nothing more than to kill him until the Texas Ranger had called it out.

"Yes, Lucky John. I'm Willie, your ol' Saint Joe buddy. Now fill your hand you sonuvabitch. Let's see how lucky you are today," Willie demanded as he kicked the Ranger's pistol toward where John was standing on the boardwalk.

"I'm no gunslinger, Willie," John said, not knowing how he would be able to come out of his current predicament alive.

Tom Burton rushed up closer to the action and motioned from the boardwalk across the street for John to stay up on the boardwalk where he was. Jasper had come to the window and was watching from inside the General Store not sure how he could help. The man lying dead in the street was the Texas Ranger who had questioned him about Willie Dunhill, the man who had gunned him down and who now stood with a pistol on his pard.

"Put the gun down, Willie. I have you covered," Bert Blackwell yelled with pistol in hand as he came fast stepping up the street from the Mustang Saloon.

Willie knew whoever was coming up behind him had the drop on him. Deciding he had nothing to lose, he spun with blinding speed and fired twice. Bert, ready for the move, fired simultaneously. Both Willie and Bert went down.

Once again, Willie seemed bulletproof as he brushed his stub across the front of his shirt and laughed out loud. What no one, not even Willie, had realized until that moment was that the money belt stuffed with gold coins Willie had stripped off José Rodriquez's dead body and had wrapped around his own had acted like a bulletproof vest, saving his life twice. None of the bullets that had stuck him in the midsection had gotten beyond the multiple layers of solid gold.

John, seeing his chance, dove for the Ranger's pistol and came up firing at Willie. Willie turned and fired once, just missing John, who lay next to the dead lawman in the middle of the street. John then took aim and hit Willie in the right shoulder spinning him around. Recovering from the hit, Willie took aim and fired, but nothing happened, only the sound of a dull click. John, knowing Willie had had him dead to rights, was surprised at his good luck. Without missing a beat, he quickly took aim and fired. The bullet nearly took Willie's head off, as it ripped through his left eye and out the back of his head. Willie's single right eye grew wide and crazed as he reflexively pulled the trigger on his pistol over and over again, its empty chambers spinning round and round, offering nothing but a series of dull clicks, until, like a windup toy that finally ran down, he hit the street a dead man who had written his own destiny long ago.

Knowing the custom of leaving the first chamber under the hammer's firing pin empty to avoid accidents, John, in thinking back over events, suddenly realized Willie had fired five shots in his gun duels, leaving his six-shooter empty. John lay in the street, amazed he was still alive and having to admit he had just earned his nickname, Lucky John. He wondered just how long that luck might hold.

Bert, his left shoulder bleeding, came up the street with a sour look on his face and rolled Willie's body over with the toe of his boot. As the body turned over, a growing pile of gold coins spilled out of Willie's shredded, bullet-riddled shirt. Bert quickly understood the reason why the man had been able to take several gunshots to his midsection without so much as receiving a nick. Though the face he looked down at was now missing its left eye and had been bloodied, Bert could still easily identify it as Willie Dunhill's. He was sickened by the high price Phil Roberts had paid for tracking down the wily, one-armed gunslinger. Bert had his own theory on Willie's probable paymaster for all the gold that now laid in a pile next to his lifeless body.

"Well son, you best give me that pistol now," Bert said to John, who was still lying in the middle of the street, pistol in hand.

Taking the pistol from John, Bert turned and was surprised to find Tom Burton on the boardwalk nearby. Looking at Burton, Bert motioned toward Willie's dead body and then toward John, and asked, "These two yours?"

"John Barton there is one of my best riders. I've no idea who the one-armed *hombre* was," Burton said, meeting Bert's stone-eyed glare with one of his own.

"I met the man in a saloon in Saint Joe two months ago. I don't know him other than he had a friend who liked to fight," John volunteered, hoping he wouldn't need to say more.

"Did he always wear such fancy duds?" Bert pressed, looking at John.

"Not sure. I guess he did. I thought he was a cowpuncher," John said shrugging his shoulders.

Recognizing the fancy hat and vest Willie was wearing as once belonging to José Rodriquez, John's mind raced to understand what might have happened between the two men. That Willie also had José's distinctive eyepatch around his neck seemed to confirm he had probably killed the man. When and why, John had no idea.

"A one-armed, left-handed, gun-slingin' cowpuncher who liked to wear fancy duds and wrap himself in gold coins. Well, it takes all kinds, I guess," Bert said, letting everyone in earshot know he wasn't happy with the answers he was getting or with how things had worked out.

With Willie's death, Bert's only lead on the Mexican cattle-rustling raid had also died. He knew of no one else who could tie the raid to Tom Burton. It was certain none of Burton's men would talk for fear of reprisal. How Burton and Dunhill happened to be in the same town on the same boardwalk at the same time seemed too coincidental, but then there was the question of the link between Willie Dunhill and John Barton, a link Barton himself had acknowledged.

The ugly twist in the tale that soured Bert's stomach was that he would now have to pay John Barton, the man who had conveniently severed his mysterious link with Willie Dunhill with a bullet to the man's brain, the two-hundred-dollar reward for bringing Willie in. Whatever their link had been, it was clear the two men hadn't exactly been friends.

Bert had to shake his head and grudgingly accept there would remain many questions unanswered when it came to the mysterious Willie Dunhill. That he had been a one-armed man had come as a shock, considering he had somehow been a cowpuncher according to Barton. Looking back at Willie's dead body sprawled out in the street, Bert took note of the ornate eyepatch that hung around the man's neck, which triggered yet another question for which he had no answer, and for which he expected he never would. He had to concede that only a higher power would be able to answer the question of how Willie Dunhill had known he would be needing an eyepatch in hell.

After arriving in Tascosa, Pedro Hernandez had drifted through the town in search of the man who had killed the traitor José Rodriquez. He had spotted a one-armed man wearing what appeared to be José's vest and hat headed up the boardwalk just when a Texas Ranger bounded out of the sheriff's office and barked the name Willie Dunhill. Pedro had watched as Dunhill gunned down the Ranger after clearly being outdrawn and taking several gunshots to his own body. Amazed, Pedro witnessed a miracle as the *pistolero* Dunhill, seemingly unharmed, then called out another man from across the street.

Just as Dunhill moved into the street to take on the other man, he once again was confronted by a Texas Ranger coming up the street behind him. Again, he took lead to his midsection, but was able to brush off the bullets, taking down the other Ranger before turning back to the other man. In the meantime, the other man had dove into the street and entered into a gun battle with Dunhill, resulting in Dunhill's death.

After the smoke cleared, Pedro joined the crowd of townfolk that vied to get a closer look at the body of the *desperado*, Willie Dunhill. Looking down at the prostrate body sprawled out in the street, Pedro found what he had been searching for hanging around the dead man's neck, José's distinctive eyepatch. Finding the eyepatch on a dead man meant only one thing, the quest of Don Enrico Martín Lopez to even the score with Don Tomás Burton had come to an abrupt and violent end.

Pedro remembered the night at the Longhorn Saloon in Pleasanton, when he had passed a heavy pouch of gold coins to José Rodriquez. The image of all those precious gold coins now tossed without a care into the middle of the street summed things up well, Pedro thought, as he headed to his horse and his long ride back to Mexico.

May 20, 1884

No Man's Land, Cimarron Territory

Every Man for Himself

"Head 'em up! Move 'em out!" Tom called out, sending his riders into motion.

On cue, Kit Larson firmly nudged the lead steer forward until he was encouraged enough to take up the challenge. Once he moved forward, the rest of the herd soon followed. After weeks of hard work, the herd had been broken to the trail, making the riders' work much easier as the number of quitters decreased by the day.

After spending only two days in Tascosa, the plan was to cross the Canadian River just outside of Tascosa and then to follow the river east to a point near Canadian, Texas, where they would turn the herd north toward Indian Territory and the Cimarron River. From there, they would drive the cattle north to Dodge City and the Arkansas River.

Baagahni and Bishop had been sent ahead of the herd to look for water between the Canadian and Cimarron Rivers. If Beaver Creek was flowing, they figured they would have no problems. Their problem was that due to the low average rainfall in the High Plains region, the creek's water often flowed under the sand. Should this be the case, they would need to find an alternative source of water. If none could be found, which was a high possibility, they might be confronted with a series of dry camps until they reached the Cimarron River, a dire situation with ten thousand thirsty longhorns on their hands. Controlling the herd in a dry camp would be next to impossible, as the animals would become increasingly dehydrated in the dry, high-plains-desert heat.

Taking the drive west into Colorado and then north had been an option. With renegade Comanche on the prowl, Burton had opted to take the drive through No Man's Land west of Indian Territory. Burton figured losing a few horses and a few head of cattle to small bands of Cherokee and other bandits in the lawless wastelands was preferable to losing his scalp and everything else to a marauding band of Comanche out for blood as much as treasure.

Burton couldn't believe his luck in the way things had turned out in Tascosa. How John Barton, one of his wild Jokers, had turned a losing hand and probable trouble with the law into a winner was nothing short of a miracle. Burton was always amazed at how unseen forces seemed to work their magic in the world beyond the control of mortal men. He had learned long ago that the destiny of people, things, and even events tended to become entangled, one with the other, in ways that were impossible to avoid, and more often than not impossible to fully comprehend. That Willie and John would have a final showdown had been written in their destinies from the moment of their first meeting in Saint Joe; there had been no way to predict how or when, only that it would happen. Tom believed how things played out depended on timing and circumstance and the whims of spirits unseen, and of course the pleasure of Lady Luck.

The Lady shined on his Jokers; he could see that the first night they met. It had been obvious the boys had run into trouble on their way to San Antonio; Jasper's split lip had made that clear enough. The kiss mark on his neck hinted the trouble might have been over a woman, which seemed fitting considering their ages. It had also been pretty obvious they had somehow come out the winners. He was pleased his bet on signing up the two inexperienced boys as the Jokers in his hand was paying off.

The unexpected bonus, which even he had thought not possible, was that the boys had demonstrated they could hold their own as leather-tough cowpunchers and do a man's work. He had to admit they had turned out to be damn good all-around cowhands, as good as any man in his outfit, and that was saying a hell of a lot.

With the prevailing wind coming from the northwest, the drag riders enjoyed fresh, dust-free air for several days in a row. Their lot in life was, at least for a time, a damn sight better than the one they experienced on the trail to Tascosa.

"Life can be good, pard," Jasper said breathing deeply.

"It surely can, pard," John said mimicking Jasper as he took a deep breath before chuckling.

"Well, you can make fun of me all you like. All I know is that this beats the hell out of the dusty trail we followed north to Tascosa," Jasper said.

"That it does, pard. No denyin' that it does," John said.

John had wanted to ask Jasper about Maryanne, but every time he had brought up the subject, Jasper had quickly found other pressing things to do or talk about. He wondered what Jasper was holding back.

"Pard," John said.

"Yea."

"You wantin' to share anything?"

"Share? Share what?"

"Oh, anything."

"I have some chew. You want some?"

"No. No. I mean on your mind."

"My mind?"

"Yea. Anything on your mind?"

"No. No. You?"

"Yea. I have you on my mind."

"You do. Why?"

"Cause, you have something on your mind."

"I do?"

"Yea. I think you do; but you don't want to share it with your ol' pard."

"That ain't so."

"Well, it seems so."

"It ain't."

"I shared the two-hundred-dollar Willie Dunhill reward with ya, didn't I?"

"Yea, you did, and I told ya not to."

"But I did. Cause you're my pard. Pards share everything."

"I share too. So, what're you sayin'?"

"It's sharing time."

"What do you mean?"

"Time to share, pard."

"Share what?"

"To share what's on your mind, that's what."

"I still don't know what you're talking about."

"Well, does the name Maryanne ring a bell?"

Jasper looked over at John with an expression on his face that John had never witnessed before. John could see the man was struggling with something he wasn't sure how to handle.

"Never mind, pard. Let's just drop it. How about a dip of that chew?" John said, deciding it would be better to drop the topic.

"You don't chew, pard. It's not a good habit to start."

"Come on pard, I smoke, I might just as well chew. Give me a dip."

"You don't want a dip of chew. You want to know about Maryanne. Ain't that right?"

John felt a little ashamed for having pressed Jasper on such a private matter. He knew Jasper shared nearly everything with him when he thought the time was right. Jasper's relationship with Maryanne really was none of his business.

"Well I thought I did, but I decided you have your reasons for not talking about her just yet. I'm fine with that. You're right, it's none of my damn business."

"Damn right it's none of your damn business, pard. But, I really do want your advice. I have for some time, but, well, I, I'm not sure how to ask or what you might say."

"You're like a brother to me, pard. You can trust me to give you the best advice I can, though I can't promise it'll be the best thing to do every time."

"Fair enough. I feel the same way about you."

"Well?"

"Well, I'll just come out and say it, I guess," Jasper said and then seemed unable to speak as he struggled to find the right words.

"Alright, go ahead," John encouraged his friend.

"Maryanne . . . she's, well, she's, well I think she's, well you know, in that way," Jasper stammered.

"What way?" John asked, just as it dawned on him what Jasper was trying to say. "Oh, damn, pard. Are you sayin' she got a little bun in the oven?" John asked, not knowing what to think about the sudden turn of events.

"Yep, that's right. My little heifer, Maryanne Fairmont, is carrying my child," Jasper said as though he was relieved to finally get a heavy weight off his chest.

Still processing the news, John wanted to support his pard however he could. He also wanted to support his decision, whatever it was. To avoid any hint as to what he might think, and at that point he wasn't quite sure, he said, "What are you going to do?"

"Do? I'm going to go back to Kansas City and marry that little heifer as soon as I draw my pay at the end of the drive," Jasper said excitedly.

"Then what're your plans?" John said curious to find out if Jasper had thought things through.

"We can go back to Iowa where I can work and save money. We could even live with my parents for a while if we need to. Like you, pard, I plan to stake my claim in one of these new western territories," Jasper said. "As soon as I can, I plan to ride out and find a place to homestead. Maybe in Colorado, Wyoming, or Montana, or even in No Man's Land where I could stake a claim right now. I heard a fella named Owen G. Chase is working on making No Man's Land into a new territory called Cimarron Territory, where families have already started settling by the thousands."

John could see that Jasper had a plan and was a man content with the direction his life was moving.

"I couldn't be happier for the both of you," John said truly meaning every word.

They rode in silence for several minutes; the air dry in the high plains desert. A pair of vultures circled in the distance. The trail-broken cattle plodded forward, no longer resisting, having accepted their plight as members of the herd.

"Hell, maybe we'll be neighbors in Dakota Territory someday," John added.

"Now wouldn't that be a hoot," Jasper said as both men broke into a good laugh.

"Hey, what's all the chatter, ladies?" Junior called over with a big grin on his narrow face.

"Jasper's moon-eyed over a little heifer in K.C.," John called back. "Can't stop talking about her."

"Like the rest of us, the only moons in his eyes are the rump ends of all the heifers we've been staring at for the past two months," Junior yelled and then gave out a hoot.

"I'm sure she's prettier than any of these mangy-lookin' long-horned heifers," Clay chimed in and gave out a loud chuckle.

"That she is, my friend," Jasper shouted out and then beamed. "She's the prettiest gal this side of the Mississippi. No brag, just fact."

"Like I said gentlemen, the man's the luckiest devil on earth," John shouted, causing everyone to hoot and holler.

As the day wore on, every time John and the other two men looked at Jasper, they knew he was a lucky man if he had someone to love who loved him back just as much. To a man, they too wished for such a woman.

Bert Blackwell, his left arm in a sling, sat in the Tascosa sheriff's office with his boots kicked up on the edge of the sheriff's desk as he leaned back in his chair, stewing in his juices. Having to pay John Barton the two-hundred-dollar reward for bringing in Willie Dunhill, a man who by all accounts may well have been in cahoots with Tom Burton in the biggest cattle-rustling scheme that had ever been pulled off, burned like a red-hot Mexican tamale in Bert's belly.

Burton's herd of longhorns numbered over ten thousand head and was made up of recently bob-tailed animals, something a rancher did to unbranded mavericks until he could get them branded. That these cattle now all bore fresh Rocking T brands only confirmed the cattle had nearly all been mavericks until very recently. Bert held no doubts that the herd was made up almost entirely of Mexican mavericks. His problem remained that there was no way to prove it.

Now that Burton had driven the animals across the Texas state line into No Man's Land, he had slipped beyond the reach of the law, but not the reach of justice, Bert thought. If Burton couldn't be held to justice for stealing Mexican cattle, Bert was determined that he would be held to justice for the death of Phil Roberts, a man who had been Bert's best friend for many years.

Bert shifted his broad shoulders and his stout frame as he stretched out, balanced on his chair's two back legs and the edge of the desk. The lines in his face ran deep; his skin was weathered, with the texture of tanned rawhide. Drawing his jade green eyes into a narrow squint he made the decision he had been pondering since Burton pulled his stolen herd out of Tascosa.

His shoulder would heal in time; he had no concern about that. He also knew where Burton was headed, so there was no need to worry about tracking the man down. Bert accepted all these things and swore to all that was holy in heaven and hell that the day would come when he would mete out the justice Tom Burton so sorely deserved, no matter how long it might take.

Getting up, he took off his Texas Ranger badge, laid it on the sheriff's desk, and walked out into the midday sun, a man on a mission.

"We're entering No Man's Land. Be on the lookout," Kit Larsen call out.

His words were soon repeated up and down the column of cattle which moved steadily north. The riders had been warned to keep a sharp eye out for renegade Indians, bandits, and cattle rustlers. For the next two to three days, they would need to double the night guard, and everyone knew they would be getting little sleep. Being outside the reach of the law of the surrounding states and territories, No Man's Land was an island unto itself, a land of utter lawlessness befitting its name. If trouble broke out, there were no official authorities to call on for help.

One of the main tenets of the Missouri Compromise of 1820 was the prohibition of slavery north of the thirty-six-and-a-half parallel. Hence when Texas entered the Union as a slave state in 1845, it was forced to cede any claim on its lands north of the thirty-six-and-a-half parallel, lands that had stretched as far north as Wyoming. The odd rectangular-shaped strip of land that was left between the Colorado and Kansas borders to the north and the Texas border to the south and the Oklahoma and New Mexico borders to the east and west, came to be known as "No Man's Land."

This unclaimed strip of land measuring at 5,746 square miles, an area larger than the state of Connecticut, became a land in limbo. Indeed, it wouldn't be until 1890 that No Man's Land, then known as Cimarron Territory, would be incorporated into a newly organized Oklahoma Territory as its panhandle.

Burton, planning on trouble ahead, had hired five additional cowpunchers in Tascosa: one rider to replace Teddy Ingles and four other riders to take up positions on both sides of the herd as flank riders. All five men were experienced cowhands, and to a man good with a gun. If trouble came, Burton wanted to have men who knew how to fight and who were not afraid to do so. The new riders were all being paid triple for their services, and Burton hoped for their loyalty as well.

Bishop rode in with Baagahni at his side and informed the camp that Beaver Creek turned out to be bone dry. They would have a dry camp the next night and then, God willing, push on all the way to the Cimarron River the next day.

"You're absolutely sure there's no water between here and the Cimarron?" Burton said, his voice hard as he considered his limited options.

"We rode twenty miles in every direction, there's not a drop of water out there, other than a few springs dotted here and there, not near enough water for ten thousand head of thirsty longhorn cattle," Bishop said.

"Well, we have little choice but to push on," Burton said. "We'll head out at daybreak and try to get as many miles under us as possible."

"We also found signs of a fair-sized band of Indians. From the looks of things, our Comanche brothers may have allied themselves with local Indian Territory renegades," Bishop said.

"How many are we talking about?" Burton said, not liking what he was hearing.

"There're at least twenty to thirty, maybe more is our guess," Bishop said, looking over at Baagahni for confirmation.

"With the lack of water, it might not be advisable to run the cattle too hard, if the Indians decide to strike," Bishop added, with Baagahni nodding in agreement.

"What d'ya suggest?" Burton asked.

"We move out early, like you said, but we try to make contact with the Indians and see if they would like a present of fifty head of choice beef for free passage," Bishop suggested.

Bishop had cut such deals in the past and felt it was worth a try. Fighting it out with the heavily armed warriors would cost lives and possibly the herd. If the cattle stampeded and if more hostiles decided to join in the turkey shoot, the survival of every rider on the drive could be at stake.

"I say we give it a try," Burton said without hesitation. "Bishop, you and Baagahni try to make contact. If it's a deal, ride to where we can see you and signal with this red bandana. If it looks like a double-cross, fire your pistol three times and ride like hell back to us as quickly as you can," Burton added, handing Bishop a red bandana.

Without another word, Bishop and Baagahni turned, mounted their horses, and were gone. The space where they had been standing near the chuckwagon was suddenly empty, as if the two men had never been there. John and Jasper had stood with the other riders on break and listened to find out what they might be up against. John had seen a lot since he left Iowa, he had even had to kill a man. He wasn't sure how he would respond to an all-out gun battle, one that may well be for the survival of every man in their outfit. As the memory of Willie Dunhill's face flashed through his mind, he was confident he wouldn't hesitate to shoot and shoot to kill, if he had to.

That evening, Cookie spent his time loading rifles and preparing ammunition. He also brought out several sticks of dynamite Burton had tucked away in the chuckwagon. Burton had instructed him to keep the powder dry until they needed it. From all indications, Cookie figured they might be needing it soon. Burton brought along several sticks of dynamite on every cattle drive. He had found dynamite useful when big things needed to be moved. He had never used it in battle.

Cookie convinced Burton the dynamite might be key to turning the tide if they ever found themselves in a fight where they were outmanned and outgunned, a fight like the one they might now be facing.

The next morning, in the rose-colored light of the early dawn, Kit Larsen called out, "Head 'em up, move 'em out."

With that, the herd reluctantly moved forward as the stars faded into the brightening sky. By noon the herd was moving at a good clip when, without warning, everyone heard three pistol shots fired in rapid succession. The meaning was clear. The Indians had declined Burton's offer of free beef and decided to take on the intruders.

"Patrols right, patrols left," Kit yelled out.

As had been discussed with the new riders, the command meant the two hired guns on each side of the herd would swing further out to check for any sign of possible hostiles and to check the perimeter on both sides of the herd. No one knew where the attack might come from.

The riders at the front of the herd were the first ones to see two riders galloping at full speed coming out of the west. A large cloud of dust was not far behind them. Shots rang out as the patrolling riders on the west side of the herd shot at the dust cloud to provide the incoming riders a degree of cover. Soon shots rang out from all directions. It suddenly became clear to Burton's men that they had been surrounded.

"Keep pushing the cattle forward!" Gus yelled out, his pistol in his right hand as he sought out a target.

John and Jasper, along with Clay and Junior, kept pushing quitters forward and watched for possible hostiles. They heard more and more shots being exchanged, but hadn't received any fire themselves.

What John saw next would be something he would never forget. Out of the east came a young brave in full warpaint. As if in slow motion, the bareback warrior rode directly at John, shooting his rifle from his shoulder as his legs gripped the sides of his painted war horse. One of the warrior's bullets took John's hat clean off, grazing the top of his head. Without thinking, John found himself pulling this pistol and firing at the crazed warrior. Two of his shots hit the warrior with one of them hitting him square in the chest, blowing him off his horse. John had no more than watched in disbelief as the man fell limp into the brush, than he found himself confronted with a second warrior out for his scalp. Wheeling around, John fired directly into the face of the second man. There was no doubt the man was dead before he hit the ground.

Jasper, too, was busy trying to stay alive. He had been thrown from his horse and forced to fight one of the warriors, hand to hand. After dispatching the warrior with his trusty Bowie knife, Jasper, with blood running down his face, fought on, firing his Winchester at marauding warriors as they continued to attack, first one side of the herd and then the other.

As quickly as it had started, it ended. Silence reigned until Burton hollered for the men to sound out.

"Answer to your name," Kit yelled.

Kit decided to call out the names of the new gun hands first, since they had been hired to confront any challenge head-on. He needed to know how many of the hired guns they could still count on.

"Jesse Givens."

"Here," Givens called back.

"Colt Watson."

The silence was deafening.

Colt!" Kit repeated.

Nothing, only silence. It was clear Colt was no longer riding for the brand.

"Dusty Crawley."

Again, nothing.

"Shorty Simons."

Again, nothing. At this point, Kit became worried about how many of their own men were still alive.

"Chase Roberts."

"Here!" Roberts yelled.

After the rest of the riders sounded off, the body count was not promising. Three of the five hired guns were dead. As for the rest of the outfit, four riders failed to respond, Clay Olsen, a young drag rider; two flank riders, Lester Beaman and Wayne Garcia; and a swing rider, Lance Freeman, which hit Kit Larson hard. Lance had been one of Kit's best friends and a trusted hand for many years. That Lance had been killed, after everything they had experienced together over so many years and so many hard drives, was tough to swallow for Kit Larson. Lance's fate reminded everyone how fickle the gods could be when it came to a man's life.

Losing seven men was a heavy toll and Tom Burton knew it. The hostiles had lost many, many more. He had counted at least twenty warrior bodies littering the ground around the herd; he suspected they had lost even more than that. The estimated size of the war party had been far short of what they found themselves up against.

"Bishop, what d'ya think?" Burton said.

"They're crafty sons of bitches. They had hidden their main fighting force. We got our asses kicked, but we held the line. We need to keep the cattle moving," Bishop said without emotion.

"How many do you think we got?" Burton said.

"Thirty, possibly more. We have no idea how many more warriors they have. They'll lick their wounds and take a second bite. We need to be ready," Bishop said looking at Burton with eyes that shined with the determination of a man who wouldn't go down without a fight.

"I need good men to ride with me west," Baagahni said, motioning to a high bluff to the west. "They'll come from the north; we'll circle and attack them from behind."

"It's a good plan," Bishop said as he assessed Baagahni's tactics.

"Yes, if they come from the north, it could work," Burton said having fought in the Civil War.

He knew flanking the enemy would give them the advantage, even if they were vastly outnumbered, which, without a doubt, they were. He also knew they would need a further edge, if they had any hope to survive the coming onslaught.

"Cookie!" Burton yelled "Bring out our little babies!"

Cookie soon came carrying several carefully wrapped bundles. The way Cookie cradled the bundles and stepped softly, careful not to jiggle anything, made everyone think the bundles must be extremely fragile. Everyone wondered what kind of "babies" Cookie might be carrying.

"Gentlemen, meet our babies," Cookie said as he unwrapped one of the bundles. It soon became clear that their "babies" were homemade explosive devices rigged up by Cookie, who had served in a naval artillery unit during the Civil War. Packed inside dynamite-charged clay jars were nails and other shards of broken ceramic and glass that would rip through anything in a fifty-foot radius when the jars exploded. For the homemade grenades to be effective, selected riders would need to ride in close and lob them near targeted groups of hostiles.

After a rider lobbed his jar, he would need to get out of the way as fast as possible. A well-placed gunshot would detonate the jars. The best option would be to throw the jars in the path of charging warriors, which could then be detonated in the middle of the targeted band. The riders liked the flexibility of getting the jars close and then exploding them when the hostiles were in the right position since there was no predicting the ebb and flow of the battle or how it would unfold.

Jesse Givens and Chase Roberts were the first two riders to step forward to volunteer to take one of the four clay jars. Gus McKay attempted to step forward but was stopped by Kit Larson who knew the outfit couldn't afford to lose Gus now that their other swing rider, Lance Freeman, had been killed. Gus and Kit were the only two men who had the experience necessary to take the herd through. After a good deal of debate between the riders, two flank riders, Pete Russ and Frank Lee stepped forward. The four men soon carefully packed the explosives in their saddle bags, mounted up, and prepared to ride out with Baagahni toward the bluff to the west.

"Godspeed gentlemen," Burton said as he stepped forward and tipped his hat to the volunteers like a General saluting his troops. The remaining men watched as the five riders rode toward the distant bluff, every man wondering if he would survive to tell the tale of the coming battle.

Darkness came early as an angry storm brewed in the west spitting out flashes of lighting while jet black clouds blotted out the last rays of the evening sun. Ten miles south of the Cimarron River, darkness made it impossible for the herd to push on.

"Bunch the herd! We'll have a dry camp tonight," Kit yelled, his commands echoed by riders up and down the column. The riders knew getting the cattle to settle down wouldn't be easy since they hadn't been watered all day. Going without water overnight wouldn't set well with the more cantankerous members of the herd. Kit and Gus turned the lead steer in circles until the herd started milling and then began settling down for the long night.

"Cookie, get the chuckwagon set up, we'll need to keep a double guard up tonight. You'll need to put on plenty of coffee," Kit said as he rode up next to Cookie, who was already pulling up his rig.

"Aye aye, Captain," Cookie said as he waved a loose salute.

Though the other men worried about the coming battle, Cookie couldn't wait for the smell of gun smoke to fill the air. He loved nothing more than a pitched battle that placed one man against another with survival as the only prize. It was his unquenchable lust for the ultimate blood sport that had driven the course of Cookie's life since the end of the Civil War. He had sought out and fought in one battle after another over the years and had loved every one of them.

The wind came up and the rain came down as fingers of lightning flashed across a pitch-black sky. Riders drenched to the bone rotated in pairs for short breaks at the chuckwagon. After a quick bite to eat, a smoke, and a cup of coffee, they returned to patrol duty. Few men spoke, with every man's mind focused only on the job at hand. There was no room for light banter. Every man feared that the Grim Reaper himself was stalking the camp, selecting his coming harvest. No one wanted to tempt fate.

It was Joe Bishop who first noticed a brightening in the sky to the east. Dawn soon followed and with it a wall of painted warriors charging at the herd from the north, just a Baagahni had predicted. Gunshots erupted as warriors and riders collided in combat.

Firing his Winchester from the back of his horse, John hit more than one target. Jasper was also firing as the number of warriors seemed to multiply by the second. Cookie's wagon had been set ablaze, while Cookie could be seen locked in a hand-to-hand struggle with a young Brave. There was little anyone could do to help him, with every man locked in his own life-or-death struggle.

"Here comes our cavalry," Gus yelled before whooping wildly.

Looking to the west, John watched five riders fanned out as they came down the slope of the bluff, closing off the warriors' possible escape routes. Several warriors pivoted their horses and charged back toward the oncoming riders. Within seconds, John witnessed the first of their "babies" as it exploded with a deafening blast, knocking down five or six warriors and injuring many more. A huge mushroom cloud rose into the air as the riders continued to charge toward warriors at the rear of their band.

The Indians, clearly shocked by the unexpected explosion, became enraged and redoubled their attack. The impact of explosion had also rippled through the herd causing the longhorns to begin to drift away from the loud sounds and growing commotion. A group of warriors once again attempted to pivot to fight off the riders closing on them from their rear. The crossfire was taking a toll and the warriors knew they needed to neutralize the handful of riders that had somehow flanked them.

Just as the warriors seemed to have the upper hand, Baagahni gave out a war whoop signaling the riders to charge the oncoming warriors with guns blazing. Jesse Givens bolted ahead of the other riders and lobbed his clay jar in front of the oncoming warriors. The warriors, oblivious to the threat, continued to gallop forward until Jesse put a bullet into the jar right in the middle of the marauding Indians. The explosion once again rocked the countyside as nails and razor-sharp glass and ceramic shards few out in every direction.

The surrounding ground was instantly painted red as pieces of flesh, bone, and blood sprayed out in every direction. As a mangled mass of injured war horses and Indian warriors twitched and cried out in pain, the surviving warriors, dazed and confused, wheeled their horses in circles as they sought to recover from the blast. In the midst of the mayhem, the five riders had moved in close, where they soon found the confused Indians easy targets. They fired without mercy, until all return fire fell silent.

The battle had continued along the northern and eastern sides of the herd. Several riders were down. The bodies of the warriors littered the ground and yet they continued to fight. Cookie, clearly bloodied, with several open wounds, continued to fire his Winchester like a marksman taking down one savage after another.

"One last push men! Take down Big Chief Red Paint!" Kit hollered in hopes of breaking the spirit of the remaining warriors.

Throughout the battle, it became clear that the leader of the war party was a warrior painted almost entirely in red and black. He had led many of the charges and had been the most fearless in battle. Kit figured, considering the warrior party's heavy losses, if their leader could be taken down, the remaining warriors might break and run.

Taking up Kit's call, Chase Roberts, with Jesse Givens and five or six other riders, headed straight for the warrior painted in red. John watched as Chase took multiple gun shots to his chest. As he slumped and then fell from his saddle, the jar he was carrying tumbled to the ground and bounced off into a shallow ravine.

Seeing Chase go down, Frank Lee signaled that he had the last "baby." Holding it under his left arm, he spurred his horse into a full gallop as he rode out toward the big chief. Just as he heaved the jar toward the group of Indians, he was caught by multiple gunshots, several in the chest and one in the head, taking him and his horse to the ground. The jar had fallen short and laid undetonated as the battle raged on. One of the warriors who had witness the other explosions now understood the white man's new trick and fired his rifle repeatedly until one of his shots hit the jar, causing it to blow up harmlessly.

John knew there was no time to lose. Chase's jar was still good. It was up to him to retrieve it and lob it as close as possible to the warrior in red paint. Working his horse to the spot where Chase went down, he stepped off his horse and pulled the animal down on its side, an old cavalry maneuver his father had taught him long ago. Using the horse as a shield, he crawled to the shallow ravine and retrieved Chase's "baby." Sliding into his saddle while his horse still laid on its side, he waited until the warriors gathered to make a final charge. Without warning, he rose as one with his horse and charged directly at the main body of warriors.

His sudden appearance as he popped up out of the low-lying brush caught the warriors by surprise as they took increasing gunfire from all sides. Quickly closing the distance between himself and the warriors, John threw the jar toward the big chief, pulled his pistol from his holster, and began firing at the jar as soon as it hit the ground. Just when the warrior in red paint realized what was happening, one of John's pistol rounds hit home.

The warrior in red paint's eyes grew wide in shock and horror at the realization of what was happening just as the jar exploded, nearly skinning him alive as hundreds of nails and razor-sharp shards ripped across and through his body, killing him before what was left of his shredded carcass hit the ground. Seven other nearby warriors also went down while the remaining handful of survivors wheeled their horses around and hightailed it in the opposite direction.

Riders continued to fire at the receding targets until Tom Burton bellowed at the top of his lungs, "Hold your fire! Hold your fire! We've won damn it! We've won!"

The victory had come at a steep price: of the five extra guns hired by Burton in Tascosa, only Jesse Givens remained alive. Of the original riders, Lance Freeman, Lester Beaman, Wayne Garcia, Frank Lee and the young drag rider, Clay Olsen, had also died. Cookie had been wounded, but not seriously. Amazingly, none of the other riders had any gunshot wounds or injuries in need of immediate medical attention beyond the need to tend to a few more serious cuts and scrapes.

"We lost nine men in the two attacks. I don't need to tell ya, this puts us in tough shape," Burton said. "Tomorrow we need to push the herd across the Cimarron River and then on into Kansas."

"Bishop, I want you to ride out tonight for Dodge City to hire six to eight good men and then hightail it back to the herd as quickly as possible. We'll have a hell of a time holding ten thousand head of cattle without more riders. One big lightning storm might scatter this herd to hell and gone. Gathering this many animals scattered across No Man's Land, so close to Indian Territory, would be next to impossible. The Indians who attacked us aren't the only ones who'd like to take us down in this lawless land. We're vulnerable right now, we have no time to waste," Burton continued, his face and manner deadly serious.

In the coming days, a skeleton crew of riders worked relentlessly as they pushed the herd further and further north. Six days after Bishop rode out, he rode back into camp with six hard-looking men. Cookie, his head and left arm bandaged, was awake and ready to serve the hungry, trail-weary men when they arrived.

"Joe, good to have ya back," Cookie said as he greeted the riders. "Step down gentlemen, I have coffee brewing, fresh biscuits in the basket over there, and stew in the pot. Help yourselves, and be sure to dig deep, puppy's in the bottom," he added with a chuckle.

"Cookie, it's good to be back. Glad to see you haven't learned how to sleep yet," Bishop joked.

"Always ready to serve, Captain," Cookie said with a mock salute, drawing a good-humored chuckle from everyone.

"Yes, it's good to have you back," Tom Burton said as he stepped out of the shadows and joined the group around the campfire. "I see you had good luck in hiring some new hands. Be good to get introduced.

"I'm Tom Burton, trail boss. I'm sure Joe's filled you in. I need four or five of you to ride flank and one of you to ride drag. Rotating these duties between yourselves would be fine with me. Please work out who's doing what. I can agree with whatever you decide. If one of you has experience as a swing rider, we could use your skills," Burton added.

After a lively discussion, the men decided that Tim Scott, Ned Mumford, Will Grey, and Leo Paris would ride flank, and Jimmy Compton would join the other young drag riders. Of the six new riders, Darrel Bland had the most experience in herding cattle and had been a swing rider on several drives. Burton, Kit Larson, and Gus McKay agreed to give Bland a try. Burton was relieved he had a fully manned outfit once again.

The drive had cost ten men their lives. The loss of one or two men on a drive was not unusual. Losing over half an outfit, less than halfway from their goal, was a very steep price, steeper than any Burton had ever seen paid. He wondered how many of his men might quit once they reached the railhead in Dodge City. From there a man could go nearly anywhere. He wouldn't blame any of his men if they decided to quit and head out to more peaceful environs. Moving cattle shouldn't cost so many good men their lives.

Five days later and without further incident the drive reached Dodge City. After crossing the Arkansas River, the cattle were bunched along the river two miles from town. Several other herds from different trail drives were being held along the river. Poaching cattle from one herd to another would be fairly easy and profitable for those who could pull it off. Animals, even those with the wrong brand, once herded onto a boxcar in Dodge City, would mean little as far as the law was concerned once the train pulled out for beef-hungry markets in the east. Taking no chances, Burton saw to it that riders were posted to keep a close eye on things until they pulled out.

With all the other herds in the area and with cattle from other herds having grazed the same land in recent weeks, Kit Larson estimated the herd had graze enough for no more than three to four days. Tom Burton, wanting to avoid any more trouble and wanting to continue the drive north as soon as possible, announced to the riders that they would spend only three days in Dodge City.

John and Jasper couldn't wait for their turn to go to town. John wanted only to take a hot bath and get drunk for the first time in his life. He couldn't shake off the sight of the mangled bodies of the Indian warriors who had taken the brunt of the full blast of Cookie's homemade "babies." Too many men had been killed and he had been the instrument that had brought death to far too many of them. His journey from Fort Dodge, Iowa to Dodge City, Kansas had been a bloody one.

When he set out on his quest, he had never imagined becoming a man would require a baptism in the blood of other men. Baptized in blood he had been; he only hoped a hot bath would help him scrub off all the sins that now stained his soul—his own and those of every man whose life he had taken.

Having survived, he no longer had any doubt that he was a man; a man able to face whatever life threw at him and accept whatever the outcome, on his own terms. He wasn't sure, however, that he knew what kind of man he had become. As he looked toward the glow of city lights in the east, he prayed that Dodge City might help him forget the ghosts of the dead who now haunted his dreams.

Jasper wanted only to get to the cowboy mail drop as soon as he could. Though he too had looked death in the face, the only "baby" on his mind was the one that grew inside the love of his life. He too felt he had become a man. He too wondered what kind of man he had become. He too hoped Dodge City might help him answer that question.

June 2, 1884

Dodge City, Ford County, Kansas

Halfway to Nowhere

TWO DAYS AFTER ARRIVING in Dodge City, John and Jasper were finally able to take their turn to visit the town.

"Jasper, I know you'll be headed straight to the mail drop. Post this letter for me to my ma and pa. I need to let 'em know we're alright. Don't worry, I told 'em only the good stuff," John said, passing his letter over to Jasper as they rode for town.

"I was wondering when you'd finally send a letter home. Your first one since San Antonio, isn't it?" Jasper said as he took the letter.

"Well, I figured your letters have been shared with my folks. No need in repeatin' everything."

"You got a point there, I guess. I'm sure your ma doesn't agree. She'll love hearing from her little boy," Jasper said as he tucked the letter in his inside vest pocket. "Where're you headed when we hit town?" he added.

"Straight to the nearest bathhouse. I want to soak the trail dust out of my bones, pard," John said with a ring of determination. "I plan to pick up a whole new set of clothes, socks, bandana, and the whole shebang, and get my old ones laundered. I feel downright filthy and just want to know what being clean feels like, even if it's only for a day or so."

He felt the stench of death smeared all over him and wanted nothing more than to have it scrubbed off his body and, God-willing, off his soul too.

"Let's meet up over at the Long Branch Saloon later this afternoon. Everyone says it's the place to go," Jasper said with a smile.

"Sounds like a plan. Meet you there after lunch," John said, signaling he needed a little time on his own until later in the day.

John watched Jasper ride straight to the sheriff's office; he hoped the news from Maryanne would be good. He was truly happy for Jasper, who could think of nothing other than Maryanne, their child well on its way, and their future together. He wondered if he would ever be able to see the world in such blissful simplicity. He envied Jasper for being able to do so.

After shopping for his new duds, some tobacco, and other essentials, he rode up the street to find a good bathhouse.

"Hey, cowboy, you lookin' for company?" a pretty little gal asked as she leaned on a porch post wearing a dainty, frill-trimmed dress with pink ribbons. Her eyes flashed when John looked at her. He noted her rosy cheeks seemed to glow with excitement.

"No, just lookin' for a hot bath," John said.

"We have the best bathhouse in town. Plenty of hot water, soap, and you can even hire scrubbin' services," she said as she stepped off the boardwalk into the street.

"Must be expensive," John said, feeling strangely attracted to the young woman.

"No, just three dollars for the bath and a shave. If you want more services, well, we have a menu. Full bath services, including scrubbin' and such, are ten dollars," she said as if she were the concierge in a grand hotel.

"Ten dollars!" John exclaimed, surprised at the outrageous price.

"Now, that would cover everything—and I mean everything, you know—the works as they say. You can always take a less, well, shall we say, enjoyable course of services," she purred as she reached up and took hold of his horse's bridle and looked up with her big hazel eyes. When their eyes met, she batted her long eye lashes, causing John's face to flush.

"Well, I need to get this trail dust soaked out of me. Lead the way," John said as he let her lead his horse to the hitching post in front of the China Doll.

Not paying attention to where he was, or the type of establishment he was about to enter, John gathered up his things and headed for the door. His escort soon led him into a private room with a large iron tub full of steaming hot water.

"Your wish is our command," she said as she gestured to the tub. "I'll leave you to it." With that, she left him alone, standing in the middle of the room holding his bundle of things.

He soon stripped and slid into the tub. The hot water felt good as the tension in his muscles relaxed. He lit up a smoke and as he soaked he felt like he had the world by the tail.

After a short series of gentle raps on the door, a maid entered the room carrying an empty bucket and a full bucket of steaming hot water. John quickly covered himself as she first scooped out a bucket of water from the tub with the empty bucket and then dumped the bucket of near boiling hot water into the tub, causing the heat of the water in the tub to shoot up considerably. John felt his skin sting and prickle at the heat, a feeling he had never experienced and one he pledged he would, from that day forward, never live without.

As he soaked in the steaming hot water, his mind drifted as his body yielded willingly to the indulgent and decadent pleasure of the moment. He wasn't sure when his escort slipped back into the room, but her hands felt good as she scrubbed his shoulders and back. It wasn't long until he felt her hands scrub his sides and chest and then plunged down to scrub his inner thighs and legs all the way to his feet and to each toe, one by one.

His escort then shaved him slowly and skillfully, her hands delicate, yet firm, ever cradling and caressing his head as she rotated his face under her razor-sharp blade. His body and mind were so at ease from her gentle touch that he didn't notice when the maid came back once again to dip water out of the tub before pouring yet another nearly boiling hot bucket of water in. By now, John felt as limp and weak as a kitten. He yielded to his escort's touch as she massaged his shoulders and then worked her slender fingers down his body until she gently embraced his manhood which had grown aroused by her touch.

"About those services, would you like the full course," she whispered into his ear, before turning his face to kiss him hard on the mouth while she deftly cupped his privates in the palm of her hand.

"Yes, yes, the full course," John heard himself say.

He had never felt so good and had never experienced anything like her.

She took her work seriously working her fingers like a true professional masseuse until she brought him ever so slowly, and with agonizing pleasure, to the promised land. After drying her hands off on a towel, she slipped the straps of her dress off her shoulders and let it drop to the floor exposing her young firm breasts and well-proportioned body. Standing unashamed in her nakedness, she asked if he would like to partake of additional services in her private boudoir upstairs. John, floating as if in a trance, could only stare at her naked beauty through the foggy steam. He had never seen a woman more desirable; she was a true frontier Venus de Milo, a temptation John found nearly impossible to resist.

Regaining his senses, he realized where he was and that he had already received more services than he had expected or could afford. Stepping out of the tub on wobbly legs, he lied and told his escort he had business to attend to and would try to come back later that night. She just smiled, touched him gently on his cheek, and then grabbed the back of his head and kissed him hard on the mouth, her tongue slashing though his closed lips, like a hot knife through butter. Releasing him, she picked up her dress and left the room as naked as a jaybird, without turning to look back. His mind spinning, he suddenly found himself in an empty steam-filled room naked and alone. Drying off, he quickly dressed and hightailed it for the door.

Before he could clear the front counter, a fixture he hadn't noticed on his way in, he was collared by a scare-faced behemoth with an ornery disposition who made it clear he meant business when he asked John to pay ten dollars for services rendered. With his coin pouch a ten-dollar gold piece lighter, John stepped out on the boardwalk, dressed in his new duds and holding a bundle of dirty clothes under his arm. Clean-shaven and smelling of lye soap and rose water, he headed up the street.

Dropping off his laundry with an elderly Chinese gentleman who ran the Lee Family Laundry just off Main Street, he headed for the Long Branch Saloon. He had never felt more refreshed in his life. Expensive though the services had been, he now understood why so many men were so easily lured to places like the China Doll. His father had warned him about following such a path. Once a man starts thinking of women as something to be purchased, he soon finds himself unable to appreciate a good woman when he finds one. His inability to treat a woman as a partner, a person equal to himself, eventually leaves him unable to truly love or be loved. Though he may find corporeal pleasure aplenty, he will never know the bliss of a shared love between a man and a woman.

Even so, John would never forget his escort's beautiful face, the perfection of her nude body, or her delicate touch. He regretted having never asked her name and yet he was glad he never did. She would forever be his mysterious Dodge City Venus. Though his memory of her would always be a fond one, he pledged he would never enter such a place again as long as he lived.

Jasper was bellied up to the bar when John bucked through the batwing door of the Long Branch Saloon.

"Hey, partner. What's the word?" John said as he took a bar stool next to Jasper.

"What the hell's that godawful smell?" Jasper said jumping back on his stool while pressing his index finger under his nose to block the strong bouquet of scents wafting off his partner.

"That, pard, is what a man smells like when he's been scrubbed clean," John said with a huge smile on his handsome, clean-shaven face.

"Not sure I like it," Jasper said, leaning forward to take another sniff.

"Each to his own," John quipped.

"Right you are. Each to his own. How about a drink?"

"Now that sounds like a great idea."

"Bartender, two cold beers."

Two cold mugs of beer soon came sliding down the counter. John grabbed the first and Jasper the second.

"Four bits," the bartender said.

Jasper slapped a fifty-cent piece on the counter which the bartender scooped up without missing a beat.

"May the drive north be without trouble," Jasper said holding up his mug.

"I pray it so," John said as they clinked their mugs together and both took a long draw.

"Ah, now that's a mighty fine beer," Jasper said licking the foam off his upper lip.

"That it is, my friend, that it is. Now, what's the word?" John asked as he too wiped his upper lip.

The beer was good and cold for a change and John couldn't wait to have another.

"She's doing fine. She said she's not showing much yet, but will be soon. In my letter I posted today, I told her to tell her boss that we were already married and that she'd like to stay on until I get back in the fall. That way, she can claim my name and avoid the shame of a single woman with child," Jasper said like a man that had everything under control.

"We'll get to Dakota Territory in no more than two months according to Kit," John said. "If all goes well, we can cover the five hundred fifty miles to get there in as little as forty-five days, they say," he added trying to sound encouraging.

"Maryanne and I'll need the money, so I have no choice but to stick it out," Jasper said, worried about all the things that could go wrong between now and when he finally was able to return to Kansas City and Maryanne.

"It's going to work out, pard, I can feel it in my bones," John said as he elbowed Jasper in the ribcage. "How about another beer?"

"Now, that sounds like a hell of a good plan," Jasper said, the volume of his voice getting louder as the alcohol started to kick in, loosening his inhibitions.

Burton watched his two young Jokers as they joked with one another at the bar. They had turned out to be better cowpunchers than he could have ever expected. He was pleased they had both held up well under fire. Bravery, he thought, must run in the Barton line. John was very much like his father had been during and after the war. He had showed he was a man of action and one that wouldn't run from any fight, even when the odds were stacked against him.

His gunning down of Willie Dunhill and his quick action to deliver the decisive blow to the leader of the renegade Indian war party made the decision Burton had been considering an easy one. The clincher had been Barton's ability to hold his tongue when he clearly recognized José's clothes and eyepatch on the corpse of Willie Dunhill. Burton would offer John Barton a full-time position once they arrived at his new ranch: The Lazy Cheyenne in southwestern Dakota Territory.

Getting up, he made his way to the batwing door. Just before bucking through to the boardwalk beyond, he was dumbstruck at the sight of Bert Blackwell headed with a hurried stride straight toward the Long Branch Saloon with a determined look etched into his hard features. Burton backed away from the swinging door and quickly checked his pistol, sliding an extra cartridge into its empty chamber under the hammer.

Busting through the batwing door, Bert Blackwell scanned the patrons of the Long Branch Saloon until his eyes locked onto Tom Burton, standing not five feet to one side of the batwing door.

"So, we meet again," Bert said, his voice dry.

"I see you're not wearing your badge. Lookin' for work?" Burton quipped.

"No, as a matter of fact, I've been lookin' for you," Bert said through clenched teeth.

"I didn't know we had any unfinished business," Burton said, knowing damn well the man had come to kill him for the death of the Ranger Phil Roberts, who Burton had learned had been Bert Blackwell's best friend for many years.

"I know those cattle you're driving to Dakota Territory came straight out of Mexico," Bert said, his face growing red. "I also know Willie Dunhill and them cattle and you are all tangled up together somehow."

"Not sure I know what you're talkin' about. I'd never seen Willie Dunhill before that day in Tascosa. I have no idea who the hell that one-armed *desperado* was. Let's have a drink and discuss it. I have a few questions of my own," Burton offered, gesturing the way to the bar with his left hand, while keeping his right hand free and close to the butt of his pistol.

"I'd rather we step outside and discuss things, man to man," Bert growled as he motioned with his left hand for Burton to join him in the street.

Burton realized Blackwell was on a mission; a mission to level the score, a mission he had already decided to see to the bitter end. He looked like he could handle a gun, but Burton doubted he had a quick draw. What Blackwell seemed not to know was that Tom Burton had a lightning-fast draw and had killed a dozen men in toe-to-toe gunfights over the years. Burton had no fear of facing down Bert Blackwell. He was confident Blackwell would meet his maker on this overcast, hurry durry day in early June if he continued to insist on a gunfight.

John and Jasper and every other patron of the saloon soon followed the two men outside. Stepping into the street, the two men squared off not ten yards apart. People lined the boardwalks on both sides of the street to witness the duel. Having seen lawmen patrolling all over town since he arrived, John noted, now that there was trouble, there was no sign of the sheriff or any of his numerous deputies.

"You sure you want this?" Burton said, hoping to dissuade the aggrieved man.

Burton knew he could outdraw Blackwell if the man went for his gun, but he had no desire to kill the man. He wanted nothing more than to avoid what seemed increasingly inevitable.

"Yes, Burton, I'm sure. Now draw you sonuvabitch," Bert growled, his eyes narrowed, his face set in stone.

Burton and Blackwell stood like statues carved in granite, as their right hands hovered over the butts of their pistols for what seemed like an eternity. Seeing that Blackwell had no intention of backing down or drawing first, Burton twitched his left hand, ever so slightly, knowing this would cause Blackwell to go for his gun. It was an old trick that gunfighters used to get their opponents to make the first play. It ensured that what any onlookers would see was that the other man drew first and that the gunfighter had no choice but to gun him down, making the killing a clear case of self-defense.

Blackwell's right hand pulled his pistol faster than Burton had expected, but not near fast enough. Burton's pistol cleared leather in blinding speed and barked twice before Blackwell could get off a shot. Blackwell, with two large holes in his chest, wore the expression of a man who realized too late that he had been blinded by his burning desire to set the world right, when in truth he could have done so much more good if he had lent a helping hand to his best friend's widow and her small children who now had no one to save them from the harsh realities of frontier life. Dead before he hit the ground, Bert Blackwell lay in the street, a man whose mission had been abruptly terminated. The crowd continued to look on until the sheriff suddenly materialized with two of his deputies and confirmed Bert Blackwell was dead.

After polling a number of witnesses, the sheriff concluded it was a clear-cut case of self-defense. Burton was allowed to go after giving a statement. To all concerned, including the sheriff, it was a mystery why Bert Blackwell, a former Texas Ranger in good standing, had come all the way to Dodge City, Kansas gunning for Tom Burton, a well-known Texas cattle baron. The sheriff, having to deal with drunken Texas cowpunchers nearly every day, concluded Texans killing one another over the damnedest things was far too common to try to suss out.

John and Jasper returned to the bar for another beer, both men knowing that to some degree the chain of events that had led to the gunfight that killed Bert Blackwell had all started with a mean drunk named Rudy James and a barfight in Saint Joseph, Missouri. Neither man understood how they had survived all that had happened or how things had worked out, and yet both men looked forward to brighter days with confidence.

Thinking about everything, John recalled Timothy Gillam telling them time and again how he had observed that the younger the person, the more likely they were able to shrug bad things off and move on. He always ended his remarks on the subject with his favorite quip, "Such is the perpetual optimism of youth."

John realized it was the resilience of his and Jasper's youth that had enabled them to shake off failures and to fight through tough times and, most importantly, to see the promise in a new day. With age he imagined people lost their will to remember life's simplest truth: Life begins anew with every next moment.

June 15, 1884

Laredo, Webb County, Texas

Rangers Never Forget

SOUTH OF LAREDO, CAPTAIN Jefferson Scott Baily stood looking out over the Rio Grande with a sour look on his weathered face. The narrow ribbon of water below his perch marked a tense boundary between two hostile nations. His men had been forced to increase patrols along the river due to the increase in cattle-rustling raids from Mexico since *La Incursión Fantasma Blanco,* known on the U.S. side of the border as The White Ghost Raid.

According to Mexican estimates, over ten thousand head of cattle were stolen in The White Ghost Raid. Though these estimates were thought to be too high, the unofficial Ranger estimate was at least eight thousand head, including an unknown number of horses—an unprecedented number of animals taken in a single foray across the border. Fact was, nothing like it had ever been pulled off before.

What seemed clear now was that Tom Burton may have been the mastermind behind the raid and that his Rocking T Ranch had been used to ready the herd before Burton moved it north. Captain Baily had approved Bert Blackwell's plan to track down Willie Dunhill, a cowpuncher Blackwell suspected had been involved in The White Ghost Raid. Blackwell had been certain Willie would eventually lead him to evidence that Tom Burton had been behind the raid. Baily had also approved having Phil Roberts join Blackwell on his quest as backup. Word from Tascosa and Dodge City concerning the events leading to the deaths of both Roberts and Blackwell didn't set well with Captain Baily.

That the *desperado* Willie Dunhill had gunned down Phil Roberts in a gunfight surprised Baily, considering Roberts had been known as one of the fastest draws in Texas; there were few men who would have tried to take Roberts on toe to toe. That Willie Dunhill had cut him down in a fair gunfight forced Baily to reconsider who Dunhill might have really been. Learning Dunhill had been left-handed and had only one arm only increased the mystery.

What surprised Baily even more was that Blackwell had resigned from the Rangers to pursue Tom Burton on a personal vendetta, only to be killed in a gunfight with Burton in Dodge City, Kansas witnessed by half the town. To a man, those who witnessed the gunfight said Blackwell drew first. Burton had given a statement and was now somewhere in Nebraska or further north in the Dakota Territory.

The formal complaints against Tom Burton filed by Don Enrico Martín Lopez and General Luis Perez Figueroa had been forwarded to Austin and on to Washington D.C. However, no real action had been or ever would be taken. There was simply no evidence Tom Burton had been involved in the raid. On top of this, all branded cattle had been returned to their rightful owners in Mexico. As to the number of mavericks or feral longhorns that had been driven across the border, there was no way to know for sure. Officially, there was nothing Baily could do.

As he considered his dilemma he understood why Blackwell had decided to take things into his own hands. Baily, however, could care less about some Mexicans losing their mavericks to marauding *gringos*. Fact was, he delighted in the thought. What caught in his craw was that two good men, two Texas Rangers, had lost their lives. Word had spread. Tom Burton may have gotten away with his *La Incursión Fantasma Blanco*, but he wouldn't get away with the deaths of two good Texas Rangers, no matter how much political pull he may have in high places back in Austin. Baily knew all too well, as should Burton, that Trans-Nueces justice may be delayed, but it was never forgotten.

With that thought in mind, Captain Baily saddled his horse and set out to make his rounds to the spike camps his men had set up along this stretch of the Rio Grande. He had learned long ago how to bide his time, how to let things come to him, how to look for opportunities without seeking them, how to be ready without preparing. He had every confidence,

Tom Burton would be back in the Trans-Nueces and that justice would find him. As certain as the sun raises every morning, he was confident that day would come. He grinned at the thought.

July 1, 1884

North Platte, Lincoln County, Nebraska

Toughest Miles

SINCE PULLING OUT OF Dodge City, Tom Burton had become a man possessed with a single goal in mind: he needed to push through to the Dakota Territory as fast as possible. According to the telegram he had received from George McFarland, his ranch manager at the Lazy Cheyenne, the Fremont, Elkhorn, and Missouri Valley Railroad was ahead of schedule and already nearing completion of a new line from Omaha, Nebraska to the newly established town of Chadron, Nebraska on Bordeaux Creek, where the FE&MV Railroad planned to build a hub for future regional branch lines. The first branch line would run to the frontier town of Casper in Wyoming Territory. The news was welcome, as the new hub would open up markets to the east for cattle coming out of the southern hills. His bet on building up his herd at the Lazy Cheyenne was looking better all the time.

What had riled Tom Burton up was the fact that a branch line running northwest from Chadron along the eastern edge of the Black Hills to the frontier boom town of Rapid City was already being surveyed, with the future plan to push the line north to Deadwood. Additional branches stretching to other northern hills towns were also planned. This news didn't sit well with Burton who was locked in a frantic competition with cattle barons on the northern plains who were already moving into the vast grasslands in eastern Montana Territory, northern Dakota Territory, and the eastern Wyoming Territory, virtually encircling the Black Hills.

His ranch in the southwestern hills was only one of a growing number ranches in the surrounding region. Taking advantage of the open grasslands along the Pine Ridge and Niobrara River in Nebraska, an increasing number of cattle operations had started to crop up.

Lands east of the Black Hills to the Missouri River however had yet to be settled, with the Lakota Sioux resisting further encroachment by the white man and his iron horse into their tribal lands. With all the would-be cattle barons vying for dominance in the region, tens of thousands of cattle had already been pushed into the vacant grasslands surrounding the Black Hills, replacing the now-decimated herds of wild buffalo that had once covered the land in numbers beyond counting.

Burton wanted to establish his own town and rail hub in the southern Black Hills and to build it into the main cattle center in the upper Great Plains. The new FE&MV Railroad link would help cattle, mining, and timber resources from the Black Hills and the surrounding region to quickly reach lucrative and resource-hungry markets in the east. North of the Black Hills, the town of Minnesela had emerged as a potential competitor as a cattle center, with the FE&MV, Northern Pacific, and other rail lines vying to expand to reach the newly established town.

Burton had heard that a man named Seth Bullock, a would-be cattle baron from Montana Territory, was promoting his own town called Belle Fourche, a newly established stage-stop on the main road to Deadwood from the town of Medora on the Northern Pacific's Transcontinental Railroad. Bullock wanted Belle Fourche to be the main rail hub and cattle center for the whole region.

Burton considered Bullock's plans for Belle Fouche a real threat to his own plans, since the location of the railhead Bullock had offered to the Northern Pacific was smackdab in the middle of Bullock's own stockyards which would give him an unfair advantage, the same kind of unfair advantage Burton himself was working to finagle in the southern hills.

With the speed of settlement and with rail spurs reaching into the region at breakneck speed, Burton knew he had no time to waste. He pushed Kit Larson and his riders to keep the herd on course and at a steady pace. Covering ten to fifteen miles a day, they crossed the Pawnee River, Smokey Hill River, South Fork and North Fork of the Solomon River, and Republican River as the herd plowed directly north from Dodge City until they arrived at the Platte River in the middle of the state of Nebraska. Crossing the Platte River at the town of North Platte, near Fort McPherson, Burton offered his riders a once-in-a-lifetime treat.

While stocking up on badly needed supplies in North Platte, Burton allowed his riders to visit Scout's Rest, the home of the legendary Wild West showman, William F. "Buffalo Bill" Cody, whose fame had grown worldwide since his first stage performance in 1872. There wasn't a man alive who hadn't heard of Buffalo Bill Cody, especially since the launch of his Wild West Shows the year before.

Spending only two days in North Platte, Kit once again pushed the lead steer forward as the herd followed the Platte River northwest across the scorching hot and parched landscape of the sand hills of central Nebraska. It wasn't long before the dry conditions and relentless pace caused the hooves of the cattle to crack. Several riders had also noticed heel flies swarming around the cattle, laying their eggs on the legs of the animals.

If left unattended the eggs would hatch in a week or so and grubs would burrow themselves into the animals' hide. After a month or so the mature grubs would resurface, causing considerable damage to any infected animals. The cost of having the herd infected with heel flies wasn't anything a rancher could afford to ignore. The lost weight and stamina of the sickened animals as the grubs took their toll could be the difference between profit and loss when it came time to sell. Burton was keenly aware he had to move quickly if he wanted to avoid the worst.

Sending Baagahni downriver to search for a natural mudhole, or a hollow in the bank of the river that could serve as one, Burton ordered his riders to push every animal in the herd through the mudhole up to their bellies, once everything was set up. The idea was to coat the legs of the cattle with mud up to their bellies to help protect them from the heel flies attempting to lay their eggs. Though this maneuver may not stop the relentless insects, it would definitely slow them down.

The operation took all day with animals having to be driven, one by one, through a makeshift mudhole blasted out of the bank of the river with dynamite Burton had picked up in North Platte. By the end of the day, the fly infestation had dropped off considerably. Burton, impatient to keep things moving forward, wondered out loud what else could go wrong. He was, of course, well aware that the number of potential problems were too many to list, as he had seen more than his share of trouble over the years. He also knew the last miles of any journey always seemed to be the toughest.

Arriving near Chimney Rock, nature's signpost for every pioneer that ever traveled the Oregon, California, and Mormon trails, Kit turned the herd north once again. After turning due north away from the North Platte River into what appeared to be a vast wasteland, the riders were pleasantly surprised when after going only a few miles they pushed the herd across Red Willow Creek, leading nearly every rider to believe they would continue to have good water all the way to Dakota Territory. They soon found out water was a scarce commodity in the panhandle of Nebraska. They knew they would find plenty of water when they reached the Niobrara River. The problem was, the Niobrara River was nearly one hundred thirty miles north of Red Willow Creek.

For the second day in a row, word was passed down the column that they would have a dry camp that night.

"Not sure we can hold these critters for another day," Jasper said, his face caked in dust.

Since crossing Red Willow Creek, the herd had found little water. By the mile, the ground had become increasingly dry and the air deathly still without the hint of a breeze of any kind, leaving the drag riders in a perpetual ball of dust. Quitters had increased as thirsty animals grew thirstier.

"Baagahni was sent to scout for water, but hasn't been back in two days, and no one seems to know what happened to Bishop either," John said, concern etched into the dirt-caked lines on his face.

"What the hell we goin' do if they can't find water?" Jasper said.

Jasper's question hung unanswered in a pall of dust. Both men knew the cattle couldn't continue without water. If the herd had to go a third day without water, the trail-weary, dehydrated animals would start dropping like flies. Several of the older animals had already given out. Cookie had butchered the first few animals that gave up the ghost, but as the number of dead cattle increased, their carcasses had been left as tribute to whatever vermin roamed the godforsaken land that stretched out around them in every direction.

Off to the far west, John could see huge thunderheads building along the horizon and prayed for rain. They had crossed many dry creek beds and empty, mud-cracked natural ponds that would quickly run full of fresh water with a good gully washer.

"Looks like rain on the way," Jimmy Compton said as he rode up next to John. "I can smell it in the air," he added, pulling his bandana down to sniff at the air.

"You think those clouds are headed our way?" John said doubtfully.

He had watched similar clouds build for weeks, yet none of them seemed to come their direction or shed a single tear of rain for their troubles. Believing Jimmy could smell rain in the air was also a stretch of anyone's imagination, considering there was no wind and the ball of dust that enveloped them smothered everything.

"No doubt about it. Look at the birds. They're already starting to hunker down. The wind should come up soon," Jimmy said as he pointed to a flock of birds racing to land in a grove of twisted cottonwood trees lining a small ravine nearby.

"I'll be damned Jimmy, I think you're right," John said suddenly sensing a storm brewing.

"Look! The dust yonder is being kicked up. The storm's headed our way!" Jimmy yelled as he looked to the west.

Jimmy had no more than gotten the words out of his mouth when a strong gust of cool damp air hit the herd from the west. As the storm front rapidly passed across the herd, pushed by strong gusts of wind, the riders soon found themselves fighting to keep the herd in line as dust devils sprang up out of the prairie in every direction.

"Mill the herd! We're goin' to mill the herd!" Kit shouted, his command repeated by riders down the column.

Kit worked to turn his big lead steer into a broad circle as the wind steadily picked up with lighting and thunder rolling ahead of the rushing storm.

The sky, once cloudless and calm, grew dark as riders found themselves under angry clouds that seemed to boil and churn with malevolent intent. Several funnels hung low from the belly of the swirling beast and swung first one way and then another with menacing potential. Every rider feared the sight of such clouds as they could soon develop into a twister that could reach to the ground, destroying everything in its path.

John and the other drag riders worked hard to keep the herd bunched as flank riders pushed the long column of cattle into a tighter and tighter bunch while Kit and the swing riders worked to keep the lead steer turning in a circle. Just when everyone felt they had the herd under control, the storm opened up like nothing anyone had ever seen before.

John stared in disbelief as he watched the belly of the dark clouds at the head of the storm turn jade green as flashes of lightning arched in long jagged fingers that clawed at the dome of sky. He knew the ominous meaning of the jade-green shimmer in the clouds rolling above the herd; he had seen it before back in Iowa, but nothing on this scale.

"Hail!" John heard a rider shout, his voice swallowed by the wind.

As though on cue, hail stones the size of silver dollars rained down from the heavens, peppering everything in their path. The milling herd the men had been so confident they had under control, soon broke free into an all-out stampede as animals ran with the wind to escape the relentless torrent of hail stones of increasing size that pelted their hides, driving them into a frenzy. Frightened and confused, animals ran from the oncoming storm as though pushed by the wind itself.

"Let 'em run! Get the hell out'a their way and let 'em run!" Kit yelled as the swing riders sent the order down the column.

Flank riders made way as cattle scattered to the northeast with the angry storm hot on their tails. Several riders had been thrown from their mounts while others had been slashed by a sea of flailing horns as the mindless, raging animals tore through everything in their path. Hailstones peppered the riders and their mounts, leaving both man and beast with serious cuts and bruises.

"The remuda!" Charlie Wingate yelled, his horse streaking past the drag riders with Jesse Givens riding close on his tail.

John, Jasper, and Jimmy quickly whirled their horses around and followed the galloping duo. Junior, having been bucked off his horse, could only watch as the other drag riders struck out after the stampeding horses.

John could see Rowdy Thompson working to corral their spare team of cantankerous mules as he flew by at a full gallop. In the distance he could see Bo Thompson attempting to keep the horse remuda from scattering in every direction as the agitated animals fled from the raging storm.

Charlie and Jesse, riding full out, had flanked the remuda on both sides. Riding hard for several tense minutes, John, Jasper, and Jimmy finally closed the gap between themselves and the charging horses. Splitting up, they worked to help the other riders slow down the remuda and to bring the animals into a manageable bunch. Bo had signaled for everyone to drive the horses into a shallow ravine where they might be easier to corral. The horses, having been driven as a bunch into the narrow ravine, where they were somewhat protected from the wind, soon began to mill and calmed down. The riders continued to patrol the perimeter of the remuda, driving back quitters until the storm blew over.

The other riders, drenched, wind-wiped, hail-bruised, and without a herd to patrol, gathered around Cookie's chuckwagon to weather the storm. After hunkering down for several hours, the wind calmed as the rain let up. Scattered clouds in the west were soon lit up in crimson, silver, and gold ribbons of light that streamed from a setting sun that slid toward the western horizon, while in the east, a perfect double rainbow arched across the sky as showers continued in the distance. The men all stood staring in awe at the unfathomable beauty of nature, thankful they were alive to witness such splendor and knowing only God could create such wondrous things.

As John patrolled the perimeter of the horse remuda, he gazed in disbelief and understood for the first time what Gus McKay meant when he had told him that though a cowpuncher may be as common as dirt, his soul is as close to the natural rhythm of God's creation as any man could ever hope to get. Witnessing nature in its raw, untamed beauty, John had to agree.

"Well, boys, stop yer standing around gawkin' at the pretty sunbeams and rainbows and dig some of that dry firewood out of the possum belly," Cookie grunted as he started banging pots and pans around in preparation for the evening meal. "Some of us have to work around here," he added with a chuckle.

Having broken the magical spell that had held everyone in its grip, the riders all started talking at once about what they needed to do next to round up the herd. Junior, the youngest rider in earshot of Cookie's request, quickly ducked under the chuckwagon to dig out a pile of firewood from its possum belly. A fire was soon started. Cookie wasted no time in getting a huge pot of coffee put on to brew. The men were damn happy Cookie's chuckwagon had a possum belly and would refill it with dry firewood the first chance they got.

The riders gathered around the chuckwagon all applauded when Bo Thompson rode in and announced the horse remuda was intact and the men could count on having good horse flesh under them for the coming gather. Saving the remuda had been the silver lining in a storm that had taken its toll. Without good horses on rotation, the riders would never be able to chase down over ten thousand head of cattle halfway across the Nebraska panhandle.

After nearly two days of tracking down strays, Kit Larson called for a head count. Tom Burton, Kit Larson, and Gus McKay made their tallies and came back to the chuckwagon to compare notes. All three men came back with a number over one-hundred head short. Several riders had seen

Indian hunting parties during the gather, and it was suspected they were most likely Lakota, the tribe that had claimed this part of Nebraska as their natural hunting grounds and the tribe with the closest Indian reservations.

If they had poached some of the cattle, it would be a small price to pay, Burton figured, especially, if a direct confrontation could be avoided. Burton insisted, however, on having Baagahni and Bishop track down one of the hunting parties to let them know, we are leaving them some of our cattle as a gift. It was agreed this would put the Indians on notice without openly challenging or threatening them. Either way, Burton had expected the possible need to gift some his cattle to the Lakota in order to pass through these as-yet-disputed lands. All and all, he tallied up the loss of the cattle as a wash, a small price to pay for safe passage.

The rain had filled many of the natural holding ponds on the numerous small creeks that dotted the countryside. The water had been a godsend. Taking advantage of their brighter prospects, Burton drove the men hard to keep the herd moving north. Three long weeks after pulling out of North Platte, the news Burton had prayed for finally came.

"Niobrara River ahead!" Baagahni yelled as he rode in from the north.

"How far?" Burton called back, anxious to get there.

"Maybe two miles," Baagahni said as he pulled up next to Burton. "Oh, and Bishop was able to speak to one of those Lakota hunting parties and they graciously accepted our gifts," he added with a smirk and without further comment.

"I suspected they might," Burton replied drily with a grunt.

Burton was glad to hear his message had been delivered to his new Lakota neighbors. He just hoped the Lakota never developed a taste for beef, unless of course he could get their government tenders to pay for it. For paying customers, he would be more than happy to supply all the beef they could eat. The thought of securing a lucrative government contract to supply beef to the numerous Indian reservations in the region put a broad Cheshire cat smile on Burton's trail-weary face for the first time in many weeks.

July 25, 1884

Chadron, Dawes County, Nebraska

Pine Ridge Mirage

CROSSING THE NIOBRARA RIVER, the riders could see pine-covered ridges rising up from the flatlands on the northern horizon.

"Are those the Black Hills?" Jasper asked as he pointed to the dark tree-covered hills in the distance.

"Kit calls those hills Pine Ridge. According to him, those ridges stretch across the northern Nebraska panhandle all the way to the Lakota Pine Ridge Indian Reservation in southwestern Dakota Territory," John said, recounting what he had learned from Kit Larson the night before.

"Those pine covered ridges look mighty fine to me. I just hope we're almost there," Jasper said.

"The Black Hills are just north of the Pine Ridge. It won't be long now," John said with excitement in his voice.

"Those hills look like heaven to me," Jasper said.

John and Jasper's excitement became infectious as the drag riders all swapped stories about how close they thought they were to the end of the long drive and what they planned to do with their hard-earned money once they got paid.

Driving the herd over the Pine Ridge took a full day as they followed what appeared to be a wagon trail that wound itself back and forth up the south face of rocky ridges and finally down the north slope of the formation just north of the new town of Chadron, Nebraska.

The first thing Burton took note of were the shining ribbons of steel leading east all the way to the horizon, confirming the new rail line had already reached Chadron and would soon reach towns in both the Wyoming and Dakota territories. To Jasper the sight of the train rails leading east from Chadron, gleaming in the afternoon sun, was an answer to a prayer. Those shiny rails meant Maryanne was closer than he could imagine. He had figured that once he arrived in Dakota Territory, he would have to ride back south to catch a ride east on the Union Pacific's Transcontinental Railroad. Backtracking south to catch a train was no longer necessary. Amazingly, the region now had its own rail link with Omaha and points beyond. He couldn't be happier about the serendipitous turn of events.

"Hey, pard, I heard they're already calling the new line the 'Cowboy Line.' Looks like you're the kind of customer they're looking for. With all the cattle filling up the range, beef and cowboys have become a booming business," John said, watching as Jasper eyed the new track.

"Yeah, well, this is one cowboy who'll be headed east to pick up a heifer, rather than to sell one," Jasper said with a wink and chuckle.

"Heck, you're getting two for the piece of one from what I understand," John said, winking back.

"It might even be three for the price of one," Jasper said, sharing the surprise with John for the first time.

According to Maryanne's last letter, the doctor had confirmed she was carrying twins.

"Oh my Lord. The man's already got himself a small herd started," John quipped. "Damn Waites always were a fertile bunch."

"When you meet your little heifer, you'll wanta get things started too. Mark my words: your days are numbered," Jasper said with a knowing grin.

The two men continued their banter until word came down the line that they would drive the herd north of town and stay over in Chadron for two days to resupply before pushing into Dakota Territory and on to the Lazy Cheyenne Ranch.

Riding into town with Kit Larson and Tom Burton, John, Jasper, and a number of other riders passed by the new train depot. Cattle pens and chutes built with fresh-cut timber had been readied for the growing cattle trade to come.

"Tom Burton! Mr. Burton, is that you?" an elderly gentleman dressed in a fine top hat and coat called out as he stepped into the muddy street and attempted to flag down the riders.

"Yes, I'm afraid you have the advantage, sir," Burton said as he pulled up his horse and looked down at the elderly gentleman who looked out of place in the rough frontier town.

"My name is Finnegan R. J. McMichael from Boston, sir, and I would like to make you an offer you may find of some interest," McMichael said in a surprisingly stout voice for such an elderly and frail-looking gentleman. Before Burton could answer, McMichael continued, "Meet me at the depot. I'm sure you'll find our chance meeting more than profitable."

With that, the old man waddled back up onto the boardwalk and briskly walked back in the direction of the new train depot. John and the other men watched the incongruous sight of a well-dressed gentleman, with top hat and cane, make his way down the rickety boardwalk lined with roughed-out buildings, surrounded by a scattered collection of ramshackle shanties, covered wagons, and canvas tents.

Burton motioned for his riders to go on into town and then turned his horse toward the train depot. It appeared to John and the others that Mr. McMichael was a cattle buyer looking to strike a quick deal with Burton. If so, it would be the quickest and easiest money Burton ever made. John wondered if he would ever be in the right place at the right time to cash in so easily. Things always seemed to work out for Burton. John had learned a lot about the man and had witnessed his darker side more than he wanted to. Burton was a gambler who wagered big bets and liked to win and never lose.

To hedge his bets, he used the talents of other men. John still wondered how and why José Rodriquez had been killed. That Burton never mentioned his death, even though he knew John had recognized José's clothing and eyepatch on Willie Dunhill, made it clear that the high-stakes gambles Burton so willingly made all too often involved betting the lives of other men.

The drive had been the learning experience of a lifetime, and the pay would go a long way in helping him stake his claim in the Dakota Territory. John, however, wanted nothing more than to get away from Tom Burton, who had cost more than a dozen men their lives in the past three months. Jasper would be going back to Kansas City to start a new life. What John wanted most was to explore the Black Hills and the surrounding region to search for his opportunity to make his mark in the new land.

Tying up their horses at one of the newly installed hitching posts with watering troughs along main street, Jasper headed straight to the sheriff's office while the rest of the men sought out the local saloon. John ambled up the boardwalk toward the General Store, taking in the sights. With so few townfolk on the boardwalks, John walked carefree, not really paying attention to anything as he breathed deeply. After months of sucking in nothing but trail dust, he always found it a treat when he could fill his lungs with nothing but clean, fresh air. Just as he turned to look into the front window of a small shop, he found himself bumping into a young lady who had suddenly sprung out of the shop door right into his arms.

Startled by suddenly finding themselves nearly nose to nose with a stranger, they both froze for a beat as they stared into each other's eyes. Being too close to focus on what or who they were looking at, they stepped back almost simultaneously in an attempt to quickly size up the situation.

"Oh my, my apologies ma'am. Are you alright?" John asked, flustered and embarrassed.

In front of him, straightening her bonnet and dress, was the prettiest girl he had ever seen. Like the old gentleman he had seen earlier, she seemed completely out of place in the midst of such a grubby frontier town.

"Oh no, it was entirely my fault. I was saying good-bye when I stepped out of the shop without watching if anyone was on the boardwalk," she said graciously, her voice steady and under control.

Her red cheeks however betrayed her embarrassment and possibly something else John felt, as he found himself unable to stop staring at her.

Unsure what to do next, he ventured, "My name is John Barton. I just arrived in town from Texas."

"So, you're with the longhorn cattle we saw north of town this morning. I hope you have a good stay in Chadron. Good day to you, sir," she said and started to walk away.

"And your name ma'am? I didn't catch it," John asked, desperately wanting to learn more about the enchanting creature he had accidently corralled.

"I didn't give it, sir. It wouldn't be ladylike to be so forward with a stranger," she quickly countered.

"But we've already met. Sharing our names would only be natural," John said, surprised he could say anything with his heart lodged in his throat.

"Interesting point for a common cowpuncher," she offered as a retort.

Once again, she started to turn to walk up the boardwalk.

"Yes, ma'am, I am indeed common, but I still have common decency," he said, casting his own barb, having been offended by her sharp rebuke.

"You have disarmed me, sir. My name is Sarah. My mother owns this shop. I'm afraid I must be on my way. Good day, sir," she said with the slightest hint of a smile on her full and inviting lips.

"Sarah. A lovely name. Good day to you, ma'am. Until we meet again," John said as he bowed slightly and touched the brim of his hat.

His smile, unlike hers, was broad and beaming. His cheeks, however, matched her scarlet hue. John watched, lightheaded, as she made her way up the boardwalk until she turned toward one of the only finished homes in the town.

"Yes sir, she's a looker, that one," a short middle-aged man wearing round spectacles and a shopkeeper's apron said as he stood next to John with his hands on his hips. The man shook his head with lips pursed as he too watched Sarah until she turned the corner.

"My name is Alford Wentworth. I run the General Store," the man said offering John his right hand.

"John, John Barton. I just rode in with Tom Burton's outfit," John said as the two men shook hands. "I was just headed to your store when I ran into the young lady," he added.

"Lucky you. No one around here has had a chance to meet the young lady. She arrived several days ago. I heard she attended some finishing school back east," Wentworth said.

"Oh, that explains it," John said.

"A woman like that is a rare sight in this part of the country and would be a rare catch, if a man ever got the chance to land her," he said with a frustrated look on his pasty shopkeeper's face.

John noted the man's thinning hair was parted in a perfect ten-ninety just above his right ear. The extreme comb over did little to hide the fact that he was as bald as a billiard cue, despite being only middle-aged.

"Would you gentlemen please move along? You're blocking the entrance to my shop," Matilda Bell scolded as she came to the door to shoo the two men away from the entrance of her Sewing Emporium.

"Of course, Mrs. Bell, we'll move immediately," Alford said in earnest.

"Why it's you, Mr. Wentworth. You just missed my daughter Sarah, who went home to prepare lunch. She'll be back this afternoon. Please do drop by again," she said in her politest of tones.

Pretending she had been utterly surprised to see that one of the men blocking her shop door was Mr. Wentworth, the owner of the General Store, she gave him her most sincere smile and bowed slightly as she closed her shop door.

The fact was, Matilda, as Sarah's mother, had high hopes that Alford Wentworth would get up the courage to come by her shop to meet her daughter. She had asked Alford many times to drop by her shop. She had watched the General Store across the street all morning for any sign of Alford. When she saw Alford finally get up the courage to head across the street to her shop, she had told her daughter to quickly hurry home. Just as her daughter headed out the door, Matilda had distracted her so she wouldn't see Alford coming across the street. Unfortunately, a stray cowpuncher had somehow come out of nowhere, spoiling Matilda's best laid plans. She had hoped Sarah would run headlong into the arms of Alford, which she had hoped would jumpstart their romance.

Though Alford wasn't much to look at, he was the wealthiest man in town. He was also an eligible bachelor of a somewhat agreeable age. Just the kind of man Matilda hoped her daughter would be able to land. As for the dirt-covered cowpuncher, she gave him little thought.

As John and Alford crossed the street to the General Store, John said, "That lady is a fine-looking woman. I can see where Sarah gets her looks."

"Yes, she is very attractive and a widow. I had my sights set on her, until her daughter came back home. Mrs. Bell seems more interested in getting her daughter married than finding a new husband for herself," Alford moaned.

"Well, it seems you'll have to take the bull by the horns, or should I say the heifer," John said with a chuckle.

"Easy for you to say. That ol' gal scares the hell out of me," Alford said.

John could see the man wasn't lying. The look on the man's face told him all he needed to know; Alford Wentworth was the kind of weak-kneed man that would fold like a tent with a broken center pole at the first sign of pressure. He wondered what Sarah thought about the situation. It seemed, be it mother or daughter, Mr. Alford Wentworth was destined for the altar.

Reaching home, Sarah couldn't help but look over her shoulder to see if she had been followed before entering the house. She had half hoped to see the handsome, witty cowpuncher, John Barton, hot on her trail. She had grown up on the frontier and though her mother had plans to marry her off to the richest man she could corner and hogtie, Sarah had other plans. Though she knew her mother meant well, she longed to be free of her mother's overbearing ways and endless schemes.

She knew her mother had her sights set on Alford Wentworth as Sarah's future mate. Though Alford was a fine man and would be a good provider, he wasn't a man who had sought to make his own mark in the world. Security and stability had been, and would forever be, his battle cry. That he owned the only General Store in a frontier boom town was more an accident of birth than personal initiative. His father had lent him the money and still regularly came out from Omaha to look in on things. Alford was more a manager than an owner, more a follower than a leader. In many ways, he was the perfect match for her mother, who insisted on controlling the lives of everyone around her.

Sarah wondered how she might turn the tables on her scheming mother. Alford was thirty-seven years old, much closer to her mother's age than her own. Though her mother might not be able to give Alford children, she could damn well take the place of his father as the controller and chief of his life. Of course, should the couple want children in the future, adoption would always be an option.

Many frontier families lived on the edge of survival as they worked to prove up their homesteads and build a new life in a hostile land. When times became unbearable, they were often forced by circumstances to give up their younger children to adoption when they were no longer able to take care of them. If Alford and his mother wanted children, they would have no problem adopting as many as they wanted, at whatever ages they preferred, a real plus for her controlling mother who would then have a whole tribe to boss around.

She had seen how Alford stared at her and her mother from afar. She had often wondered why he hadn't dropped by the shop to introduce himself. It wasn't long after she came back that she discovered Alford wasn't the kind of man who ever took the bull by the horns. She would need to find an innocent way to meet Alford and to delicately direct his attentions toward her mother, who, Sarah had to admit, was still a very shapely and attractive woman. If she played her cards right, her mother would never see Alford coming, she thought, as a wily little smile slowly creased her elfish face.

When she thought of a man like John Barton, Sarah's heart raced. His tall, trim build, rugged good looks, and razor-sharp blue eyes had caught her by complete surprise. She had never had such a feeling of familiarity for a stranger before, a feeling that intrigued her, a feeling she wanted to learn more about. Where it might lead, she had no idea. She was sure, however, it might well lead to a place far, far away from her mother's scheming designs.

Burton had followed the elderly gentleman to the depot where, to his surprise, the man had a fully appointed office with all-new furnishings. It seemed the railroad had thought of everything, including providing office spaces above the new depot.

"Please be seated, Mr. Burton," McMichael said as he stood and offered Burton a large leather upholstered chair facing the desk.

"So, what's on your mind, Mr. McMichael?" Burton asked as he settled into his seat.

"I'd like to buy five hundred head of your cattle for twenty-two dollars a head. That's eleven thousand dollars Mr. Burton, money I could pay you today," McMichael answered taking out two large cigars and offering one of them to Burton.

After lighting their cigars, the two men sat back in silence as they enjoyed the flavor of a good smoke. Burton was in no hurry to reply and McMichael seemed to be in no hurry to hear one. Silence reigned until Burton blew out a plume of smoke and then leaned forward, rubbing his chin as though in deep thought.

"That's a handsome offer, Mr. McMichael, a very handsome offer indeed. A bit on the light side, however. I'll cut out five hundred of my fattest cattle for twenty-five dollars a head," Burton countered as he met McMichael's eye.

"They said you wouldn't take twenty-two a head. Alright, let's split the difference. I'll go twenty-four dollars a head for a total of twelve thousand dollars, not a dollar more," McMichael said as he leaned back in his chair and took a long pull on his cigar, releasing the smoke in a long plume that hung high over the heads of the two men.

"You have yourself a deal, Mr. McMichael. I'll get the cattle ready and deliver them day after tomorrow. We can go over to the bank later today to have the papers drawn up, if that works for you," Burton said with a deep timbre in his voice.

Burton couldn't believe the unexpected stroke of luck, considering he had been wondering how he was going to pay his riders once they reached the Lazy Cheyenne. He had transferred money from Tascosa to the bank in Chadron, but he knew he was well short of what he needed. The twelve thousand dollars he would soon receive from Mr. McMichael would completely cover the cost of the drive and then some, leaving him with roughly ten thousand head of stolen Mexican cattle and two hundred horses free and clear, and with the whole kit and caboodle safe and sound in the Dakota Territory. Life could be good, and things could work out, if you just went out and took the bull by the horns, Burton thought.

His plans for establishing a northern plains cattle empire were well underway. With the two herds numbering over forty thousand head already grazing at his ranches in eastern Wyoming and northeastern Colorado, and now with his Dakota operation soon to be up and running, he would have over a hundred thousand head of cattle after calving season next spring. If he could hold things together, he would be able to once again double that number in another year. At twenty-five dollars a head or better, his two-hundred thousand head of cattle would be worth over five million dollars, more than a man would ever need. But then, he already owned more than any man would ever need; fact was, need had nothing to do with his desire to accumulate wealth. It had always been about the power it could buy, and he knew it.

The thought of ever having enough, made him smile; he knew there would never be enough for the likes of a scoundrel like Tom Burton. Blowing out a large plume of smoke, he got up from his chair, and told Mr. McMichael he would meet him at the bank in an hour.

Once again, John and Jasper found themselves standing at a bar in yet another saloon, in yet another cow town, drinking the brew they had both come to look forward to enjoying every chance they got: beer, glorious beer.

"Damned if this stuff doesn't go down smooth over a parched throat," Jasper said as he finished his second mug.

"Damned if'n you ain't right as usual," John said, laughing at his partner's serious, matter-of-fact manner.

It felt good to laugh as the men let the stress of the past several weeks drain out of their bodies as the liquor flowed in.

"Damn it, I mean it. They're puttin' something in this stuff," Jasper said still acting dead serious.

"Yep, they call it alcohol. It'll lubricate damn near anything, especially if'n you drink enough of it," John said still laughing at his partner.

"It's sure working on you. Hell, man, you're not only loose, you're acting crazier than a horse on locoweed," Jasper said as a broad toothy smile spread across his face before he too started to laugh uncontrollably, unable to keep up his serious act.

Jasper and John, unable to stop laughing, tried not to look at one another until they both caught their breath. Finally getting themselves under control, they ordered another beer and decided to take a seat at one of the tables in the back of the room.

"Now that we're lubricated, pard, what'd that little woman of yours have to say for herself," John asked as the two men sat facing one another.

"She said all's fine, and though she's showing considerable, she's still working at the tavern," Jasper said.

"You'll be with her again soon," John said, seeing a worried look come across Jasper's face.

"I know. We'll be fine. No need to worry," Jasper said and then added, "There is just one thing I need to get your advice on."

"Oh. What's that?"

"Not sure how you'll take it."

"What'd ya mean?"

"Maryanne has an uncle in Wyoming."

"Yea, so?"

"He wants to expand."

"Oh?"

"He says there's plenty of good land and his livestock's doin' well."

"This all sounds great, Jasper. Is that what you wanted to tell me?"

"He's making a good living."

"Sounds even better."

"Well. The critters he's raisin' ain't cattle."

"Oh? Is he raisin' horses?"

"Nope."

"Pigs?"

"Nope."

"Well, is he raisin' some kind of fowl? Like chickens or geese?"

"Nope."

"Damn, Jasper, you goin'a keep me guessin'? What's the man raisin'?"

"Sheep," Jasper said as though the word left a bitter taste in his mouth.

The taboo word, once uttered, hung suspended between the two men; John unwilling to touch it and Jasper unable to think of anything further to say.

"Yea, that's right, pard, sheep. The damn man is a sheepherder," Jasper moaned with a forlorn look on his face.

"Sheep. Well, sheep ain't that bad, pard. You get to sell their wool every year and the meat's popular back east," John said with a sense of encouragement he didn't really feel.

"They stink, pard and you know it," Jasper said shaking his head.

"Man can get used to the smell of anything, if'n he's making a living from it. Hell, we think a stockyard full of cow dung smells like money," John said, still trying to cheer up his partner.

"Yea, well," Jasper moaned again.

"Tell me more about Wyoming," John said, unsure what to think about Jasper going into sheep herding, but excited to learn more about the vast open lands to the west.

Both men knew there had been a running range war between cattlemen and sheepherders as long as anyone could remember. The unbendable belief held by most cattlemen was that sheep overgrazed the land, making it useless for cattle. The truth was that the range wars were more about access to water and vast public grazing lands then about whether sheep and cattle could graze the same ranges.

Sheep actually did better on the semiarid ranges of the high plains. Sheep favored grazing on brush and could survive on ranges with scarce water resources, both conditions common in northeastern Colorado, eastern Wyoming Territory, as well as southwestern Dakota Territory for that matter. Cattle tended to graze near water and were selective grazers, favoring long grasses, while sheep tended to prefer drier rangelands where they could graze on a variety of bushes and plants. Sheep could also go without water for days, where cattle needed nearly daily watering.

Despite these realities, the range wars were real and violent. More than a few men had lost their lives. What concerned John was that most of the men who had lost their lives had been sheepherders who tended to be outgunned and without political clout. In the west, cattle were the undisputed kings.

"He's settled in Thunder Basin north of the headwaters of the Cheyenne River, just west of the Black Hills. He has over two thousand head of sheep and would be willing to help get me started in the business. With the railroad coming, I'd be able to ship wool and meat to eastern markets in coming years. It'd be the fulfillment of my dream, pard," Jasper said, starry-eyed.

"But sheep, pard. Can you really make the switch?" John said in all seriousness.

"We'd be near Maryanne's kin. With two young'uns coming so soon, having kin nearby would be a comfort. Heck, man, to make her happy, I'd become a damn frog-rancher if'n she asked me to," Jasper said, as he looked to his partner for support.

"Frog-ranching? Yea, I can just see you hoppin' to take care of your herd. Would you keep your bullfrogs in a separate pasture?" John said with a chuckle.

"Come on, pard, I need your advice," Jasper said in desperation.

"You said you wanted to settle in one of the new territories out west and damned if you didn't fall into it. You'll also be staying near the Black Hills, near where I plan to stake my claim. I was afraid you might actually be thinking of staking a claim in the lawless lands of Cimarron Territory," John said.

John was relieved that Jasper's talk about settling in No Man's Land would come to nothing. He was happy that Jasper and Maryanne now seemed to have a real chance of making a life together. With two little ones on the way, John knew Jasper needed to make his decisions fast. Winter would be coming to the northern plains in just a few short months.

"No Man's Land! Are you kidding? We barely got out of that godforsaken wasteland with our scalps," Jasper blurted. "I was never serious about wanting to settle there, though I might have thought about it."

"Well, I thought you were kind'a partial to that high plains desert land," John chided.

"No, pard, the plan now is to have Maryanne come to Chadron. I sent her a telegram earlier today to asked her to buy train tickets and to head our way as soon as possible," Jasper said with the biggest smile John had ever seen.

"Now that is news," John said surprised by the turn of events.

"We'll get married here and then move to Wyoming, where we'll winter with her uncle and his wife and young'uns," Jasper said, excited to share his plans. "I'll buy me a small herd of sheep and learn the ropes over the winter. Me and Maryanne can set up our own place next spring."

John could see that the man had a plan and he was already looking deep into his future life with Maryanne and their growing family. Jasper was truly happy, and John saw no reason to be anything but happy for him, sheep be damned. A man had to make a living, and the truth of it was, no one should have anything to say about how he did it, especially if it made him happy and it was honest work.

August 1, 1884

Burton, Fall River County, Dakota Territory

The Promised Land

AFTER TWO DAYS IN Chadron, the drive continued its way north into Dakota Territory. On the afternoon of the fourth day on the trail, the call came down the line that they had arrived at their destination: the Lazy Cheyenne Ranch. John and Jasper had been in awe of the natural beauty of the deep canyons and pine-covered bluffs of the southern Black Hills. John thought he could imagine how God's chosen people must have felt upon seeing the promised land. He was certain they couldn't have been any happier than he was upon seeing the Black Hills for the first time. After traversing endless miles of nearly featureless windswept prairie, free of trees in every direction for hundreds of miles, the lush, pine-covered Black Hills that rose out of the bleak landscape surrounding them were a mystical wonder to behold.

Why the Lakota viewed these hills as the spiritual center of their nation was no longer a mystery to John. He knew of their origin story and would seek out Wind Cave the first chance he got. He grinned at the thought of bumping into Inktomi somewhere in those hills. Who knows, he thought, the tricky shapeshifting spider might materialize in just about any form. He felt deeply that there was much more to these mysterious mountains than gold. He had much to learn.

Once the cattle were herded along the Cheyenne River where the grass stood belly-high, the riders were put on rotation duty to patrol the herd. Burton then gathered everyone around Cookie's chuckwagon at the center of their makeshift camp.

"Gentlemen, it's been a damn tough drive, but we finally made it," Burton said as the men settled in to listen to what he had to say. "Cookie, break out a couple of barrels of brandy and some cups. These men deserve only the best," Burton ordered, looking around for Cookie.

"Aye aye, Captain!" Cookie barked as he hustled to dig out two small barrels of brandy and pass around tin cups.

"Kit Larson will set up a table here tomorrow morning to get everyone paid. I promised a hundred dollars a man plus wages for work south of the border and three dollars a day for the drive. We'll count the drive as a hundred and twenty days. That'd add up to three hundred sixty dollars plus the hundred and wages for eight days in Mexico for a total of over four hundred and eighty dollars for each man who rode with the brand all the way up from San Antonio. I told Kit to make it an even five hundred. For you other riders, your total wages will vary depending on when you joined the brand and on what terms," Burton said as he surveyed the faces of the men gathered around him.

"Gus and I've talked to Tom and we all agreed to giving every man who survived our battles in No Man's Land an additional one-hundred-dollar bonus," Kit said. "The bonus will come as little comfort to those we lost. And it won't help to wash away their blood or bring 'em back; they're gone forever. It's meant to give comfort to those of us who survived and must continue in our journey on this earth without 'em."

Kit's voice trailed off at the end and John thought he saw the man wipe away a tear. It was clear, the memory of Lance Freeman's death was still raw for Kit Larson.

The men, at first, had no reaction; they sat silently, each man deep in his own thoughts as he recalled the faces of the many men who had lost their lives on the drive. Each man counted his blessings and wondered why he had been chosen to live and not any of the men who had lost their lives. The men somehow knew that the calculus of the gods that weighed the value of each man's life was beyond the purview of mere mortals. Blessings, life, death, and the reasons for each were questions no one had answers for.

Breaking the silence, Jesse Givens stepped forward and said with enthusiasm, "Now that's a damn generous bonus, if'n I don't say so myself. A man might get spoiled having so much extra cash in his pocket. Come on, men! Show your appreciation!"

With that, the men gave out a raucous cheer as the brandy began to warm their guts and brighten their spirits.

Jesse had been hired as an extra gun and would be paid handsomely for his role in fighting the renegade Indians. As far as he was concerned, the one-hundred-dollar bonus made his payday all the better. He had no regrets about the men who had been killed. In his mind, whether a man lived or died depended on the luck of the draw. If a man didn't make it, he simply drew poorly or failed to cheat enough to make a winning hand for himself. For Jesse, life had always been a gamble and, as he reminded anyone who cared to ask, his fate had always been in the hands of the devil himself.

After paying all the men, Burton still had nearly four thousand dollars left over from his quick sale to Mr. McMichael. He figured the old shyster already had a buyer in Omaha that would pay him thirty dollars a head or better, which would give him a quick three-thousand-dollar profit. Such was the luck of those being in the right place at the right time. The clever old devil had somehow learned Burton's herd would be coming through Chadron and took the initiative to cash in.

Burton respected the old fella. He had of course burnt the old bastard for being unwilling to meet his price. Finnegan McMichael had taken advantage of him. Burton knew he should have gotten at least twenty-five dollars a head for his cattle. To make up the difference, the five hundred head Burton had cut out for the sell had been on the scrawny side and riddled with heel fly grubs. Finnegan McMichael would need to learn that cheating Tom Burton wasn't something any man did without paying a price, Burton thought. Fact was, Burton had already started scheming on ways he might bring down the old bastard completely, the first chance he got.

The men worked on repairing and stowing their gear and cleaning up after they got paid the next morning. In the late afternoon, many of the riders headed straight to the Standard Gauge Saloon located in the future town of Burton which had been crudely laid out just up the trail on a high bank along the Cheyenne River. Burton and E. J. Bishop had agreed to work together to attract a railroad to the new town, which would one day sit, like Seth Bullock's little town of Belle Fouche, smack dab in the center of Burton's own stockyards.

Bishop had a lot riding on whether the area would attract a railroad. He had not only invested in setting up a hotel with a saloon in the future town of Burton, which had become a stage stop on the Cheyenne and Black Hills Stage and Express Line, he had also invested heavily in Minnekahta, a new resort town just thirty miles away. Bishop supported Fred Evans's dream of commercializing the natural mineral springs that boiled up out of the native stone in that part of the hills.

Evans believed that Minnekahta, with its natural mineral waters, was the perfect location for bathhouses and health spas like the ones popularized by Europe's elite classes. Burton, like Bishop, could clearly see that as the nation grew richer and the Great Plains became settled, the southern Black Hills held the potential of becoming a hub for business and high society, a place where socialites would swarm to resuscitate at the hot springs and take the water for its many health benefits.

Bishop seemed to have plenty of money and wasn't looking for a partner; the hold Burton had on him was that the man wanted to expand his investments into the cattle business, something he knew nothing about. Burton had agreed to help him and had taken on Joe Bishop, E.J.'s nephew, who had been a cavalry scout. Joe had come out to the Dakota Territory from Oskaloosa, Iowa after resigning his commission in the U.S. cavalry. To hear him tell it, he had had a bellyful of fighting Indians and wanted to stake his own claim in the west.

Joe had taken his pay in cattle for the past several drives to Wyoming and Colorado, slowly building a herd of his own which he grazed near the entrance to Red Canyon on the north side the Cheyenne River not far north of Burton's own holdings. Burton knew this guaranteed the Bishop family would do everything in their power to ensure the railroad came to the future town of Burton. For his plan to happen, Burton knew he would need all the allies he could gather.

E.J. stood at the batwing door of his rickety saloon to welcome riders as they came in. He was thankful it was a cloudless sky, considering the roof of the Standard Gauge Saloon's main room leaked like a sieve ever since the last rowdy group of miners and cowpunchers shot it full of holes.

"Come on in, gentlemen. Step up to the bar. We have the best whiskey and beer this side of the Mississippi," E.J. said with a broad smile as the men filed in.

The men had been drinking for several hours when the late stage from Wyoming pulled in just before sundown. Much to everyone's delight, one heavenly beauty after the next emerged out of the stagecoach door as blurry-eyed cowpunchers gawked from the saloon's batwing door. All feathers, frill, and femininity, the women moved like a gaggle of geese into the saloon to the uncontrollable whistles, cheers, and catcalls of the drunken cowpunchers who to a man hadn't been near such sweetness in a coon's age, and for more than a few, had never been near any woman the likes of these.

Seeing a business opportunity, E.J. quickly collared the man who seemed to be the ladies' manger to work out a deal. Edward Millhouse, a gambler by trade, told E.J. if he stayed out of his card game, the ladies would work for drinks and tips. E.J. and Millhouse agreed on a fifty-fifty split. E.J. assigned the ladies two upstairs rooms in the back at no charge for private transactions.

"Just be sure not to stiff the house, comprende?" E.J. said to Millhouse with raised eyebrows.

"Fifty-fifty. Just stay clear of my card game. What I make there is mine," Millhouse said drily, looking at E.J. and signaling the point wasn't negotiable.

"No problem. We have a deal," E.J. said. "Oh, and you'll have to pay for your own drinks."

As far as E.J. was concerned, business was business. There were no free riders. With negotiations complete, Edward Millhouse gathered his ladies, stepped up in front of the bar, and turned to face the rough-looking tangle of cowpunchers who crowded around.

"Now settle down, gentlemen. Let me introduce the ladies, who I might add are as thirsty as a longhorn after a dust storm," Millhouse began.

"We'll buy 'em a drink," several cowpunchers hollered, as the crowd pressed in closer to the ladies.

"They're hopin' you do, and more than one," Millhouse quipped. "The ladies drink only champagne for a dollar a glass, which E.J. here has especially imported for such occasions as these."

Having the men's attention, he ran down the full menu of available services, "Dances are two dollars each. Private consultations upstairs, ten dollars for ten minutes. Tips of course are always welcome."

Millhouse then paused to let things sink in. The room had fallen silent as the men waited eagerly with money in hand.

"Now before we get started, let me introduce the ladies. First off, we have with us tonight Miss Bonney Blue, known far and wide as one of the finest singers in the West."

Bonney stepped forward, curtsied, and step back into line.

"Next we have, Miss Brandy, Queen of New Orleans, Miss Rose, Queen of San Francisco, Miss Estelle, Queen of Saint Louis, and last but by far not least, Miss Maria-Louisa, Queen of Santa Fe."

Each lady followed Bonney's lead with a shallow curtsy when introduced.

With introductions complete, the piano player in the corner of the saloon hit up a well-known tune and Bonney was soon singing to the music. As champagne flowed and the ladies, one by one, escorted tipsy cowpunchers up the back stairs for private consultations, E.J. couldn't help but grin as the money started rolling in.

Johnny Ritter, known as Mutton Chops because of his huge bushy sideburns and mustache with clean-shaven chin, was the bartender at the Standard Gauge Saloon. He had seen a lot of wild nights over the past couple of years and a lot of money spent by drunken miners and cowpunchers, but nothing to compare to what he was witnessing unfold on this crazy night. Men were throwing money around like there was no tomorrow. The ladies had been up and down the back stairs countless times, causing him to wonder how many men they could service in a single night.

"Mutton Chops! How about another champagne for the lady?" a red-faced cowpuncher barked.

The man had already bought Miss Rose five drinks and still hadn't ushered her upstairs for additional services. His hands had inspected every inch of the merchandise, yet he continued to monopolize her time.

"The ladies have a three-drink limit per customer," Mutton Chops said, hoping to avoid a scene.

"My money's as good as any man's. Now give the lady another drink," the man demanded as he slammed a silver dollar down hard on the counter and grabbed Miss Rose's left breast, causing her to screech in pain.

"I'd step away and let the next man buy the lady a drink," Roland Bishop said, as he squared up his shoulders and stood in front of the drunken man.

Roland was E.J.'s younger brother and had spent some time as a professional boxer back east before coming out to join his brother to assist in his many and growing business ventures.

The temper of the drunken cowpuncher flared as he swung wildly at Roland with his balled-up fists. Stepping back to allow the man's haymakers to purchase only air, Roland dodged and bobbed until he came up with his own one-two combination which stopped the man dead in his tracks. Hitting the floor like a two-hundred-pound sack of potatoes, Roland grabbed the man by his collar and dragged him out of the saloon. After taking the man's pistol, he left him knocked out cold in the middle of the road.

Returning to the saloon, he surveyed the now-quiet room.

"Just took out some trash, gentlemen. Don't let it ruin your evening," he said with a broad smile, in hopes the man's friends, if he had any, would leave well enough alone.

The piano soon started up again with Bonney belting out another popular tune. As if reanimated by the music, the room once again roared with laughter and the high-pitched giggles of young, lively ladies.

Millhouse smiled as he peeked at his cards: three aces, a one-eyed jack, and a deuce. He had prayed the short fight with the cowpuncher wouldn't send the whole damn saloon to into an all-out brawl just when his luck had turned. The game had ebbed and flowed all evening in ways he couldn't fully explain. He had employed all his skills just to stay ahead. He figured he was over three hundred dollars up, not bad for an evening's work, but he knew he should have done better. The pot in the center of the table had swelled to over two hundred dollars, and he was confident it was his to win. He had been the last player to call on the last bet, when the fight broke out.

"I think we're ready to show our cards, gentlemen," Millhouse said as he looked around the table.

One by one the men laid their cards on the table: a pair of kings; two pairs, jacks and trays; deuces, three of a kind; two pairs, tens and eights; queens, three of a kind. Millhouse was the last man to show his cards. He grinned as he laid his cards down one at a time, knowing he had won the pot: deuce, jack, ace, ace, ace. When the last ace hit the top of the table, Jesse Givens jumped up out of his chair, pistol in hand.

"Millhouse, I'm calling you a goddamn cheat," Jesse growled through clinched teeth.

Millhouse, taken by surprise, stayed seated, his arms extended away from his body with his hands palms out.

"I think you're mistaken. I wasn't the dealer of the last hand. You were," Millhouse said as he stared back at Jesse.

"That's right, I dealt the last hand and I gave you two aces right off the bottom of the deck. I know because I have the other two right here in my shirt pocket," Jesse said as he slowly pulled two aces out of his shirt pocket and tossed them on the table while keeping his pistol aimed squarely at Millhouse's chest. The other players looked on, unsure of where things might be headed.

Millhouse realized too late that Jesse Givens was a card shark and a damn good one, since he hadn't suspected or seen any of his moves all evening. He now understood the reason why he hadn't won as much as he had expected.

"So it seems you, sir, are the cheater. It was you who dealt from the bottom of the deck," Millhouse said, desperate to find a way out of his untenable situation; his argument weakened considerably by the fact no deck of cards had five aces.

How Jesse had dealt him two aces and had put the other two in his shirt pocket was a mystery to Millhouse. The bigger mystery was how Jesse had known a fifth ace had been cycling in and out of the game all night. By dealing him two aces, Jesse had tricked him into trying to slip in his fifth ace for the big win. Millhouse cursed himself for having taken the bait. He had to admit, it had been a damn clever play on Jesse's part.

"Haven't you heard, buckaroo, it takes a thief to catch one," Jesse said. "Now stand up slowly and drop your gun belt. You can also ease that peashooter out of your right sleeve while you're at it."

Millhouse slowly brought his hands to his sides and then quickly flipped the table over in Jesse's direction as he sprung to his feet and reached for his gun. Anticipating the move, Jesse sidestepped the table and fired three times directly into Millhouse's chest before the man's pistol could fully clear its holster. Dead before he hit the floor, Millhouse had palmed his last Ace. Jesse, looking down without remorse, flipped Millhouse's lifeless body over with the toe of his boot and reached down and scooped the dead man's money pouch out of his inside suit jacket pocket.

While Jesse divided up Millhouse's money pouch with the other players, Bonney Blue nonchalantly sashayed over to E.J. to reconfirm their arrangement. E.J. patted her on her substantial yet shapely bottom and assured her their fifty-fifty deal was still good and that Roland would ride with the ladies to Deadwood to get them settled in for a small fee. Bonney patted E.J. on his bony backside, giving it a gentle squeeze. She then winked and blew him a kiss, sealing the deal, leaving both parties looking forward to its consummation later that evening.

Roland unceremoniously dragged Millhouse's corpse out through the batwing door, while once again piano music rang out, with Bonney Blue belting out yet another popular tune. The night was still young, the cowpunchers still had plenty of money to spend, and the ladies still had the gumption to take them on one after another without missing a beat.

Pouring one glass of champagne after another and witnessing the countless dances the ladies had endured and the number of service calls they had each made up and down the back stairs, Mutton Chops could only marvel at their undeniable, near superhuman stamina.

August 29, 1884

Chadron, Dawes County, Nebraska

Ladies Lucky

SHE STOOD LIKE THE statue of a Greek goddess at the Chadron train de-pot surrounded by a towering pile of steamer chests and luggage with no golden chariot in sight. Her natural, chiseled beauty caught the attention of everyone who looked her way, leaving them to wonder from whence this vision of splendor had descended into their earthly realm. She had arrived on the noon train and had expected her husband to be waiting for her. The pine-covered ridges to the south were beautiful compared to the endless stretches of barren land she had crossed since leaving Omaha.

As the other passengers were being greeted by friends and family, she caught sight of a carriage pulled by a matching team of white horses speed-ing its way toward the depot at a full gallop. Pulling up hard in front of the depot, the carriage wheels and horse's hooves threw up dust and stones in every direction.

"Whoa, whoa there, big fellas," the driver called out as the matching team of white stallions skidded to a stop.

Getting the team under control and settled down, the driver hopped down to greet his passenger.

"What in the world? Who are you, sir?" she asked.

"Sorry, ma'am. I'm running a little late. My name is John Barton. We've made arrangements with the local hotel," John said.

"Hotel? I was expecting to visit the Lazy Cheyenne," she demanded.

"The main house isn't finished yet, ma'am," John said wishing he hadn't been singled out for the task of greeting the high and mighty Mrs. Alivia Kristine Harrington Burton.

"Where is my husband?" she demanded, confused.

"We received your telegram only two days ago, ma'am. Mr. Burton was up in Minnekahta and was expected back at the ranch today. We sent a rider to bring him straight here," John said trying to explain.

"Two days ago? I sent that telegram four days ago," she said even more confused and angry.

"They got the message here in Chadron and had to bring it by horse-back to the ranch. We don't have a telegraph out there yet," John said wondering why the woman couldn't understand she had left civilization behind when she pulled out of Omaha.

"When will Mr. Burton arrive?" she questioned, still uneasy about the unexpected reception.

"Tonight, ma'am. He should be here sometime tonight, if'n they don't have any trouble," he said, immediately wishing he had learned how to keep his thoughts to himself.

"Trouble? What kind of trouble? Are the Indians causing trouble again?" she asked, clearly upset.

"No ma'am. There won't be any trouble with the Indians. He'll be here tonight," he said with conviction, turning away quickly to load her many steamer chests and various pieces of luggage onto the carriage and wondering how he would make it all fit.

After getting Mrs. Burton settled into the High Ridge Hotel, the only hotel in town, John walked over and sat down on the boardwalk bench in front of the General Store in hopes of make himself scarce. The last thing he wanted was to be run ragged by Mrs. Burton, who, it had quickly become obvious, loved to boss people around for no good reason.

Lighting up a smoke, he noticed Sarah peeking out of the shop window across the street. At first he pretended not to see her, not knowing exactly what he should do or what she expected. Unable to act nonchalant with her spying on him, he broke down and waved to her. She waved back and then disappeared. The unexpected exchange left him unsure what to think of the encounter.

Sarah had heard the latest gossip that had spread through the town like wildfire: the wife of Tom Burton, one of the biggest cattle barons in the region, had come all the way from Austin, Texas to Chadron on the noon train. Her arrival from Omaha had confirmed for everyone in town that they were no longer an isolated frontier outpost. Their link to the east was real and would soon change all their fortunes. Burton's shipment of five hundred head of cattle from Chadron just the month before had demonstrated they had all made the right bet in investing in the new town.

Her mother was wild-eyed when she had shared the gossip about Mrs. Burton's arrival. Matilda Bell was determined to have Mrs. Burton visit her shop, which would make her the envy of every woman in town. Seeing that the driver of Mrs. Burton's carriage was the same young cowpuncher Sarah had accidently run into the month before, she asked her daughter to see if she could encourage the young man to bring Mrs. Burton by her shop before supper. Of course, after Mrs. Burton had a chance to freshen up from her long trip, her mother had added. Sarah had her doubts about getting Mrs. Burton out of the hotel before her husband arrived, but found that she still wanted to meet John Barton again and that this gave her a perfectly innocent excuse to do so. She had to giggle to herself at the thought that her mother, in all her twisted conniving, had been the one to suggest she pursue the handsome cowboy.

Alford Wentworth had also noted that the young cowboy who had driven Mrs. Burton's carriage from the depot and who was now sitting in front of his store was none other than the young man he had met in front of Matilda's shop when Burton's cattle drive came through town. He had noticed the cowboy's little exchange of waves with Sarah as she peeked out of her mother's shop window across the street. He wondered how long their little secret romance had been percolating. In this, he saw an opportunity to further his own love interests, the conquest of Mrs. Matilda Bell.

He only had to figure out how to encourage the young cowpuncher to help him corral and rope his prized heifer. Matilda seemed to have showed her interest in him by always asking him to drop by her shop. Though she had used her daughter as an excuse, he believed he had noticed her own flirtatious manner. He might be five years her junior, but from all appearances, he had to admit, she looked a damn sight younger and in better shape than he did. He wanted nothing more than to hold her fulsome figure in his arms and to have her teach him how to make love. He longed to be her eager pupil.

Jasper rode slowly across the rolling countryside leading from the southern canyon lands of the Black Hills to Chadron nestled in the foothills of the Pine Ridge. His mind raced as he went over and over his plans for the future. Maryanne would be arriving on the train from Omaha at noon the next day, August 30th, and things would need to move quickly after that. With Maryanne five months pregnant, they would need to get to her uncle's place in Thunder Basin as soon as possible to allow her time to settle in before the twins came in early December.

He had promised Maryanne a church wedding and had visited Mrs. Matilda Bell at her Sewing Emporium to have her start work on a wedding dress for a young lady in a motherly way. Mrs. Bell had assured him of her discretion and that she would be able to design an appropriate dress for the occasion. He had also engaged the local preacher and had reserved the church. He had even purchased a covered wagon with a good strong mule team and had already stocked the wagon full of provisions. He planned to swing by Burton on the way to Wyoming to pick up his other two horses. With wedding rings in his shirt pocket and a hotel room in Chadron reserved for the next few days, he was confident he had his ducks in a row.

He had no idea how the telegram with news of Mrs. Burton unexpected arrival would impact his own best laid plans. The news had exploded with the force of one of Cookie's famous "babies," sending riders flying out of the Lazy Cheyenne in every direction. Knowing there would be no one to meet Mrs. Burton when she arrived, John had struck out of the ranch driving a horse-drawn carriage like a man possessed. Jasper wondered if John made it, and if so, what had happened? With John needing to tend to Mrs. Burton, Jasper had resigned himself to the new reality that he may not have a best man at his wedding on Sunday, August 31st, only two days away.

Burton hadn't been in Minnekahta as everyone had thought: he had been up in Deadwood trying his luck at the blackjack tables. When word of his wife's imminent arrival in Chadron finally reached him, it was far too late for him to get to Chadron in time for her arrival. Riding out on the fastest horse he could buy with Tommy Water Horse at his side, the messenger who had finally tracked him down, Burton hoped to reach Chadron by late evening on August 30th. He wasn't sure how upset his wife might get, considering she expected everything to happen on time and as she had planned. He was certain being more than a day late for her arrival wouldn't go down well.

He had married Miss Alivia Kristine Harrington for the political clout she could leverage with her father, a serving judge on the Texas Supreme Court and a former Senator for the State of Texas who had served in Washington D.C. Though their marriage had been a loveless arrangement for too many years, her connections in high places in Austin had come in handy and kept the couple together, with her providing political leverage and Burton providing the financial means for her to live a life of carefree comfort and style.

He wondered why this creature of Austin social circles would suddenly come all the way to the yet-unsettled Dakota Territory in such a mad rush. The only two things he could imagine that would prompt such bizarre behavior was that she either needed money or she wanted a divorce. Burton saw neither prospect as very palatable, though a divorce wouldn't be all that unacceptable, now that he was on the verge of become a multimillionaire. Once his fortunes no longer depended solely on Texas politics, his wife's connections would become a damn sight less valuable then they had once been.

Burton followed Tommy as his horse picked its way up the side of a rocky knoll. The sky was clear and the smell of pine rich in his nostrils. The more time he spent riding through the stone-capped ridges and picturesque meadows of the enchanted Black Hills, the more he fell under their spell. Crystal-clear water seemed to bubble out of every hillside crevasse. The sights and sounds of a forest teeming with wildlife enveloped the two riders.

Burton noted how the hills became drier and the tree cover less dense as they moved further south. There was no doubt the southern and northern hills, though separated by no more than a hundred miles, had very different climates and landscapes. Picking up the pace, the riders spoke little, each man content in his silence. Burton knew all too well his peace and quiet would end abruptly once he reached Chadron and met the hailstorm Alivia Kristine Harrington Burton head-on.

Sarah had watched as John finished his smoke and entered the General Store. She decided it was time for her to be bold and take the bull by the horns. She needed a number of dry goods and there was no reason she couldn't just go over to the General Store to shop. With that in mind, she marched out of the Sewing Emporium straight across the street and into the General Store. Upon arriving, she realized she had forgotten to bring her purse and hadn't covered her head.

Standing just inside the front door, she also realized she had been in town for over a month and had never set foot in the place. The mixture of smells was the first thing that hit her as she took in a panoramic view of the wide variety of goods stacked and hanging everywhere. She had to admit it was a well-stocked store, and a goldmine considering it was the only store of its kind in the region.

"Miss Bell, I do declare. What a pleasant surprise," John said as he turned from a display of tobacco products just to the right of the front door.

John was in disbelief at his good fortune. He had wanted to find a way to meet Sarah again and now here she was in her full glory.

"Is that you, John? John Barton, right? I thought I saw you earlier. I, I came by to do some shopping," she stammered, her face and neck suddenly flushed.

John took little note of her distress as he struggled with his own.

"I came to town to pick up Mrs. Tom Burton who arrived today on the train from Omaha," he said, hoping to engage Sarah in a longer conversation.

"Yes, the whole town is talking about nothing else," she admitted.

"Tom Burton is on his way and should be here tonight or tomorrow," John said.

"We're all so honored to have such a fine lady visit our small town," she ventured.

"Oh, I can see how she might cause a stir," John said, wanting to change the subject.

"Will she tour the town?" Sarah asked with such an innocent look on her face that John knew there must be something behind the question.

"Yes, will the lady take a look around our fine town?" Alford chimed in, suddenly popping out from behind a stack of dry goods.

"Oh, Mr. Wentworth, how nice to finally meet you," Sarah said with a grand smile, having avoided an introduction for over a month.

"The pleasure is all mine. Your mother has often said we should meet. How is your mother, by the way?" Alford said, hoping to bend things his way.

"She's fine. She often speaks kindly of you," Sarah said.

Seeing Alford's eyes brighten at her remark, Sarah wondered how she might steer Alford's interest in the right direction.

"Oh, she does? Well, I'll be sure to drop by the shop. It's been some time, since I last visited," Alford said, charging forward.

"Yes, please do," Sarah said with a genteel smile.

Her mouth racing ahead of her thoughts, she then heard herself add, "You know my mother loves to stroll, but it's not ladylike for a woman to walk around town unescorted. Have you ever asked her for a stroll?"

The words had so quickly and innocently slipped from her lips, she had been unable to hold them back. She knew by asking such a potentially embarrassing question, she had risked everything. If Alford had no interest in her mother, Sarah knew her strange forwardness may be taken badly. Indeed, the consequences of her question were tough to calculate, though she knew none of them would be good if Alford found the question objectionable.

Caught flatfooted, Alford seemed stunned by the question. For several beats, he stood motionless, his mouth half open, with a look on his face which was difficult to read. As though he were shaking off a heavy blow to the chin, he rubbed his jaw and begin to speak.

"I, well I, I think I would like to do so," Alford mumbled and stumbled until he was finally able to answer.

As beads of sweat suddenly broke out through the thin strains of hair plastered to his bald head, Sarah and John both pretended not to notice. Mr. Alford Wentworth showed every indication that he had a strong desire to know Mrs. Matilda Bell better and that a stroll with her had long been on the man's mind.

"Flowers always help win a lady's attention," John offered, looking sideways at Sarah and hoping she would think his suggestion was helpful.

Both Sarah and Alford looked at John and wondered how the three of them came to be having such a conspiratorial conversation about the courtship of Mrs. Matilda Bell.

"Yes, bring flowers when you ask her for a stroll," Sarah said, quickly winking at John when Alford looked down at his shuffling feet.

"Yes, that, that would be a good idea. When . . . ?" Alford ventured with a look in his eyes of a man desperately in need of advice.

"Tomorrow morning might be a good time," Sarah said, knowing Jasper Waite's bride-to-be would be coming to the shop in the afternoon for a final fitting of her wedding dress, leaving her mother's morning free.

"Tomorrow? Tomorrow morning . . ." Alford mumbled, his head spinning with the pace of unfolding events.

"John, if you could have Mrs. Burton tour the town this evening before supper, perhaps Alford could escort Mrs. Burton over to the Sewing Emporium after she toured the store here. That way, he could introduce Mrs. Burton to my mother. And then, when Alford came back tomorrow morning to ask my mother for a stroll, it would seem no more than natural," Sarah said, her mind racing a mile a minute as she put a workable plan together on the fly.

"Good idea, I'll find a way to convince Mrs. Burton to tour the town before supper," John said, unsure of his probability of success.

"Alright then, it's all set," Sarah said looking back and forth between the two men.

"Yes, it's all set," both men answered on cue, neither knowing how the conversation had started nor how they had agreed on everything Sarah had outlined.

"Now, Mr. Barton, you seemed to have asked me to take a stroll. I accept. Shall we?" she said.

Looking at John, she lifted her left arm and pointed toward the door with her right hand. Offering his right arm, she took it and then remembered her head was uncovered.

"May I?" she asked as she plucked a colorful scarf off a display stand propped up on the counter and quickly covered her head, tying the scarf's loose ends under her chin.

"Yes, yes, by all means," Alford said without thinking, his mind still in a whirl.

With that, the young couple dashed out of the General Store and up the boardwalk toward the stables at the far end of town.

Alford watched his co-conspirators go, arm and arm, his heart pounding hard. As he dabbed the sweat running down his forehead, he was determined he would make his play tomorrow morning. He couldn't wait to stroll around the town, arm and arm, with the lovely Matilda Bell.

His hopes were high for the first time in his life. He was resolved to muster up the guts to go out and get what he wanted the most for a change. He wanted Matilda and he felt she could come to want him, if she would just give him half a chance. He was determined to take the bull by the horns, or heifer as it were, he chuckled.

"Well, that couldn't have worked out better, and yet, I'm not sure how it all happened," John said.

He couldn't be happier about having the beautiful Sarah Bell on his arm. What he couldn't quite understand is how it all fell into place.

"Some things are just meant to be a mystery," she said innocently. "I had no idea Alford had eyes for my mother. I had come to ask you about having Mrs. Burton take a tour of the town before supper. That her tour of the town could be used to further Alford's efforts to court my mother, well, the idea seemed natural once it became clear he fancied her."

John still wanted to question her further, but was content to remain silent as the couple walked stride for stride until they reached the stables at the far end of town.

"Maybe you would like to see some of the horses," John ventured, pointing at the enclosed stable just off the boardwalk.

"Horses? Why yes, of course. Yes, that would be nice," she stammered, her face suddenly warm as her cheeks grew rosy red.

Entering the enclosed stables, Sarah became aware they were completely alone for the first time. When John lightly touched her hand to guide her to one of the stalls, it caused goosebumps to run down her back.

"This horse's name is Stinker," John said with a smile.

"What kind of name is that?" she asked.

"Well, I'd just like to warn you to avoid getting' downwind from him. He's a real gas bag," John said with a chuckle.

"John, you're not being serious," she said, leaning into him and punching him lightly on the chest with a balled up fist.

"No, I'm serious. He's a great horse, but he never fails to remind you why he's earned his name," John insisted, as he took ahold of the halter of the large strawberry roan that Junior had sold to the stable owner the month before.

"He's beautiful," Sarah said as she reached up and stroked his nose.

As if on cue, Stinker let out a long, rippling juicy fart.

"Oh my," she screeched holding her left hand over her nose, while pulling John away from the horse stall.

John stumbled after her and then caught her up in his arms as they both laughed with abandon.

"My goodness, that horse needs help," she said as she tried to catch her breath.

"Do you think I need help?" John said holding her in his arms.

"No," she said as she pressed herself against his chest, feeling the strength that surged within him.

His muscular arms were thick and comforting as they held her in a gentle embrace. Looking up into his eyes she felt as though she could see their future together there and wondered how their souls had found one another. John melted into the crystal-clear pools of her baby blue eyes. Hypnotized, he leaned forward and kissed her deeply, experiencing a physical jolt of energy he would never forget.

"My God, you're so beautiful. You could have any man you set your sights on. I'm just a cowpuncher with little to offer any woman," John said, stepping back.

"You're my cowpuncher, big fella, and don't you ever forget it," she said as she threw her arms around his neck and kissed him like he had never been kissed before.

The two remained in the stable for over an hour before they returned back downtown with Sarah hurrying to her mother's shop and John hurrying to the hotel.

It took John some doing but he finally convinced Mrs. Burton that it would be a real honor for the leading merchants in Chadron if she would take a short walk around town and drop by a few shops.

"The place is so primitive and dirty," Mrs. Burton said, still having her doubts.

John had stroked her vanity in every way he could think of to convince her to take a short walk around town. That she hadn't dismissed the idea offhand give him hope he might be making progress.

"That, ma'am, is why having someone as sophisticated and cultured as you tour their makeshift town is like receiving a royal visit to these frontier bumpkins," John said, adding yet another coating of honey on his request.

"Well, alright. But like you said, a quick tour of the General Store and the Sewing Emporium should suffice," she said as she straightened the pleats in her Parisian gown, with its elaborate overskirt gathered in a large bustle in the back.

The bustle protruded so far from the woman's bum that John thought it made her look like a female centaur. He marveled at how the large bustle could be held up without another set of legs under it.

"Shall we?" John said as he stepped aside to allow Mrs. Burton to lead the way out of the hotel.

Noting how her skirt brushed the floor with every step, he wondered if their little jaunt through the grubby town might ruin the expensive gown. He quickly brushed his concerns aside, wanting nothing more than to have his and Sarah's little scheme play out as planned. Boldly, he led her down the boardwalk, pointing out one sight after another until they arrived at the General Store.

Alford Wentworth stood in front of his store in his best Sunday suit.

"Welcome, welcome, Mrs. Burton, welcome. It is indeed such an honor. My name is Alford Wentworth, owner of the Chadron General Store," he babbled, amazed John had been able to pull off bringing such a fine lady to his humble establishment.

"Thank you, Mr. Wentworth. I told John I would like to tour the town and I am delighted to have the opportunity," she said with such conviction that for a fleeting moment, John himself even believed her.

"Please let me show you around," Alford said, so excited his hand shook as he pushed the door of his store open to usher her inside.

After a quick tour of the General Store, Alford escorted Mrs. Burton across the street to the Sewing Emporium, where Mrs. Matilda Bell stood with her daughter on both sides of the front entrance.

"Ladies, I am honored to introduce to you Mrs. Alivia Burton, all the way from Austin, Texas," Alford said in his stoutest voice. "I insisted Mrs. Burton pay a visit to your shop, Matilda. I knew Mrs. Burton would appreciate meeting Chadron's most stylish and cultured citizen."

Matilda's cheeks momentarily flashed red with the unexpected compliment. Quickly catching herself, she covered her embarrassment by giving Mrs. Burton a shallow curtsy.

"Mrs. Burton, I am indeed honored. My name is Matilda Bell, and this is my daughter Sarah," Matilda said delighted to have such a fine lady visit her shop.

She knew the visit would bring every woman in town to her shop to hear all about Mrs. Alivia Burton. There was no denying the visit would be a boon to her business. She truly appreciated Alford's consideration and complimentary introduction. She had to admit she had underestimated the man.

Alivia and Matilda seemed to hit it off immediately as the two found much to talk about. John and Alford, like a couple of cigar store Indians, stood mum and motionless just inside the shop's entry as Matilda showed Mrs. Burton around her shop, the two chattering like old friends about the latest fabrics and fashions. Sarah, acting as the gofer, dug out one fabric, pattern, or dress after another.

"Oh, is this a wedding dress?" Mrs. Burton asked as she looked over the gown on the dress form at the back of the shop.

"Yes, this is a wedding dress for a young bride to be married on Sunday," Matilda said.

"She must be a big girl," Mrs. Burton remarked, taking note of the amount of material wrapped around the middle of the gown.

"Well, to be honest, I understand the bride is five months going on six months pregnant, with twins no less," Matilda said. "I'll have to make the final adjustments tomorrow after she arrives from Omaha. The groom is on his way here now. He's a cowpuncher who works for your husband."

"Sounds like the wedding will be just in time," Mrs. Burton said without any hint of maliciousness in the tone of her voice. "Tom, that is, Mr. Burton, and I never had any children," she added as she fingered the gown's material with a distant look in her eyes.

"Yes, it will be the first wedding held at our new church," Matilda said. "Everyone will be there."

"This Sunday, you say? That's the day after tomorrow. If the whole town is attending, Tom and I would also like to attend," Mrs. Burton said, looking straight at John.

"I'll be sure to make the arrangements," John said. "As it happens, I am the best man at the wedding. Jasper Waite, the groom, is my cousin. We joined the drive from San Antonio and have been through a lot together."

"Well, well. Isn't the world a small place," Mrs. Burton said, her thoughts racing to examine the fresh insight that flashed into her mind. "Very well then, I look forward to seeing you all again at the wedding."

"Yes, it will be a glorious day," Matilda said, truly meaning it.

She couldn't believe that Mr. and Mrs. Burton would be attending the wedding. Front row seats would need to be arranged. Sarah could help John Barton with the details. Once again, she found herself having to reassess someone she had dismissed. John Barton turned out to be much more than just another mangy cowpuncher.

John escorted Mrs. Burton back to the hotel while Alford marched back to his store with his chest out, a changed man.

"Well done," Matilda said looking squarely at her daughter. "I'm not sure how you swung it, but things couldn't have worked out better."

Sarah could see an actual glow come off her mother. She had never seen her so delighted.

"What did you think about Alford," Sarah asked.

"Alford?" Matilda asked, acting as if she was unsure she heard correctly.

"Yes, Alford."

"What about him?"

"What did you think?"

"Of him?"

"Yes."

"What do you mean?"

"You know he fancies you."

"Me? It's you he fancies."

"No mother, it's you."

"Why do you say that?"

"Because he can't take his eye off you."

"Oh really, Sarah. I think you're seeing things."

"No, I see just fine."

"I'm not looking for a man."

"That, Mother, has nothing to do with it."

"You really think the man fancies me?"

"Yes."

"What are we going to do about it?"

"Question is, what are *you* going to do about it?"

"Me?"

"Yes, you."

"I'm not sure how I feel."

"Do you like Alford? He clearly likes you."

"Yes, he is a fine man. A little uncertain at times, but a solid businessman."

"Sounds like a match made in heaven."

"Don't be cute."

"Really, Mama, with your determination and his money, the two of you could go far."

Sarah's words hit Matilda hard, causing her mind to spin as she seriously considered the possibility of marrying Alford Wentworth for the first time.

"What about you, honey?" Matilda said worried for her daughter's future.

"Don't fret about me, Mama. It's your turn to be happy. I'll do just fine. There're plenty of prize fish in the sea," she said with a giggle.

"And we'll net a big one, for ya" Matilda said, joining her daughter in a good laugh.

The next morning Sarah repeatedly peeked through the shop window, wondering when Alford would gather up enough courage to come calling. Just when she had given up hope, she spotted Alford standing out in front of his General Store straightening his suit jacket before picking up a huge bouquet of wildflowers and heading across the street with a determined look.

"Mother, I see Alford headed this way," Sarah said slyly.

"Bring him on," Matilda said wearing just a touch of rouge and dressed in one of her finest gowns.

With her bonnet and parasol positioned strategically near the front door, it wasn't long before Mrs. Matilda Bell and her new beau, Mr. Alford Wentworth, walked arm in arm down the boardwalk. Sarah had to marvel at how life seemed to insist on its own way sometimes.

As noon rolled around, Jasper and John stood waiting for the train from Omaha. It wasn't unusual for the train to be late, but for Jasper, who pranced back and forth like a caged cat, the delay was nearly unbearable. More than an hour late, the train finally chugged into Chadron. The train had no more than pulled to a stop, when Maryanne came bounding out of her coach straight into Jasper's waiting arms.

She was already bigger than an October pumpkin. For John it seemed as though a lifetime had passed since he and Jasper first met her at the tavern in Kansas City. He and Jasper had been through a lot over the past five months; he could only imagine the many worries Maryanne had suffered as her belly grew by the day, not knowing if she would ever see Jasper again.

The couple embraced for the longest time as John gathered her luggage up and loaded it in the carriage. The chatter between Jasper and Maryanne was nonstop as the lovers caught up and made plans for the future.

Dropping the lovebirds off at the hotel, John took the carriage back to the stables, where to his surprise he found Tom Burton looking trail-weary after his long, nearly nonstop ride from Deadwood.

"John. I'm glad we could meet before I got to the hotel," Burton said having learned from Tommy Water Horse that it had been John who rushed to Chadron to greet Mrs. Burton when she arrived.

"Yes, Mrs. Burton has settled in and taken to Chadron just fine," John said. "She was a bit upset when she arrived, but she is looking forward to the wedding tomorrow and seems to be in a good mood."

"Wedding? Good mood? You sure you're talking about my wife?"

"Yes sir, she hit it off with the local seamstress and decided to attend Jasper Waite's wedding tomorrow."

"Jasper's getting married? When did this happen?"

"He's had plans to get married since meeting Maryanne in Kansas City."

"I'll be damned. Well, that explains the kiss mark I saw on his neck back at the Rocking T Ranch."

"You noticed that?"

"Yep, and the split lip too."

"Well, we were young," John said, causing Tom Burton to laugh.

"That you were, son, that you were," Burton said. "But no longer from what I've seen."

With that, Burton helped John put up the carriage and feed and water the horses before the two men walked over to the hotel. Burton couldn't wait to shave and get a hot bath.

"John, run up and tell Mrs. Burton I've arrived and will join her for dinner. I need to scrub some of this trail dirt off before I meet her," Burton said as he stepped into the General Store to pick up a razor and toiletries and a fresh set of clothes.

John no more than turned to head for the hotel when he saw Sarah headed in the same direction on the other side of the street. He figured she was headed to the hotel to fetch Maryanne. There was little time left to do a final fitting on her wedding dress before she headed for the altar. Jasper and Maryanne would be surprised when they discovered the whole county turning out for their wedding, led by Mr. and Mrs. Burton, who he and Sarah had arranged to have seated in the positions of the father of the groom and mother of the bride on both sides of the aisle in the front row.

Since John would be the best man, he had asked Sarah to be the maid of honor. He was thrilled when she accepted. He and Sarah also agreed

Matilda should catch the bridal bouquet, now that Alford Wentworth had signaled his courtship by strolling with her around the town that morning. To hedge their bets, Sarah would make sure Maryanne knew what to do when the time came.

As they moved toward the hotel, John waved and winked at Sarah and she mirrored him. They both smiled as they hurried along the boardwalks on both sides of the street. She waited in front of the hotel for him to cross the street.

"Mr. Burton has arrived," John said.

"Well, it seems the gang's all here," she said with a grin.

"You're enjoying all this intrigue a little too much," John said, matching her knowing grin.

"Yes, I truly am," she said. "But then, if all my machinations hadn't worked out, you'd just be another lonely cowpuncher down on his luck, and me, well, I'd be married off to some rich handsome gentleman and destined to live a life of luxury."

"Pity things seem to be working out," John said, deadpan. "If things keep going well, we just might end up on a Wyoming sheep ranch like Jasper and Maryanne."

"Sheep!"

"Yep."

"Oh, my Lord. Well, they love each other, right?"

"Yes, that they do. Love conquers all," John said. "Even if you have to become a lowly sheepherder."

"Sheep, sheep, sheep. At least, the little lambs are cute," she said shaking her head.

"So, you're saying, Mary had a little lamb, little lamb, little lamb. Mary had a little lamb whose fleece was white as snow . . . ," John began.

"And everywhere that Mary went Jasper was sure to go," Sarah said, finishing John's witty little lyric with a twist of her own.

"You are way too clever for your own good," John quipped.

"Another thing about Wyoming," she said. "Women have had the right to vote over there since 1869. Wyoming Territory is the first place in the world to grant women's suffrage."

"You're pullin' my leg. Women voting; that seems unnatural," John said, not sure he wasn't serious.

"Nope. Women have been voting over there nearly fifteen years now. You just wait, Johnny boy, women'll be the equals to men everywhere some-day," she said matter-of-factly, ready for a fight.

"Equals. Heck, they'd have to come down a notch to be equal. Women have been smarter than men since the garden of Eden," he said with a chuckle.

"Just you remember that, John Barton. And don't forget, I'm your new pard, now that Jasper's gettin' hitched," she said with a wink.

"I don't deserve you, but I'm yours," John said, meaning every word.

"And I'm yours. I'll see you at the altar tomorrow," she said, as she turned to head into the hotel where Maryanne was waiting.

After Sarah went her way, John soon ran upstairs to inform Mrs. Burton her husband had arrived and would join her for dinner. Finding Jasper sitting in the lobby, John decided to take Jasper over to the local saloon to have at least one beer to celebrate. It didn't take much to talk Jasper into the idea. His nerves were shot. He agreed a little lubrication might just be the remedy for what ailed him.

The dirty, dilapidated saloon was a far cry from the bustling saloons, where they had drunk beer from Saint Joe to Dodge City. As they worked on their second mug of beer, both men found the lubrication just as effec-tive as any they had drunk over the past five months. Always a couple of happy drunks, they couldn't help but laugh until they cried about all that had happened to them, the good and the bad.

Neither man could have ever predicted the journey they had taken, from boyhood to manhood, but they had traveled that bumpy road of hard knocks and both had arrived as men, fully formed. What tomorrow would bring neither man knew; the only thing they were certain of was that they had each found a good woman that loved them, and that the future be-longed to those willing to go out and grab it. They were both determined to continue to be the kind of men who would do just that.

August 31, 1884

Chadron, Dawes County, Nebraska

Hidden Truths

THE LITTLE TOWN OF Chadron had never been so busy. Buggies, carriages, and riders on horseback all dressed in their Sunday finest had descended on the town from every direction. The church, built to seat fifty souls, had over seventy packed into its pews, with at least another fifty taking up makeshift seats on planks and sawhorses just outside the open windows on both sides of the church. The Reverend had at first protested against the bride wearing white and to having the ceremony in his holy church when he learned she was in a motherly way. Indeed, that very morning, he had lectured John and Jasper, in no uncertain terms, that these principles had been ordained by God and formed the bedrock of his faith and that he couldn't risk the sanctity of his church, no matter what.

When he saw the number of souls that had gathered in and around his church for the wedding, he soon tossed his objections and bedrock principles out one of the church's open windows, assuring himself that God would understand, given he intended to pass the donation tray before and after the service.

When the wedding carriage, drawn by matching white stallions, pulled up to the church decorated in flowers, ribbons, and bows, it was met with a chorus of oohs and aahs from the assembled congregation. A rendition of "The Wedding March," played by an impromptu orchestra made up of townfolk who had brought a collection of musical instruments, including trumpets, banjos, guitars, fiddles, mouth harps, and accordions, rang out as John and Sarah escorted the bride to the church door, where Mr. Burton stood with his arm bent and ready to receive her.

Jasper stood at the altar next to the Reverend and watched as Maryanne, dressed like an angel, was walked down the aisle arm and arm with Mr. Thomas Burton himself. No one seemed to notice the bride was coming as a package deal; her twins kicking all the way. The ceremony went long when the Reverend Robert P. Mason, with spittle-rimmed lips and emotion-filled and reddened face, decided to use the occasion as a promotional opportunity. He spoke for nearly forty minutes about the need for the followers of the Lord to encourage others to attend church and become members. John had seen enough preachers in his day to know they never failed to encourage every member to get a member. The business of soul saving no doubt required volume, John concluded.

At the end of the ceremony, music once again rang out, as the now-married couple hurried down the narrow aisle and outside into the open carriage. As rice rained down on the happy couple, John and Sarah quickly hopped up on the buckboard and John snapped the reins, setting the carriage rolling. John almost laughed out loud when he thought about why everyone threw rice at weddings: the main reasons were that everyone believed being showered in rice increased prosperity, fertility, and good fortune for the married couple, he recalled.

Little did the assembled town folk know that Jasper and Maryanne already had two of the three reasons well covered. As for prosperity, however, they could have used more than just a light shower of rice; a full bath wouldn't have hurt, he thought as he smiled. John drove the couple to the hotel for their wedding reception as the attendees led by Mr. and Mrs. Burton made the journey from the church to the hotel by marching straight down the middle of Main Street.

The wedding ceremony and lavish reception was more than Jasper and Maryanne could have ever imagined. As the evening grew late, the big moment came for the bride to throw her wedding bouquet to all the single maidens that could be gathered.

"Now, Mama, come on, we'll both join the other maidens," Sarah urged.

"You go now, this is for young maidens, not for mature women like me," Matilda insisted.

"You're still young and you're single," Sarah said not willing to take no for an answer. "And don't forget, Alford is watching."

Reluctantly, Matilda was pushed into the group of maidens all crying and jumping up and down, with each one urging Maryanne to throw the bouquet to her.

As Maryanne turned around with her back to the assembled ladies, Jasper yelled out, "One, two, three, let it go!"

Just before turning around, Maryanne had spotted Matilda on her far-right side and at the back of the assembled ladies. Calculating Matilda's position at the back of the scrum, Maryanne threw the bouquet over her left shoulder as hard and as high as she could. As the bouquet flew over the heads and extended hands of the ladies in the front and sailed in a high arch directly toward Matilda, her daughter, unnoticed by the other ladies, lifted her mother from the waist with both hands at the last second.

When Matilda caught the bouquet, which hit her square in the face, the room exploded into uproarious applause and cheers, as Alford, who had clearly drunk more than his share of spiked punch, raced forward red faced and embraced Matilda, kissing her square on the mouth. Stunned, Matilda found herself lost in the moment amidst the cheers and kissed Alford back, giving out a wild cheer of her own.

Sarah and John looked on in amazement until they caught each other's eye and soon disappeared to a more private setting, where they too kissed with abandon and then consummated their love for one another for the first time.

The next morning, John found Tom Burton waiting in front of the hotel with a buggy.

"Good mornin'," John said as he greeted his boss. "Thank you for everything yesterday. And thanks to you and Mrs. Burton, Jasper and Maryanne will never forget their wedding day and their fabulous wedding reception."

"Good mornin'. No problem. It surely was quite a day and quite a party," he said with a broad smile. "After talking to Alivia, we agreed to give the couple a good send-off. I think we did just that. I have to admit, it didn't hurt in our building good relations with the townfolk either."

"Good morning, John," Mrs. Burton said as she came out of the hotel.

John no more than helped her into the buggy when Tom Burton snapped the reins and took off. John watched them head south toward the Pine Ridge and wondered why the couple had suddenly gotten the urge to tour the area.

Still walking on cloud nine, having partaken of the wondrous delights of the beautiful Sarah Bell, he brushed aside the Burtons' morning outing and gave it no further thought. Feeling exhilarated, he rolled a smoke, lit up, and took a seat on the front porch of the hotel. He had never felt more alive. In the midst of endless trials and tribulations and unexpected disasters at every turn, life was still a wondrous thing, he thought, as he enjoyed watching the plume of smoke he exhaled merge into the cool morning breeze until it disappeared.

As the buggy pulled out of the town of Chadron, Tom held his tongue until they were well beyond the last shanty. Following the road leading to the Pine Ridge, Tom finally said, "Now, why all the secrecy?"

Alivia had cautioned him she wouldn't tell him why she came to Chadron until they could ensure their conversation wouldn't be overheard.

"Remember your little foray into Mexico back in April?" she asked.

"What foray?" he said, hoping his face wouldn't betray him.

"You know damn well what foray, Tom."

"Well, some of my men might have taken a dip across the Rio Grande. Hell, ranchers do it every day. What's the problem?"

"Two Texas Rangers are dead and the powers that be in Austin find it difficult to cover you on this one."

"I had nothing to do with those men's deaths," he said, wondering where things were heading.

"They found the dead body of José Rodriquez next to the body of Rudy James, a well-known sidekick of Willie Dunhill, at the spot where a large number of cattle had been driven out of Mexico across the Rio Grande."

"So."

"So. It was Willie Dunhill who gunned down Phil Roberts and shot Bert Blackwell in Tascosa. In a gunfight you witnessed. Am I right, so far?" she asked, her voice rising with every word.

"Yes, but . . ."

"Yes, but . . . you still don't see the problem. Well, here's the problem, darling. One of your men gunned down Willie Dunhill, which caused Bert Blackwell to resign his commission as a Texas Ranger and attempt to track you down to serve his own justice."

"Yes, but . . ."

"Yes, but . . . you still can't see the problem. For one, you killed Bert Blackwell in a gunfight in Dodge City. Yes, yes, it was a fair fight, as testified to by every witness, but it doesn't change the fact that Rudy James and Willie Dunhill were partners and it was well-known that José Rodriquez was your righthand man on the Rocking T Ranch—the ranch, by the way, where the Rangers now think the stolen cattle were prepared for the drive north."

"This is a lot of circumstantial evidence. You should be able to smooth things over in Austin, like you always have. What's the trouble this time?" he complained, not accepting the seriousness of the situation.

"The trouble is they have issued a warrant for your arrest. It seems a Don Enrico Martín Lopez has been very helpful to the Rangers, especially in the identification of the body of José Rodriquez, a critical piece of evidence that points to you as being the cattle baron behind the whole incident."

The truth in her words hit him hard; he was in trouble and not sure how he might slip the noose.

"What's the charge?" he asked.

"Well, they couldn't get you on murder, but they have charged you with treaty violations and are demanding restitution for the Mexican ranchers who are claiming they lost over ten thousand head of cattle, not to mention over two hundred horses," she said, still shocked by the size of the theft and the brashness of her outlaw husband.

"I might be willing to give 'em two dollars a head to make this go away, but the Rangers want more than that, don't they?" he said.

He knew that killing Bert Blackwell had been a bridge too far. The Texas Rangers would never forgive him. They wanted his blood, nothing else would do.

"Yes, they want more—your head in fact," she said, confirming his thoughts.

"What do you want?" he asked.

"I brought papers with me that will transfer all of your Texas holdings, your ranches, cattle, and investments, including those in Tascosa, into my name. My lawyer has postdated these documents to November of last year. That way, we can try to avoid any legal battles over these assets," she said as she ticked off what she came for.

"I have also brought divorce papers. You need to sign these to make our marriage final as of the end of last year, long before any of these recent events. Lastly, I need you to also sign an affidavit that clears my name of any involvement in any of your business dealings, past or present," she concluded.

Tom absorbed her list of demands and nodded his acceptance. He then turned the buggy around and headed back to town, a man in need of a plan for a life on the run, a life he hadn't expected. With the Lazy Cheyenne located in the Dakota Territory nowhere near Texas, he had little concern about Texas Rangers or bounty hunters considering the charges against him. He would need to give up his Texas holdings and focus on his ranches in the northern plains.

He figured the setback would have little impact on his grand plan. His herds would number over two-hundred thousand head with their natural increase over the next two years. He could always change his name and move to California or even overseas once he cashed in. Looking over at his stylish wife, he wondered if she might be in the mood for a final tryst between the sheets before heading back to Austin. She had always been good in the sack.

The next day, Jasper pulled his fully outfitted covered wagon up to the hotel and John helped Maryanne up next to Jasper on the driver's bench. John stepped up on his horse while Sarah, Alford, and Matilda and half the town lined the streets to bid the couple farewell. John insisted on accompanying the couple to Wyoming, convincing Jasper that he wanted to look up Gus McKay who had set up a ranch in the Thunder Basin region. John also saw the journey as a way to further explore the Black Hills on his way back to the Lazy Cheyenne after Jasper and Maryanne got settled into their new home.

Tom Burton had surprised everyone when he insisted that Jasper take a good bull and four cows with him as a wedding gift, claiming a cow-puncher simply couldn't live herding sheep alone. The plan was that John would round up the five cattle, while Jasper picked up his horses on the way through Burton.

At the end of the first day on the trail, John, Jasper, and Maryanne relaxed around the campfire after dinner as they watched the puffy scattered clouds, hanging in the western sky, like papier-mâché lanterns, light up in brilliant hues of yellow, orange, and crimson as the sun slipped beyond the horizon.

The trio sat silently, each recalling how far they had come and knowing they had only taken their first steps into new lives they had yet to live. The twins kicked. Maryanne reach over and placed Jasper's hand and then John's hand on her swollen belly. Both men felt the next generation stir.

"They're eager to begin," she said.

"So are we," Jasper said. "So are we."

Suddenly, overcome with emotion, John could only nod as a tear worked its way down his cheek. At that moment, he wanted nothing more than to hold Sarah tight in his arms. His only thought when he felt the babies move inside Maryanne's belly was how fragile life really was and yet how tough it had to be to survive.

January 9, 1887

Hot Springs, Black Hills, Dakota Territory

Whiteout

IT HAD BEEN TWO and a half years since Tom Burton brought his last herd of Texas longhorns up from San Antonio. Though John wanted nothing more than to make a clean break with Burton, who was now a wanted man in Texas, he had reluctantly stayed on with the Lazy Cheyenne to build up his grubstake and to be close to Sarah Bell. Since her mother's wedding to Alford Wentworth after a whirlwind courtship, John and Sarah had become more serious about their own future together.

The long dry summer of 1886 had burned off the green grasses of spring earlier than anyone ever remembered, leaving the landscape barren. Frequent prairie fires had also reduced grazing land that had been abundant in past years. The cattle barons who had built huge herds on the vast prairie grasslands of the upper Great Plains became increasingly concerned as they entered the fall without enough feed to maintain their herds, now numbering in the hundreds of thousands.

Unseasonably cold weather, brought by stiff northern winds, descended on the region early. As once-lush grazing lands were turned into powder-dry deserts covered in nothing more than brown stubble, Tom Burton became desperate. In hopes of finding graze and finding it fast as the winter swiftly approached, he sent riders out in every direction.

Despite the risk of running into Indian resistance, John had ridden up the Cheyenne River halfway across Dakota Territory all the way to the Missouri River in search of graze and had found none. Riding alone in the silence of his thoughts, he found himself falling in love with the mysterious and majestic lands of the Mauvaises Terres, as Pappy had always called them. Though the drought had left the lands bare and lifeless, John could see that the Badlands weren't all bad. He saw great promise in the lands to the east of the Black Hills.

Failing to find any graze, he took the opportunity to scout out a location where he might stake his homestead claim in the future. He was well aware he had ridden into the lands of the Great Sioux Reservation when he headed east across the Cheyenne River. Though no railroads had been able to penetrate these lands, he knew this would not always be the case. When the railroads finally came, the lands would be settled. Of this he had no doubts.

Once he finally quit Burton's ranch, and he prayed that day would be soon, he would need to find a place to settle; a place he and Sarah could call their own, where they could raise their future children; a place where he could fulfill his boyhood dream. He wanted that place to be in the Mauvaises Terres, the Badlands of the Dakota Territory.

Just southwest of two rivers, the point where the Belle Fouche River flows into the Cheyenne River, John Barton found his Shangri-La nestled in the rolling countryside. Having ridden over a series of rolling ridges after crossing the Cheyenne River, he came upon three large cottonwood trees lining a creek that fed a small kidney-shaped pond at the bottom of a shallow valley. He immediately christened the unique setting as Three Tree Creek and the small pond as Barton Lake. To symbolically stake his claim and to mark the location, John stacked up a pile of stones next to a tree at the edge of the pond. The pond was the only one John had found with any water still in it in the vast, bone-dry rolling grasslands, making the location ideal for future settlement.

Until the vast stripe of land east of the Black Hills and west of the Missouri River was officially surveyed for homesteading, there was no way to officially claim the land. Indeed, the land was still considered hostile territory with the Lakota resisting any further reduction of their reservation lands or encroachments on their native hunting grounds.

To protect his claim, he pulled out an eagle feather he had tucked under the inner brim of his hat that Pappy had given him long ago as a good luck charm and as a reminder of his membership in the Otoe Eagle Clan. He then wedged the eagle feather under the base of his stone marker. Satisfied he had marked his claim well and had done what he could to ward off any evil spirits, he knelt next to the stone marker and said a final silent prayer before mounting his horse.

John rode back down the Cheyenne River and took the trail west through Buffalo Gap, so he could ride down between the Dakota Ridge and the Black Hills to the Fall River. From there, he followed the river up through a narrow, winding, red-cliffed canyon that led to Hot Springs. Originally named Minnekahta, meaning warm waters in the Lakota language, the town's promoters had only recently changed its name to Hot Springs, a name more easily understood by the well-healed tourists they hoped to attract.

After fighting bitterly cold winds for several days, John looked forward to soaking in the warm waters of the town's mineral baths. He was in no hurry to return to the Lazy Cheyenne, knowing Burton wouldn't be happy to learn there was virtually zero graze east of the Black Hills.

John had no more than ridden into Hot Springs when the north winds picked up, sending the temperature plunging and bringing heavy snow flurries that blanketed everything in their path. John decided to settle in at the new Minnekahta Hotel to wait out the storm until he could make his way south to the Lazy Cheyenne. By daybreak the next morning, John found the town buried under a mountain of snow.

The winds howled and the temperature continued to plunge, as townfolk fought to dig themselves out of their homes in a vain effort to get to their stranded horses and livestock. John could only imagine what damage the storm had wrought back at the Lazy Cheyenne, situated on the open plains where many of the cattle had already been starving when he rode out the week before. He knew there would be heavy losses from the severe cold and deep snow.

What he didn't realize was that the blizzard of 1887 had buried the Great Plains, from Montana and Wyoming to Colorado and Dakota, with over sixteen inches of snow. Temperatures dropped to more than fifty degrees below zero, making survival on the open plains next to impossible for weakened, underfed, and starving longhorn cattle accustomed to warmer climates. The massive herds that had been built up on fenceless open ranges since the late 1870s and early 1880s had nowhere to run as the storm swallowed them whole.

John had to wait nearly a week before he was able to make his way back to the Lazy Cheyenne. Snow covered everything, causing John to squint and shield his eyes from the blinding glare as he surveyed the open land southwest of Hot Springs. As his horse ploughed through the snow, nothing moved in any direction. Even the birds were silent with none brave enough to take flight. The deathly, bone-chilling air caused his horse's breath to hang in misty puffs as John nudged him forward through the featureless landscape. After two days, John rode into the Standard Gauge Saloon nearly frozen to death.

"My God man, where'd you come from?" E.J. said as he helped John off his horse and into the relative warmth of the rickety saloon.

"Hot Springs," John managed. "There's nothing moving out there. Nothing at all."

"Hot Springs! And you struck out in this. You must be crazy," E.J. blurted. "Nothing movin'? Hell, man, there ain't nothing alive out there."

John would later understand that no truer words had ever been spoken, when with the spring thaw they would discover the open range littered with countless carcasses of rotting cattle. Spring showers would clog rivers and streams with the rotting animals, compounding the catastrophe by spoiling scarce water resources. Many cattle barons, including Tom Burton, would discover they had lost everything.

April 1, 1887

Burton, Fall River County, Dakota Territory

Fool Me Twice

JOHN, GEORGE MCFARLAND, AND five other ranch hands, including Jesse Givens, sat around a large wooden table in the main room of the two-story brickhouse, built the year before on Burton's Lazy Cheyenne Ranch. Burton had asked his men to gather now that a full assessment of the condition of the herd had been completed. With stooped shoulders and looking older than John remembered, Burton coughed as he entered the room and shuffled to his chair at the head of the table. Taking his seat, the large wooden chair with its ornate cravings of wild beasts seemed to threaten to swallow its small and frail occupant whole at any second. His dead, beady-eyed stare, hollow cheeks, and the deep dark shadows under his eyes gave him a ghastly, ghostly appearance that sent a shiver down John's spine. It was clear to every man present: Tom Burton was dying.

"The final count is fifteen. That's right, gentlemen, there are only fifteen head of cattle still alive on the Lazy Cheyenne. Of those, seven have severe frostbite and may not make it," Burton said before going into a long coughing jag.

After struggling for some time to catch his breath, he calmed his cough by taking a couple of big gulps from a tin flask he pulled out of his vest pocket.

"Word from Colorado and Wyoming is no better. They've not found a single cow alive in Wyoming and only a hundred and fifty head or so in

Colorado. Many of those are believed to be mavericks from other herds in the area," he continued, trying to keep his voice steady and strong.

After a long pause, with Burton's labored breathing filling the room with a gurgling wheeze and no one else daring to speak, Burton finally said what needed to be said, "I'm busted, gentlemen, busted all to hell. Flat broke."

John thought he saw a tear run down the man's cheek which he quickly wiped away with the side of his shaking hand when he took another long pull on his tin flask.

Burton had amassed over two hundred thousand head of cattle on his ranches in Colorado and the territories of Wyoming and Dakota which he had intended to sell right down to the last steer after the coming spring calving season. His secret plan had been to sell out completely, so he could start a new life south of the boarder in Argentina, where he had been advised by his attorney he would be able to live the life of a *patron* with servants and vast land holdings. Burton's Spanish was nowhere near fluent, but being from Texas he could speak the language and figured in time, he would improve.

Unlike Mexico, in Argentina the European population made up the majority, a place where a *gringo* with a new identity might more easily blend in. Unable to return to Texas and tired of looking over his shoulder for the law, he saw South America as a real option for a wealthy man on the run.

No one was surprised the next morning when they found Tom Burton dead, lying in his bed, dressed in his finest suit, with his pistol in hand, its barrel in his mouth, and his brains sprayed all over the headboard. By noon, without ceremony or wasting time to read over the remains, the men buried his body in a shallow grave behind the brickhouse. Led by Jesse Givens, the men searched the house for money and jewelry and found little. They then quickly emptied the house of anything and everything of value.

It was estimated that roughly 90 percent of the cattle on the open range were killed in the blizzard of 1887 which forever reshaped the Great Plains by heralding the end of the era of cattle barons and the birth of family farming and the permanent fencing of grazing lands.

For John and Sarah, the blizzard of 1887 had also changed the course of their lives. John had suddenly found himself out of work and dead broke. He had saved money over the years which Burton had held onto for him and for the other ranch hands. He had counted on his sizable grubstake and the backpay Burton owed him to make his final break with the man.

Burton had promised to pay all his ranch hands when he started shipping cattle in the summer. With no cattle to ship and Burton penniless when he died, John found himself without the cash he needed to strike out on his own.

John's share from the sale of the things the ranch hands had stripped from the brickhouse amounted to little, considering he had lost all of his savings from the past two years and all the money he had been owed in back wages. Though Sarah had become the local schoolmarm in Chadron, her job paid little. John decided if they wanted to make a go of it, he would need to find a job and fast; not just any job, but one that paid well.

John cursed the day he ever signed on with Tom Burton. Burton had tricked him and Jasper into risking their lives during the dangerous cattle rustling foray into Mexico and now had stolen all his money and back pay. He also cursed himself for not heeding one of the simplest lessons his father had ever taught him: Fool me once, shame on you; fool me twice, shame on me.

With the clarity of hindsight, he knew he should have made his own clean break with Tom Burton at the same time Jasper had left for Wyoming two years earlier. Rather than crying over spilt milk, he headed for the Standard Gauge Saloon. He had heard there might be an opening for a guard on the Cheyenne and Black Hills Stage that was having trouble with bandits in and around the Black Hills. John figured if there was work with the stage company, E.J. Bishop would know all about it.

Arriving at the Standard Gauge Saloon, John was a man with no time to waste. Stepping through the batwing door, John was surprised to find the place completely empty. E.J. stood behind the bar and offered John a beer and gestured to a table in the back of the room.

"Damn pity about what happened to Tom Burton," E.J. said as he handed John his beer and the two men took their seats at the table.

"Have any of the other ranch hands come by?" John asked not knowing for sure what happened to the men since they ransacked the brickhouse and split the proceeds.

"Yea, some came through, but no one stayed long. Like yourself, they're all in need of work and there ain't any around here," E.J. said as he sipped on the whiskey he had brought for himself.

"Does the stage still need a man to ride shotgun?" John asked, hoping the job might still be available.

"Shotgun rider. On the stage? No, the stage went bust when the FE&MV Railroad reached the Black Hills and Wyoming just before the snow flew last year. They do still make gold runs from Deadwood to Cheyenne with the Monitor. I'm sure you don't want anything to do with that job," E.J. said, confident no one with half a brain would risk his life riding shotgun on a wagon full of gold.

"They pay well?" John said.

"Yea, they pay well alright, if'n you can live to collect."

"What do you mean?"

"They've lost three guards on the Monitor in the last couple of months."

"And . . . ?"

"Well, those boys are all dead or they might just as well be. The last one's lost an arm, an eye, and still has more lead in him than they could dig out."

"What's the job pay?"

"You serious?"

"Yep."

"It pays a hundred dollars for a roundtrip run."

A hundred dollars a run was a sum tough to turn down for a man desperate for a fresh start and who had nothing more to show for his labors over the past three years than a few loose coins in his pocket.

"Where do I sign up?" John said, not having to think about his decision. He'd made up his mind long before he walked into the Standard Gauge Saloon.

"You are serious. Hell, man, I'm sure you can ride with the next Monitor run headed to Cheyenne where you can sign on official like. I'll send a note with ya as an introduction," E.J. said, shocked John would actually risk his life for a hundred dollars a run on the deadliest trail in the west.

"When's the next Monitor due?" John asked, eager to get his life back on track.

"Actually, you're in luck. It'll be here tomorrow," E.J. said. "Relax and have a couple beers on the house, you can bunk in the barn."

E.J. knew damn well the kid didn't have any money, having heard how Burton had died penniless.

"Thanks, E.J. I won't forget it," John said, meaning it and determined to pay the man back someday.

The Monitor from Deadwood pulled in early afternoon the next day. Jumping down from the driver's seat, Ned Bronson, popping dust off his trench coat with his gloves, told the guards they would pull out as soon as they could get the team switched out. The Monitor was an ironclad coach with an iron strong box bolted to the wagon bed. Guards took turns running to the outhouse and inside the Standard Gauge Saloon for a quick bite to eat while others remained stationed in and round the coach during the brief stop.

John was introduced and, leaving his horse with E.J., climbed up next to the driver to ride shotgun for the trip south to Cheyenne, capitol of Wyoming Territory. Whether the coach carried gold or not was unknown to the men. All they knew is there were at least two runs for every shipment of gold with one of them acting as a decoy. According to the guards this did little to deter bandits who figured a fifty-fifty chance at riches was pretty good odds, either way.

With John riding next to him on the driver's seat, Ned Bronson felt better knowing he had another gun hand onboard, especially one recommended by E.J. Bishop, a well-known and respected station master.

"Ever kill a man?" Ned said as he pushed the team hard toward their next stop: Mule Creek Junction, just across the border in Wyoming Territory.

"I killed Indians in Cimarron Territory and shot a man in a gunfight in Tascosa," John said trying to sound more worldly than he actually felt.

"You never get over killin' a man," Ned said thoughtfully.

"No, you never do," John had to admit.

"Good to know we have an experienced gun hand with us. Things've been downright dangerous recently."

"Any trouble this run?"

"We had a couple of yahoos try to take us on in Red Canyon, but we taught 'em a lesson they won't soon forget."

"What happened?"

"They tried to get the wagon to stop."

"And . . . ?"

"And . . . well, we ran the bastards over. Never stopped. Just rolled right over the top of 'em. Might have killed one of 'em. Can't be sure, but I heard a hell of a lot of screamin' and bones crackin' as the wagon bucked over the two of 'em," Ned said and then gave out a hearty laugh.

John surveyed the sage-brush-covered countryside stretching out in all directions and promised himself he would quit riding shotgun on the Monitor as soon as he had a thousand dollars saved. Risking his life and running men over with a wagon full of gold was not the safest way to make a living, even if it was legal. He knew if Sarah got wind of his decision, she might have second thoughts about their engagement. John believed, however, that he had no other choice, having lost everything he had worked to build up over the past three years. Riding shotgun was a gamble, but his life had been a series of gambles that in many cases had been no less dangerous.

A lone hawk soared high in the empty sky, marking their passing as Ned pushed the horses hard toward the transcontinental railhead at the town of Cheyenne on Crow Creek north of the Colorado border. With Fort Laramie and its large contingent of cavalry on the North Platte River roughly halfway between Mule Creek Junction and Cheyenne, John figured the chance for bandits or Indians making a try on the wagon during the Wyoming leg of their run was low. The real danger lurked along the steep trails and in the narrow canyons in the Black Hills where *desperadoes* plied their trade without fear of the law, of which there was damn little, if any at all.

August 15, 1887

Deadwood, Lawrence County, Dakota Territory

Fool's Gold

THE MONITOR MADE A round-trip run once every other week, never stopping at any of its way stations for very long. John grew accustomed to the grueling routine, which for the most part thus far had been uneventful. An Indian hunting party and several groups of rough-looking men had shot at the wagon on different runs, but hadn't made any serious efforts to launch a full-scale attack. Spending time in Deadwood every other week, John soon discovered it was a town that never slept as miners, merchants, gunslingers, whores, and rogues all looking to make their fortunes collided in a never-ending and volatile churn of potential violence. Gunfights weren't uncommon, with the law more often blinder than the justice it was sworn to serve.

John stood at the bar in the Deadwood Gulch Saloon, one of the regular watering holes for Monitor guards, enjoying his favorite brew: a mug of rich foamy beer.

"Hear the news?" the bartender, Lame Johnny, said as he hobbled around behind the bar.

Johnny Benson got his nickname because of his gimpy right leg, a gift he received from a knife-wheeling Apache, he told everyone who cared to listen or ask.

"No. Somethin' happenin'?"

"The Fremont, Elkhorn, and Missouri Valley Railroad will finally complete its rail spur into Deadwood next year. It's gonna change everything. Passengers'll be able to ride straight into the whorehouses and gambling halls. Should make shuckin' 'em of their cash even easier," Lame Johnny said with a big belly laugh.

"It's goin'a shake things up, that's for sure," John said, having learned that Monitor runs would soon be a thing of the past once gold started to be shipped by rail.

The news made him think seriously about what he would do when riding shotgun on the Monitor was no longer possible. He had saved well over his goal of a thousand dollars, since he started, and had already stayed on longer than he had promised himself.

"John, you in there?" Ned called from the batwing door.

"Hey, Ned? That you? Come on in and have a beer," John called back.

"Been lookin' for ya," Ned said as he took a stool at the bar while Lame Johnny slid him a full mug of foamy beer.

"Put it on my tab. I'm feelin' generous," John said as he clinked mugs with Ned, each man taking a long pull on his beer.

"Always hits the spot," Ned said, smacking his lips.

"That it does, every time," John agreed.

"We'll be pullin' out bright 'n' early tomorrow mornin'," Ned said in a low voice, looking around to see who might be in earshot in the nearly empty saloon.

"Not many more runs, Ned. The train may close us down soon," John said.

"Doesn't change a thing as far as runs go. They'd kill us for the gold just the same, whether it's our first run or our last," Ned said.

John knew the man was right. As long as they made runs, the risks would remain the same. Ned had seen a lot over the years and had taken more than a little lead. He knew every time he hauled a load to Cheyenne it could be his last. John had been lucky to have built back his grubstake without serious incident; he just hoped his luck would hold out a little longer.

He had made up his mind, this would be his last run. When he got to Cheyenne his plan was to resign and ride up to Thunder Basin for a visit with Jasper, Maryanne, and the twins. He would then swing back down to Chadron and into the arms of the beautiful Sarah Bell, the love of his life. He looked forward to holding Sarah again and to getting his life back on track.

Having been the first man to search Tom Burton's room, Jesse Givens had ridden out of the Lazy Cheyenne with far more money in his pockets than any of the other men. It didn't take him long to parlay his ill-gotten grubstake into a good living in Deadwood. From bushwhacking and claim jumping to gunslinging and card-sharking, he had built up a sizable bankroll. His dream was to become a Deadwood business tycoon. He could see no end to the wealth miners were pulling out of the earth and no end of ways to pull that wealth out of their pockets and to put it into his own. When he got wind of a chance to buy the Franklin Hotel, he decided it was time to go after the kind of capital he would need to run his own gambling establishment.

Soon after arriving in Deadwood, Jesse had learned how to stay on top of things. His best sources of information had proved to be bartenders, waitresses, and whores who tended to be ignored by customers when they talked about matters confidential, especially when they were drunk. Jesse had no problem greasing a few palms to learn what he needed in order to pull off one of his swindles or to simply find his next fat mark. Lame Johnny had become one of his most reliable sources.

It seemed the Monitor would be making one of its last runs to Cheyenne before the railroad took over gold shipments. With the next gold shipment going out the next morning, and knowing there wouldn't be many more runs until the railroad took over, Jesse decided he couldn't afford to wait any longer.

Wasting no time, he dusted off his old plan to take down the Monitor, a plan he had worked out in detail long ago when he first arrived in Deadwood. He was confident the plan would work, if followed to the letter. He truly believed he could succeed; that is, that Jesse Givens, the devil's own, could succeed, where so many others had failed. The very thought of sitting on a pile of ill-gotten, blood-stained gold bars brought a ghoulish grin to his cold, wicked, hard-featured face.

The next morning, Ned and John sat up on the driver's seat while the Monitor was loaded. With guards stationed inside the carriage and horse mounted guards on both sides, the Monitor pulled out of Deadwood in a driving rain. Moving through the narrow canyon leading out of Deadwood always worried John. Beyond the obvious risk of bushwhackers, rockslides were always a concern.

"We're makin' good time. This rain might become a problem, though," Ned barked through the driving rain.

The creeks had already started running high. Should the rain come down any harder, washed out roads and bridges could become a real concern.

Clearing the canyon, Ned drove the wagon south through the mining town of Hill City and over a series of winding ridges and open valleys until descending into Custer on French Creek, where gold was first discovered in the Black Hills in 1874. Pulling out of Custer, rather than heading east to the new route that skirted the eastern edge of the Black Hills, Ned headed the wagon west until turning at four-mile corner to follow the Pleasant Valley Trail.

John had always enjoyed this part of the old route, because of the sudden change in the color of the rocks and soil, from grey and sandy brown to burnt orange and bright red, that marked the boundary between the northern and southern hills. As the wagon traveled further south, white gypsum capped bluffs of bright red soil became the dominant feature in the surrounding landscape.

Though the Red Canyon stage route had been abandoned ten years earlier, Ned often chanced taking the old route as a shortcut, figuring bandits would never suspect the Monitor would ever take the forbidden route nowadays. The deep canyon, with its long, narrow, and twisting trail, had made the route so dangerous in the past that the company had been forced to abandon the old route in favor of a new one that skirted the Black Hills to the east.

Taking the safer eastern route, however, added a great deal of time and difficulty to the journey due to the many river crossings along the way. The rivers that flowed off the Black Hills all ran due east to meet the Cheyenne River as it made its way northeast across the Badlands to the Missouri River. Trails running north and south along the edge of the Black Hills had to cross each of these tributary rivers. Because of the heavy rains and the likelihood of heavy flooding, Ned had decided it wouldn't only be quicker, but it would be a damn sight safer to take the old route through Red Canyon where they could stay high and dry and come out at a place on the Cheyenne River that was easy to cross in dry or wet weather. Once they crossed the Cheyenne River they would be able to roll on into the Standard

Gauge Saloon in Burton. From there, they could continue their journey west to Mule Creek Junction in Wyoming Territory and then south to Fort Laramie and Cheyenne.

Ned and John, up on the driver's seat, each carried a messenger's gun, an eighteen-inch, side-by-side, double-barreled shotgun. The purpose of these high-powered weapons was to cut-down anything at close range. John also carried two pistols and a Winchester, and Ned always had his trusty Winchester next to him on the driver's seat. Tucked under the seat was a stack of ammunition. The other guards were also heavily armed and ready for battle.

The rain had continued to pour down all day and the logic of Ned's decision became clear. There would have been no way they could have crossed the flooding rivers on the new route that ran down the natural valley between the Dakota Ridge and the Black Hills since many of the bridge crossings were no doubt already washed out. Driving the wagon's team hard through blinding rain, Ned never slowed up to read the faded hand-scrawled sign at the entrance of Red Canyon that read, "*Abandon hope all ye who enter here*," though he was well aware of the sign's warning and the risk they were taking.

As the wagon rolled deeper into the canyon, John looked up as the wind howled high above their heads and rain continued to shower down from the canyon rim. Suddenly, as if the sun itself erupted from the canyon floor, a massive explosion consumed the Monitor's charging team of horses. In the blink of an eye, John witnessed the six charging stallions nearly evaporate into a bloody mist. The wagon, following its forward momentum and no longer able to be steered, careened into the canyon wall, throwing Ned and John high into the air. The escort guards quickly pulled their horses down into defensive positions as rifle fire erupted from every direction.

John found himself a good fifty yards from the Monitor that now lay badly damaged on its side. He could see guards struggling to open the rear doors from the inside, as rifle fire rained down on the Monitor from above. Ned lay another ten yards further up the canyon with his right leg bent in an unnatural position. Blood ran down his face. In an effort to direct John's attention, Ned motioned with his arms to where several of their rifles lay scattered on the canyon floor nearby.

With the rifle fire from the canyon rim above concentrated on the Monitor and the escort guards, who now lay prostrate, cavalry-style, behind their horses, John risked jumping out from behind several large boulders, to grab a messenger's gun and two Winchesters before quickly scampering back behind the boulders. In the meantime, Ned had somehow crawled to a similar defensive position behind boulders piled up against the opposite wall of the canyon. Catching Ned's eye, John tossed one of the Winchesters to him. He was relieved when Ned caught the rifle mid-air and gave him a thumbs up.

The gun battle raged for more than half an hour as the gunmen high above slowly picked off the guards one at a time. The two escorts were the first to die, followed by two guards from inside the Monitor who had tried to escape the damaged wagon. John and Ned had stayed out of sight, knowing they had no chance to fight sharpshooters who could easily cut them down from above.

"In the wagon, come out now and we'll let you live," a loud voice echoed down from the canyon rim. "One minute, gentlemen. One minute, or we burn you alive."

To drive home the point, barrels of lamp oil crashed down on and around the Monitor. Even in the driving rain, a single spark would set the whole thing ablaze.

The two surviving guards in the wagon stepped out with their hands high in the air. John physically jerked when two rifle retorts rang out as the two men fell over dead. The echo of laughing men bounced down off the narrow canyon walls as John and Ned remained quiet, each man's heart pounding hard.

"Well, boys, let's go get the gold," the same voice called out, followed by a loud burst of cheers and laughter.

Listening to the group of *desperadoes*, John tried hard to gauge the number of bandits in the group. He was certain he heard at least three distinct voices respond to the leader's call. John and Ned could plainly see each other. Both men wondered how they had been missed by the bandits. The only thing John could figure was that the bandits had all been positioned high on the canyon rim behind where they attacked the wagon. The boulders Ned and John crouched behind had apparently blocked the bushwhackers' view from that angle. He also figured, now that they were entering the canyon from the direction the wagon had come, being hidden behind boulders deeper in the canyon in front of the wagon just might give Ned and him the necessary advantage to take down the ruthless killers who had found pleasure in gunning down unarmed men, men whom Ned and John had known as friends and comrades.

Jesse Givens, riding a grey roan, led his bandit trio into the canyon. Stepping down from their horses, the men quickly set to work. The gold chest was bolted to the Monitor's bed and chassis making it impossible to simply lift it out.

"She's sitting tight, with her skirt still on," one of the bandits yelled out from inside the Monitor.

"We'll just have to encourage her to lift that skirt," Jesse said with a chuckle.

John instantly recognized Jesse Givens's voice. He had bumped into Jesse in Deadwood more than once in recent months. The two men had even shared a beer or two. On one such occasion, John now recalled how Jesse told him that he had helped Cookie make his famous "babies" for their battle against the renegades in No Man's Land. John realized that Jesse had used that knowledge to take out the wagon's team. He shivered at the thought that Jesse had calculated the blast of nails and broken glass from his "baby" wouldn't only take out the horses, but would take out anyone on the wagon's driver's seat as well. John now understood the reason the bandits hadn't spent any time looking for Ned and him. They clearly believed the two of them had been blown to hell and gone in the same blast that had ripped through the wagon's team of horses.

The canyon once again reverberated, when a sizable charge of dynamite exploded. Rocks, dust, and smoke shot out in every direction. John and Ned were pelted with stones and engulfed in dust and smoke as the blast cloud billowed out to fill the narrow confines of the canyon in both directions.

"Whoa, Dick, what the hell are you thinkin'?" Jesse barked as he fought to control his horse.

"Well, I might've encouraged her a touch too much," Dick said with a grunt.

"A touch," Jesse growled. "I'd say that was a might more than a touch. Hell, man, that was a serious spankin'."

With that, Jesse gave out a loud laugh, with the others soon joining in.

"Well, Jim, duck in there and see if'n her skirt's been stripped off," Jesse said.

"By God, we did it. She's as naked as a jaybird! Her skirt's been blown clean off and she's got a heart of gold!" Jim cried out, his voice cracking with excitement.

"Wiley, bring up them pack mules. Let's get loaded and get the hell out of here," Jesse barked, taking charge of the operation.

John and Ned continued to lay low. Their next move depended on which direction the *desperadoes* decided to ride. If they turned back toward Custer, striking them from behind might be tricky, considering the bandits would be mounted and able to make a run for it while Ned and John were afoot. With Ned unable to stand, there would be little chance of taking down all four men. If the bandits followed the trail south toward the Cheyenne River, Ned and John would be able to flank the bastards when they rode by. In such a scenario, the fact Ned was unable to move quickly would make little difference.

With the pack mules loaded, the riders mounted and turned their horses south.

"We'll ride south. Once we cross the Cheyenne, we'll hightail it straight into Wyoming Territory. We can split up the gold south of Newcastle," Jesse barked. "Now, move out."

As the bandits filed past, one by one, John pressed his body low against the side of the canyon wall and held his breath. After the third rider passed, John took the chance to motion to Ned to get ready. Just when they thought the fourth rider would ride past, three gunshots rang out in rapid succession. The horses of the first three riders, startled by the loud echoes, reared up, throwing their limp riders to the ground. John could see that one of the riders had fallen badly, breaking his neck. He watched in disbelief as the other two riders, bleeding from gunshot wounds in their backs, struggled on the ground as they tried to reach for their pistols, only to be shot again at close range.

The last of the two riders to stop moving had caught sight of John hiding behind his boulder at the last second before his death. In the fleeting instant their eyes met, John had seen a knowing grin run across the man's face. John guessed the bandit died content knowing his double-crossing partner would soon join him in hell.

John and Ned waited a beat before simultaneously rising from behind their boulders on each side of the canyon trail.

"Drop your gun, Jesse!" John commanded.

Surprised by the sudden appearance of men popping out of the canyon walls on both sides, Jesse attempted to fire at the first thing he saw. John and Ned weren't in the mood for a long gun battle. They both fired their Winchesters at Jesse's chest from behind the relative safety of their boulder hideaways. Jesse, on the other hand, sitting high on his horse, was exposed with nowhere to hide.

John could see that Jesse had taken several hits in his chest, but refused to go down. Finally, knocked off his horse, he charged John's position like a crazed animal, growling and cussing and firing his pistol while attempting to draw another from his belt. Just as he reached John's boulder hideaway, John rose up with his messenger's gun and delivered a final love letter. With the blast hitting Jesse square in the face, what was left of his near-headless body ended up thrown back in a bloody heap on the canyon floor.

When the smoke cleared, John rounded up the bandit's horses and the four pack mules. Ned insisted he would be able to ride if John could help splint his leg and get him up into the saddle. After dragging all the bodies into the Monitor, John did the best he could to seal up the windows and doors to keep varmints from scavenging. There was no way for one man to bury ten bodies, let alone dig holes in the middle of the rocky Red Canyon trail.

With John busy moving bodies, Ned leaned over to check the loads and the ropes on the pack mules, while holding onto his saddle horn and willing away the pain in his broken leg.

"How much gold is there?" John said as he stepped up on his horse.

"None," Ned said, shaking his head.

"None? What d'ya mean, none?" John said confused.

"Iron pyrite, ever hear of it?" Ned said.

"Yea, they call it fool's gold," John said, knowing the Black Hills had a lot of the stuff.

"That's right. It looks like real gold; it's even found where gold's found," Ned said.

"Yea, so?"

"So, these packs are full of fool's gold. All these shiny gold bars ain't worth a red cent."

"You sayin', we were the decoy?"

"That's right. And Jesse Givens and his bandit trio were the fools."

August 15, 1890

Edgemont, Fall River County, South Dakota

Dry Goodbye

It had been three years since John and Ned Bronson rode into the Standard Gauge Saloon in Burton trailing four pack mules loaded down with bags stuffed full of bars of iron pyrite. Not long after, John resigned his position with the Cheyenne and Black Hills Stage Company and returned to Chadron, where he took a shopkeeper position at the Wentworth family's General Store. John still held on to his boyhood dream of homesteading in the Mauvaises Terres. Believing his dream would one day come true, he followed developments in the Dakota Territory with keen interest. Sarah and John wanted to marry and start a family together as soon as possible. John knew they had waited long enough.

With statehood for South Dakota, John believed the land in its west river region east of the Black Hills would soon open up for homesteading, just as lands west of the Missouri River in North Dakota had long ago. It had been thirteen years since the 1877 Treaty, following the Great Sioux War that forced the Lakota to cede a fifty-mile-wide strip of land along the western border of Dakota Territory, including the Black Hills and all the land west of the Cheyenne and Belle Fourche Rivers. The land John had claimed when he piled up his stone marker during the winter of 1887 was located just east of the Cheyenne River on the then-Great Sioux Reservation, which at the time included all the land between the Missouri and Cheyenne rivers.

A new act of Congress passed in March 1889 had subdivided half the land of the Great Sioux Reservation into five smaller reservations and opened up the other half of the land—over nine million acres or fourteen thousand square miles—for public purchase and homesteading. Reading the news, John had been excited to set out for Three Tree Creek right away, until he learned that the Lakota hadn't fully accepted the new boundaries of their diminished reservation lands and had continued to resist settlement into western South Dakota. Though the settlement of the newly opened lands was being encouraged by the railroads and the government, homesteaders remained wary of the many nonagency Lakota bands that continued to roam across the region.

John began to wonder if the lands of the Mauvaises Terres would ever be safe for settlement. He had learned only recently that a kind of spirit dance called the Ghost Dance, taught by a Paiute spiritual leader named Wovoca, promised believers that if the spirit dance was properly conducted, it would bring back the spirits of the dead to help drive out the white invaders, bringing a return of peace, prosperity, and unity to all native peoples.

Wovoca claimed the spirit dance ceremony came to him in a vision during the total solar eclipse on January 1, 1889. He taught his vision to many native tribes west of the Mississippi. Many Lakota bands adopted the practice as spiritual support for their continued militant resistance to the expansion of settlements into their native lands.

Bucking through the batwing door of the Standard Gauge Saloon with a strong thirst for a tall mug of cold beer, John found the place completely empty.

"Hello! Anybody here?" John called out, wondering how the saloon could be empty, considering there was an army of thirsty men working on the many new buildings that had sprung out of the prairie around a new railroad depot within walking distance of the Standard Gauge Saloon.

John had ridden up from Chadron to see the new town of Edgemont that had been established with the arrival of the Burlington Northern Railroad. The new rail line ran from the Transcontinental Railway in the south all the way across the Nebraska Panhandle up to Edgemont and on into Wyoming's Thunder Basin region. With Edgemont acting as the regional hub, a direct spur to Deadwood had also been completed. The construction of a roundhouse for train engine repairs in Edgemont was well underway. There was even talk of setting up a wool mill in the new town, making John see the logic of Jasper's decision to raise the wooly little critters just across the border in Wyoming. With the new rail link into Thunder Basin, Jasper now had a direct link to markets in the east.

"One beer coming up," E.J. said as he walked out of the back room and took up the bartender's position behind the bar.

E.J. knew John loved beer and figured the man must be thirsty. He'd never known him not to be.

"E.J. Good to see you again! Where's everyone?" John said, looking around while extending his hand for a hearty shake.

Without answering his question, E.J. slid a mug of foam-topped beer across the bar to John and poured himself a whiskey.

"On the house," E.J. said as he clinked glasses with John and took a sip of his whiskey. John followed by taking a long pull on his beer, draining about half the mug.

"Now that hit the spot," John said.

"Have you had time to look around our new town?" E.J. asked, taking another sip of his drink.

"Tom Burton knew this would happen one day," John said matter-of-factly.

"That he did. It's a damn shame it all came too late," E.J. said. "I plan to sell out myself."

"What? Why sell out now? Looks to me like this godforsaken stretch of prairie has turned into a boom town," John said.

"The good citizens of Edgemont haven't given me much choice," E.J. said bluntly draining his glass in a single gulp. "Prohibition was passed at the end of October last year."

"Prohibition. You must be jokin'," John said shocked.

"That's right, from October 30th to November 2nd, 1889, the railroad came, the town of Edgemont was born, the territorial legislature passed Prohibition, and we became a state. It all happened over a three-day period. And now they have their railroad, their town, and their state, and since the state legislature has just met and passed an enforcement bill, the civilized citizens of Edgemont want their law enforced as well." ,

"I'll be damned. I hadn't heard South Dakota was a dry state," John said.

"Unfortunately, it is," E.J. said.

"You could move to Mule Creek Junction just across the line. I'm sure saloons over there will become damn popular with the thirsty menfolk from South Dakota in coming years. Wyoming's still wet, isn't it?" John said.

"Yea, they're still wet over there and probably always will be. And of course, there's always Deadwood. They ain't givin' up their booze no matter what. Rather than fight it, I've decided to focus on my investments in Hot Springs. It's booming up there too," E.J. said, seemingly unconcerned with the sour turn of events.

"How're Joe and Roland doin'?" John asked, deciding to change the topic.

"Roland's up in Hot Springs lookin' after things and Joe's rebuilt his herd and is livin' in the brickhouse on Burton's old place. Being able to ship cattle from Edgemont should help him make a go of it."

"Not sure you've heard, but FE&MV rail service to Belle Fouche just opened last week," John said. "Cattle from Seth Bullock's ranch and other ranchers up north will be coming through Chadron on the way back east soon, just as Tom predicted."

"Now that's news Joe will want to know," E.J. said, surprised that things were moving so fast and that competition from ranchers in the northern hills had already arrived.

"Seems the railroad originally had plans to run track from Whitewood to Minnesela, which caused land prices to soar in the new town. Ol' Bullock outfoxed 'em all by offering the railroad free land in his new town of Belle Fouche just a few miles away," John said. "Again, it played out just like Tom predicted."

"Damn man was a prophet," E.J. said shaking his head, wondering what might have been if the blizzard of 1887 hadn't happened and Tom Burton had lived.

On the other hand, E.J. was a realist. He never wasted much time pondering all that could have been. He preferred to focus on what might be.

As John rode out of Edgemont, he thought about how far he had come since leaving Lizard Creek. Though it had only been six and half years since he and Jasper had ridden south on their journey to Texas, it felt like a lifetime. He was twenty-two years old and wondered how much longer he would have to wait to fulfill his boyhood dream. He understood why the Lakota continued to resist; people down through history had resisted the invasion of their lands, since the beginning of time.

As a boy, back in Webster County he had been fascinated by the many huge mounds that had been built on limestone bluffs overlooking the Des Moines River and Skillet Creek valleys. His father had told him the mounds were older than any of the Indians who had lived in the area before it was settled by white men.

The figures of men and animals carved in the sandstone cliffs along the Cheyenne River in the southern hills and in Red Canyon that Joe Bishop had showed him years earlier also predated any of the Indian tribes that claimed the Black Hills. Who were these ancient peoples? Who had driven them from their lands? There was no easy answer other than men had roamed the earth from the beginning of time, with different peoples settling new lands and sometimes resettling the same old lands over and over again down through the ages. The land may be eternal; its people, however, were forever destined to be mortal.

Turning his horse south, he decided it was high time he got on with his life. He would take Sarah Bell back to Iowa where they would marry. He had enough money to buy a farm near his father's place on Lizard Creek. He and Sarah could start their family, while he planned his next move. As surely as the cycles of the moon follow one after the other, the lands of the Mauvaises Terres would one day be ready for settlement. When that day came, he knew exactly where he would head as fast as he could get there; he had placed his stone marker on the exact spot long ago. Looking up he saw a lone eagle soar high overhead and prayed his eagle feather had done its magic to protect the land he believed would be his one day.

December 16, 1890

Pennington County, South Dakota

Dancing Ghosts

ANGERED AND BROKENHEARTED OVER the sudden and senseless death of Sitting Bull at the hands of reservation police made up of fellow Lakota tribesmen, Yellow Elk fled Standing Rock Reservation and rode south to join Chief Big Foot's band for the winter. Coming to a small pond, he slid off his horse to let it drink. As he knelt to take a drink of the clear water, he noticed a pile of stones next to a tree near the water's edge. The stones had clearly been piled up by someone who had marked this spot. He had seen this kind of marker before. It was the kind of thing white men did to mark a place they wanted to claim as their own. Enraged by the thought, Yellow Elk nearly struck out to topple the stones until he drew back upon seeing an eagle's feather wedged under the bottom edge of the stone pile.

The eagle was the strongest and bravest of all birds to the Lakota people. Eagle feathers were given to honor warriors and were worn with pride. Yellow Elk recalled the day he received his first eagle feather and how much it had meant to him. Looking down at the marker, Yellow Elk couldn't help but wonder why the white man who had piled up his stone marker to claim this land had chosen to use an eagle feather, one of the holiest of all symbols, to act as its protector. The position of the feather was clearly intentional, yet it hadn't been placed in accordance with Lakota custom.

On further thought, Yellow Elk found himself considering a potential deeper meaning for the marker. The stones had been there for some time, meaning this intruder had passed through these lands when they were still part of the Great Sioux Reservation, a time when the Lakota had defended these lands from outsiders without mercy. Even so, this man had boldly stacked up his pile of stones to mark land he had no right to claim.

Yellow Elk had to admit the location was a good one, with fresh water and firewood from the trees and bushes along the small creek and surrounding the pond. The rolling land also provided a natural barrier from the howling winds of winter. He nodded his head as he looked over the lay of the land and determined that it was suitable for a man looking to live in one place as the white man seemed to prefer.

Searching the banks of the small creek, he picked up four stones of roughly the same size and a couple of hands full of small pebbles. He had selected four stones of differing color to represent the four cardinal points and their meanings: the Yellow stone represented the East for enlightenment; the Black, West for insight; the White, North for wisdom; and the Red, South for innocence. He placed the colored stones at the base of the stone marker, one at each of the four cardinal points. He placed the small pebbles one by one in a square around the whole arrangement to represent the Earth. He then placed the last of the pebbles so they emanated out from each corner of the square to represent the Four Winds.

When he finished, he stood back and studied his handiwork. Satisfied with his *uname* design, one of the Lakota's holiest symbols, in which he had enshrined the alien stone marker and its eagle feather, he held up his arms with open palms to the four directions of the wind and said a silent prayer. After taking one last look, he turned, mounted his red and white pinto pony, and rode south across the snow-dusted prairie toward Wounded Knee Creek on the Lakota Pine Ridge Indian Reservation to spend the winter.

Though the Ghost Dance had caught the imaginations of some Lakota people who longed for the old days, Yellow Elk knew no amount of dancing in a circle would ever bring back the glory of the past; his people's challenge was not in finding a lost past, but in dealing with an uncertain future that had already arrived. As surely as the sun rose in the east, an endless stream of white settlers would continue to flow from the distant eastern horizon until they filled up the lands of his ancestors.

October 17, 1902

Prairie Creek, Webster County, Iowa

Teddy, Man of the People

OVER TEN YEARS HAD passed since John and Sarah returned to Iowa. Alford and Matilda Wentworth, Jasper and Maryanne Waite with their growing family of five children all came back to Iowa for John and Sarah's wedding in the spring of 1892. With the rapid spread of postal service, the telegraph and the telephone, and the ever-expanding network of train lines, travel and communication had improved by leaps and bounds.

John sat on the front porch of his house enjoying a smoke when his brother Benjamin rounded the gate and rumbled into the yard in a horseless carriage. John had used steam-powered machinery on his farm for some time, but still used his horse and buggy to get around. Noisy motorized contraptions like Benjamin's were becoming common in larger towns like Fort Dodge; John hadn't seen many this far out in the countryside, however.

"Johnny! Take a look at my new motor-buggy," Benjamin called out as he pulled up and turn off the noisy engine.

"Benny! Good to see ya! That thing safe?" John called, grinning.

"Hell yea, it's safe! I built the damn thing," Benjamin said, looking indignant.

Benjamin had become well-known for his many mechanical innovations. John wasn't surprised he was getting into building motorized buggies. He had a hand in nearly every new-fangled contraption that came along.

"It's the latest thing in motorized transportation," Benjamin bragged. "There'll be one of these motorized buggies in front of every home in these here United States in the near future."

"What's pa think?" John asked drily.

"Well, you know, he still thinks it'll be tough to replace the horse and buggy," Benjamin said. "Of course, he still marvels at the telephone."

"Benjamin, I thought I heard your voice," Sarah said, coming out of the house holding little Billy in her arms.

William Rueben Barton, named for his grandpas on both sides, had been born six months before. John and Sarah had hoped to have a big family by now, but when that hadn't happened, after nearly ten years of marriage, they started considering adoption. Their first child, little Billy, came as one hell of a surprise since Sarah had given up trying to get pregnant. Now that their first child had come, John and Sarah once again looked forward to having more children.

"How's my favorite nephew?" Benjamin said.

"He's hungry all the time. Like someone else we all know," Sarah quipped.

Benjamin was notorious for his huge appetite and never failed to visit right at or around mealtime.

"Smells like dinner's on. Got room for one more?" Benjamin said, taking her barbed remark in stride.

"For you, always," Sarah said with a knowing grin. "Come on in and get cleaned up. I'll set another place at the table."

The conversation over dinner covered the full range of topics of the day. Teddy Roosevelt, at age forty-two, had suddenly become the nation's youngest president with the assassination of William McKinley, the year before. Bringing his wife and six young children into the White House had become the talk of the nation overnight. His focus on breaking up the large trusts was wildly popular.

"Did you hear the latest?" Benjamin said, always excited to talk politics.

"Something on the coal strike?" John said.

The coal strike had people worried about winter fuel supplies. The strike in the anthracite mines in eastern Pennsylvania had dragged on for months with no resolution in sight.

"You might have heard that Teddy was plannin' on goin' down to the mines to kick some asses," Benjamin said. "Well, he did just that and got 'em to end the strike! Workers got more pay and the shorter hours they've been wanting. It's the first time the President of these here United States of America ever stepped in as an arbitrator for the working man."

"Now that's the kind of square deal he promised," John said. "It's his experiences in the Dakota Badlands on his Elkhorn Ranch up there on the little Missouri River that shaped him. Ol' Teddy knows what it's like for a man to have to fight to survive."

"Do you really believe his Dakota experiences shaped him that much?" Benjamin wondered.

"He's a man who has known loss. He lost his wife and mother in 1884. And a few years later, in the winter of 1887, he lost most of his cattle, just like the rest of us," John said with a distant look in his eye.

"I heard he lost over twenty-thousand head of cattle," Benjamin said.

"That's right. Even so, he made sure his ranch hands didn't suffer for it," John said. "A hell of a different story than what that shyster Tom Burton left us with when he lost his cattle."

"I've heard all the stories. There's no doubt, Burton had been nothing more than an outlaw, but at least he led you to Sarah. Joining his drive to Dakota Territory wasn't all bad, was it?" Benjamin said as he dished up a hearty second helping.

"Well, it seems to have worked out pretty good for you anyway," Sarah said with a grin looking straight at Benjamin as she pursed her lips and puffed a loose strand of hair out of her eyes.

"You caught me, Sarah," Benjamin said, a serious look on his face. "Your cookin' has ruined me. I swear, I may never find another woman to measure up."

"I've heard you say the same thing to your mother," Sarah said as she stared at Benjamin. "In fact, it was just last week when we all got together."

"She's got ya there, Benny Boy, and I'm staying out of this one," John said, looking back and forth between the two of them, grinning.

"Oops, caught me again," Benjamin said, pretending to look innocent.

After a beat, all three broke into a hearty laugh. John thought he even heard little Billy giggle.

"Seriously, what's next with Teddy?" John said. "When's he goin' to open up western South Dakota?"

"No idea." Benjamin said. "The papers say he'll take a western state tour next year. Emigrants from Europe are pouring into the country and they're hungry for land. All the lands surrounding western South Dakota are already nearly filled up with homesteaders."

"Without a railroad, folks ain't gonna be heading into the Badlands of South Dakota," John said. "A few brave souls've settled along the Missouri River and some ranchers graze cattle out there in the spring and summer, but the land is still empty for the most part."

"When you gonna try to go back?" Benjamin said.

"I plan to stake my claim as soon as a railroad reaches someplace near two rivers; someplace near the stone marker I stacked up next to Barton Lake fifteen years ago," John said, meaning every word.

John had never given up hope of one day staking his claim in the Mauvaises Terres. With Teddy Roosevelt's love of the region and his desire to settle the lands to the west, John was confident he would finally be able to stake that claim in the coming years.

Riding out of Fort Bennet to the southwest, following the Cheyenne River along its southern banks, Lt. Robert Powell led his small troop of twelve men on a patrol of the southern border of the Lakota Cheyenne River Reservation. It had been nearly a dozen years since the cessation of hostilities in 1890 after the battle at Wounded Knee and the 1891 ratification of the 1889 Treaty that had permanently partitioned western South Dakota into five distinct Indian reservations, each with specific boundaries, freeing up the remaining land for public use.

In the beginning, it had been hard to convince the Indians that the public lands no longer belonged to them and that they needed to stay on their own reservations. For years, ranchers had complained of cattle rustling by bands of Indians living off the established reservations. The few sodbusters who had tried to homestead in the isolated and arid region found it difficult not only because the soil and rainfall were poor, but because they feared the Indians who frequently roamed the land in silent protest.

Because there had been rumors of trouble in the area, Lt. Powell wanted to show the flag as a reminder to everyone, white man and red man alike, that the Army was ready, willing, and able to enforce the law. Arriving at the convergence of the Belle Fouche River and the Cheyenne River, he steered his men straight south for several miles before turning back east to once again take a course paralleling the southern bank of the Cheyenne River, a course that would lead them back to the Missouri River and Fort Bennet on its western bank.

Though the prairie at first glance appeared as flat as a pancake to the untrained eye, the actual terrain rolled up and down, making it impossible to see what might be over the next rise. This feature had always concerned Lt. Powell, since without sending out scouts in every direction there was absolutely no way to ensure safe passage when out on patrol.

Being west of the 100th Meridian, he knew the annual rainfall was less than twenty inches in the region, making the growing of crops difficult, if not impossible. The 100th Meridian that ran down through the middle of the states of North Dakota, South Dakota, Nebraska, Kansas, Oklahoma, and Texas had become the recognized dividing line between the moist East and arid West.

In South Dakota, it turned out the Missouri River, which ran from north to south across the state exactly along the 100th Meridian, divided the state almost perfectly in half. The two halves came to be called East River and West River, each half being very different in climate, character, culture, and economy. While sodbusters prospered in the East River, Lt. Powell had witnessed hundreds of abandoned homesteads in the West River where settlers had been unable to make the arid land yield a living. He had begun to wonder if the Badlands of South Dakota would ever be fully settled.

After climbing and descending an endless series of rolling rises and finding nothing in the ravines and valleys beyond, Lt. Powell was delighted to come upon a creek lined with three huge cottonwood trees that ran into a small pond at the bottom of a beautiful hidden valley. Reaching the spot, he dismounted and tested the water and found it both sweet and good. With nightfall coming, he ordered his troops to settle in for the night. Walking around the kidney-shaped pond, he came upon a pile of stones next to a tree that struck him as very odd.

He had seen may Lakota ceremonial sites including the arrangements of buffalo skulls used in the Sun Dance and the Sweat Lodge. He had witnessed many ceremonies and dances and knew a lot about the symbols and art of the people. He had never known the Lakota to build stone monuments of this kind, however. Clearly, he thought, the construction of the stone pillar and the stones arranged around it was a kind of cultural hybrid.

The central stones were piled up in the manner of a territorial or place maker. This was common among Europeans. The four colored stones at the cardinal points at the base of the maker and the square design made up of smaller pebbles around the whole arrangement was definitely Lakotan in origin. Indeed, someone had made the whole arrangement into an *uname*, a holy symbol of the Lakota. The pebbles that radiated from each corner of the square confirmed the symbol's Lakota meaning, being that of the Earth and the Four Winds.

Studying each element, Lt. Powell took note of an eagle's feather wedged under the base of the central pillar. He knew the eagle feather was a powerful totem to ward off evil. He was perplexed seeing it pushed under the stones, since he had never known the Lakota to use eagle feathers in such a way. Kneeling down, he took a rosary he had carried for many years out of his jacket's inside pocket and wound it carefully around the central stone pillar, tying the beaded necklace so as to leave the crucifix hanging down on the eastern side of the stone monument. Saying a silent prayer, he stood and looked at his handiwork one last time and then returned to his men, who had bedded down on the other side of the pond.

At daybreak, Lt. Powell took one last look across the pond at the stone maker he could just make out near a tree at the edge of the water. He smiled at the thought of the man who had built the original marker someday returning to claim this land; a land of spirits, a holy land, now blessed by both peoples.

As he led his troop east toward the Missouri River, he couldn't help but wonder when this vast untamed land would finally be settled. With immigrants continuing to pour into the country at record numbers and Teddy's burning desire to make all the lands in the nation productive, he figured homesteaders would fill the land sooner than most people imagined.

December 25, 1906

Lizard Creek, Webster County, Iowa

Time Waits for No Man

IT HAD BEEN MANY years since the Barton clan all gathered together for Christmas. Lucy had been baking and cooking for the past two days with Alda, Linda, and the twins' wives pitching in. The menfolk had been chopping wood, decorating the house, and putting up the Christmas tree with no little help from an army of grandchildren all wanting to pitch in to make decorations and put them on the tree. The many spicy aromas and scents of Christmas filled the air. Everyone was excited and knew how special this Christmas holiday had become.

With the table set and the food all arranged down the middle and on several side-tables, Bill and Lucy took their seats at the head of the main table with John and Sarah on each side. Their two children, Billy and Alva, sat at the children's table in the living room. Alda and her husband Jack Watson sat next in line at the main table, one on each side, with their five children—Jack Jr., Tim, Terry, Susan, and Larry—gathered around the children's table in the living room with Billy and Alva.

Benjamin sat at the far end of the main table. Still single at age thirty, he failed to bring a female friend with him much to his mother's displeasure. He hoped that sitting out of her direct earshot at the opposite end of the table might make for a more pleasurable dinner, seeing how she never stopped hounding him about his marriage plans, or rather his lack thereof.

The twins, Charles and David, who had been only five years old when John and Jasper rode off to Texas, were now twenty-seven and married.

Charles and his wife Cinthia had three children—Doug, Robert, and Nancy. The couple sat at the main table and their three children took up seats at the children's table.

David and his wife Ariel had two children—Terry and Mason. David slid in next to Charles and Ariel next to Cinthia at the main table, while their two boys joined the children's table.

Linda, born in 1884, was twenty-two and still single, much to her mother's constant concern. She had attended Northwestern University in Evanston, Illinois, and now worked at the First National Bank in Fort Dodge. Lucy had hoped her daughter would marry a local boy, but Linda was determined to transfer to the bank's Saint Louis office, where she had been offered a promotion. Linda sat at the far end of the table across from Benjamin, content to be away from to her mother's relentless nagging. She could see Benjamin felt the same way. Indeed, the two had conspired to take seats at the opposite end of the table from their mother and gave each other a knowing grin when they finally settled in.

Clifford, was the youngest of Bill and Lucy's children and had been born in 1893 soon after John and Sarah's big wedding after their return from Chadron, Nebraska. At thirteen, the same age as Alda's oldest son, Jack Jr., Clifford sat at the children's table.

Once everyone was seated, the room soon became awash in conversations as everyone tried to talk at once. So much had happened since their last gathering, the stories soon filled the air. After about ten raucous minutes, with the volume growing by the second, Bill stood up and tapped his butter knife against his water glass to get everyone's attention.

"May I have your attention, please?" Bill said with a broad grin on his face. "Give an old man a chance to say a few words."

"Not sure you ever lacked a chance to prattle on, pa," Benjamin said in good humor, causing everyone to laugh.

"Well, that might be son, but in your case I had'ta do a little extra prattling to give ya all the instruction I could," Bill said as if to remind everyone of Benjamin's deficiencies. "And as anyone can see, a man can only do so much."

The comment set off another round of laughter as everyone enjoyed the friendly jabs.

"Touché," Benjamin said, raising a glass to his father, causing even more laughter.

"Now let a man say a few words, please," Bill said, raising his glass in a toast and giving Benjamin a nod and a wink. Everyone soon quieted down.

"This is the first time in a long time we've had everyone together for Christmas. It's hard to believe we've been blessed with twelve grandchildren and from what I can tell we have more on the way," Bill said with a smile, raising his glass to Ariel and Sarah, who were both visibly carrying members of the next generation. He then quickly looked at Linda and winked. She smiled back. No one else seemed to take note of the exchange.

"It's not since Pappy passed away five years ago that we all came together. It was a somber time," Bill continued. "Let's all make this gathering a happy memory, one that recalls all the good times we've shared together. John and Sarah will head out to South Dakota early next year. Linda will head to Saint Louis for a promotion and a new position with the bank. Benjamin has accepted a position with Ford Motor Company up in Michigan, where I am sure he'll invent the next generation of horseless carriages. David and Ariel are headed to California, where they plan to start a wine vineyard. I can't wait to get the first bottle of Chateau de Barton."

Everyone laughed at the remark.

"Charles and Cinthia are headed to Oregon where Charles has been offered a good position with a printing company. It seems the Bartons are branching out into many other parts of this great land. May we never allow distance to keep us apart," Bill concluded.

"And I'll not let my children and grandchildren run off on an empty stomach," Lucy said stoutly, as a tear ran down her cheek. "Now Bill, please lead us in grace."

Bill could see she was taking it hard knowing so many of her children would be moving away and that watching all her grandchildren grow up would no longer be possible. Bill also knew Lucy understood this day would come.

Having one's children set off into the world was all part of what it was to have children: the joy of watching them grow up, test their wings, and one day leave the nest to strike out on their own. Even so, Bill felt as Lucy did. He never wanted to let them go. He knew, however, for their children's sake, they would have to learn to fly on their own. Becoming a whole person is all about learning to stand on one's own. For any child to do so, the parents must learn to let go. Success and failure were both good teachers. Bill and Lucy had long accepted that letting their children go was all part of how they matured and continued to grow. For frontier folk, it had been that way since the beginning of time.

Bill had always used the same prayer when he was asked to say grace; it was the only one he had memorized as a child, not having been a church going man.

Bill and Lucy folded their hands on the edge of the table with the Barton children all following suit; even the little ones on the children's table folded their little hands and bowed their little heads just like the adults.

"Come, Lord Jesus, be Thou our guest and let this food to us be blessed. Amen," Bill said.

"Amen," everyone said, after a beat, and in unison.

The Bartons' meal prayer had become a family tradition long ago. Everyone loved the fact that they knew it always would be.

"Benjamin, since you're now a professional mechanic and all, please carve up those three huge turkeys and that mother of all hams," Bill said as he pointed to the huge platters of steaming meat in front of Benjamin.

"Must I remind you, pa, a mechanic isn't a lowly butcher," Benjamin scolded his father in jest. "A mechanic, my good man, is nothing less than an artist."

"Well, put your artistic skills to use and lop some meat off them chitters and start passing plates," Bill said with a chuckle which caused a ripple of laughter to roll around the table.

"Come on, Uncle Benny, hurry up. I'm mighty hungry," Jack Jr. called from the children's table.

"Yea, Benny, let's get the plates movin'," Clifford chimed in, grinning at Jack and elbowing him in the ribs.

Jack Jr. was thirteen going on fourteen and soon to be a man and was the oldest of the grandchildren. He and Clifford were both nearly as big as their fathers. They had both grown up listening to Pappy's many stories before he passed; stories that had ignited in them a wanderlust to travel beyond the horizon. They both dreamed about heading to Alaska the first chance they got. They wanted to live their own stories, create their own destinies, just as their grandfather and great grandfather before them had done.

"Why yes, Master Jack and sidekick Uncle Cliff. How about big juicy drumsticks for the both of ya?" Benjamin replied as he adroitly carved two drumsticks off and slapped them on a couple of plates.

With the first two plates on their way around the table to gather all the fixings, Benjamin barked, "Next order!"

Soon everybody was placing orders as Benjamin carved off meat, sending plates flying around the table, each getting a helping of mashed potatoes and gravy, stuffing, sweet peas, candied carrots, fresh buns and butter, and so much more.

Sarah, Cinthia, and Lucy were pushing plates over to the children's table as Ariel and Linda helped get the main table all served. With the first helping all dished up, once again the room erupted into a cacophony of voices, belly laughs, and giggles as the Barton clan put on the feedbag and tore into their Christmas feast.

John had decided the timing was right to head for the Mauvaises Terres of South Dakota when he learned that the Chicago and North West-ern Railway Company would complete its line from Pierre through the new towns of Philip and Wall and on to Rapid City by mid-summer 1907, just six months away.

Studying a map for the new rail line, John noted that the new town of Wall, by coincidence, happened to be located just south of the land where he had piled up his stone marker during the winter of 1887. He figured if he could get his wagon there by train in the spring, he could make his way north to his claim before anyone else grabbed it.

Emigrants, mostly from Germany, were pouring into Nebraska and some had already headed into western South Dakota by wagon.

Not wanting to miss out on the coming boom, the Chicago, Milwau-kee and Saint Paul Railroad Company announced it planned to complete its own new rail line from Chamberlain to Rapid City along the White River through the new towns of Kadoka and Interior sometime in late 1907.

Both railroads, in hopes of boosting the population along their new rail lines, had been advertising nonstop from New York to California, and even across Europe, to entice as many new immigrants as possible to come and settle in South Dakota with the promise of free farmland. John knew he had no time to lose.

After President Roosevelt had taken his 1903 Grand Tour of the West, the public's interest in settling the more arid western regions of America had finally been piqued. Owning a ranch on the Little Missouri in western North Dakota since 1884, Roosevelt loved visiting the vast grasslands of the northern plains. Wanting to preserve their many wonders for future generations of Americans, he authorized the Antiquities Act, which passed through Congress in 1906, giving the the president the power to set aside national monuments.

Impressed by its mysterious and unique geological features, the presi-dent chose Devil's Tower in Wyoming, located just north of the Black Hills and not far from his Elkhorn Ranch in North Dakota, to become America's first national monument. What excited John most was that the president had also expanded the Homestead Act to permit land grants of up to six hundred forty acres to farmers and ranchers to encourage cultivation of the more arid lands west of the 100th Meridian. John hoped this expansion included the lands of the Mauvaises Terres in western South Dakota.

Whether the new rules would apply to land in the Badlands of South Dakota or not, John intended to buy additional land, if necessary, after homesteading the one hundred sixty acres of land allowed by the original Homestead Act. He figured he would need at least three hundred twenty acres to make a go of his new farm in the Mauvaises Terres. Either way, the first thing he needed to do was to get to the Mauvaises Terres as soon as possible to file an official claim on the land where he had set up his stone marker long ago.

April 28, 1907

Prairie Creek, Webster County, Iowa

Mad Dash

SPRING CAME EARLY IN 1907. John had been preparing for his journey into the Mauvaises Terres for months. The Chicago and North Western Railway Company would soon reach the newly platted town of Wall, said to be named for the wall-like rock formations nearby. The rail line was already carrying passengers and commerce from Pierre across the Missouri River into western South Dakota to the newly platted town of Philip. The railroad planned to have the new line reach all the way to Rapid City, the gateway and growing rail and commercial hub for the Black Hills, before the end of summer.

John decided to set out the next morning for Philip, South Dakota. He figured if immigrants are already flowing into the Philip area, just thirty miles east of Wall, he had no time to lose. Once he got to Philip, he could camp out while the track was laid further west. He would then be able to board one of the first trains headed to Wall. From there he would gallop north on horseback to stake his claim.

On his way north out of Wall, his plan was to search for a possible trail he could use to bring wagons to the new place. Benjamin had offered to pitch in, insisting he had to see the Mauvaises Terres for himself. He too had been hooked on the mysterious region after listening to Pappy's many stories as a child. John appreciated the help and the company. Benjamin also offered to drive a second wagon which would make establishing John's homestead faster than a man who was working alone and had only one wagon and one load of supplies. Sarah and the children would wait to come out until late summer, to allow John and Benjamin time to get a place ready.

The sun stood high in a clear blue sky as a lone rider surveyed his herd that had stretched itself out, speckling the rolling prairie with cattle for miles in every direction. He knew other riders were posted further out to keep the herd from straying too far. They would let the cattle feed in the area for a couple of weeks and then move them further south. It had been a wet spring and the graze was good. Clay McCall was satisfied, something his men had learned was the way they needed to keep him. With the temperament of an angry badger, he wasn't the kind of man anyone wanted to cross or rile up.

Clay had grazed his cattle in western South Dakota since the mid-1890s. With the cessation of hostilities after Wounded Knee, grazing cattle in these virgin lands became routine for ranchers in South Dakota along the Missouri River. Ranchers further south along the Niobrara River in northern Nebraska also took advantage of the free open grasslands to graze their cattle in western South Dakota during the summer. The vast grasslands of the Mauvaises Terres were virtually empty of settlements outside of the defined Indian reservations. With few competitors to challenge those bold enough to enter, the nearly unlimited grazing lands were a boon.

It had been some time since he grazed his herd along the south side of the Cheyenne River that ran east to the Missouri River and formed the southern border of the Lakota Cheyenne River Indian Reservation. Though there had been no problems with the Indians in years, he suspected more than a few of his missing cattle over the years had been poached by Indians off the reservations; there simply weren't many other suspects to point to. Clay was a man with little tolerance for anything he didn't agree with or understand. He believed the Indians had had their day and should now stay out of the way so the rest of the country could get on with building the nation.

Teddy's Grand Tour had brought unwanted attention to the region from Clay's point of view. He liked that Teddy had been a cattle man, but he didn't like that he now wanted sodbusters to settle good range land. Looking out over the open range, he feared the day would come when barbed wire fences would spring up out of the prairie, cutting off ranchers like himself from the free and open use of the vast grasslands.

He had at first been heartened by the course chosen for Teddy's Grand Tour of the West, which in many ways followed the old borders claimed by the Great Sioux Nation as spelled out in the Fort Laramie Treaty of 1868. The treaty had granted the Lakota Sioux all the land bounded by the Yellowstone River in the northwest, the Missouri River in the east, and the North Platte River that ran from central Wyoming southeast all the way across Nebraska to the Missouri River.

The Great Sioux Nation, with the Black Hills at its center, covered much of what was now western North Dakota, eastern Montana, eastern Wyoming, the northern half of Nebraska, and all of western South Dakota. At the time, Clay had been pleased the president had made a symbolic statement that these vast lands were now part of the United States of America.

What he now understood was that Teddy had been trying to drum up interest in the homesteading and farming of these arid lands more than in making any statement as to their new ownership. With immigration at record levels and the railroads laying track into western South Dakota at a feverish pace, Clay had to accept there would be no holding back the coming tidal wave that would soon wash up a tangled mess of filthy foreigners looking for free land.

The news from Washington D.C. was that Teddy was now claiming he wanted less immigration and wanted the tens of millions of immigrants already in the country to learn to speak English and adopt the American culture over the cultures of their native lands. Clay saw these proclamations as meaningless, since the door to new immigrants hadn't been closed; indeed, under Teddy, immigration had continued at record levels.

What he feared most was that foreigners might soon outnumber real Americans in the lands out west. As their numbers continued to swell, the political clout his family had built up in the state of South Dakota over the years might soon go the way of the land itself.

With his head filled with foreboding about the future of his ranching empire, Clay rode into a beautiful little valley with a crystal-clear pond at the end of a small creek lined by three large cottonwood trees nestled tranquilly at its bottom. Though he had grazed cattle in this area in the past, he couldn't recall ever finding such a wonderful place.

Stepping down from his horse, he knelt at the water's edge to taste its freshness. The water was cool and sweet. He drank deeply. As he let his horse drink while filling his canteen, he noticed something flicker with a shiny sparkle on what appeared to be a pile of stones by a tree on the other side of the pond.

Posting his horse to let him graze, Clay walked round the kidney-shaped pond to investigate the sparkling object. What he found took him by complete surprise. Arranged in a kind of primitive reliquary were an array of religious and spiritual relics. Stepping back, her surveyed the whole shrine. He noted that the whole construction was anchored by a central pile of stones that had been crowned with a delicately carved turtle. Wound around the stone column were the beads of a rosary, the leather strap of a medicine bag, a gold chain with a golden Star of David pendant, a silver chain with a silver crescent moon and star pendent, and a woven braided cord with a silver Saint Francis medallion.

At the base of the stone pillar, four different colored stones had been placed at the cardinal points. Around this arrangement a square of small pebbles had been established with additional pebbles laid so as to stream out from each corner. Numerous feathers, including eagle feathers, had also been woven into the chains on the main pillar. Indian head pennies, buffalo nickels, and Mercury head dimes had been balanced on many of pebbles around the base. On the black stone lay a brass slave bracelet, probably left by a Buffalo Solider serving in the 10th Cavalry that had patrolled western Dakota Territory or by a freed slave who had by chance passed this way. Clay couldn't believe his eyes and could only wonder at the meaning of such an elaborate religious shrine in the middle of nowhere.

He found himself searching for answers to his many questions: How had so many people found this spot in the middle of nowhere? Why had so many visitors felt compelled to add to the reliquary? What did it all mean?

Search as he might, he could find no answer other than after being in the shrine's holy presence, he too felt the need to kneel and pray, something he hadn't done since he was a child. He somehow understood in looking at the reliquary that this land now belonged to everyone, to those who came long ago and to each successive wave of immigrants.

He stood so he could survey the shine as a whole once again. Wanting to add to the shrine, he studied every element carefully as he considered his own contribution. Pulling a small pouch out of the inside pocket of his vest, he removed his lucky talisman, given to him by his grandfather when he was only a boy. Kneeling once again, he placed the delicate jade double happiness pendent carved long ago in distant China at the base of the stone pillar on the yellow stone, facing east toward the rising sun.

Clay McCall rode back to patrolling his herd a changed man. He now accepted that sodbusters would come to take possession of the land, as had others before them. Even the Lakota were only recent landlords; their conquest of the Mauvaises Terres, the Black Hills, and the vast grasslands further north, south, and west had come only after their equestrian way of life started in the 1770s, when horses first came into their hands—a relatively short period of time in the greater scheme of things. Coincidentally, in many similar ways, the Lakota and the original thirteen colonies gained their freedom around the same time.

Though the Lakota and other native peoples had lived nomadic lives that crisscrossed the northern plains for thousands of years, the undisputed control of vast tracts of land hadn't been possible until the horse upset the balance of power in the region.

The rapid mobility of the horse brought with it the ability to move bands of warriors over vast distances in a short time, something which had been impossible for native peoples who had lived for millennia afoot with only dog-drawn travois to ease their labors on the vast rolling grassland of the Great Plains. Now, the iron horse provided an even speedier deployment of new invaders, and with them the birth of a new age.

Clay McCall had made peace with the coming tide. He would welcome the newcomers. Looking out over the empty prairie in its pristine, untouched natural state as sun beams streamed out of the bellies of thick blue-grey clouds in the west, he recalled the admonition uttered by wise King Solomon, long ago: "This too shall pass."

He had no doubt it would.

Arriving in Philip, South Dakota, John and Benjamin soon learned that the new rail line to Wall would begin operations the next day. Neither man could believe their dumb luck. Philip wasn't much of a town to write home about. The hundreds of covered wagons that had been unloaded from a steady stream of railcars filled the streets in front of the many empty plots of the newly platted town. John heard a number of foreign languages churning in the air, from German and Norwegian to others he couldn't identify. Many of the immigrants were clearly new arrivals in the New World, their dress and mannerisms strange and foreign. For John, he knew these people would soon become his new neighbors, the first crop of hearty homesteaders to finally settle the Mauvaises Terres.

"John, I got us a place on the first train to Wall tomorrow morning," Benjamin said as he walked up to where they had parked their two fully loaded wagons.

"How in the world did you swing that?" John asked, surprised Benjamin had taken the initiative to secure train tickets only an hour after they had arrived.

John had been told upon arrival that in no uncertain terms train tickets wouldn't go on sale until tomorrow morning. The railroad wanted its settlement of the free land in the region to be as orderly and as fair as possible, considering they were dealing with future long-term customers. He had been asked to put the names of his party on a slip of paper and to submit it to the ticket office for the random drawing the next day. John had asked Benjamin to submit their entry.

"Well, it seems the station master loves Ford automobiles," Benjamin said with a devilish grin on his face. "I promised to ship him a new 1908 Ford Model T at a discount."

"Didn't know Ford had a Model T."

"He didn't either. He wanted a Model K."

"I've seen one of them. They have shiny brass radiators and a lot of fine craftsmanship. Aren't they a little expensive?"

"Well, I talked him out of a Model K."

"So, you're telling me you sold him on a Model T that doesn't exist yet."

"Yep, not until next year anyway. The Model T is the reason I'm joining the Ford Motor Company," Benjamin said proudly.

He had been designing automobiles for several years and Ford liked what he could offer. Henry Ford's idea was to "democratize the automobile." To do that, the price had to come down.

Just as Benjamin had predicted, the first Model T rolled off the Ford production line in 1908 with a price tag of eight hundred fifty dollars. Model Ts continued to roll off the production line until 1927. By 1925, assembly-line production brought the price of a Model T touring car down to less than three hundred dollars. Popularly known as the "Tin Lizzie," over fifteen million Model Ts were produced, accounting for over 40 percent of all automobiles manufactured in the United States at that time.

"So, he trusted you to deliver an automobile that doesn't exist yet."

"Yep. The man's a saint."

"A saint who just happened to have a couple of train tickets to Wall with our names on 'em, right?" John said, matching Benjamin's devilish grin.

"Be damned if he didn't."

"Do you already have these magic tickets?"

"Not exactly. I have his word. He'll draw names from a hat tomorrow mornin'. Ours will come right off the top of the stack. I watched him stack up the name slips myself. We'll have tickets number one and two for passengers, freight and livestock."

"You, little brother, are a wonder."

"I've been told that all my whole life," Benjamin said, meaning every word.

Benjamin had been told many times he had been born with a veil, a very rare occurrence that was widely believed to portend special talents and good fortune. His father, Bill Barton, never failed to remind Benjamin of his auspicious birth and how the family hoped for big things from him.

"That may be, but facts are facts. You really are a wonder. You're the only shyster I know who could've pulled that off."

Both men, with a glint of the devil in their eyes, broke out into a hearty laugh that they found nearly impossible to stop, as every time they looked at one another they started laughing all over again. John could only shake his head in wonder when he thought about Benny Boy getting them the first tickets to Wall.

Finally catching his breath, John turn to Benjamin and said, "We're getting close, Benny Boy, so very close. I can feel the place calling me."

"The station master said there's a land office in Wall that has a map of the townships that cover all the land from the Cheyenne River in the north and west to the White River in the south which forms the northern border of the Pine Ridge Indian Reservation," Benjamin said, excited to share the additional good news. "We could check the map, and if you could identify your land, you could file an application for your claim as early as tomorrow morning."

"You're kidding," John said, not expecting to be able to file so easily. He had thought he might have to ride out to his claim first and then come back to file.

"Nope. That's how it's done. These folks around us are new to these lands, for the most part, and have no idea what's out there. You, on the other hand, know these lands well. If you think you can find your land on the map, you could claim your land and we could head there tomorrow."

"Seems unbelievable."

"Believe it, brother. If all goes well, we could reach Three Tree Creek by tomorrow night."

"That's fantastic news. I need to make a telephone call to Sarah to let her know things are moving faster than planned. She's excited about settling the new place. The little ones don't understand yet, but their lives are about to change. They'll soon be the children of the Mauvaises Terres, the children of the Badlands of South Dakota."

"I heard that Alda's husband, Jack, was going to farm your place in Iowa."

"For now. We all agreed it would be the best way. He wants to buy more land and this way he can crop our land to make some of the money he'll need."

"What's on our dance card once we get to Barton Lake?"

"The sooner we get started on the house, dig a well, and put up a fence for the livestock, the better. Winters can be damned hard in these lands. There really is no time to lose."

"I don't need to be back in Michigan until December 1st, so we should have plenty of time to get things ready for winter."

"I hope you're right. Last thing we need is for Sarah and the kids to face a winter like the one in 1887 without a warm house and a good roof over their heads."

"Wasn't the winter of 1887 when you piled up your stone marker near Barton Lake?" Benjamin asked, recalling the many times he had listened to John tell stories of his adventures in the Wild West, from cattle rustling in Mexico and gunfights in Texas to Indian battles in No Man's Land and the great Red Canyon stage robbery in the Black Hills, and so many more. He often wondered how many of the events in his big brother's wild stories of the Wild West were actually true.

"It surely was. That was twenty long years ago. I wonder if the marker's still there," John said wondering if his eagle feather totem had done its job.

He harbored no illusions that his stones would still be piled up as he had placed them; anything could have happened over the years. He was excited just the same at the thought that his marker may have withstood the test of time and that his eagle feather would still be where he placed it. By tomorrow night, a fact he still couldn't fully accept, he just might have his answers.

After a restless night, the next morning John found himself in the middle of a mob of men all hoping to get a seat on the first train to Wall.

Gunther Swensen, the station master, a short, plump little man with a high-top cowboy hat and shiny cowboy boots, marched out of the new depot building carrying a black derby hat upside down and covering its open side with his other hand. He quickly stepped up on a small platform that had been set up in front of the main entry.

"May I have your attention!" Gunther barked.

The mob fell silent instantly. No one wanted to be blamed for holding up the proceedings. Everyone was eager to get to Wall as quickly as possible: the lure of free land was just too irresistible.

"The name slips you filled out yesterday are right in this here hat. I'll pull out the slips at random and read the names. My assistant, Nena Bamberger at the depot ticket counter over there, will get you sorted out," Gunther said as he surveyed the men's faces.

Catching Benjamin's eye for just instant, Gunther quickly looked passed him without seeming to recognize him or anyone else in the mob of men jockeying for position. He then unceremoniously reached into the hat and pulled out the first slip of paper, holding it up high for everyone to see.

"Benjamin and John Barton, party of two," he shouted, so Nena could hear him.

Without further fanfare, he then picked out the second slip.

"Fredrick and Natasha Meyer, party of two," he shouted.

As John and Benjamin worked their way to the depot building, other men glared, wondering how the Barton brothers got their names picked first, but no one protested. Many in the crowd simply figuring, there's just no accounting for dumb luck.

The slip drawing and name shouting continued as Nena wrote names down in the order received, while arranging the ticket fares for the line of men that grew as more names were called out.

"So, you're the lucky duo to get the first tickets," Nena said with a wink.

John wasn't sure what to think until he noticed her wink wasn't about them being picked first. Her eyes were locked on Benjamin who she seemed to find particularly interesting. John soon noted that Benny Boy seemed to like the attention, and for a grown man soon to be thirty-one years old, he started acting like a school kid still wet behind his ears.

"Yes, ma'am. There's no accounting for dumb luck," Benjamin said.

Watching the exchange, John noted that though Benny Boy's cheeks were not exactly flush, they had definitely grown visibly rosy.

"I've always liked lucky men, they tend to always be in a good mood," Nena said as she ever so slowly calculated their train fare, her eyes repeatedly flashing back and forth between her paperwork and Benny Boy's smiling face.

"Nena, are your folks homesteading near here?" Benjamin ventured with a notable quiver in his voice.

"Yes, just three miles from here. I took this job to help out," she said nearly in a whisper.

"They hold dances around here yet?" Benjamin pressed, hopeful, never taking his eyes off her.

"They plan to have a big dance next month, when they finish the church," she said, acting nonchalant, the goose bumps on her neck and her bright red cheeks betraying her manner.

"I'd like to ask you to that dance. I could come back this way in a month. I'd really like to see you again," Benjamin said earnestly, unable to take his eyes off of her.

Benjamin found himself unable to think of anything but her voluptuousness, a fact not-so-well-hidden under her rough pioneer costume. Her full and inviting lips and her soft, blemish-free, milk-white skin were alien to the harsh lands surrounding the depot. To him, though she was a foreigner, she was irresistible. He felt like she was his Delilah, though he was certain there was no treachery in her.

"Yes, Benjamin, I too would like to see you again," she said boldly, briefly touching his hand as she passed him their tickets.

Her German accent came through in her final words, making her all the more alluring to Benjamin.

"The dance then," Benjamin said with excitement.

"Yes, let's meet at the dance," she replied, batting her eyes with a broad smile that nearly knocked Benjamin off his feet.

As Benjamin and John moved off, several of the others in line grumbled about all the time it took to sort out some people's train fares. Though the two men let the barbed remarks roll off their backs, they couldn't help but notice the line move rapidly once they were out of the way. John had to chuckle at the noticeable bounce in Benjamin's step as the two men headed for their wagons.

"What's your problem?" Benjamin asked, knowing damn well why John was snickering. He knew how foolish he had acted at the ticket counter with Nena, but then he knew he would have done anything just to see her again. That she had agreed to meet him at the upcoming dance had put him on cloud nine.

"Problem? I have no problem, Benny Boy. It seems you might be headed for a pretty little bundle of problems from what I could see," John said with a chuckle.

"Well, you have to admit, the woman is a beauty, and smart too," Benjamin said, defending himself and Nena's honor.

"No doubt, no doubt," John said, happy his little brother, a devout bachelor, had finally been bitten by the lovebug.

The two men soon had the wagons and livestock loaded on the train. John found a phone at the post office, where he could make his call back to Iowa. Holding the candlestick phone with its mouthpiece close to his mouth and its receiver next to his ear, he couldn't help but remember how his father told him about the first time he learned about the telephone back in 1876 and how he believed at the time that the telephone would change everything. John had to admit that it quite literally had.

Being about to talk directly with Sarah in Iowa hundreds of miles away didn't seem like any miracle to John; it was something everyone had come to take for granted. Fact was, running a country as large as America wouldn't be possible without the telephone. And yet, for his father's generation, the telephone remained a magical wonder they still couldn't believe actually worked.

Sarah had been pleased things were going smoothly. She was also thrilled to learn that Benjamin might have finally met his match. She insisted on telling Lucy the first chance she got. The two things that occupied Lucy's mind were Benjamin and Linda and the fact neither had yet married. The news that Benjamin might have found his future bride in the wilds of the South Dakota Badlands would no doubt send Lucy over the moon.

The call had been expensive, but John felt good that he had had a chance to talk with Sarah and with both little Billy and Alva, who had jabbered on about a collie dog, Buster, they wanted to bring with them to South Dakota. He couldn't wait to have the family together on the new place in the Mauvaises Terres.

Coming out of the post office, the thought suddenly dawned on him: if Wall had a land office than Philip must have one too. Doing a quick three-sixty of the town, he spotted the Philip land office. With the train ready to pull out soon, he wasted no time. Running to the land office, he found himself in the middle of a crowd of men waiting with filled-out applications in hand.

"Hey, no cutting in line, mister," a sour-looking man said as he tried to block John's forward progress.

"Only want to look at the maps," John said crisply.

"Go right ahead. All the good parcels have already been taken," sour puss said with a taunting grin.

Squeezing inside the door, John saw two huge maps on the wall, each map with a thick book of parcel descriptions sitting on a small table in front of it. The maps were divided into townships, each township measured six square miles and was made up of thirty-six sections, with each section measuring one square mile or six hundred forty acres. Each section was divided into quarters measuring one hundred sixty acres each.

Under the Homestead Act, anyone twenty-one or older could claim one hundred sixty acres, or a quarter section of land. To prove up the land and gain title to it, the claimant needed to live on the land five years and make improvements, including building a dwelling, digging a well, fencing, and farming at least ten acres.

Staring at the two maps, John could see that the one intended for homesteaders wanting to settle near Philip was covered in red marks, indicating all the parcels of land that had already been taken. The other map for Wall also had red marks but these tended to be in and around Wall itself. Quickly studying the Wall map, he found the township where he figured his parcel must be located. The township had been designated as Rainy Creek. Looking closely, he noted several small ponds in the northwest corner of the map near two rivers. Three of the ponds were inside the Rainy Creek Township. Like a beacon, he noted that one of the ponds was clearly kidney-shaped. He had no doubt that this was the location of Barton Lake.

Checking the book of parcel descriptions, he found exactly what he was looking for. Beyond giving the coordinates for the one-hundred-sixty-acre parcel, the description stated the parcel had a three-acre pond fed by a creek with three large cottonwood trees. Rushing to the counter, he grabbed a pencil and a land application. He quickly filled out the document while trying not to draw too much attention. Satisfied he had what he needed; he quickly closed the parcel description book. He then carefully folded up his application, tucked it into his inside jacket pocket, and headed for the depot. Rather than waste time searching on the map in Wall, he would get in line to file his claim the moment they arrived.

As the train pulled out for Wall, the platform was lined with people waving to those on board. Among the many faces, John noticed Nena energetically waving a white handkerchief as she ran to pass it to Benjamin, who leaned out of the train car window with his right arm extended as far as he could reach. Seeing the precarious situation, John grabbed ahold of the back of his brother's trouser belt to avoid having him spill out of the window. Just as Benjamin snatched for Nena's handkerchief, she kissed it before passing it into his hand. Holding her handkerchief tightly in his hand, Benjamin could still feel the softness of her skin that his fingers had brushed only momentarily. The love-struck couple stared at one another until the train engine's billowing clouds of smoke and steam blocked their view.

Settling back in his seat across from John, he pressed the handkerchief to his nose.

"Lavender," he said, pleased, his eyes half closed as he took in the scent.

"What's that red smudge?" John said, seeing something red smeared on the cloth.

Looking down at the handkerchief, Benjamin let it lay flat. On it was the perfect imprint of Nena's farewell kiss forever pressed into the cloth in ruby red lipstick.

"So, the girl really seems to like you, Benny Boy," John said, impressed again with the speed his brother lived his life.

On further thought, John had to admit to himself that his first encounter with Sarah Bell had not been much different, nor had Jasper's with Maryanne Fairmont. When a man is smitten, he's smitten; there is no logic to it. How and why two people become attracted to one another, and thereafter become blind to everything and everyone else, would, it seemed, forever remain a mystery to him, and for that matter, to everyone else in the human race.

As Timothy Gillam said on that train to San Antonio, years ago, quoting the French poet Victor Hugo, "To love or have loved, that is enough. Ask nothing further. There is no other pearl to be found in the dark folds of life."

John still had to wonder how two people find one another, and when they do, they somehow know by instinct they have found their other half. Perhaps Victor Hugo, happy to have found his other half, decided there was no point in searching further in "the dark folds of life" for the source from whence that love came. For Victor, love was enough. Considering everything he had learned about life; John was inclined to agree.

May 2, 1907

Wall, Pennington County, South Dakota

Into the Mauvaises Terres

As the train rolled down the track, the two men looked out at the vast empty prairie that stretched to the horizon in every direction, deep in their own thoughts. John still couldn't believe that trains would soon be run through the heart of the Mauvaises Terres on a regular basis. The vacant lands the railroad companies were trying to settle consisted of a broad corridor bounded by the Missouri River in the east, the White River in the south, and the Cheyenne River that ran north from the southern Back Hills in the west to the greater Cheyenne River in the north, from where the Cheyenne River and Belle Fourche River merged and turned east toward the Missouri River.

The land on which John had piled up his stone marker was situated at the far northwestern corner of the targeted region just southeast of two rivers. Having worked for the railroad as a gandy dancer for a time in Nebraska, where he became familiar with survey maps, he had no difficulty in finding the coordinates of his quarter section of land on the government survey map.

He figured most newcomers would want land away from the heart of the Badlands, where towering cliffs of mud and sediment consumed the countryside for miles, creating a dead zone where nothing could take root. These barren lands were directly south of where John had found his Shangri-La. The new town of Wall was located on the northern edge of the wastelands. This fact would encourage homesteaders arriving in Wall to naturally look north for good arable land, right in the direction of the land John wanted to claim.

Figuring there would be a mad dash once they arrived in Wall, he was determined to be the first one off the train. He would head directly to the Wall land office to file his filled-out claim application. His single-minded goal was to secure his claim before anyone else had the chance to grab it for themselves. His advantage was that, for him, finding his homestead hadn't been a matter of luck, nor had it depended solely on some vague description in a land parcel book; he had seen the land he wanted to claim with his own two eyes and knew exactly where it was located. He was sure the parcel described on his filled-out claim application was the right one, the land he had claimed with his stone marker long ago.

Tim Olsen had watched with no little interest as John Barton, the same John Barton that had received one of the first tickets on the train to Wall, studied the Wall land map at the Philip land office. What piqued his interest was the fact Barton seemed to be interested in only studying the map for the Wall area, and further, only the far northwestern corner of the surveyed lands on that map. He was also taken by how excited Barton seemed to get after he studied the book containing parcel descriptions for that area. Olsen knew he was on to something when Barton frantically grabbed a claim application and filled it out on the spot, tucking it into his jacket's left inside breast pocket before heading to board the train to Wall.

Sensing an opportunity, he too studied the area where Barton had been looking. What caught his eye was that not all the land in the region was completely arid, there were a few ponds in the corner of map, where Barton had focused his search. Olsen was certain it was one these parcels, one that had a pond, that Barton somehow knew was the prize he sought.

Calling ahead to Jeffrey Dale, his partner in Wall, he recounted what he had witnessed and instructed Dale to pick the left inside breast pocket of Barton's jacket, the moment he jumped off the train in Wall. Since the application in that pocket had already been filled out, all Dale would have to do is file the document before Barton could make out a new one. Olsen figured the claim might be worth several hundred dollars, if they played their cards right.

They could sell the claim to Barton or to someone else in need of good land with water. In this part of the country, that would be just about everybody. He smiled to himself when he thought about how easy the pickings had been since the railroad created a land rush in the region. Swindling naive sodbusters, especially foreigners unfamiliar with American ways, had been like taking candy from a baby for a scoundrel like Jeffery Dale. Musing about the friendly Wall welcome they had in store for the unwitting Mr. Barton, he couldn't help but chuckle to himself as he twisted the ends of his well-waxed mustache.

The thirty-mile journey between Philip and Wall took only an hour. During the trip, John informed Benjamin that he had visited the Philip land office and had located the parcel description for the land he wanted to claim. Benjamin was surprised to learn that his big brother already had his claim application filled out and would file it as soon as they arrived in Wall.

Just before the train pulled into the station, John tapped his left jacket pocket and said, "Wish me luck. I'll be back to help with the wagons and livestock as fast as I can."

"Good luck, big brother. I know this is a dream come true for you," Benjamin said, proud of how resourceful his big brother always seemed to be.

To Benjamin, there seemed to be nothing his big brother couldn't overcome. Unlike his younger twin brothers and little Cliff, Benjamin had been raised by John and his big sister Alda. The three of them had spent a lot of time together. John hadn't been able to teach his younger brothers how to ride a horse or rope or be a cowboy the way he had taught Benjamin. Little Cliff hadn't been born and the twins had been too young when John left for Texas in 1884.

The day John and Jasper rode out nearly broke Benjamin's heart. He always believed John would come back one day. When he did, no one could have been happier. Being able to share an adventure with his big brother, in the mysterious Mauvaises Terres no less, was a dream come true for Benjamin. After hearing so many of Pappy's stories and those of his father, and even those of John himself, Benjamin longed for the day when he would be able to tell his own stories of the west and about what it is to become a man and a rider of the Mauvaises Terres.

As the train pulled to a stop, John sprang to his feet and headed for the door. Benjamin, having no need to rush, watched John descend the steps to the platform. Just as John hit the platform, a man in a tan duster with his hat pulled down low, bumped squarely into him nearly bowling him over. After a quick beg-your-pardon, the man swiftly turned and headed away from the depot.

John, having seen similar moves during his days in Deadwood, quickly checked his pockets. Unable to believe it himself, he discovered the application in his left inside jacket pocket was gone. Spinning around quickly, John frantically searched the crowd for anyone wearing a tan duster.

"Over there!" Benjamin shouted as he pointed to a man who was trying to shed his duster, while hurrying toward the center of town.

Benjamin could clearly see the man in the duster moving through the crowd from his higher perch in the rail car. Following Benjamin's directions, John finally caught sight of the man, and before launching into pursuit, yelled back to Benjamin, "Bring a gun!" With that, he was gone at a full run.

Running headlong, he quickly closed the distance between his target and himself. Dodging in and out from behind the tangle of people, horses, and wagons that filled the crowded streets, John worked to avoid tipping the pickpocket off that he was being followed.

Shrugging off his duster and without missing a beat, the pickpocket tossed the duster onto a bench in front of a lively dinner set up in a large tent. In a quick flowing move, the pickpocket then deftly exchanged his hat with a new one hanging on a peg in a hat display outside the front door of the newly built General Store.

If John hadn't witnessed the man's smooth moves, he wouldn't have been able to recognize him, even if he had run into him in the middle of an empty street. That not being the case, he now knew exactly what the scoundrel looked like and how he was dressed. Figuring two could play at the same game, John grabbed the discarded duster on his way by. Keeping his distance, John continued to shadow the pickpocket who, thinking he was in the clear, had slowed his pace.

Acting nonchalant, the pickpocket strolled down the street as if he hadn't a care in the world. Slowly, step by step, he made his way to the Wall land office where men holding filled-out claim applications stood in a long line. The pickpocket walked up the line to a man dressed like a cowboy and handed him a folded piece of paper. John now understood this was a sophisticated operation with an unknown number of associates.

That they had known he was carrying a filled-out application in his jacket's left inside breast pocket meant someone in Philip had been watching him and had called ahead to relay the information. They had been ready for him when he arrived in Wall. It was clear to John their larceny wasn't a random act, but one well-orchestrated.

"Here," Benjamin said over John's right shoulder as he slipped John a loaded pistol. "Did you keep an eye on him?" he asked, still standing behind John, not wanting to attract attention.

"Yes, he gave the application to the man dressed like a cowboy standing in line just outside the front door of the land office," John said, not turning to look at Benjamin.

"Where'd the pickpocket go?" Benjamin asked, his voice tense.

"He's standing in front of the barber's tent smoking a cigar acting the part of a man without a care," John said through clinched teeth.

"I see him," Benjamin said with a growl. "And I'll take care of him. He has no idea who I am or that I'm even in the mix."

John had never heard Benjamin talk tough or even utter a harsh word; it didn't surprise him however that Benjamin had the sand to take care of himself. Bill Barton would have taught him all the same moves he had taught John; the martial moves of a trained soldier with one goal in mind, victory at all cost.

Benjamin peeled off from behind John and walked slowly across the busy street, where there was a line of men sitting on benches waiting for their haircuts. Benjamin took a number off a spindle near the front tent flap and sat down in line on the furthest bench.

Seeing Benjamin was in place, John slipped on the duster, stepped from behind the porch post where he had been standing, and moved quickly across the street, rushing up next to the cowboy. Before the man knew what was happening, John rammed a pistol barrel hard in his ribs.

"If you want to live, follow me," John hissed in a near whisper and then laughed out loud, slapping the cowboy on the back, his shoulders jerking up and down in good humor.

For those witnessing the encounter, it appeared the two men were good friends who had just shared one hell of a good joke. The startled cowboy looked into John's smiling and laughing face and found a pair of stone-cold eyes staring back at him. He realized instantly he wasn't dealing with some would-be sodbuster from an unknown foreign land; he was staring into the eyes of a stone-cold killer who wouldn't hesitate to kill again.

Reluctantly at first and then at a pace, he followed John's insistent directions. When the pickpocket realized what was happening to his cowboy confederate, he set out after the two men. Benjamin got up from his seat, returned the number he had taken, and followed the pickpocket at a distance. What Benjamin hadn't told John was that he too had a pistol and knew how to use it.

John guided the cowboy behind the General Store, one of the only buildings in town that had been fully constructed. Once they were out of sight from the street, John demanded the claim application, which the cowboy quickly handed over. Checking the document, John could see it was just as he had filled it out.

"Hold it right there, big fella," the pickpocket barked as he came around the building his pistol drawn and pointing at John.

"Looks to me like we have a Mexican standoff. I'll kill your man here if you fire on me," John said coldly.

"I could care less. I'd still shoot you and get the claim application. I win. There's no standoff, Mexican or otherwise," the pickpocket said.

"Oh, I beg to differ, little man," Benjamin growled as his shoved his pistol barrel hard up against the back of the pickpocket's head.

After a long beat, the pickpocket was the first to try to make a move. Ducking low he tried to swing around to punch Benjamin in the midsection. Anticipating the move, Benjamin sidestepped the pickpocket's swing, causing it to go wide. Just as the pickpocket attempted to regain his balance, Benjamin smashed his pistol butt into the man's temple, dropping him where he stood.

The cowboy, seeing his partner go down, turned to John with a look of utter fear in his eyes. Seeing how scared the man was, John saw an opportunity to reduce the chances of any future retaliation.

"Who's your man in Philip?" John barked, shoving his pistol barrel harder into the cowboy's ribs.

"I don't know, mister. Jeff there never told me," the cowboy said with a shaky voice. "What are you going to do with us?"

"Answer my questions and you have nothing to worry about. If you don't, well, there's no saying," John hissed. "Now, what's Jeff's full name? And where's he from?"

"Jeffrey Dale. He's from Pierre," the cowboy said, ready to cooperate.

"And the man in Philip?"

"Tim Olsen. He comes from Sioux Falls."

"And you?"

"Lester Ray. I'm also from Sioux Falls."

"So, you and Olsen are ol' buddies?"

"Yes, we grew up together."

"Are there others?"

"No, just the three of us. Though Tim might have someone else in Philip. I don't know."

John considered his answers and figured the man was so afraid he was probably telling the truth. He hadn't hesitated before answering every question. If he was lying he was damn good at it. John hoped knowing the men's names and where they came from might give them pause should they ever consider retaliation. He had lived through one set of men seeking revenge and wanted to avoid another one, if at all possible.

"Well, here's how it's gonna be," John growled slowly. "You, Jeff, and Tim are gonna let this thing drop, right here, right now. You're gonna put it behind ya. If you don't, we may have to go to the law, or more'n likely we'll just track ya down and kill ya ourselves, *comprende*?"

"Yes, yes, I understand. We're sorry for all the trouble, mister. Damn sorry," Lester babbled, his eyes wide with fear and full of tears as John dug his pistol barrel deeper and deeper into the man's ribs.

Knowing he had pushed Lester to his limits, John suddenly pulled his pistol back and in a single sweeping move struck the man hard on the back of the head with the butt of the pistol dropping the man where he stood.

"Whoa! Damn, man, I wasn't sure where all that was going," Benjamin said.

Without saying a word, John quickly went through the cowboy's pockets and found little. Benjamin, seeing what his brother was doing, quickly searched the pickpocket, also coming up with nothing of note.

"We'll need a good length of rope and several bandanas. Good thing we're behind a General Store," John said. "Go get what we need. We need to buy ourselves a little time."

Benjamin wasted no time running into the General Store and buying what they needed. After they hogtied and gagged the two unconscious men, they piled crates and boxes around and on top of their prostrate bodies and left them to the elements or to whatever vermin might come along. There was no telling how long they would remain unconscious or how quickly they would be able to untie themselves when they came to. John's hope was that the two rogues would hightail it out of town as soon as they were able.

It took John nearly an hour to get his claim filed. In the meantime, Benjamin had worked feverishly to get the wagons off the train, the two teams of horses into their rigs, and the livestock—two milk cows and two extra horses—tied to the back of wagons for their long journey north to Barton Lake.

With receipt in hand, John ran and hopped up on the driver's seat of his wagon. Having readied everything for a quick departure, Benjamin was already up on his wagon's driver's seat and ready to go.

"Move'm out!" John yelled as he snapped the reins and the team moved his wagon forward.

Benjamin followed suit, happy to put Wall behind them as quickly as possible. By noon, they had come seven miles from Wall. The ground had been relatively level, though John knew it would become increasingly rolling as they went further north, which would slow their pace as they climbed each successive hill.

John's wagon was in the lead. As he pulled his wagon over, Benjamin followed. The spot John selected to pull over at was near a dry creek that still had water in a series of small pools. John thought it would be a good place to take a break, unsure of where they may find standing water again.

"Let's dip some water for the horses and livestock and have something to eat," John said as he hopped down from his wagon.

John hadn't talked with Benjamin since they split up after tying the two con men up behind the General Store. For John, the speedy filing of his claim had been his highest priority. There had simply been no time to talk before their departure. John figured once they put Wall behind them, they would have plenty of time to chitchat about all that had happened. He still felt he needed to keep a wary eye out for the two snakes they had tied up. He also worried about any other possible confederates that might be trailing them. It had been a close call in Wall, and he knew he should have been more careful. He was damn glad he had had his brother with him. Had he been alone, he would have lost everything.

"Well, pard, we got out of that little scrape pretty slick," John said, looking at his little brother in a new light and with a new level of respect.

Benjamin was not only gifted in things mechanical; he was as tough as they come on the frontier. John wasn't the only child of Bill and Lucy

Barton; Benjamin had received the same upbringing he had and had lived on the same frontier. And like John, he had turned out as tough as nails.

"Pard, is it? Not Benny Boy?" Benjamin said, his eyebrows arched.

"You'll always be my little brother, Benny Boy, there's no changing that," John said as straight as he could. "What we experienced today makes you a pard in my world."

"Well, pard, we kicked a couple asses and it felt damn good. I could get used to this wild, reckless western life," Benjamin chuckled.

"You're a Barton alright. We all have a little *desperado* in us," John said with a grin and a wink.

John still wondered if his father would ever tell him the real story of how he got mixed up with Jesse James and Cole Younger right after the Civil War. John suspected his father had been more than a little wild. He had a hunch his father had been an outlaw. That Tom Burton, a true outlaw, had owed his father a favor seemed to confirm John's suspicions.

"Think they'll follow us?" Benjamin said.

"I'm not sure they care all that much about jumping claims. They're playing the extortion game," John said. "Once they get a stolen claim filed in their name, they offer it to the person they stole from, for a price of course. If that doesn't work they sell it to the next guy."

"They might hold a grudge," Benjamin said, wondering if they had anything to worry about.

"People always carry a grudge around about something. They have other fish to fry. I don't think they want anything to do with us again," John said. "I made it pretty clear to our cowboy friend that we could have just as well killed 'em both."

John's words hit Benjamin hard. He realized his brother wasn't kidding. Killing the men had been an option, one his brother had obviously considered. It had never crossed Benjamin's mind. In this he realized John's stories of his adventures into the Wild West may be truer than he ever believed. His brother had killed men. He had been hunted by men who wanted to kill him. These were experiences Benjamin was grateful he hadn't had and prayed he never would.

After the two men fetched water for the horses and milked the cows, they checked their wagon loads. Finally, able to relax a little, they had a lunch of corn beef and sourdough biscuits they had bought from one of the many tents selling cooked meals in Wall. John had been surprised to find so many settlers eager to make a little extra money before driving their wagons out to their homesteads.

Finishing lunch and after getting everything packed up, John decided to ask his brother about Nena.

"What're you going to do about Nena?" John asked as he poured himself a coffee from the pot they had hung over a small campfire they built along the dry creek bed.

"I'm going to waltz the pretty legs off that fine-looking filly at the dance in Philip on Saturday, June 15th," Benjamin said matter-of-factly.

"Well then, we best be gettin' to Barton Lake and puttin' you to work as soon as possible, if'n you're plannin' to run off to chase some wild filly across half the state of South Dakota in six weeks," John said with a grin.

"She didn't seem like she'd be needin' all that much chasin'," Benjamin said with confidence.

"Wait till you've tasted some of that delicious fruit and she decides to make you work for a second helpin'," John said. "You'll chase after her; it'll be the only way she'll know you're serious."

Taking the white hanky out of his shirt pocket and holding it up to his nose, Benjamin said, "I'd chase that woman to the end of the Earth and beyond if'n I had to."

"Damn right you would. That's the way of it, pard. There ain't no other," John said.

As the day grew long, the two men drove their teams over land that had never been trod upon by horse-drawn wagons. John thought over time a road would be established and along it small towns may even one day spring out of the grasslands. Change was coming to the Mauvaises Terres; transplants from Europe and across America had converged with the shared hope they and their descendants would take root in this alien land.

The weather had been mild all day, with puffy clouds dotting the sky, drifting in unison as if painted on a blue canvas that was being rolled up in the east. Time crawled as John and Benjamin fell into the rhythm of their teams. The sunset was glorious as the puffy clouds burst into red balls of fire, rimmed in yellow and gold, before slowly dimming to ashen grey.

Evening came and lasted over an hour until the men found themselves in a night as dark as any they had ever experienced. The stars shone brightly, the Milky Way so clear and close it seemed just out of reach. Shooting stars streaked across the heavens. No longer able to see far enough ahead, John once again pulled up his team, with Benjamin pulling up beside him.

"We had a near full moon last night," Benjamin said.

"The full moon should rise in a while. Let's rest up until we can see again," John said. "From my guess, we're very close."

A lone coyote howled; his call answered by a duo of howls far off to the east. The night was abuzz with insects, though none seemed interested in them.

"I'm going to take a horse to scout the land ahead," John said. "I'll be back soon. Put on some coffee."

John's concern was they might have strayed off the course he had plotted with the agent at the land office in Wall. He had triple-checked his compass readings throughout the day and was certain they had stayed on track. If so, according to the land agent, they would arrive at Barton Lake without so much as a turn.

As it happened, his claim lay directly on the township line that ran straight north from Wall. The agent was convinced this line would become the established market road for the whole area one day. John was thrilled to learn of the lucky break. Having the market road lead directly by his place would make life a damn sight easier in coming years.

John rode no more than a mile when a brilliant full moon suddenly popped over the eastern horizon. What had been nearly invisible in the inky black darkness was now lit up in stark contrast, creating moon shadows that stretched long, with the moon still low on the horizon. The shadows grew shorter as the moon climbed into the starry sky.

Riding another mile over several rises, John saw the shiny surface of Barton Lake as he looked down into a small valley, exactly as his compass coordinates had predicted. The beauty of the moon-lit sight brought tears to John's eyes. His breast filled with emotions he had held in for many, many years. He had finally done it; he had staked his claim in the Mauvaises Terres. His boyhood dream lay bathed in moonlight, appearing as a surreal mystical place beyond the realm of mere mortal men.

A shiver ran down John's back as he urged his horse to enter the serene sanctuary that spread out before them. Riding down the gentle slope into the small valley, John soon arrived at Barton Lake. The moon's reflection on the mirror-like surface of the lake was like nothing he had ever seen. An owl hooted from somewhere in the direction of the three large cottonwood trees lining the creek that fed the pond. The trees' thick, waxy leaves shimmered in cascading layers as a cool breeze rippled through their foliage.

The moonlight illuminated everything with a soft, dim, sepia glow. Stepping down from his horse, John walked to the edge of the pond. A frog croaked and then hopped, splashing into the water, causing ripples to spread slowly across its placid surface. John's eyes, mesmerized by the effect, followed the outer ring as it grew larger, its crest catching the moonlight until it washed up against the opposing bank of the pond, causing a backwash of ripples that created a sparkling dance at the water's edge as opposing rings collided.

It was then that he saw the stone marker he had stacked up twenty years earlier in hopes of one day claiming this land as his own. As unbelievable as it seemed, the marker had somehow stood in defiance of the elements, silently awaiting his return.

Walking around the edge of the pond to the marker, the closer he got, his heart quickened in anticipation. What he found was a reliquary of religious and spiritual objects the likes of which he had never seen before in his life. His simple stone marker, still resting on the eagle feather he had wedged under its base, had been transformed into a symbolic totem of the beliefs of many peoples, cultures, and religions from around the world. How over the last twenty years this remote spot in the middle of the Mauvaises Terres, where few men had ever tread, had become a crossroads of worldwide spiritual belief was beyond his understanding.

The totem seemed a natural fixture in this mysterious moon-lit place. After saying a silent prayer in front of the bizarre reliquary of religious and spiritual artifacts, he felt the spiritual power of its conglomerated objects surge through his body. As though a veil had been lifted, he sensed the totem's deeper meaning. He thought about the color of the stones and knew their meaning to the Lakota people. Looking at the brass slave bracelet resting on the black stone and the jade pendant on the yellow stone, the meaning of the red and white stones seemed clear to him. Bathed in moonlight, the colors nearly merging one with another, the colored stones had taken on another layer of meaning, one beyond their original spiritual significance. For John, the colors represented perfectly the four races that now made up this land.

The Mauvaises Terres, a land of infinite mystery, now belonged to everyone. Looking at the Lakota *uname* symbol that framed the reliquary, he knew the deepest native spiritual roots of this land would never be washed aside or forgotten as had those of so many other native peoples in the course of building a new nation. He felt truly fortunate to have staked his claim in such a place, one that now belonged to all humankind, and yet would forever be the Mauvaises Terres, a mysterious place, a spiritual place, a place of awe and wonder.

Riding back to Benjamin, he had decided they would push on to Barton Lake tonight, rather than wait for the morning. His main reasons being that tonight the sky was clear, the moon was full and bright, and the pond was a mystical place beyond the horizon of mere mortals. He wanted to share that magic with his new pard; it was the least he could do for his little brother, Benny Boy.

May 2, 1912

Rapid City, Pennington County, South Dakota

A Boy's Dream

JOHN BARTON STEPPED OUT of the Pennington County Register of Deeds Office with a huge smile of satisfaction on his face. After five years of hard work, he had proved up his claim and had in his hands the registered patent on his homestead in the Mauvaises Terres. In addition to his homestead's one hundred sixty acres of free land, he had purchased an additional one hundred sixty acres for two hundred dollars at a dollar and twenty-five cents an acre. The government's only requirement for the low acquisition price had been that he live on the land at least six months. With a full half section of land, three hundred twenty acres in all, he had been able to turn a profit on his crops for the past couple of years and provide plenty of feed for his livestock. He was confident he would be able to make a go of it.

As he walked back toward the center of town, the sun was out, the sky was clear, and the temperature brisk. John felt good. The hustle-bustle of the busy streets in the booming hub of the Black Hills made him confident in the future of the region. Tin Lizzies puttered up and down the streets and were parked everywhere. The age of the automobile was in full swing.

John thought of his brother and was proud to know the role he had played in bringing the automobile to the common man. Just as Benjamin had predicted, the price of the Model T had come down every year. The car's low cost, durability, adaptability, and especially its ease of maintenance, had been a boon to sales in the remote regions of South Dakota, where the need for self-reliance was essential for survival in the sparsely populated lands so far from the major commercial centers in the east.

On the corner of 6th and Main, John walked into "Big Jack" Clower's Saloon to have a beer or two to celebrate having obtained the full and clear title to his land. He had heard Big Jack served his beer ice cold. John remembered when he and Jasper drank their first beers lukewarm in Saint Joseph, Missouri. Even as warm and as flat as the beer had been, they both grew to love the taste. He had to smile when he thought of Jasper and all the adventures they had shared together.

John planned to take Sarah and the children to Wyoming to visit Jasper and Maryanne and all their children during early summer after he had planted all his crops. He had arranged to have his place looked in on by his neighbor, who had also offered to take care of his livestock while he was away. Jasper and John were cousins and had grown up as neighbors back in Iowa. They had been like brothers in everything. In those days, the Waite and Barton children had been very close. He wanted his children to know their Wyoming cousins and to stay close. Though each generation had continued the march west, John didn't want the excuse of physical distance to cut the ties that bind them as a family. To John, like his father and his father before him, family was everything.

His plan was to take a grand tour around the Black Hills, visiting Hot Springs and then on to Edgemont, Newcastle, Sundance, Devil's Tower, Belle Fourche, Spearfish, Sturgis, and Rapid City. He wanted his children to know about the Black Hills and to have a chance to see their natural wonder from every direction. Before returning back to the Mauvaises Terres, he planned to also take them into the hills to visit the Needles and Wind Cave, birthplace of the Lakota people.

Billy, now ten years old, was the same age John had been when he made up his mind to stake his claim in the Mauvaises Terres, the enchanted lands of Pappy's many stories. Billy longed to homestead in the Black Hills itself. Being a child of the prairie, he longed to live in the pine-covered hills that had forever been just beyond his reach. Stories about the mystical power of the *Paha Sapa* had captured his imagination.

Though new lands for homesteading hadn't been offered in the Black Hills proper, there were those who demanded Pleasant Valley be made available for settlement. John hoped that one day those lands would become open for homesteading and that Billy would be able to fulfill his boyhood dream. He knew from his own experience—nothing would be more satisfying.

Situated in the southern hills, Pleasant Valley stretched for miles, with huge tracts of virgin meadowlands ready for the plow. John had to agree it would be the ideal location for homesteads. The Pilger Mountain area just north of Red Canyon was particularly promising. John himself had often thought about the area's natural features. Game had always been thick in the hidden valleys and canyons in the region and had always included a mixture of both plains animals, like pronghorn antelope and mule deer, and their forest-dwelling counterparts, whitetail deer and elk.

John knew the area well since the Pleasant Valley Trail had been part of the Cheyenne and Black Hills Stage Route, which had run from Mule Creek Junction to Bishop's Standard Gauge Saloon, through Red Canyon and Pleasant Valley to Custer, and then straight north through Hill City to Deadwood. He had to admit, his son's dream was a good one. The thought of his son one day settling on Pilger Mountain in Pleasant Valley, one of the most beautiful places in the Black Hills, sounded better every time John thought about it.

Sitting at the bar, John gazed out the front window of the saloon and watched the mix of people made up of many races and backgrounds, all bound in common cause, each chasing his own individual errands. Watching them come and go on the busy street, he realized they were America's living reliquary, the embodiment of the mysterious shrine created by people from many different traditions he had found on his claim. It would be their descendants who carried forward the American dream. He believed it would be those with pioneer spirit who continued to lead America beyond the horizon. He prayed his children would be among them.

Unconsciously, he found himself reaching up to touch the newly issued deed to his land tucked in his jacket's inside breast pocket. Reassured it was still there, he smiled to himself, never feeling more content. As he thought about everything that had happened to bring him to this point in his life, he could only shake his head and wonder at what might come next. Taking a long pull on his second mug of ice-cold beer, John wiped the foam off his upper lip with the back of his hand and had to admit, lukewarm or ice cold, it was as delicious as ever.

Epilogue

THE STORY OF JOHN Barton continued long after he staked his claim in the Mauvaises Terres. John had seven children in all—three sons and four daughters—and homesteaded on Three Tree Creek in the Rainy Creek Township near the little town of Creighton, Pennington County in western South Dakota from 1907 until 1932, when with the sudden death of his wife and his worsening eyesight he was forced to sell out and move with his youngest son, Francis, to live with his eldest son and his wife, Bill and Kate Barton, on their homestead on Pilger Mountain in the Black Hills.

John's oldest son, William (Bill) Reuben Barton, named for his grandfathers, was born in Fort Dodge, Iowa in 1902. From age five, he grew up in the Mauvaises Terres. He married Kathrine (Kate) Busskohl, the daughter of German immigrants, who also homesteaded near Wall. John became postmaster of the Creighton Post Office located about halfway between his father's homestead on Three Tree Creek and the town of Wall on the section line road.

Bill and Kate Barton had three children—two sons, Harold and John, and one daughter, Velda, my mother. From 1929 until 1935, Bill and Kate Barton homesteaded on the last available free land near Dewey on Pilger Mountain in Pleasant Valley, Custer County, Black Hills of South Dakota, not far from where gold was first discovered on French Creek in 1874.

Many of the children, grandchildren, and great grandchildren of Bill and Kate Barton have continued the family's relentless quest to go beyond the horizon. Members of the family now reside in North Carolina and Texas, and those who continued the move westward now live in South Dakota, Montana, Oregon, Washington, Hawaii, and even further west, beyond the dateline, in Japan.

Based on historical records, I included mention of Bishop's Standard Gauge Saloon and the original plans for the establishment of the town of

Burton at the current location of Edgemont, South Dakota. What John Barton and E.J. Bishop could not have known at the time they met in the 1880s was that their Dakota descendants would one day marry and that their great grandchildren would continue the relentless quest of both the Bishops and the Bartons since arriving in the New World: the quest to venture ever westward, beyond the horizon.

www.ingramcontent.com/pod-product-compliance
Lightning Source LLC
Chambersburg PA
CBHW051147030726
47504CB00004B/1081